A GRAVE MISTAKE

A GRAVE MISTAKE

KATE MACLEAN

Copyright © 2026 by Kate Maclean

All rights reserved.

This book was written entirely by the author without the use of artificial intelligence tools.

No portion of this book may be reproduced in any form without written permission from the publisher or author, except as permitted by U.S. copyright law.

The story, all names, characters, and incidents portrayed in this book are fictitious. Any resemblance to actual persons (living or deceased), places, buildings, or products is purely coincidental.

For Leselle, who loved this idea first and never let me forget it.

PROLOGUE

myPAGE

Mandy Simon is listening to love story again!! *2 hours ago*

| Wall | Notes | Info | Photos |

all about me ;P
November 29, 2008 at 10:13pm

Rules: Once you've been tagged, write a note with FIVE random things about you. Then tag FIVE people to share their own. If I tagged you it's because I want to know more about you!

I was tagged by <u>Jason Emmerson</u>. Here goes!

1. I love Taylor Swift and already know every single word to every song on her new album
2. chocolate is my favorite food
3. I've never had any pets but I want a dog so bad
4. I'm a Hufflepuff
5. I'm probably the worst dancer you'll ever meet

I tag <u>Christina Hamilton</u>, <u>Kaylee Pierce</u>, <u>Jamie Gonzales</u>, <u>Rachel McKinney</u>, and <u>Adam White</u> keep it going guys!!!

CHRISTINA HAMILTON:

HUFFLEPUFF??

you know there's no sorting hat telling you you're a hufflepuff right??

like you know you get to choose??

                                  MANDY SIMON:

                              Hufflepuffs are loyal!

CHRISTINA:

and LAME

                                    MANDY:

          loyalty is important! we could use more hufflepuffs

          what friend is gonna be your ride or die? help you bury a body? a hufflepuff!!

CHRISTINA:

well then come over here asap and help me bury a body

aka figure out how to get hair dye out of my carpet before mom gets home

seriously come over right now i need you!!!

1

My phone buzzed again from its resting place in the bottom of my bag, and I pointedly kept my gaze forward, ignoring it. My eyes tracked the movement of Carol Hodges's powder pink lips, but my ears only took in the sound of the phone's vibrations. Beneath the table, my feet grabbed my purse and tugged it backward, my patent leather pumps squeaking against the fabric as they shoved the bag back beneath my chair, toward the wall and away from the woman now frowning at me from across the table.

"Mrs. Perkins?"

I blinked, panic flooding my senses. "I'm sorry, can you repeat that?"

I tore my gaze from her lips and forced myself to listen as Carole Hodges, Senior Recruiting Coordinator, the woman whose socks I needed to positively knock off today, repeated herself. "I said, your dissertation work is certainly impressive. Everything on your resume is impressive, really. But it's all very much geared toward a career in academia. I'm a little surprised to see a candidate like you in our interview pool for this entry-level position, and wonder what it is about a career as an actuary that interests you?"

I swallowed and stammered, "I like math. I've always been good at it. I, um, realized a lifelong career in academia wasn't for me, and when I took stock of my options, an actuarial career stood out as one in which I could marry my mathematical expertise and academic experience with real-world problem-solving." I gained confidence as I spoke, and by the end of my rehearsed answer my voice was steady once again.

Ms. Hodges peered at me through thick, orange-hued lenses with rhinestones around the edges, the corners of her mouth pulled just slightly down. My heart thudded against my ribs, a certainty building that she could see right through me. I felt entirely sure that her dark brown eyes could read my thoughts, and imagined her seeing me Google "highest paying math jobs" the week before while drinking too much wine and wondering if I could get my teaching position back if I groveled enough.

Just when I was about to open my mouth and spew more made-up reasons a thirty-two-year-old woman would be seeking an entry-level job, Ms. Hodges dipped her chin in a short, sharp nod and said, "Right. Can you—"

My phone vibrated again, and Ms. Hodges paused. "Do you need to get that?"

"I'm so sorry," I mumbled. "No. It's not important."

Ms. Hodges gave me another discerning look, then placed her palm down on the table atop my printed resume. "Mrs. Perkins—"

"Ms." I couldn't stop myself from correcting her, but when her eyebrows shot up in surprise, the remaining words froze in my windpipe and I coughed trying to get them out. "I'm separated."

"Right." She cleared her throat. "Ms. Perkins. I appreciate your interest in Asterales Insurance, and I admire your decision to make a change in your career and find a position more aligned with your personal goals. However, I am unconvinced that a position as an actuarial analyst with Asterales is truly what you want. I wish you all the best in your pursuit of employment, but I'm afraid I do not think you are the right fit for this role, and as such I must terminate this interview."

My mouth hung open as I gasped like a fish desperate for

oxygen. I'd had plenty of unsuccessful interviews in my life, but in none of them did the interviewer tell me during the interview that they weren't hiring me—that always came later, after I'd had at least a few days to stew in my anxiety. I braced my hands on the walnut table and tried to form a sentence that would convince her to change her mind, but my phone sent another vibration through the floor.

"In future interviews," Ms. Hodges said with a stern look down her nose at my bag, "I'd advise you to turn your phone all the way off."

She rose and waited for me to pick up my purse, then escorted me, still shell-shocked, to the elevator bay. "Thank you for your time," she said and extended her hand.

I shook it, then boarded the elevator, unable to meet her eyes while she watched me press the button. As the doors shut and I began to process the rejection, tears bit at my eyes.

"Shit," I muttered. Then, louder, "Shit!" I fumbled in the dark interior of my purse for my phone.

Four missed calls from Christina filled the lock screen, and one text message.

Christina: SOS I need you to help me hide a body

2

The phone rang for so long I thought for sure it would go to voicemail. Just before I gave up and hung up, Christina answered, her voice breathy.

"Finally!"

"You just cost me a job." I stepped from the air-conditioned building lobby into the Arizona sunshine, squinting and bringing a hand up to shade my face. "Four phone calls? Seriously?"

"What job?" In the background, I could hear a scraping sound, like something heavy being dragged.

"What is that?"

"What job?" she repeated. "Last weekend you were barely a third of the way into that book about figuring out what you want out of a career. You can't have finished it already."

I cocked my head to hold my phone between my ear and shoulder, using both hands to keep the pieces of my superglued key fob together while I unlocked the rust bucket of a car I now called my own. Despite the superglue, if I wasn't careful with the pressure, the fob popped open, spilling the contents onto the sidewalk for me to pick up and reassemble while watching a YouTube tutorial later. Ask me how I found that out.

"I can find myself and figure out what I want out of a career during the evenings and weekends and get a different job down the road. In the meantime, there's rent, and—"

"You didn't have to move out!" I flinched at her sudden outburst, and she let out a long exhale before continuing softer.

"We told you we were happy to let you stay as long as you needed. You didn't have to go move into the first place you found that was up for rent, and you don't have to jump at the first job opportunity you find, either."

That might have been true—they were happy to have me stay as long as I liked, or at least they wouldn't tell me otherwise. But I wasn't happy staying in my friend's pool house any longer than it took to find a place that would take me on as a tenant with no proof of income. My life may be imploding around me, but I wanted to stand on my own two feet amidst the swirling chaos I'd created. I certainly wasn't going to let it impact my friends.

"I appreciated the offer, and still do," I said. "Anyway, what's going on? I'm heading over now."

"No!" There was a clatter, like she'd put the phone on speaker and set it down. "Not yet. But can you come over later tonight? After dark?" Her voice got further away as she spoke, and the words were punctuated with light grunts.

I tried to imagine what crisis Christina might need my help with after dark. She'd requested my help with many "bodies" over the years—from the very first time I helped her rearrange her bedroom furniture to cover the bright red hair dye stain on the carpet before her mom came home from work to more recently sourcing a replacement for the wedding china she'd accidentally dropped and broken before her husband Hudson realized it was missing. Now, I wondered if we were finally going to get back at Maureen down the street for letting her dog poop on Christina's lawn every morning.

Every day, without fail, Maureen walked her Chihuahua down the street, and every day, without fail, Sprinkles picked Christina's lawn to do his business. And every time he did it, Maureen bagged it up, then left the bagged poop sitting on the lawn.

"Why doesn't she just take it with her?" Christina had bemoaned over the phone one morning, peering through the blinds and watching Maureen drop the bag on the grass before continuing on her walk. "It would almost be better if she just walked off without bagging it. Why bag it if she's going to leave me to deal with it?"

It had been going on the entire time Christina had lived there, ever since they'd moved so Hudson could run for district supervisor. I theorized that Maureen had been in conflict with the previous homeowners and didn't realize the house had new occupants, but Christina said she and Hudson had brought over pie their first week.

"We brought pies to every house on the block," she'd lamented. "Do you know how long I spent baking? All my clothes were still in boxes, but damned if I didn't bake thirty pies within days of moving in."

"Maybe she doesn't like pie," I'd suggested.

After months of brainstorming ways she could get her revenge, I wondered if we were finally going to enact my plan—scavenge the pet waste receptacles on the trail near their neighborhood and then cover Maureen's front porch in bagged dog poo.

"How's seven?" I proposed.

Christina hummed, then said, "Make it eight. Wait—actually, let's say eight-thirty."

MY CAR TURNED heads at every stoplight as I crossed town. The AC didn't work, so I had all the windows down and could hear better than anyone the various noises coming from under the hood. One of Hudson's former colleagues had planned to give it to his son when the son turned sixteen, but the kid had raised ever-loving hell and the dad bought him a Beamer instead. I couldn't blame him.

The clunker looked right at home in front of my new home, the left side of a green stucco duplex I was renting. It was tiny, and it didn't seem like the landlord had ever once cleaned it before I moved in, but it was mine, and after I'd spent three days scrubbing it from top to bottom, I didn't mind spending time in it.

The Rightsides, as I called the family who occupied the right half of the duplex, were friendly enough. We smiled and waved if we saw each other coming or going. I ignored the sounds of their soap operas constantly drifting through the thin walls and they ignored the sounds of my crying breakdowns when I remembered the current state of my life, and we lived in harmony. The dad gave me a jump once when my car wouldn't start, and I brought over a six-pack in thanks, which he'd graciously accepted.

I parked across the street and down the block in the only open spot and started to walk towards the house, my mind flitting between satisfying thoughts of Maureen's face when she discovered bags of dog poo covering her front porch and panicked dismay at the idea of being back at square one in my job hunt. Tires screeched behind me and I whirled to see a car turning sharply onto our street just as he honked his horn at me. I ran the few remaining steps across the street and jumped up onto the curb but tripped, sending myself sprawling onto the sidewalk and my car keys flying.

"Asshole!" I screamed at the car, long gone already, and threw my middle finger up.

"Hey, are you okay?"

I lifted my head to see the door of the house whose yard I'd just landed in open and a man in a tank top and athletic shorts run out.

"I was getting ready to head out for my run and saw you fall. Are you hurt?" He crouched beside me, frowning. His hair hung in dark curls over thick eyebrows creased in concern. All the moisture left my mouth, and I opened and closed it while trying to remember where I was.

"No, I, um, I'm fine." I pressed myself up onto my hands and knees, and he quickly stood and offered me his hand to help me to my feet. Once I was standing, I realized I was still holding it and quickly let it drop. "My keys," I said suddenly, patting my pockets and scanning the ground.

"Uh," he said, holding up the keyring with only half the fob still attached. "Was it like this before?"

I cursed and got back down on the ground where he'd picked up the ring. "It falls apart like that sometimes." I pawed at the ground, looking for the other half of the fob and the lost internals. The man got down on the ground next to me and began to search, too. "You have to hold it just right when turning it in the ignition to keep it together. And not throw it on the ground."

"You know, they sell those. You could get a new one."

"But then I'd lose my key fob jigsaw puzzle Friday night activity."

When we'd collected the pieces to my key fob, the man extended his hand again. "Francisco."

"Mandy." My gaze went to our hands, his swallowing mine in a firm shake.

"You new to the neighborhood? I haven't seen you around before."

I nodded. "I moved here about two weeks ago." I pointed up the block and said, "I'm in that lime-green monstrosity," then immediately regretted it. What if he turned out to be a murderer? I'd just told him exactly where to find me. But then I turned back to him and saw his crooked smile and thought I might be okay with him finding me.

He took a step backwards and said, "Well, Mandy, if you're sure you're okay, I'm going to take off for my run. But maybe I'll see you again sometime."

With a wave, he was gone, and I stumbled up the sidewalk and into my house. I tossed the pieces of my key fob onto the gray plastic folding table I was using as a combination dining table and desk, then walked into the kitchen, filled a glass with boxed wine from the fridge, and downed half of it in one go. "What the hell was that?" I muttered.

Dave and I had had a good marriage. A fine marriage, at least. Nothing was ever *wrong* with our marriage. Nothing was ever *wrong* with our relationship in general, which was why, after six years, I agreed to marry him in the first place. We never fought. We liked the same TV shows. We were comfortable and happy and had reasonably good sex twice a week. But, much like my math PhD and subsequent professorship, my relationship with Dave was something I started because someone said I should—my roommate freshman year met him playing intramural soccer and thought he and I would make a good match—and then stayed in because there was never any good reason to leave.

The fact that I left without a "good reason" was also why Dave firmly believed I would be coming back to reconcile once I'd come to my senses and continued to text me with concern for my well-being. *News flash, Dave: not everyone who abruptly quits their job just as they're about to get tenure and ends their happy marriage to move across the country is having a mental breakdown they'll soon regret.*

I slammed the microwave door hard after pulling out the frozen lasagna I knew from experience was likely still half-frozen but would somehow burn my tongue anyway. Then I grabbed my laptop and set up at the folding table—basically my only furniture save for a second-hand loveseat—to watch a YouTube tutorial and put my key fob back together while I ate. When I opened the computer, six browser tabs were already open, all of them job search related. One was a page on how to nail an interview. I closed out of it quickly, stomach sinking as the image of Ms. Hodges's disapproving face flashed in my mind, but left the other tabs open to revisit before going to Christina's later. The sooner I found a job and got myself established here, the sooner Dave would see I was serious about staying here and not just spiraling out before running back to him.

Hours later, with a put-together key fob and a head full of actuarial analyst job listings, I shifted my thoughts to mischief and changed into dark clothes. I pulled my long, brown curls into a ponytail, fired off a quick "On my way" text to Christina, then drove north to her fancy neighborhood in the foothills. Once on her street, I slowed, taking stock of whether there were any evening walkers or runners out who might notice us. Christina's house was dark except a light in one of the back rooms, dimly visible through the window above the front door. When she opened it to let me inside, her face was pale and glistening.

She'd cut her hair short a year ago, and now instead of touching the middle of her back it barely grazed her chin. The straight blond strands fell over her ashen cheeks and emphasized their lack of color.

"Are you okay?"

"I'm fine." Without elaboration, she led me down the hall and toward the second, less formal living room on the back side of the house.

"I was thinking we should try that trail you took me walking on the first week I was here. We saw so many dog walkers, those trash cans have to be—"

We turned off the hallway into the living room where the ceiling opened up to double-height and massive windows overlooked their pool in the daylight but were filled with our reflection now. Just inside the room was a massive cedar blanket chest. It was one Christina's mother-in-law had given her and Hudson when they married, with floral motifs carved on the lid. Hudson had played in it as a child.

Christina gestured to the chest. "I need you to help me bury this."

3

While I processed her request, my eyes took in the rest of the room for the first time and landed on the pair of shovels leaning against the sliding-glass back door. One was tall and covered in uneven stains from having been used in the past. The other was tiny, two feet long from the tip of the bright blue shovel to its handle, and squeaky clean, its barcode sticker still intact.

"You need me to what?" I asked, looking from the shovels back to the chest.

"Help me bury this chest." Her voice was short, like she didn't have time for nonsense like questions. And that was one of the two rules that went with our "hide a body" code word: if one of us asked the other to hide a body, the first rule was that we showed up, and the second rule was that we didn't ask any questions. Rule number two had been implemented when I asked her to hide a body once and she showed up to find me panicking in front of a virus-infested laptop. What exactly I had been doing to contract those viruses was none of her business, and thus the rule was born. When one of us asked, the other one helped, no questions asked.

Still, being handed a blue children's shovel and directed to grab one end of a four-foot-long wooden chest to help haul it outside was so far outside of the realm of expectations, I had to work hard to bite my tongue.

Christina slid back the door, and the sound of crickets

replaced the thick silence. "On the other side of the pool," she directed. "By the shed."

I stepped through the door and surveyed the area she indicated. "How?"

Christina whirled on me and hissed, "What do you mean, how? We dig, Mandy!"

"Your yard doesn't have any dirt, Christina," I hissed back. "It's all fucking rocks!"

I was standing on the first flagstone in the path that led to a stunning pool in the center of the yard. On the other side of the pool there was a pool house to the left, a studio apartment that Christina used as an art studio and had let me stay for two weeks after I blew up my life in Michigan until I found my rental, and a small potting shed to the right. Along the left side of the pool was a pair of loungers with a hanging egg chair in between them, and to the right was a concrete pad with a fire pit in the center, surrounded on two sides by a stunning outdoor sectional. Two more outdoor chairs in the same finish dotted the patio. String lights hung overhead, strung from poles along the stucco walls surrounding the entire space.

Where there wasn't luxurious furniture, the yard had been professionally xeriscaped with saguaro cacti, giant aloe vera, and other native plants. And where there was neither furniture nor plants, there were pretty beige pebbles. The open space Christina was pointing to on the far side of the pool, between the potting shed and the patio, was entirely covered in gravel, and I was guessing it wasn't soft, loamy soil underneath.

"We'll dig up the rocks. Come on!" Christina said.

We each took one end of the chest and heaved it as high as we could, just a few inches off the ground, then waddled awkwardly over toward the proposed burial site. By the time we'd maneuvered it across the yard, I was sweating despite the fifty-degree weather and we were both out of breath.

"Come on," Christina said again, and picked up the larger of the shovels. I watched as she put the tip to the ground and stomped on the step as hard as she could. The blade sank a measly inch into the ground. She cursed and repeated the sequence, then admonished me, "Are you going to stand there or are you going to help?"

"What am I supposed to do with this?" I raised the children's shovel into the air.

"Dig!"

"It's two feet long! I can't even use it standing up."

"Go look for something else in the shed, then." Christina made another, more successful, attempt with her shovel, this time moving several inches of gravel and sandy soil, a tiny hole beginning to take shape.

Using my cell phone flashlight to guide me, I pulled back the door of the small shed and peered inside. The beam illuminated spiderwebs, and I remembered the one time I'd floated the idea of moving to Dave, back when we were finishing up our graduate programs and applying for teaching jobs.

"You want to move to Arizona? It's so hot there, and there are black widows everywhere."

I took an involuntary step backward at the memory. "I don't know, Christina."

I heard her frustrated exhale, then her steps on the gravel as she came up behind me. "Here." She thrust her shovel into my hand and took my phone, stepping into the shed with no fear.

I returned to the small hole she'd created and tried to imitate the motions I'd seen her make, placing the tip of the blade against the ground and stomping on the top, forcing it down into the dirt. My first attempt threw me off balance and shot a sharp pain up through my ankle, a lightning bolt through the dull ache in my joints that never seemed to go away. I cried out as I stumbled forward.

"Quiet!" Christina hissed as she emerged from the shed. "Here, I found this."

When I turned around, Christina was holding up a pickaxe.

"Why do you have a pickaxe?"

She shrugged. "Hudson got it in his head that we were going to do the landscaping ourselves after we moved in. He bought a handful of tools, but it only took one afternoon for him to give up on that dream and call the professionals."

Christina held the pickaxe out to me and I took it, bending with the weight, and gave her back the shovel.

My first swing with the pickaxe was nearly as bad as my attempt with the shovel. I planted my feet and raised it over my head against the protestations of my shoulders. When I swung it down at the ground in front of me with a grunt, it left a bogglingly small divot in the earth. I swung a few more times, getting a feel for the motion and pushing through the ache building in my muscles.

We switched off, trading the shovel and pickaxe between us. When we'd dug out an area as large as the chest's footprint, I paused to catch my breath. "How deep do we need to put it?"

Christina frowned at the six-inch hole we'd managed so far. "I don't think we're going to get to six feet." With no further answer, she picked up the pickaxe and resumed swinging, breaking up the dirt so I could move it with the shovel.

When the moon was fully overhead and sweat had soaked through my t-shirt, I mumbled that I needed the bathroom and slipped back into the house to find my purse hanging by the front door. I pawed around inside it with my dirt-covered hands until I found my joint cream, then desperately rubbed it over my throbbing joints before popping two pain pills in my mouth.

"You can do it," I muttered to myself. "Almost there."

"You okay?" I jerked my head up to find Christina standing at the other end of the hallway.

"Yep! Just looking for some gum in my purse." I hung the bag back up and hurried back outside to where Christina had already picked the pickaxe back up and resumed swinging.

As the hole deepened, we slowed down. Between every swing of the shovel, we looked from our hole to the chest and back, eyeing it up.

"Do you think it's deep enough?" I asked.

Christina climbed out of the hole and stood beside the chest, rubbing her finger along the fabric of her jeans, smearing a line of dirt marking the height of the chest. She stepped back down into the hole and both of our hearts sank when we saw the line several inches higher than the top of the hole. Resigned, we continued to dig in silence, Christina checking the depth against the line on her jeans every so often.

"Look!" she finally said, pointing down to her pants. The side of the hole came up just above the line she'd made.

It crossed my mind that our hole might not be an even depth all the way around, but as Christina climbed out of the hole and scrambled over to the chest, I kept that to myself. I wasn't about to inflict more digging upon us. We would put the trunk in the hole, and if one side wasn't deep enough, we'd just pile dirt over the top and act like her yard had always had a hill in it.

The sky was just beginning to lighten as we heaved the trunk over to the hole. We lowered my side down first, then hers, and as it slid into place, the top of the chest just below the rest of the ground, I felt my shoulders drop in relief.

"Oh, thank goodness," Christina breathed. With just that single second's pause, she picked up the shovel and began to cover the top of the chest.

"What are we going to do with all the dirt?" I asked when we were finally smoothing gravel over the top of the freshly covered hole. We'd packed some of it back in around the sides of the chest, but there was an impressive pile left behind.

Christina sized up the pile, then ducked into the house and came out with a roll of huge black trash bags. One by one, we filled them until they were just at the brink of being too heavy to lift, then lined them up by the house.

"I'll take these to the dump tomorrow." Christina looked up at the rapidly lightening sky. "Or today, I guess."

As we tied the strings on the last bag, I muttered to myself that I thought the dump would have been a better solution for getting rid of the chest, too.

"Mandy!" Christina called out when I'd thrown my purse over my shoulder on my way out. I turned, and she waved and said, "I'm sorry about the interview."

I waved back before climbing into my car and sinking down into the seat, groaning in a combination of pain and pleasure at finally sitting down. I started the car and pulled away from the curb. Just as I did, headlights came on behind me, and I blinked into my rearview mirror just in time to see another car swing out from the curb and speed past me.

4

I slept for sixteen hours after shedding my clothes during the walk from the front door to my mattress on the floor and woke late in the evening, naked except for my underwear and entirely disoriented, my body screaming in pain. I rolled over with a whimper and felt the sheets soaking wet beneath my skin. When I threw a hand over my forehead, I could feel it burning up.

Great. Pushing myself up and standing left me breathing heavily, and I padded into the bathroom and sipped cold water straight from the tap before splashing it over my face. I slathered more joint cream over my skin and downed two more pain pills, then crawled back into bed without bothering to change the sheets.

When I woke again, the sun was just beginning to rise, nearly twenty-four hours after I'd arrived home covered in dirt. While my body still ached all over, the fever had subsided and I was starting to think clearly. Clearly enough to notice my gnawing hunger.

Clearly enough to wonder why Christina had put me through hell to hide that chest.

I poured cereal into a bowl and wolfed it down standing at the countertop. Then I poured another bowl, this time taking it to the table and sinking down into the matching gray plastic folding chair. Between bites, I fired off a text to Christina.

Mandy: Morning sunshine. Slept all day yesterday after you

put me through bootcamp. When I can lift them again, my arms are going to be jacked. Want to get lunch later?

In the light of day, maybe she'd open up.

I washed my bowl—the only one I owned, along with one plate, and one of each utensil—and took a shower. The water ran a sludgy brown, dislodging the soil from where it had caked into the creases in my skin. I scrubbed and scrubbed and still emerged with dark, dirt-stained cuticles.

My phone buzzed on the bathroom counter and I snatched it up, but instead of a response from Christina, it was a message from Dave.

Dave: Hey Mands, hope you're doing well. I'm packing up the latest of your mail to forward to you. Are you still staying with Christina or is there a new address I should use? If you want to talk, I'm here. I still love you and I always will.

Before I'd even finished reading the message, my face broke and I found myself wiping tears from my eyes.

"Fuck you," I muttered and threw the phone across the room onto my mattress. I didn't want him fishing for my address, and I really didn't want him to be the good guy right now.

When I'd stripped the bed and gathered up my laundry to take down the street to the laundromat, Christina still hadn't replied. I was trying to balance my laundry hamper on one hip and fumbling with my key in the lock when a shout startled me.

"Hey! It's you again!" Francisco was jogging up the street under the pink dawn sky, bare-chested and dripping sweat and carrying a t-shirt in one hand. "Another early bird?"

I forced my eyes not to follow the bead of sweat dripping down from his collarbone. "Um, I guess?" I swallowed and tried to remember what I'd been doing. "I couldn't sleep any more so I figured I'd get a few things done."

Francisco took in my laundry basket with a raised brow and chuckled. "Been rolling around in the dirt?"

"No!" My response was too defensive, and he recoiled, surprised.

"Whoa, just teasing." He watched me curiously as he turned back toward his house. "I'll let you get to it. See you around?"

My jaw dropped when I rolled up to the laundromat. I'd expected the early hour to mean I had the place to myself, but it seemed like all of Tucson had decided six in the morning was laundry time. The space was packed, and I waited in line for a single washer to become available, then tried in vain to cram everything in together to get it all done in one load. While I waited, I glanced up at where four televisions were mounted along the back wall above the dryers. Two of them were tuned to news stations, one local and one national, while the other two played the History Channel and the Food Network. I fired off another message to Christina before settling in to watch a historian theorize on the identity of Jack the Ripper.

The historian had gone through two candidates, convincing me in turn that the Ripper was a woman and then that the Ripper was H.H. Holmes, an American. I had pulled out my phone to look up whether he'd ever traveled to the UK when a machine beeped across the room and I made a beeline with my hamper.

As I stood from shoving my sheets into the machine, a familiar face on one of the other television screens caught my eye. On the local news channel, Christina's husband's face took up half the screen. A news anchor wore a stern expression as she spoke next to Hudson's photograph. I blinked, trying to take in the subtitles.

"...his colleagues on the Board of Supervisors last saw him at work on Thursday. Colleagues at the law office where he has continued to practice part-time since his election to the Board of Supervisors say he attended a partner meeting Friday morning. Police say they have no reason to believe there is any cause for concern, but local activists continue to gather outside the administration building demanding to know why their district supervisor failed to attend their scheduled meeting Friday."

The chyron read, "LOCAL SUPERVISOR HUDSON SCHUPPERT MISSING?"

5

The picture of Hudson disappeared, the anchor reclaiming the full screen as the story switched to coverage of a recent high-profile lawsuit featuring a large pharmaceutical company. I stared at the screen, willing it to switch back, desperate for more information, but an over-the-shoulder graphic insert popped up featuring a different man's face, and the anchor continued talking.

"...family is protesting outside the company's headquarters, stating they believe the pharmaceutical company is responsible for Mr. Hall's suicide."

I turned away from the screen, already dialing Christina's number as I stopped the washers and loaded my sopping wet, still half-dirty clothes back into my hamper.

"Pick up, pick up, pick up!"

When she didn't, I called again, and kept up the attempts while I scrambled to my car and threw it into drive.

Christina's house in the Catalina Foothills was a twenty-minute drive from my neighborhood, but I made it in fifteen, calling on repeat the whole way there. I was still trying to call her when I stormed her front porch and knocked like crazy. I told myself it was early, still barely dawn, and Christina was never an early bird. We'd been up all night just a day ago; she was probably sleeping in this morning to make up for it. But the harder I knocked and the more calls that went unanswered, the more my gut told me that wasn't the case.

Something was horribly wrong.

I looked around for an obviously fake rock or other hiding spot for a spare key, then remembered the key she and Hudson had given me when she'd come to get me from Michigan and told me to stay in their pool house until I figured out what I wanted to do next. I'd insisted upon giving it back to them when I found my apartment, but when I'd arrived home that day I'd found the spare key inside my purse again.

"For emergencies," Christina had said when I called her.

"I'm not going to have an emergency. I'm fine. This place is great, and I can take care of myself."

"What if your landlord ends up being a creep and you need a place to stay, but you try to come over and Hudson and I are out at one of his fancy political events? You're just going to sit on my stoop until we get back?"

I ran back to the car where my purse was tossed haphazardly on the passenger seat and rummaged through it frantically, searching for a metallic glint. My hand closed around it so tightly the teeth bit into my skin.

"Christina?" I ran inside, the door hanging open behind me, and shouted for her. "Hudson? Christina?"

Hudson is missing. Christina isn't answering. Something is wrong.

I tried to calm myself, to remind myself that the police didn't think he was missing. Some activist group was supposed to have a meeting and he didn't show, but that didn't automatically mean he was missing. Maybe he just forgot about the appointment.

My gut rejected that idea even as my brain suggested it. As long as I'd known him, Hudson had been obsessive over his schedule. If he missed an appointment without a call, something was wrong.

The growing panic clouded my ability to think, and for a minute I stood in the hallway, just calling their names again and again. A loud sports car starting up down the street brought me back into my physical surroundings, and I closed the door behind me and kicked off my shoes.

Hudson had shown up to work at his law office on Friday, the day of his missed meeting, but then never turned up to work at the Board of Supervisors. The angry activist group went straight to the press, outraged by the lack of support from their district supervisor, and the press had begun to spin a story that Hudson was missing when his colleagues at the board said they hadn't seen him at all that day. When neither Hudson nor Christina could be reached for comment, the story grew.

But being unreachable for comment wasn't the same thing as being missing.

I dragged myself up the stairs, my energy flagging as the initial adrenaline wore off and the fatigue set back in. Nothing seemed out of place in their bedroom. The bed was neatly made. I peeked into the bathroom where two towels hung on the towel racks. I reached out and felt them; they were dry.

I peeked in the other two upstairs rooms; one was set up as a guest room and the other was a game room. Both were spotlessly clean, without a speck of dust, though I'd never seen Christina or Hudson use the game room when I stayed with them and, as far as I knew, the last time they'd had anyone stay in their guest room was a disastrous visit from Hudson's parents months ago. If something had happened in this house, there wasn't any evidence of it happening up here.

Downstairs, I went room by room, not knowing what I was looking for but desperately looking all the same. I'd just seen Christina barely twenty-four hours ago, in the pre-dawn hours after burying that god-forsaken chest, and now the local news was saying her husband was missing and she wasn't answering her phone. There had to be some explanation, if only I could find it. But room after room, the story was the same: no signs of a struggle and nothing obviously out of place.

Hudson's office was the last room I checked. It was a dark room with espresso-stained wood shelves lining most of the walls and a deep teal paint coating the rest. A huge walnut executive desk occupied the center of the room. Hudson's briefcase leaned against the side of the desk, and I reached for it. With my fingers hovering over the zipper, I debated with myself. It was one thing to look around the house; it was another to rifle through a closed briefcase. But something was wrong here, and I needed to figure out what was going on.

I opened the briefcase and pulled out a laptop, a legal pad, and a small agenda book. It was too dark to make out the writing in the little booklet, so I pulled back the curtain to let in some light, then froze to the spot. Hudson's office window overlooked their backyard, and gaping at me through that window was a huge hole in the ground. An empty hole where Friday night I had helped bury a chest.

6

I instinctively jerked the curtain back into place as if that could make this all go away. As if that swift jerk of fabric could turn back time to before Christina and I had so painstakingly buried the chest her mother-in-law had given her. Before someone had taken it out of the ground. Before my best friend stopped answering her calls and vanished with her husband into thin air.

Seconds later, I tore the curtain open again to make sure I hadn't imagined it. I hadn't.

I flipped hastily through the legal pad, but nothing jumped out at me. I didn't even know what I was hoping to find. The agenda was the same story—he didn't have "disappear" written on his calendar, nor anything else that immediately leapt out as connected to his disappearance. Or Christina's.

It was rapidly sinking in that not only did Hudson seem to be missing, but so did Christina. Did the police know? When they said they didn't think there was cause for concern, did that mean they'd been able to reach Hudson or Christina more recently than Friday? Or did it just mean they thought a bunch of activists demanding to speak to their district supervisor were kooks and they didn't want to take their concerns seriously?

I slid my phone from my back pocket and dialed 911, but then the hole in the yard caught my eye again.

"911, what's your emergency?"

"I, uh—sorry, there's no emergency." I fumbled with my phone to end the call.

If the police came here searching for Christina and her husband, they'd find what looked like a grave in their yard. Granted, the grave was only four feet long and not very deep, but it would raise questions. They'd go to the neighbors, start asking around. Whatever Christina had wanted to hide, whatever I'd helped her bury, I was sure it was nothing. But as long as I didn't know what it was or what I might have been a party to, I didn't want the cops crawling around the house and looking into it.

I stepped back into the hallway and let myself slide down the wall until I was crouched on the floor with my head resting on my knees. Something was horribly wrong, and I knew the authorities ought to be doing something, but I couldn't bring myself to bring them here. I turned my head toward the front door, thinking of the last time I'd stepped through it. How had everything changed so fast?

I started to pull my phone out again, to make yet another desperate call to Christina, when I noticed something—or rather, the lack of something—by the door. The shoe rack had two empty spaces.

I scrambled to my feet. There was never open space on the shoe rack. Hudson complained that Christina bought too many pairs of shoes, and then she complained that he dragged her to too many swanky events with his law partners or local businessmen and politicians where she had to look the part—it was an argument I'd heard them have more than once. And this was the first sign that Christina and Hudson hadn't simply evaporated into thin air.

I hurried back up the stairs. I'd been looking for some clue to why Hudson and Christina might be missing, unconsciously seeking out signs of a struggle, indications that something horrible might have happened. But what if they'd just...left?

I flicked on the bathroom light, and immediately my eyes

landed on the toothbrush holder on the counter. I didn't know how I'd missed it before. It was empty.

The last place I needed to check was the closet. I pulled the chain to illuminate the walk-in closet that was nearly the size of my bedroom and looked straight to the shelf above the hanging clothes where Christina and Hudson kept their luggage. When Christina had dropped everything to come get me in Michigan and move me down here after I'd told Dave I wanted a divorce, she'd had a pink duffel bag with white stars all over it. Scanning the luggage, I saw matching sets of hard-shell suitcases but no duffel.

I reached for the suitcases, needing to be sure. My fingers came up inches shy of the shelf, and I looked around for something I could stand on. I peeked behind the door, hoping for a step stool, but found nothing. Back in the bedroom, I glanced under the bed. Maybe there would be a sturdy box I could use? Instead, my eyes landed on a soft duffel bag. Not Christina's pink starry bag, but a dark leather one. I pulled it out and unzipped it, a gasp escaping my lungs when Hudson's clothes stared back at me from inside.

I dumped the contents of the bag onto the carpet. A handful of shirts, a pair of pants, a pair of shorts, and a few pairs of underwear. A toiletry bag with the toothbrush that was missing from the bathroom and travel-sized soaps. It was the epitome of packing light, but there was no doubt that these were Hudson's things.

Unwilling to waste more time looking for a stool, I jumped, grasping for the handle of one of the suitcases and tugging it down off the closet shelf with a clatter. I then repeated the process until the shelf was empty, searching each case to see if Christina's starry bag was nested in any of them, but it wasn't. It wasn't in the closet, concealed behind hanging clothes. It wasn't under the bed with Hudson's. I went from room to room a second time, now searching specifically for the bag rather than looking for some undefined clue, but came up empty.

There was only one place I still hadn't looked: the garage. When I pulled back the door, sure enough, Hudson's Lexus was still inside. A packed bag. His briefcase and his laptop. His car. All left behind. But Christina's SUV was nowhere in sight.

I stumbled into the living room, reeling. Hudson was gone, but he'd left all his things behind. It didn't seem like something he would do if he'd left of his own volition. But Christina was gone, and I couldn't say the same for her.

What did you do?

I threw the living room curtains back, the floor-to-ceiling windows giving me a better view of the hole in the ground than I'd had from Hudson's office. The bags full of dirt and rubble were still lined up outside the house. Christina hadn't made the trip to the dump to get rid of them before she disappeared.

Even if I didn't call them, I figured it was only a matter of time before police officers came by and let themselves in. They might not have cause for concern now, but if he didn't turn up for work tomorrow, I thought it likely that they'd look into it. And when they did, I thought it might be better if they didn't find a giant hole in the ground.

Cursing her name the entire time, I rolled the bags over toward where Christina and I had spent hours digging. I slashed each bag and refilled the hole, then tried to spread as much gravel as I could from the rest of the lawn to make the refilled area blend in. It still looked out of place, but maybe not enough to draw attention, or at least I hoped not. I threw the bags away in their garage trash can, then gathered up Hudson's laptop, legal pad, and agenda to take with me. I was suddenly itching to get out of this house, but I thought maybe there was something in them that might help me make sense of this mess.

I locked the door behind me and hurried to my car. I'd

forgotten all about my wet laundry until I opened the door and the damp smell greeted me. A quick glance down at my clothes revealed how filthy I'd gotten manhandling bags of dirt to refill that godforsaken hole, so I headed home to change before returning to the laundromat. I could take Hudson's agenda and legal pad and read through them while I waited.

I was leaving with my hamper under my arm for the second time when Francisco pulled into the parking spot behind my car and waved at me. With a quizzical look, he pointed to the hamper. "Laundry twice in one day?"

"I got a little sidetracked earlier." He shifted a stack of manila folders and a laptop under his arm, and I asked, "Done with work for the day?"

"Just getting started." A smile broke out across his face. "I just landed a new lead I want to follow up on."

"New lead?"

"I'm a journalist."

The back of my neck began to tingle. "A journalist? What kinds of stories do you cover?"

His smile widened, and he stepped closer so he could lower his voice. "I've been stuck on fluff pieces for years, but I've been working on a piece on the side that's going to transform my career. This is going to be the piece that shows everyone I'm a serious reporter. It's going to change everything."

My pulse pounded in my ears as I waited for what I somehow knew was coming. "Oh yeah?"

"I've been working on a piece about a corrupt local politician. And as of this morning, the guy seems to have gone missing."

7

My stomach dropped and I tried to look nonchalant, though the flat smile I attempted to paste on felt a little crazed.

"You're kidding. Here?" I pointed at the ground and Francisco chuckled, seemingly pleased to get to let me in on what he knew.

"Right here in Tucson. KVOA reported on it this morning."

"That's unbelievable. And you said he's corrupt? What does that mean, like taking bribes?"

Francisco pursed his lips. "I shouldn't tell you that. When I finally get my piece published, I'll be sure to let you know, though."

"Oh, come on," I challenged, hoping I sounded playful and not desperate like I felt. If he knew about some shady business practices Hudson was engaged in, he could hold the clue to finding Hudson—and with him, I hoped, Christina. "Don't tease me like that. Now I'm dying to know!"

A smile crept back across Francisco's face.

"I've got no contacts in the area. I'm an unemployed former math professor who's lived here less than a month. You're going to hint that I moved into some hotbed of political corruption and not give me the deets?"

Francisco winked and said, "Everywhere's a hotbed of political corruption if you dig deep enough. Anyway, I've already said too much, and I really need to get going. See you around?" With a wave, he hustled over to his car and then disappeared out of sight.

The line at the laundromat was a sea of eagle-eyed citizens glaring at each new person who joined the queue. The moment one of the machines chimed, at least three people swarmed it, arguing over who had been there first. I took a spot behind a young man in swim trunks and a baby blue button-down, the very image of laundry day, and set my hamper down at my feet, kicking it along each time we inched forward.

I picked up Hudson's agenda to look through while waiting. *Corrupt.* I'd thought a lot of things about Hudson since Christina first introduced us, but never considered that he might be anything more than a kid born with a silver spoon in his mouth, rubbing shoulders with the other good old boys and climbing the ladder to more and more money and influence. A little bit of *you scratch my back and I'll scratch yours,* sure. Out-and-out corruption? That seemed a bridge too far.

But where did the good old boys doing favors for each other stop and corruption start?

I thumbed through the agenda, scanning each page of appointments with more scrutiny than I'd done at their house. If Francisco was right—and he gave off the confident aura of someone who usually was—then Hudson was in over his head. Because however much I did not like him for my friend, Hudson wasn't a conniving, unscrupulous, duplicitous man. He was just a boy who never had to grow up. He never seemed to have learned that the world didn't revolve around him, and while that made him a shitty husband for my vibrant, empathetic artist of a best friend, it didn't make him malicious. It didn't make him cut out to hang with truly bad people.

I flipped through weeks of appointments—Board of Supervisors meetings, court appearances, meetings with civic organizations—but it felt like looking at a *Where's Waldo* picture without knowing what Waldo looked like. I knew there had to be something to find, but I didn't know what it was. I was halfway through March, skimming Hudson's schedule from just a month ago, when something caught my eye. Sandwiched between an event with the Conservation Lands and Resources Department and a reminder to file a Motion to Continue with the court was a late-night meeting with someone named Diamond.

"Hey, you want a machine or not?" The older man behind me shoved forward, knocking me so that the agenda fell out of my hand and landed on my hamper. I looked up to see someone unloading one of the washers and hurried over to take over the machine.

Once the washer began to spin, I leaned against it and paged hurriedly through the agenda, looking for the page where I'd left off and then flipping forward from there. In the month since the first meeting with Diamond, they'd had two other meetings, both after eight in the evening. The most recent one was just last Thursday, the day before Hudson disappeared after his meeting at the law firm. The day before Christina called me to help her bury a chest and then apparently packed a bag and left.

I moved to the legal pad next. The top page was dated about three weeks earlier, and each page was filled with everything from daily to-do lists to notes from his meetings to birthday present ideas for his mother. Each page was dated, the notes printed in all caps. The first meeting with Diamond had taken place before the first notes in this legal pad, but I flipped the pages until I arrived at the date of their second meeting and scanned the yellow page. It contained notes from a meeting with a legal client, the County Health Department, and the Regional Affordable Housing Commission. Every one of those meetings was listed in Hudson's agenda. The only agenda item without corresponding notes in the legal pad was the meeting with Diamond.

I flipped ahead in the legal pad to the page from last Thursday when he'd last met with Diamond. Just as before, everything else in Hudson's schedule had notes, but the meeting with Diamond was entirely absent.

There was only one more page with writing on it, the page from last Friday. Hudson had taken notes during the partner meeting at his law firm, but there was nothing else. Sometime after that meeting, he'd gone home and deposited his briefcase, then disappeared, leaving behind his laptop and notes and a packed bag of clothes. According to his schedule, he should have met with the Redistricting Advisory Committee that afternoon and then the environmental activists after that, but apparently he never made it.

My pulse raced and I shifted my weight restlessly. I wanted to talk to the other partners at Hudson's firm, the last place I knew he'd been before going home and disappearing, to see if he'd been acting strange or said anything that might shed some light on all of this. And I needed to track down this mysterious Diamond. But first, I needed another washing machine to open up so I could get out of this laundromat.

When I finally tossed my dry, clean laundry into the hamper, skipping the folding and just cramming it in, I thought about Francisco and his lead. If he was digging into Hudson, he had better access to sources than I did, and as a journalist he would have investigative experience I couldn't compete with. But maybe I could leverage his work. No one seemed to have picked up on Christina's missing status yet, but if I could find out what Francisco knew about Hudson, maybe it would lead me to my best friend.

I turned onto our block, searching the street for Francisco's car. There was nothing wrong with a friendly neighbor dropping in to say hello, I thought. And if he happened to be working on his piece, maybe he'd let something slip. I was so focused on looking for signs Francisco was home that I didn't even notice the police officer standing on my porch.

8

My brain's full capacity was used up trying to comprehend what a police officer was doing on my doorstep, and I suddenly couldn't remember simple things like how to breathe. I sputtered, trying to suck down air as the officer turned and saw me moving toward him.

"Are you Mrs. Amanda Perkins?"

"No. Well, yes. I don't..." The whole breathing thing was still a struggle, and his question left me stumped.

Technically, yes, I was still Mrs. Perkins. I'd changed my name on all my social media profiles back to Mandy Simon during the drive from Michigan to Arizona. Christina had whooped and congratulated me, though there had still been concern behind her eyes—I hadn't given her an explanation yet for why I was blowing up my life, and she didn't ask questions until I'd been in her pool house for three days and she barged in saying, "Okay, I'm happy to drive you and all your things across the country, but your husband is blowing up my phone. He's threatening to call the police if I don't put you on the phone so he can see for himself that I didn't kill you and leave your body on the side of the road somewhere in Missouri. Before I tell him to fuck off and respect your space, I need to know what's going on."

I'd told her the story—most of it, at least. With my application for tenure starting, I'd realized I was living a life I'd stumbled into but didn't actually want. I was great at math, but I didn't actually *care* about it. I had no real passion for it. And

Dave and I were happy enough together, but it was another example of me taking too many "next steps" down a path that was comfortable and never once considering if it was the path I really wanted to be walking down. Facing down a milestone promotion just highlighted that I'd been busting my ass to get somewhere that, once I could almost taste it, I realized I didn't actually want to be.

Christina had responded by making me put on one of her bathing suits and get into their pool.

"It's March, C!"

"It's Arizona, Mandy! It's seventy-seven degrees outside."

"But—"

"You told Dave you wanted to leave Michigan, right?"

I nodded. I had, every year since grad school.

"And he decided his desires mattered more than yours, so you stayed, right?"

It wasn't just his desires. It was that we had jobs there, and his family was nearby, and moving would set us back in our careers, and if I just stuck it out, he was sure I'd get used to the snow. I squared my jaw as I nodded to Christina again.

"Now you get to show him you're doing what you want. You're in the mother fucking sunshine in a mother fucking pool because you don't live somewhere where it mother fucking snows anymore."

She'd taken a picture of me lounging on a pool float shaped like a flamingo and sent it to Dave as "proof of life" along with a stern warning not to contact either of us again. One he'd continued to ignore.

The police officer on my porch was looking at me like he was trying to decide whether to take me to the hospital. I hurried to clarify, "I'm separated from my husband." As my brain had finally kicked back in and I was now breathing and speaking like normal, he seemed to relax. "Can I help you?"

"That husband you're separated from called the station and

asked us to conduct a wellness check on you. He said he believed you to be at this address and said he had reason to believe you may be a danger to yourself."

My jaw hinged open and my fingers gripped the laundry hamper tighter. I knew he thought I was making a mistake, that I must be having some sort of mental health crisis to want to run away from my life, but I never expected him to go so far as to call the police to my home.

"I assure you, officer, I'm no danger to myself. I just haven't been responding to his messages since, you know, we're separated."

The officer was already walking down the path toward where I stood between him and his patrol car, nodding with understanding. "Next time, it might be easier just to respond. Tell him you're fine but not to contact you again."

My blood heated. "Thanks," I said drily.

"And that car you pulled up in has a headlight out. You should get that fixed."

I was barely inside the house before I called Dave.

"You sent the police to my house because I won't respond to your texts?" I demanded.

"You haven't responded in over a week. Christina isn't responding anymore, either. For all I knew, something could have happened to you. Stable women don't just—"

"Don't you start in on how I'm unstable, Dave. I am of sound mind and I can make decisions for my own life, including the decision to end my marriage to you."

"What about what I want? I don't get a say in whether our marriage ends?"

"No!" I screamed, a deranged laugh erupting from me. "That's not how it works."

"Mandy, I just want to understand. We were happy. I don't know what—"

"That's something to talk to a therapist about, Dave. I don't owe you an explanation, and I don't owe you understanding. I am sane and healthy. I am not a danger to myself. But if you send the cops to my door again because I stopped responding to your texts, I'll be a danger to you."

I'd already pulled the phone away from my face to hang up when I remembered. "How did you know where to send them?"

Dave was quiet on the other end.

"How did you know where I'm staying, Dave? You said Christina wasn't responding to your texts. How'd you know where to tell the police to go to check on me?"

The line was quiet for long enough that I thought he was going to refuse to answer, but finally he let out a long sigh and said, "The laptop."

"You tracked my laptop?" My laptop was his old one, one he'd used for two years before his grandpa died and he'd used the money he'd inherited to replace it with a nicer one.

"It had tracking enabled from when it was mine. I have it on all my devices. Look, Mandy, I—"

"Fuck you, Dave."

I hung up the phone and screamed into the threadbare cushion of the loveseat Christina had helped me bring home from the Salvation Army. Then I went to where my laptop rested on the folding table next to Hudson's. And I suddenly wondered if taking his laptop from his house was a very big mistake.

9

Hudson's laptop stared up at me, a sleek machine out of place next to my hand-me-down laptop in this tiny apartment whose furnishings consisted solely of a second-hand loveseat, a mattress on the floor, and a plastic folding table with a pair of matching folding chairs. I kicked myself for being so stupid. What was I thinking, bringing it here?

I flipped open the lid, then reared back, kicking myself again for touching it with my bare hands. I wiped at the computer with a paper towel, then surveyed the lock screen. A picture of Hudson and Christina grinning at the camera from their vacation in Greece hovered above Hudson's username. Beneath that, a password entry box. If I could get in, maybe I could see whether there was tracking software activated and disable it before the cops came knocking at my door for reasons beyond a wellness check.

With a groan, I folded the laptop shut. Who was I kidding? I didn't even know where to begin guessing his password, and once I got in, I had no idea what I was even looking for. I'd been using my own laptop for two years without realizing there was location tracking enabled.

I shoved Hudson's computer away and grabbed my own. Nothing on the screen indicated that it was beaming my location data to my ex across the country. I Googled "how to find tracking software on a laptop," but my eyes glazed over at the results. The further I scrolled, the more my anger at Dave flared. I didn't want to be digging through guides on how to find hidden programs on my laptop. I wanted to be down the street trying to figure out if the journalist with the dreamy curls was onto anything that might help me find my missing best friend.

Finally, I shoved myself back from the table with a few choice words. Dave had already traced my location; figuring out how to stop him from further tracking me could wait. I tucked the laptop under my arm and gave Hudson's one last withering glance before heading out the door for Francisco's. I couldn't stop myself from picturing Dave, bent over his own computer, watching some blinking dot representing me move across the screen as I walked down the street. I pulled my shoulders back and thrust my chin forward. *Watch me all you want, Dave.*

Francisco's house was similar in size to the duplex I was renting half of, but instead of a garish lime green, it was a cream color with a deep red-orange door. I raised my fist and knocked, then shifted my weight from foot to foot while I waited for him to answer. When he finally pulled back the door, he looked surprised to see me.

"I have a computer question," I said and held up my laptop. "Do you think you could help?"

He blinked, then pulled the door wider and gestured me inside. "I'm not exactly a technology wizard, but I can try." He led me through the entryway and into a dining room he was using as an office. It was fully furnished as a dining room—a china cabinet lined one wall, and a large polished wood table with a colorful runner and six matching chairs took up the bulk of the space—but one of the dining chairs was moved against the wall and an office chair took its space, and a desktop computer sat beneath the table with a monitor and keyboard atop the runner.

"Everything okay over there?" Francisco asked while I set my laptop on the table and settled into one of the dining chairs.

When I opened my mouth in surprise, he clarified, "I saw you talking to a police officer."

Had he been watching as I'd pulled up?

I swallowed and said, as casually as I could, "Yep, totally fine."

"The guy that lived in that unit before was a real piece of work. I guess I shouldn't be surprised to see police turning up looking for him."

"Oh, no, that's not—" I kicked myself for not just nodding and accepting his explanation, but Francisco was looking at me with curiosity now, so I explained. "My ex. He, uh, called in a wellness check on me." Francisco's thick brows shot up and his eyes widened. "When I moved here, I left behind a life that, from the outside, looked great. He hasn't taken the split well. We all know that when a woman makes a bold choice about her own life, she must be having a mental breakdown, right? He's 'concerned' about me." I drew air quotes around the word and tried to force a laugh, but it came out mirthless.

"That's awful." Francisco looked genuinely horrified, and his shock stirred embarrassment in me.

I rushed to brush it off. "It's no big deal. I up and left, and since we're separated, I wasn't responding to his messages. He was worried."

"No, he wasn't. He was trying to control you, and it *is* a big deal."

My mouth went dry, all the spare moisture having moved suddenly to my eyes. I gestured awkwardly to the laptop in front of me. "Anyway..." I breathed and forced the question out. "If there was tracking software on this laptop, do you know how I could find out?"

His horrified expression deepened. "You think your ex put something on here?"

"I'm pretty sure of it."

He pulled the laptop toward him, and I watched the muscle in his jaw flex as he clicked around. "Like I said, I'm not amazing with computers, but I think..." He trailed off, his entire focus on the screen. His eyes darted from left to right, and he opened and closed windows at a rate I couldn't follow, checking one thing after the next. A few minutes later, he turned the screen toward me and leaned back in his chair with a satisfied nod. I grabbed the computer and pulled it toward me. I should have felt relieved that Dave couldn't track me anymore, but all I could think about was Hudson's laptop back in my house.

"Could you should me how you did that? In case I ever need it."

Francisco waved a hand in the air. "You're all good. You don't need to worry anymore. It'd be a good idea to get a new laptop when you can, though. One he never had access to."

That was at the top of my to-do list for when I actually had money. It still didn't help me with Hudson's, though.

"Thanks. How accurate is that stuff anyway?"

"I promise I took care of it. You don't need to worry."

"I'm just curious. If you hadn't wiped it, if I went to a coffee shop with a laptop with tracking software on it, could the person tracking it tell I was in the coffee shop and not the library next door?"

Francisco shrugged. "Depends on the program. Maybe, maybe not. Probably not."

His phone beeped, and he looked at it and frowned, then turned immediately to his monitor, waking it up. "Sorry," he said. "I really need to—" His phone beeped again, and this time his frown broke immediately into shock. "I've got to go."

He stood, hurrying to the door, and I gathered my laptop again and followed, confused.

"I'm so sorry. A new lead that can't wait." As he waited for me to get my shoes back on, he was buzzing with energy.

I looked up at him and smiled. "I guess I'm your lucky charm. It seems like it's something really exciting," I probed, but instead of spilling his secrets, he just gave me a tight smile and checked his watch again. My cheeks burned.

"Thank you for your help." I turned to say goodbye on his front porch, but the second he turned the key in the lock, he bounded toward the curb in two great strides.

"Later, Mandy!" he called, already shutting his car door and then taking off.

Back in my home, which felt dimmer and emptier having just been inside a home with actual furniture, I set my laptop down by Hudson's and stared at it. The clock above the stove warned that I'd missed lunchtime, but the thought of a blinking dot on someone's screen proclaiming that Hudson's laptop was here in this shabby neighborhood miles from his home killed any appetite I might have had.

"All right," I said out loud to the offending device. "It's time for you to go."

I scooped it up and started on my way. When I passed Francisco's house on my way, I wondered what exactly he'd run out of there to track down. Wherever he was right now, was he uncovering Hudson's whereabouts—finding the clue that would make it make sense that he'd left without taking anything with him? And would that clue somehow also make it make sense that Christina had called me over to bury something and then disappeared immediately after?

I dismissed the nagging feeling in the back of my head. Christina and Hudson were going to reappear and it would all make sense. Francisco would publish his story about Hudson's corruption and maybe Christina would leave him and we'd carry each other through it. It would all be fine.

I was telling myself that story over and over when a billboard caught my eye and I nearly caused an accident, too fixated on the woman making come-hither eyes at me from the sign to notice brake lights in front of me. Beneath the establishment's name, the billboard encouraged the reader to "Visit Diamond, Tucson's Finest Dancer."

I waved an apology to the driver I'd nearly hit, then pulled immediately off into a gas station. I stared up at the sign. Could the Diamond Hudson had scheduled in his agenda be the Diamond on the sign? My gut immediately said yes. Everything I knew about Hudson told me he was absolutely a man who would leave his wife alone in the evenings while he visited a gentlemen's club, then come home and lament how long and stressful his workdays were while said wife brought him a beer and listened to his complaints. In short, Hudson was a dick, and I could believe in a heartbeat that he was skipping out on Christina to watch Diamond dance topless on stage.

But why leave evidence of his indiscretions in his agenda? Was he so meticulous he couldn't do anything without scheduling it in?

"Let's find out," I muttered and turned the car around.

10

The lights of Heaven on Earth gentlemen's club bathed me in a purple glow the moment I stepped inside, and the air wrapped me in its thick, cigarettes-and-perfume embrace. I looked down at the jeans and MIT shirt I'd worn to the laundromat and never changed out of and contemplated that if I'd changed for the new venue, maybe fewer heads would be turning in my direction.

I let my eyes adjust to the dim, hazy lighting. The outer edges of the room, including where I was standing, were raised, but most of the seating was down a small set of carpeted stairs on a lower level where patrons could look up at the runway stage extending from the opposite wall. Two poles rose from the stage to the ceiling, and barstools lined the entire thing. Behind the barstools were small high-top tables, and behind that were booths. Up on the U-shaped raised section circling the room, more high-top tables dotted the floor, and to my left was a bar.

Standing up on the raised level made me feel like I was up on the stage myself, and I felt my pulse quicken and my breathing shallow. I hadn't thought through this plan at all. I felt an overwhelming urge to run back to my car and go home to listen to the Rightsides' soap operas through the walls for the rest of the night. I turned to do exactly that when a motion between me and the bar snagged my attention. I gasped, a hand flying to my mouth in surprise. It was Hudson, turning and leaning in to the bar, pointing at a bottle of liquor on the shelf. I blurted, "Hudson?"

The man turned toward me and my stomach dropped through the floor. It wasn't Hudson. Just another tall man in a suit with that same self-assured posture. A wedding ring on his finger but not a hint of shame in the way he moved.

"Sorry," I murmured. "You look like someone else."

The man moved on, and I filled his spot at the bar. Not sure what else to do, I ordered a vodka soda. The bartender could have been a dancer herself. She wore fishnets under shorts that really stretched the definition of the word, and her breasts were pushed up almost to her chin in a leather corset. She placed my drink in front of me and took my card, frowning at my clothes.

This was my chance. Hudson may have met with Diamond, the dancer from the billboard, on the day before he went missing. Finding her—and getting her to talk to me—could be the key to finding out where he was. I told myself this was ridiculous; if Hudson was meeting with a stripper, he wouldn't be telling her his plans to leave town with his wife and stop answering his calls. But I couldn't bring myself to let it go. Every time I tried, my mind returned to Christina's ashen face and the chest we buried. It returned to Hudson's packed bag still under their bed. I couldn't let myself put my worries into words, but a voice in the back of my head was telling me something was seriously wrong. I needed to find Hudson alive and well. I needed to find Christina. And I needed to know what I'd helped her bury in their backyard. And since Francisco was being tight-lipped about his own investigation, I'd have to do it myself.

"Excuse me." I forced the words out before I could think it through and make a different choice.

The waitress scowled as she turned back to me from where she was making my drink and cocked her hip expectantly.

"Do you know when Diamond dances here?"

She laughed coldly. "Every night, sweetie."

"Has she already done her, uh, performance for the night?"

"You're just in time."

The bartender nodded over my shoulder, and I turned to see the most beautiful woman I'd ever seen step through the heavy black curtain at the end of the stage and make her way down the runway. My mouth dropped open of its own accord. I was entranced.

Diamond wore thigh-high boots with sky-high heels and not much else. The boots glittered, and with every step she swished her legs and slowly raised her arms until, in perfect time with the music, she arrived at the first pole with her arms directly overhead and struck a pose, left knee bent and right leg kicked out to the side. The crowd whistled and hollered for her.

Diamond grabbed the pole and began to defy gravity while I watched, amazed. I moved slowly to one of the tables close to the back curtain, but a sliver of extremely muscular man was visible through the gap in the curtain, and I knew I'd have no luck trying to follow her backstage to talk with her after her set. Instead, I took up a seat closer to the stage and pulled up a picture of Hudson on my phone.

"Hey." I leaned over toward the man to my left, who looked like I was the last woman he wanted to be talking to in a place like this. "Have you seen this guy here before?"

I flashed the phone screen at him, but he leaned away like I'd just held out a live tarantula. "I'm not getting in the middle of that," he said. "You gotta talk to your man yourself. I'm no snitch."

"He's not my man. He's a missing person."

Instead of assuaging the man's concerns, that only seemed to alarm him further. He held both his hands up by his shoulders and shook his head. "I told you, I'm not getting in the middle of whatever you've got going on."

I shoved away from the seat and left the club with one last look to where Diamond was doing dance moves upside down that I'd injure myself even attempting right side up. No one in there was going to be of any help in finding Hudson. I needed to talk to the dancers. Instead of walking to my car, I circled the building toward a metal door in the back, thinking that if I couldn't get to Diamond backstage, I could wait for her to leave at the end of the night.

That plan was immediately foiled by the twin of the extremely muscular man I'd glimpsed through the curtain backstage, who was standing guard outside the back door.

"Can I help you?" He demanded.

"I, uh—" Mercifully, I was cut off by the door swinging open and two women spilling out, cackling with laughter. They each had duffel bags thrown over their shoulders, presumably filled with the costumes they'd changed out of and into the sweatsuits they now wore.

"Night, Rob!" One of them called.

I turned toward them as they walked past muscle-man Rob and me. "Excuse me, have you seen—"

"Don't bother the girls," Rob said, cutting me off verbally at the same time he moved his body between me and the women.

One of them turned around, her red braids hanging down to her hips over her tie-dye sweatsuit. She leaned over to look at me around Rob. While she looked mainly curious, the other woman turned with a look of sympathy.

"Look, if you have to ask us if your husband was here, the relationship's dead already."

"He's not my husband. He's—"

"Even better. Then you don't even need a lawyer to leave him." She turned, grabbing the other woman's arm and dragging her alongside her.

I weighed my options as quickly as I could, Rock-Solid Rob still towering over me and looking like it wouldn't take much for him to decide to pick me up and remove me from the premises.

"He's my friend's husband."

The women turned around again, sympathy playing on their faces. I ran with it.

"You know how it is. She won't leave him without proof, but he's an ass. I'm sure he's been here. I heard him talking with his buddies." My heart hammered, and I decided to risk it. "I heard him talking about someone named Diamond."

Both women perked up at the mention of Diamond, and the one with the red braids stepped forward, reaching for my phone.

"Yep, that's him," she said over her shoulder to the other woman. "Diamond's boy."

"So he's been here?"

"Your friend's lying to you, girl. She knows that man's playing her."

"What do you mean?"

"He was here a couple weeks ago. After Diamond's set, she brought him backstage like always."

The other woman, short with a black bob that stopped just above her chin, interrupted, "I don't know why Snake lets her do that." Somehow, I wasn't surprised the enormous man I'd seen a sliver of through the curtain was named Snake. "Men see her bring him backstage and they think they can push their way back. It puts all of us at risk, just so she can have some private time with her boy toy."

The woman with the braids held up a hand, cutting her friend off. "But when Diamond was bringing him backstage, this woman comes flying from out of nowhere, yelling about how she was going to kill him and how could he betray her like this.

"He tried all the usual stuff. 'It's not what it looks like. You don't understand. Let me explain.' But Snake dragged her out and then booted the husband out, too, and then Rob here had to keep her from murdering him right here in the parking lot."

I looked up at Rob with my eyebrows raised and he nodded, confirming her story.

After I'd thanked them for the information, I climbed into my car and laid my head on the wheel. I'd found the Diamond from Hudson's agenda, but so had Christina, two weeks before he'd gone missing and I'd helped her dig a conveniently grave-sized hole in their yard. The voice in the back of my head was getting harder to ignore. I cast one last look behind me at Heaven on Earth before pulling out of the parking lot and heading home.

11

The clock on my dash had some lights that didn't work, so sometimes a seven looked like a one, or a six like a five, but it was perfectly clear when the clock struck midnight and Sunday rolled into Monday. Not even seventy-two hours had passed since Hudson had made an appearance at his law firm for a meeting, and yet in those three days, I felt like I'd stepped through a portal and into a different world. But I hadn't walked through any mirrors; I'd dug a hole. I'd dug a hole and must have fallen through it into some other realm because nothing made sense anymore.

Sitting in the car, three blocks from home because all the good spots were taken this late at night, I pulled out my phone and dialed Christina's number again. It went straight to voicemail without ringing. I threw the phone down onto the passenger seat and then banged the steering wheel with both hands.

"What the hell, Christina?" I shouted at the dash. Tears bit at my eyes, and I swiped at them. Letting my head drop back against the duct-taped headrest, I blinked up at the sagging headliner. "You're supposed to tell your best friend before you up and disappear."

With a sniffle and one last wipe at the corners of my eyes, I dragged myself out of the car and up the street towards home, surprised to find the younger of the two Rightside kids sitting on the front porch of their unit.

"Are you okay?" I asked her when I got close enough. "Are you locked out?"

"No." She stood up and crossed her arms across her front against the nighttime chill.

"Um, okay... Why are you out here?"

She shrugged. "I couldn't sleep. Why are you out here?"

"I'm not 'out here.' I just got home. I'm on my way inside." I gestured to the doorknob, my key still inside.

"Are you going to cry again?" I spun in her direction, but before I could respond, she added, "When you cry at night it's really annoying. Maybe you can try to just cry during the day when I'm at school?"

I flung my arms down at my side and let out an exasperated breath. "I'm sorry my adult heartbreak is disturbing your teenage slumber, although it seems to me like I'm getting an unfair share of the blame here, since you were out here before I even got home."

"I'm twelve," she said, pushing off the wall and crossing the gravel stretch between our two porches. "I'm not a teenager yet. Can I see your house?"

I looked back over toward her half of the duplex, hoping one of the parents might poke their head out and call the girl home. I'd never read the handbook on what to do when your preteen neighbor invites herself over. "Um, I guess that would be okay." I pushed open the door. "But then you have to go home and go inside. It's not safe to be hanging out outside alone this late."

"Why do you stay out so late?" The girl nudged past me and into the house, eyes roving around the space. "You don't have a lot of stuff."

"I haven't been here very long. I haven't had the time to furnish it." *Or the money.* My alarmingly low bank account balance had moved down on my priority list since Friday night.

The girl was standing in the middle of the room, surveying it with a frown of disapproval, and I suddenly felt defensive of my tiny, empty home being scrutinized by this preteen. With her long straight hair and black plastic choker, she was the spitting image of the cool girls I could never quite convince to like me in school, and now she was judging my home while my life was in tatters.

"Do you stay out late because you don't want to be in here?" she asked me.

"I don't stay out late, and I like my house!"

"It's late right now. You said I shouldn't be outside because of it."

"Tonight's different."

"You were out late on Friday, too."

I faltered, reaching for words until finally, I choked out, "Okay, time for you to go. And I think maybe you should get a hobby besides surveilling your neighbors."

But the girl didn't move toward the door. Instead, to my irritation, she plopped down onto my loveseat. "I sing in the choir at school. Kaylie says choir is for dorks, though, and she doesn't want to be friends with me anymore unless I quit."

My nose crinkled. "That's not very nice of her."

She just gave me another disinterested shrug. "Mom and Dad say I should pick robotics for my elective instead of choir next year, anyway. They say I'm not going to be a famous singer and that I should do something that will get me into college and pay the bills."

I looked from the door to the girl and back, then let out a sigh of resignation. "Look," I said, sitting next to her on the loveseat. "They're not wrong that it costs money to live. But you can't make all your choices based on what other people want for you. It's a recipe for disaster." *It's all fine and dandy until you wind up broke in a duplex with no job and no prospects outside of the field you don't actually want to be in.*

The girl apparently wasn't interested in my advice, however, as evidenced by the eye roll she gave me before getting up.

"Do you sell drugs?" She asked me with no preamble, hand on the doorknob to leave.

My mouth gaped open. "No," I said emphatically.

The girl's mouth twisted like she was trying to decide whether to believe me. "Mom says you must be selling drugs because a police officer was asking where you were earlier, but my dad told her it's not right to make assumptions like that and there are plenty of other reasons a cop might want to talk to you."

"Police officer?" Had Dave called the police to my house again after I'd disabled the tracking on my laptop?

"She didn't have a uniform, but she showed my parents her badge."

My hands went to my temples as I tried to make sense of what this kid was telling me. I opened my mouth to ask her what the officer had said, but the girl pulled the door wide and bounded across the gravel to her own front door before I could. Alone again, I peered through the vinyl slats of my blinds. I scanned the street up and down, but there was no one; no police officer nor anyone else.

After I peeled off my clothes, which, though I'd been there less than an hour, smelled distinctly like Heaven on Earth gentlemen's club, I lay on my mattress on the floor watching for headlights of passing cars. The list of things I knew for sure was not long, but I went through the items one by one on a loop in my mind. I knew that Hudson had gone to his law firm on Friday, come home and deposited his briefcase, and then disappeared without taking his car. I knew he had a bag packed that he didn't take with him. I knew Christina had seemed off when she'd asked me to help her bury a chest in the backyard with no explanation. And I knew that she'd taken a bag with her, or at least that her bag was missing from their home, along with her car.

After tonight, I could add to that list that Hudson had been visiting a stripper with enough regularity to annoy the other dancers, and Christina had not taken the news well when she found out. I replayed the conversation I'd had outside the club. *"Rob here had to keep her from murdering him right here in the parking lot."*

But before I knew any of these things, I knew Christina. And I knew Christina would never hurt Hudson.

I fell asleep to the image of Christina's face when I'd last seen her, pale and tinged with green. I dreamed she and I were in a hole together, twenty feet deep and still digging. "We have to keep going!" she shouted, but my joints were failing me. When I tried to tell her I couldn't dig anymore, she turned that sickly pale face on me and begged me to try, but the shovel dissolved in my hands and then she dissolved right in front of my eyes.

When I woke, the sheets were drenched again.

"I need another pair of sheets," I groaned, stripping the mattress and trying to remember if I had enough quarters to do another load of laundry. "And I need a fucking job."

I sent off four more applications while I waited for my sheets to dry, then stopped by the store and bought a second pair of sheets and a case of ramen. I was halfway home when I remembered the neighbor girl's remark that a police officer was looking for me and decided I could just as well spend the day job hunting from the library as from home.

By the time a voice came over the intercom to announce that the library was closing, it was dusk. I joined the stream of patrons filing out into the parking lot and was carrying my hamper toward my house when I heard a familiar voice.

"Mandy!" Francisco was hurrying up the sidewalk, a

messenger bag thrown over his shoulder. He pointed at the hamper and asked, "Laundry again?"

"What can I say? That laundromat's really something. I couldn't stay away." He grinned, and I asked, "What's got you so excited on a Monday evening?"

He paused, and I gave him my best conspiratorial smile. *Tell me*, I tried to telepathically beam into his head.

"I shouldn't say anything…"

Tell me.

He exhaled and looked around. "Remember how I told you I was investigating someone who'd gone missing?"

My best friend's husband, maybe-corrupt local politician and generally obnoxious guy. "I remember."

"I've just got a lead on security footage of the guy's house."

My stomach plummeted and my head spun. That security footage would show me arriving at Hudson's house in dark clothes on Friday night and leaving before dawn covered in dirt. It would show me coming back, sneaking in, and leaving with Hudson's belongings.

"I'm sorry to rush off, but I've got to follow up on this."

I waved goodbye, then slowly walked toward my house as he ran across the street and hopped in his car. The second he rounded the corner, I darted for my own and took off after him.

"If you're going to follow that lead, I'm going to follow you," I murmured. Because one thing was for sure: Francisco could not see that footage.

12

I was great at many things: decomposing partial differential equations, pushing through pain while my joints screamed out in agony, and cooking chicken without drying it out. But one thing I wasn't great at was tailing someone in a vehicle. As Francisco navigated the streets of Tucson, I tried my best to stay three cars back and one lane over, something I'd heard on a cop show years earlier. The problem was, if that was the best way to follow without being seen, it also kept me from being able to see. I lost Francisco's blue Corolla on more than one occasion, once going through a green light only to realize he was sitting in the left turn lane when I whizzed past him. Praying he didn't see me, I made a U-turn at the next opportunity and caught up to him on the next street.

As the chase progressed, I hardly took my eyes off Francisco's car, letting our surroundings pass me by without taking in the direction we were going, my focus solely on that blue sedan always on the verge of slipping out of view. *Surveillance footage.* Someone had video footage of the Schupperts' home.

I wondered whether Francisco had contacts at home security companies. If the police requested footage, maybe a contact of Francisco's had given him a heads up.

Visions of me on video emerging from the house before dawn Saturday morning, then coming back the next day and pounding on the door before letting myself in, played in my head. No, Francisco couldn't see that footage. But as we raced toward it, I suddenly wanted to see it. I desperately needed to see it.

I needed to see that footage for the same reason Francisco wanted it: Hudson's disappearance was on that recording.

In between me showing up in all black before leaving looking like I'd dug a grave with my bare hands and me showing back up, letting myself in, and leaving with Hudson's belongings, there were answers on that tape. There had to be. Sometime after the partner meeting at his law firm, Hudson had come home and then vanished. The recording might show Hudson storming off and leaving on his own, or it might show someone breaking into the house and dragging Hudson out with them.

Or, a nagging little voice suggested, it might show that Hudson never left at all. I tried to dispel the thought, but it wormed its way back over and over. What was in that chest? What had I helped Christina bury before she'd up and left?

And suddenly, I realized that the footage might show more than just Hudson and Christina leaving. That recording could shed light on what had happened to the chest after I'd left Christina's.

Had Christina changed her mind after I'd left and dug the chest up herself? Or would the security footage show someone else at the scene?

Francisco and I wound our way further and further north until suddenly we passed a Mexican restaurant with an enormous cactus statue in the parking lot out front and I realized where we were. We weren't going to the corporate office of some home security company. We were just minutes from Christina's house, speeding straight toward her neighborhood.

Traffic died down as we moved into the foothills, and I tried to keep further back from Francisco. As the sun dipped entirely below the horizon, I hoped soon I'd just be an unrecognizable pair of headlights behind him. But the closer we got, the fewer cars there were to try to hide behind. I felt exposed no matter how far back I hung. When we pulled into Christina and Hudson's neighborhood, I pulled my car over to the curb and waited until I saw him make a turn. When he had rounded the corner, I pulled away and followed, making the turn just in time to see him make another turn at the end of the street. Just in time to see him turn onto Christina's street.

I stopped my car at the end of the street instead of turning onto Christina's street, where my lights would draw Francisco's attention. When I turned the corner on foot, I could still see Francisco's taillights as he crept slowly up the street, likely searching for a particular street number. One of these neighbors had a security camera with footage of the Schupperts' house on it. But who?

Francisco's brake lights glowed when he finally pulled to a stop. I counted the houses.

No.

Francisco's door opened and one lean leg emerged. Then another. Then Francisco climbed out of the car, stuffed his hands in his jacket pockets, and shuffled with his head down to the door. I kept waiting for him to change course, to jog over one to the next house down. But he hopped nimbly up the single step to the porch and peered at the doorbell before ringing it.

The door swung wide to reveal Christina's neighborhood nemesis, Maureen.

13

I watched from the shadows as Francisco followed Maureen into her house, Sprinkles the Chihuahua nipping at his feet, then emerged only a minute later, tucking something into his messenger bag before returning his hands to his pockets. He climbed into his car and pulled away, and I waited several long minutes planning my approach before emerging from the darkness and advancing on Maureen's home. Another neighbor drove by, and I kept my face pointed down as I walked.

"I told you, I—oh." Maureen's face was flushed, gray-streaked blond curls sticking up behind the reading glasses pushed atop her head, when she pulled back the door. Sprinkles made a mad dash for the door, and she scooped the dog up and tucked him under her arm, then continued to frown at me. "I thought you were going to be... Never mind. Who...?" She peered behind me, and when she looked back she fixed her eyes on me with a level of scrutiny that made me squirm. "You look familiar."

"Hm, I don't think so." I kept my expression blank, and put on my best cheerful but serious voice. "I believe you just spoke with a man at this address. About yea high, dark hair." I gestured with my hand in the air, marking out Francisco's height. Maureen nodded, a hint of concern growing on her face. Things were going to plan.

"I'm his boss. Gretchen. Nice to meet you." At my outstretched hand, Maureen's concern deepened. I continued. "The man you just spoke with, Francisco, has been pursuing a story that was not assigned to him. I apologize for your trouble. I'll be collecting anything he received and passing it along to the appropriate reporter, but I need a statement from you detailing exactly what you gave him."

Maureen's curls bounced as she shook her head, more of them coming dislodged from behind her glasses and falling in front of her face. "What?"

"I need to know what he received from you. You've done nothing wrong. But can you tell me exactly what you gave to Francisco?"

Maureen stammered, "I got a phone call from a reporter saying he was doing a story on one of my neighbors. He gave me his name, and I looked him up so I knew he was a real journalist. He said he was seeking any doorbell or security camera footage anyone on the block could give him. No one else has any of those things. This is a safe neighborhood; having cameras up is basically telling everyone else you don't trust them."

"Do you not trust your neighbors?"

"Not as far as I can throw them!" She pulled Sprinkles tighter to her chest. "How does every horrible news story start? 'Nothing like this has ever happened here. It's such a safe town.' I don't care what anyone else thinks; I'm protecting myself."

"So you agreed to provide the footage from your security cameras?"

"It's just the doorbell cam. But yes, I told him I'd be happy to help."

I shivered, and Maureen pulled the door open wider. "Why don't you come in?"

I wanted to. Both the warmth and the look inside her home were appealing, but I shook my head. She already thought I looked familiar standing on the porch at dusk. In the light, I was sure she'd recognize me. She'd never acknowledged me when

I'd waved at her on her walks during the weeks I stayed with Christina, but she'd clearly seen me.

"That's all right. This won't take long. When Francisco called you, did he tell you which of your neighbors he was doing a story on?"

"No," Maureen said with a harrumph. "'Journalistic integrity' or something like that. But I know who it is." I raised a probing eyebrow, and she pointed across the street at Christina and Hudson's house. "She lives right over there. I told him I wasn't sure my footage would be of any use, since it only barely captures her door, but he said he wanted it anyway."

She thought Francisco was digging into Christina? Though I tried with all my might to keep my expression unrevealing, Maureen barked a laugh. "Don't worry. Your guy didn't tell me. Like I said, he was big on keeping his secrets to himself. But this neighborhood's small, and people see things."

"What kinds of things?"

Maureen put her free hand on her hip and cocked it to the side, Sprinkles dangling from the other arm. "Sounds like you're asking me for an interview now. And I'm sure the rest of the street will have the same line for you that I have: no comment."

"But—"

Maureen shook her head. "The doorbell footage was one thing, but that's all you get."

I held up my hands in surrender and switched gears. "I understand. I'll leave you to it, but I just want to make sure I know exactly what you gave my reporter. Like I said, the story's been reassigned, and he isn't exactly thrilled. I need to know that what he gives me to pass along is everything you gave him. Can you tell me exactly what footage you gave him?"

"The last month. I put it on a flash drive, like he said."

"And did you show him the footage when he came to collect it, or just give him the drive?" My pulse hammered while I waited for her to answer. If they'd watched the recording together, it didn't matter whether I could get the flash drive from Francisco.

She shook her head. "I just gave him the drive."

With a sigh of relief, I thanked her and turned to leave. Just as she was shutting the door behind her, I turned. "Wait. Just in case he's not enthusiastic about turning his materials over, do you think you could make another copy of that footage?"

Maureen's lips pursed and she looked me up and down again. "I deleted it after I put it on that drive."

I felt certain she was lying to me, but whether that footage still existed or not, it was clear she wasn't going to give it to me. Trying to disguise my crestfallen expression, I said, "That's okay. Thank you for your help."

She may not have given me a copy of the recording, but Maureen had given me two new pieces of information: the security footage Francisco had only barely captured Christina's door, and Maureen had reason to believe a reporter would be looking into Christina, not Hudson.

I drove toward home, planning ways I could get Francisco to invite me over again the next day, equal parts desperate to see that footage and desperate to keep Francisco from ever seeing it. Would he watch it as soon as he got home or wait until morning? Could I come up with a reason to knock on his door tonight? Maybe I could pretend I'd locked myself out and needed a place to wait for a locksmith. But even if I got inside his house, could I steal from him? It was one thing to follow someone to piggyback on their lead. It would be another thing entirely to take that flash drive.

A flash of blue caught my eye, jerking me out of my deliberation. I slowed the car to get a better look just as Francisco hung up the gas pump and walked from his car to the gas station mini-mart.

This was my chance. I turned across two lanes of traffic to pull into the station. If I could just grab that bag, I could—

A sleek red sports car pulled up at the other side of Francisco's pump and before I could even make sense of what was happening, a hooded figure emerged from the car, jogged around and opened Francisco's passenger door, then grabbed his messenger bag before speeding off.

14

I watched through my stained, warped blinds as Francisco walked home after parking his car. His shoulders hunched over in defeat, and he seemed weighed down though he wasn't carrying anything with him. I exhaled. He hadn't managed to recover his bag. I tried to be relieved; Francisco wouldn't see that recording. I wouldn't have to explain why I was over at the Schupperts' house. Still, the heavy weight of dread in my stomach didn't quite go away. Francisco might not have that security footage, but someone did. Someone out there did have video of me at the Schupperts' house with suspicious timing, and I had no idea who it was.

Half-baked theories looped in my head and kept me from sleep. Each time I drifted off, I jolted awake only to look over at the clock resting on the tile floor beside my mattress and see that mere minutes had passed. When I finally did slip into unconsciousness, I saw Francisco's car parked by the gas pump again, a hooded figure pulling open the passenger door and reaching inside. The figure turned toward me, giving me a full view of their face. Christina, hood concealing her short blond hair, raised a finger to her mouth and then winked at me, a sinister gleam in her eye I'd never seen in real life. Then she stepped backward and I could see what she was pulling out of Francisco's car. Instead of his messenger bag, Christina was dragging Hudson's limp body from the car, his heels scraping the concrete as she tugged him away. She paused and turned her head to me again, putting her finger to her lips a second time.

It was the sound of my own scream that woke me. I gulped air, blinking the sleep from my eyes until the textured ceiling came into focus. "I've got to take something for these dreams." My whisper came out strangled, and I worked my mouth trying to moisten it. I slept poorly enough with my body aflame with untouchable pain most nights. I didn't need to be haunted by my missing best friend, too.

Coffee was the first order of business when I hauled myself upright. Pain pills and the toilet and a splash of cool water on my face were all necessities, too, but they could wait until the coffee maker was doing its thing. I'd just dumped the grounds into the basket when three hard knocks sounded at the door. I filled the reservoir with water and flicked the machine on before searching for a sweatshirt I could throw over the tattered pajamas I'd worn so thoroughly they were riddled with holes and practically indecent. Three more knocks.

"Just a minute!"

I tugged the sweatshirt over my head and looked through the peephole in the door. A woman wearing black slacks and a maroon button-down stood squarely in the center of my porch. My eyes traveled down and snagged on the silver police badge on her belt loop. Was this the officer who'd been asking around about me? I pulled the door open.

"Look, officer, I'm sorry my ex is calling in checks on me. I'm fine. I don't know if you can make a note or something so if he calls again—"

"I think there's been some confusion." The woman cut me off, and I took half a step back. She watched me, then extended a hand. "Detective Farrah Styles, Pima County Sheriff's Department."

I took it but didn't respond.

"I'm looking into the disappearance of two Pima County residents: Hudson and Christina Schuppert. Do you know them?"

"I—yeah, I know them." My instinct was to say more, to try to be helpful and win this steely-eyed woman over, but there was nothing more I could say without risking implicating myself in something I didn't even know about.

"Your husband—"

"Ex," I couldn't stop myself from interrupting. She raised a groomed eyebrow, and I clarified, "Soon-to-be ex. We're separated."

"There was mail addressed to you at your Michigan address in a packet at the Schupperts' home. We looked up the address and called your husband. He said you and Christina Schuppert have been friends since high school."

I nodded, internally kicking myself for not looking more closely when I was at the Schupperts' house. I waited for the detective's next words to be "You're under arrest," but instead she asked, "When is the last time you heard from her?"

I tried to think of how many days it had been. It felt like another year, another lifetime, when Christina had texted me after my job interview.

"A week? Not even that long. Four or five days? We talked on the phone after I had a job interview on Friday."

Detective Styles pulled a small notebook from her back pocket and leaned toward me. "Friday of last week?"

I nodded. It was Tuesday now. Still not even a full week since I'd been humiliated in my first job interview in six years. Not even a full week since I'd dressed in all black, expecting to pull a prank on a bad neighbor. I tried to read Styles's reaction to the news that I'd spoken to Christina on Friday, but her face was inscrutable.

"How often do you usually talk with her?"

"I don't know that there's really a 'usually' right now. I just moved here. After I, uh, ended my marriage, Christina helped me move. I was staying with her and Hudson until a few weeks ago, so I saw her every day, but before that, we'd sometimes go weeks without talking." The urge to act like I knew less than I did was strong. I wanted to play it up, widen my eyes and ask, "What do you mean, they're missing?" But I'd seen enough television to know that wasn't a good idea, so I answered her questions honestly but gave her nothing extra.

"Have you tried to reach her since?"

My breath hitched as I tried to work out how I'd answer without putting a spotlight on myself. If I lied and the police ended up digging through phone records later, it would look suspicious. But if I told her I'd tried reaching Christina all weekend with no luck, she'd wonder why I hadn't bothered to report my best friend missing.

"Hey!" Both Detective Styles and I looked up to see Francisco jogging over toward us, dressed for a run. "Everything okay?"

Before I could answer, Detective Styles said curtly, "Everything is fine."

Francisco kept coming toward us until he stepped around the detective and joined me in the doorway, then turned to her. "If everything is fine, then you'll be on your way. Mandy isn't interested in talking to you any further without an attorney present."

Detective Styles's shocked expression matched my own. She pulled a card out of her pocket and handed it to me.

"Give me a call if you do want to talk." She glanced back once on her way to her car, then climbed in.

"What was that about?" I demanded. My ears burned as the shock of his outburst faded into embarrassment.

Francisco didn't look at me. His eyes were still on the detective's car as it sped away. "I don't trust the cops. As the ones who are supposed to enforce the rules, they don't care much about following them themselves." Styles's car rounded the corner and disappeared from sight, and Francisco turned to me, looking me over as if for injuries. I felt more of my skin flush under his inspection. "Are you all right?"

I nodded. The porch suddenly felt too small. I shifted my weight backward, but my heel slipped from the concrete and I found myself falling.

Francisco lurched forward, grabbing me before I landed in the bushes. "Careful," he said, returning me to solid ground. His hand lingered on my back just long enough to cause my lips to open and my breath to shallow, and then it was gone and he was stepping down off the porch and onto the sidewalk.

"What did Styles want from you?" he asked, looking from where I was leaning against the front door to steady myself back to where her car had gone.

"Oh, just my ex again." I waved a hand in the air in dismissal, and Francisco gave a small nod, though he didn't look entirely satisfied.

Inside, I leaned against the door and tried to slow my pulse. *There's nothing to worry about. That detective just wants to find Christina and Hudson, same as you.* No matter how many times my brain repeated it, my body wasn't buying it. My palms were clammy and my breathing erratic. And when I looked up and saw Hudson's laptop still sitting menacingly on my plastic table, all I felt was a jolt of dread.

I gathered the computer into my arms. I didn't let myself think about how close a call that might have been or what would have happened if that detective had found Hudson's belongings in my house. Nor did I let myself think about the warmth of Francisco's hand on my back or how close his chest had been to mine. I just threw on a pair of jeans, grabbed my keys, and tossed the laptop into a backpack before heading out. I was halfway to Christina's when it occurred to me to wonder how Francisco knew the detective's name.

15

I drove slowly past Christina's house, wondering where there might be eyes I couldn't see watching the house. Watching me. The police had checked out the Schupperts' house; did they have people staking it out now?

Hudson's laptop was concealed in my bag on the passenger seat, but I could just imagine the invisible signals it might be sending out to anyone who was looking for it. *Here I am. Come find me. See who has me.*

I drove the full length of the street and didn't see anyone sitting in parked cars obviously watching the house, but I didn't know who could be peering out a window, hiding behind their curtains. I thought of Maureen and her doorbell camera footage. *This neighborhood's small, and people see things.* Maureen knew more than she'd told me; I was sure of it. I just hoped she'd been as tight-lipped with Francisco as she had been with me.

On my second pass of the street, I knew I was likely attracting eyes. I couldn't come back a third time. I slowed down as I neared Christina's house, but I wasn't looking at it this time; I was looking at Maureen's front door. It was across the street and three houses down. Those doorbell cameras with their wide-angle lenses might have some view of the Schupperts' home from Maureen's, but there was no way it was clear from there. It might show a figure in dark clothes arriving and leaving with suspicious timing, but I doubted it would show that I was covered in dirt when I left, and it surely wouldn't show enough of my face to ID me.

I was more worried about the daylight footage from Sunday, when I'd let myself in and then left with items from inside. I made a note to retire the red-and-white striped t-shirt I'd been wearing that day. Because while there was a possibility Maureen hadn't watched the footage before handing it over, and Francisco had never had the chance to watch it, someone had it now.

A friend of mine from undergrad once interned with a home security company and told me that most burglaries happen during the day when everyone is at work and out of the house. That wouldn't be the case in this neighborhood, though. Some of the husbands might still go to work, but most of the men in this neighborhood who hadn't yet retired were "consultants," which, as far as Christina could tell, meant they worked approximately five hours per week and made upwards of a half-million dollars a year. And while the ones not currently in an office might be playing golf, their wives would all be home. Several of them were probably calling each other now to discuss the suspicious car driving too slowly down their streets.

No, I couldn't risk entering Christina's house through the front door again.

I parked on the side street just like I had when I'd followed Francisco to Maureen's, then walked toward Christina's house. My throat tightened, and all I could think about were imaginary eyes on me, curtains being pulled back as nosy neighbors whispered about who was walking down their street, then summoned Detective Styles or one of her colleagues to come have a word with me. When I reached the house before Christina's, I collected myself as much as I could and then rang the doorbell before I could talk myself out of this plan.

A woman answered. I gauged her age to be mid-fifties, but the amount of Botox in her face widened the possible age range from late thirties to early seventies. She frowned at me, or at least I thought that's what she was trying to do. It was an expression in her eyes more than an actual movement of her face.

"We have a 'No soliciting' sign. You can't come here."

"Oh, I'm not here to sell you anything. My name is Mandy." I held out a hand, but she just looked at it and hugged both arms tighter around the pink satin robe she was wearing. "I'm close friends with Christina Schuppert, your neighbor. In fact, I stayed with her for a couple weeks recently. I think she may have introduced us when we saw you outside."

The neighbor's face remained entirely still, but she let out a small noise of recognition. "I think I do remember that." I expected a "How can I help you?" now that we had established my identity. Instead, she just stood there, quite literally expressionless.

"This might come as a surprise. I was just informed that Christina is missing. Both her and Hudson." If I'd hoped to glean any information from the neighbor's reaction to the news, I'd picked the wrong neighbor. Her features remained motionless, and she said nothing. "I'm just a bit shocked. I've known her for what feels like our whole lives. I guess I was just hoping to hear from someone who was nearby in case you'd seen anything? Maybe you heard something, or maybe she mentioned to you that they were going on an impromptu trip? Anything like that?"

The woman's eyes flicked left and right, scanning the street behind me, and she shook her head. "Sorry. We don't really talk much. I don't know anything."

She started to close the door. This was my moment. I dropped to my knees and let out a cry, more than a little bit genuine—the hard concrete sent pain shooting from my knees up through my thighs. The neighbor reeled back in shock. "I'm sorry," I said, covering my face and using everything my single semester of improv acting had taught me. "I just can't believe it. I can't stop thinking about what could have happened!"

The woman turned around, desperately looking behind her into the house, but there was no one else home who she could enlist to deal with me. She took a reluctant step forward and put a hand on my shoulder, the other still clutching her waist. "It's okay," she said, though everything in her body language said this situation was absolutely not okay with her. "I'm sure she's fine. I'm sure they...went on a trip! Like you said!"

I continued to cry dramatically on her porch, and the neighbor continued to look around beseechingly for help. I turned my face up to her, hoping that in her panic she wouldn't notice it was dry, not a tear in sight.

"Can I come inside?" I asked. When she hesitated, I launched into another wail, and she pulled me up with surprising strength, looking up and down the street to see whether anyone saw this ridiculous display.

"Come on." She pulled me inside with one last check to make sure I hadn't drawn any other neighbors' attention.

The floor plan of this woman's house was identical to Christina and Hudson's, but it felt like walking into a furniture showroom or a magazine instead of a real home where people lived. All the decorations were impersonal; there wasn't a single indication of who the home's occupants were—only that they were wealthy.

I made a beeline for the living room at the back of the house, positioning myself near the back door.

"You, uh, you're close with Kristin?" the neighbor asked, following me closely.

"Christina!" I wailed, throwing myself down onto the couch. After a minute of contemplating loudly whether she might be hurt somewhere—and focusing on the dramatics of my display to avoid thinking about the reality of that possibility—while the woman watched me and anxiously fidgeted with the tie of her robe, I declared, "I need some air," and then pulled open the double French doors to their backyard.

"Of course," the neighbor said, taken aback. "Um, can I get you anything else?"

"Can I have some privacy?"

She stepped back, and the Botox was no match for the surprise; her brows shot up to her heavily highlighted hairline. "Oh, um, sure. I'll just go upstairs and finish getting dressed." She checked her watch, then said, "I need to leave in twenty minutes for a lunch appointment."

She hurried upstairs to swipe makeup across her expensive, expressionless face and probably text her husband and all of her friends that there was a woman having a breakdown on her couch, and I counted to thirty and then bolted outside.

Instead of the chain-link fences of my neighborhood, six-foot-tall stucco walls separated the properties in Christina's. I grabbed a pool chair from the neighbor's poolside and moved it up against the wall, then threw myself up onto it as quickly as I could.

From the top, it looked a long way down to the gravel beneath me. I hesitated, trying to decide whether I should scoot along the wall to try to find a better place to hop down, but then realized I wasn't sure which side of the house the neighbor's bedroom was on. If their floor plan really was the same as Christina's, she had a perfect view of the backyard and me sitting on her perimeter wall from the primary bathroom. Without another moment's thought, I jumped.

I landed on my feet, then immediately toppled over. I bit down on my fist to muffle my cry. When I stood again, my left ankle refused to take any weight, and I limped to the Schupperts' back door still biting down on my hand. Real tears were now flowing freely down my cheeks.

I pulled the spare key from my purse and prayed they had the same locks on all their doors. I was shaking both from panic and from pain. It took multiple attempts to fit the key in the lock, and when it turned, I breathed a sigh of relief before falling into the dark living room.

With Hudson's laptop back on his desk where I'd found it, I prepared to hurry back next door on my injured ankle and thank the neighbor for her hospitality. I was nearly to the door again when I stopped short. The police had already been here. If they came back and found a laptop that hadn't been here before, they'd know someone had been here. I needed to stash the laptop somewhere besides the pristine wooden desktop—somewhere someone could have missed on a first search, in case they decided to take another look.

I pulled drawers out from Hudson's desk, but none of them were big enough to fit the computer. I spun around, eyes frantically lighting on every surface, but none of them could have been missed by police. With the laptop in one hand, I used the other to steady me as I limped out of the office and then dragged myself up the stairs. I wrote half my dissertation propped up in bed; I'd probably done more work from my bed than any other single location, including my desk and the school library. Maybe their bedroom would have a good spot to stash the computer.

The wave of emotion that crested in my chest at the sight of the room caught me by surprise. The last time I was in this room, I'd come to get some answers from Christina about the chest. I hadn't come to the house expecting her to be gone, and even when I'd left—even after finding her things missing and realizing something was seriously wrong—some part of me had still expected her to call me back.

Now, I felt like I was standing in a museum or a crypt. The air inside felt different. I dropped to the carpet and saw Hudson's leather duffel still stuffed under the bed where I'd found it two days ago. A strangled cry pushed itself up through my lips as I gripped the bed and heaved myself up off the floor. I stared down at the bedspread and watched as each tear landed and soaked into the fabric. I didn't want this to be the last time I was in this house. I didn't want to live a whole life never hearing Christina's laugh again. I didn't want to spend any longer wondering if she was hurt or in danger or simply needed to get away.

I grabbed my phone out of my back pocket and willed it to ring, desperate for Christina to tell me this was all just a misunderstanding. She and Hudson had left town for a few days and she'd lost her phone. He'd forgotten his bag, but they didn't want to waste time turning back for it when they could just buy new clothes at whatever resort they were enjoying. The chest was just... I couldn't think of a good explanation for the chest, but I dismissed the thought. She could explain when they came back from their spontaneous vacation.

I limped over to the nightstand that was clearly Hudson's—it was topped with a photo of the two of them from their wedding day and a lamp and nothing else, whereas Christina's had a sketchbook, a photograph of her and Hudson from their ski trip to Banff, a photograph of the two of us from our high school graduation, and a jar of glass flowers a glassblower friend of hers had given her one birthday. The nightstand was large, and I felt a frisson of hope as I pulled the drawer open to reveal nothing but the nightstand's assembly instructions inside. This could fit a laptop.

I tucked the computer inside the drawer and pushed it closed. Now, if someone was trying to track Hudson's location via his laptop, it would ping from his own house and not mine. And if the police did another search of the house and found it, they'd just assume no one checked the nightstands during the first one.

I checked my watch; ten minutes had passed since the neighbor had gone upstairs to get ready. The clock was ticking. I needed to get back. But, unable to stop myself, I limped around the bed to Christina's nightstand first. It was so full of life with all its adornments—so *her*. I slid open the drawer and pawed through her effects, desperate for more of my friend. Desperate for answers.

Christina's drawer held a vibrator, another sketchbook, an eye mask, hand lotion, and a stack of photos that hadn't yet been put into albums. I pulled them out with trembling hands and flipped through them. They were photos from her wedding, and I remembered her talking years ago about getting them printed but needing to make an album or scrapbook of them. I thumbed through them quickly, but just before I reached the end, a set of Polaroids fell out.

These were more recent. There were three of them, all taken in the same room I was in right now. All three of them featured Christina, naked and with a man who was definitely not Hudson.

16

I instinctively looked away, as one does when confronted with surprise nudity, then looked back again because I couldn't help myself. Was I seeing things? Maybe it was actually—nope. Definitely not Hudson. The smirking face of the man who seemed to be thoroughly enjoying my best friend's body in ways I never thought I'd have to witness was handsome in a completely different way than Hudson was. He was a bad boy to Hudson's good old boy. His hair was lighter and slightly curly, tousled and untamed in a way Hudson never wore his, and in the Polaroid with the best view of his face, a scar was visible on his left cheek, running vertically from mid-cheek down to his chin.

I leaned heavily on the bed, gripping it tightly while I tried to work through this. If I'd expected to find evidence here of anyone cheating, it wasn't Christina. She was just in the parking lot of Heaven on Earth threatening to kill Hudson for cheating on her, and yet here were photographs of her doing the same, and seemingly enjoying herself in the process.

I stuffed the photos back into the nightstand, except for the Polaroids. Those I shoved into my back pocket. I didn't think anyone searching this place after me needed to find them.

The second I pushed off the bed and tried to stand on my own, a pain so hot it made me see stars erupted in my ankle. I fell to the floor, gulping down air between sobs. I glanced at my watch again. I had six minutes to get myself down the stairs, out of this house, and back into the neighbor's living room. Holding my left leg aloft, I scooched along the floor to the top of the stairs, then slid down them one by one on my ass, careful not to bump my foot.

I crawled to the back door, but once I was outside I had no choice but to push myself up and try again to walk. Just as I'd done next door, I dragged a poolside chair toward the perimeter wall, though this time I pushed it along in front of me and hopped on one foot behind, using it for stability. I lined it up roughly where I thought I'd come over so there would be a chair waiting on the other side, just feet away from the refilled hole I'd helped dig.

"Here goes nothing." I grabbed at the top of the wall and pulled myself up. Up was the easy part. It was down that was the concern, and perched atop the perimeter wall I knew there was no way I could get down without using my injured ankle. I gave myself one deep breath of preparation, then spun so I was facing Christina's and tried to lower myself down backwards instead of jumping forwards. My foot missed the chair waiting below and instead kicked it over, sending me falling with no support.

If she hadn't noticed me outside before, the clatter of the chair toppling over and my subsequent shout was certain to catch the neighbor's attention. I couldn't return the chair to its poolside home; I didn't have time, and I needed it to help me get to the house. I thrust it along in front of me, hopping behind it, then left it by the door and staggered inside. I'd just resumed my position on the couch, face pale and wet with tears this time, when the neighbor hurried downstairs, a pair of feathered and bedazzled high heels in hand.

"I need to head out for my lunch, so I'm afraid you'll need to leave." There was an air of forced authority in her words, but they wavered like she wasn't entirely sure I'd go willingly.

"Thank you for letting me collect myself. Just being so close to their house really got to me." Another tear slid down my cheek as I forced myself to my feet.

She nodded enthusiastically, ignoring my distress and leading me toward the front door. "I totally understand. I'm very glad you're feeling better." When I hadn't caught up to her, she turned back and saw me using the wall to push myself along. "What happened?"

I waved her off and tried to hasten my pace. "I'm fine. It's an old injury. It, uh, acts up whenever I get too sad."

She was so relieved to get me out of her home, she didn't question it. She just tapped her foot impatiently until I crossed the threshold, then locked the door and hurried across her yard to the car in the driveway. A moment later, she whizzed past me while I hobbled, agonizingly slowly, to my car.

The moment I slid into the driver's seat, I cried out in relief. With both hands, I gingerly removed the sneaker from my left foot, revealing a grossly swollen ankle. My instinct was to just go home, ice it, and hope for the best, but I knew I should get it checked out. I wasn't sure it wasn't broken. What if it needed surgery? And separated wasn't divorced—for now, at least, I was still on Dave's excellent health insurance plan. Might as well take full advantage. I took myself to the hospital.

I WALKED out of the hospital three hours later with a super sexy orthopedic boot and strict orders to take it easy, though I was allowed to walk with the boot on. Small blessings—I would be a danger to myself and others on crutches. I stopped at the grocery store for a pint of ice cream and to test out walking with the boot. Between the boot and the extra-strength Ibuprofen, my ankle felt as good as it normally did—that is to say, not great but serviceable.

The visit to the hospital had only reminded me of the one item on my to-do-after-moving list I was still putting off: finding a new doctor. I'd had such a terrible time finding anyone who took me seriously back in Michigan that the idea of going through the process again in a new place was just too much. No matter how important it was, I couldn't bring myself to start the process all over again. Waiting for months to see a specialist only to be told I was probably just stressed and nothing was really wrong with me wasn't exactly my idea of a good time. I grabbed a box of butterfly-shaped Little Debbie cakes to go with the ice cream.

Back in my apartment, with *Days of Our Lives* drifting in from next door, I sat on the edge of my mattress and took my boot off long enough to wiggle out of my jeans. The Polaroids fell out of the pocket when I tossed the pants to the side, and I scrambled to grab them before tucking them under the mattress and out of sight.

"What the hell, Christina?"

I strapped the boot back onto my ankle and propped myself up in bed with my pity party dinner and my laptop. A twinge of guilt wormed through me when I pulled up a web browser and searched Christina's name. Her website was the first hit. It was full of bright pictures of Christina beaming next to her art, or beaming while painting, or beaming while creating a papier mâché unicorn bust. I searched her eyes but saw nothing but my friend, warm and genuine. No sign that behind those brilliant smiles she was hiding an affair or anything else. Was I just the least perceptive person on the planet?

The photoshoot was from her studio out back, the pool house where I'd spent two weeks spiraling after blowing up my life. The pool house where I'd spent two weeks listening to them shout at each other from inside the house where they thought I couldn't hear.

Christina never said a word against Hudson. I'd hated him when she'd started dating him, and had only ever warmed to being cordial with him. But she saw stars when she looked at him and lit up in his presence. It was harder to hate him when he made her so happy. He was a moneyed lawyer, schmoozing people and climbing the ladder of power, and she was this creative spirit who couldn't be caged, and yet somehow they worked.

Unless maybe they didn't.

I told her once that I had heard them arguing. We were hiking at an ungodly hour because she wanted to see the sunrise and thought the fresh air and exertion would be good for my ailing heart. When we got to the top, I asked if things were okay between her and Hudson. When she spun around to look at me, I expected her to look embarrassed or annoyed that I'd brought it up. Instead, she looked terrified. She gave me a firm "Everything's fine," we climbed down the mountain in silence, and I didn't hear them arguing again.

Hudson carrying on with an exotic dancer was easy for me to accept. Men with money and power went to clubs like that to flex them. Having an "in" with a dancer and getting to slip into the back—it was the ultimate flex. And Christina finding out and flipping her lid was almost as easy for me to digest. She never accepted disrespect. She wouldn't plaster on a fake smile and let something go.

What was entirely out of line with everything I thought I knew about my best friend was her carrying on an affair of her own. Was it revenge? Were things really that broken in her marriage? Why didn't she feel like she could tell me?

I pulled up her social media profiles next and combed through every picture she'd shared online in the last five years. There was no sliver of an arm that might have belonged to the mystery man. No dirty-blond companion. Absolutely nothing. I reread our messages, scrolling back and back and back and looking for anything out of place. I second-guessed every word she'd sent me, wondering what else she might have been hiding. What else she hadn't been telling me.

How long had she been keeping secrets from me? And how deep could her deception have run?

Hudson's packed bag shoved beneath the bed. Christina's frantic, almost desperate energy on the night we buried the chest. The local news anchor reporting that Hudson hadn't been seen since his meeting that morning. The images flashed one by one like the pictures on a View-Master reel. *Click. Click. Click.* And with every one, I felt the puzzle pieces fitting together, revealing a picture I didn't want to see. A picture of a suspiciously grave-sized hole I helped dig for my friend on the day her husband disappeared. *Could we have...?*

The doorbell rang, and I jumped, sending my spoon clattering onto the floor.

I set the half-eaten and three-quarters-melted pint of ice cream down beside it and padded to the door. I expected to find Detective Styles and briefly considered whether ignoring her was a viable option. I peered through the peephole and was surprised instead to see Francisco looking slightly nervous on the doorstep, casserole dish in hand.

I pulled the door back, and his face brightened. In my periphery, I saw the neighbor girl sitting on the stoop again, eyes watching Francisco and me with interest. He thrust the dish toward me. "I saw you hobbling in with that boot," he said with a nod toward the boot swallowing my left ankle. "I thought maybe you'd like some company? I also brought food, since you might not be up for standing in the kitchen."

I glanced into the bedroom at the ice cream container sweating on the tile and the laptop open to the social media pages of the wife of the man Francisco was trying to write a story on. I opened my mouth to tell him I appreciated the gesture but that now wasn't a good time, but the aroma of the casserole hit my nose at exactly that moment and sent my mouth watering. Overcome, I reached for the dish.

"Sure, come inside," I offered, reaching behind me and pulling the bedroom door closed as I led him to the folding table.

17

I could imagine Francisco's eyes surveying my space as he followed me inside. I turned around, expecting judgement or pity on his face, but instead of my humble, crumbling apartment, Francisco was looking at me. His eyes flitted from the boot on my ankle up to my face and back down.

"What happened?" he asked softly.

I tried to wave it off. "I'm clumsy," I said. "And I break easily." That part wasn't a lie. My body certainly didn't take kindly to the assaults of everyday life, as evidenced by my losing an entire day in a feverish sleep after one hard night.

He frowned, but sensed I didn't want to talk about it any further and set the casserole down on the table. "It was my mom's favorite recipe." *Was.* No elaboration. I wasn't the only one with a painful past. Crossing into the tiny kitchen, he asked, "Where do you keep the plates?"

I winced. "Plate." At his quizzical expression, I elaborated. "I only have the one. One plate, one bowl, one set of silverware. I'm clearly a grade-A adult."

I pointed to the cabinet, and he pulled down the two dishes. I volunteered to use the bowl so he could have the plate, but he insisted I take the plate and fork and dished us each a serving. My heart thudded watching him, and it occurred to me that it had been a long time since someone had done something for me. A long time since I'd let them.

Dave and I had been busy. Young professors working toward tenure, we worked all the time and our schedules didn't always line up. If we ate together, it was microwave meals or something quick and cheap in the Student Union. And he didn't cook. On one of our earliest dates, he tried to make me a roast chicken but forgot about it in the oven until it caught fire. Once the fire department had left, we went to McDonald's and stayed and talked all night until they switched the menu back over to breakfast foods. I'd thought it was a cute quirk—here was this brilliant person who could hardly boil water. But looking at Francisco across the table with the taste of homemade food in my mouth, I had the sudden urge to crawl across the table into his lap.

"It's good, huh?" Amusement danced across his face, and I suddenly became aware of how quickly I was devouring my plate. "My mom dreamed of opening a restaurant. She was always cooking, but always things like this—comfort food, nothing fancy. She said the world had enough expensive restaurants with elaborate menus, but people needed a place they could go to have something simple and delicious that someone had made with love. She said not everyone had a loving home, but they still deserved a home-cooked meal served up by someone who'd remember their names."

The casserole felt thick in my throat. "She sounds really special."

"She was," he agreed with a faraway look in his eyes.

I searched for some piece of me that I could offer in return for his vulnerability. My home life had been boring; my parents were fine, but we weren't close.

"I had a friend like that," I said, despite myself. "She was into art and always talked about how it could heal. She was good—really good. Her pieces sold for more money than I ever thought people would pay for art. But she gave a lot of it away. She didn't like the thought of something that could do so much good being reserved for the people who could pay for it."

It was stupid. If he was looking into Hudson, he'd surely come across the fact that his wife was an artist. He could connect the dots. But I couldn't keep it inside.

"What happened to her?" Francisco asked softly.

The question—entirely reasonable and yet somehow unexpected—caught me by surprise, and I choked on my food. "What do you mean?" I sputtered in between coughs.

"You said you *had* a friend. She *was* into art."

"We drifted apart." I took a long drink of water and added, "She got into the college I wanted to go to. We had a huge fight. High school stuff." That was true. I swore I'd never talk to her again after that fight, but it hadn't stuck.

"She was selling her art in high school?" Tiny creases formed between his brow, and I had the sensation of wading deeper and deeper into quicksand, everything I said pulling me more firmly into its grasp.

"I, uh, found her on social media, looking to see what she'd been up to in the years since our falling out."

Francisco nodded, either accepting this statement or just letting it go. I wanted to search his face to see if I could tell what he was thinking, but I couldn't bring myself to look at him.

We finished eating in silence and then he gathered up our dishes and started washing them. Over the sound of the running water he asked, "So, what brought you here?"

"Hm?" I stalled.

He turned the faucet off and then leaned against the counter. "You left your shitty, controlling ex and moved across the country, right?"

I nodded, trying to remember how much I'd already told him.

"How'd you settle on a lime-green duplex in glorious Tucson, Arizona, for your landing pad?"

I held my arms up and said, "You mean this isn't everyone's

dream?" He laughed, and I tried to keep my tone light as I said, "I wanted someplace warm where I'd never have to shovel snow again. What about you? How long have you been here?"

"I came here for school. I followed my older brother here from Texas and stayed."

"You have siblings?"

"Just the one." Something in his tone told me not to ask any more, so I didn't.

"Well, I'm glad we landed here together. It's nice to have a friend here." Were we friends? Could we be, while he searched for the truth about a man I wasn't sure I hadn't buried? I wanted us to be. And something within me wanted us to be even more.

Francisco smiled. "Right back at you, although you might be bad luck."

"What do you mean?

"Well, you came into town and my nearly finished article on corruption in local politics got blown up by the main subjects' disappearance. Then I bumped into you on my way to chase down my biggest lead to date and ended up getting robbed. Some might say I should stay far, far away from you, Mandy." He was smirking, but I felt a guilty flush spread over my cheeks.

"You got robbed? Are you okay?" The words were pinched and high, and my flush only deepened as I pretended this was the first I was hearing about his setback.

"I'm fine. Someone robbed my car while I wasn't in it. No gun to my head or anything like that, but I lost some stuff I hadn't digitized yet and everything that source gave me. Not a great night for me."

"That's terrible." I felt the seed of an idea take root and said, "What if I could make it up to you?"

"How do you mean to do that?" He shoved away from the counter and moved toward me, and the suggestive tone of his voice made me squirm.

I blinked and forced myself to focus on the plan taking shape in my mind. "I could help you. With your, um, investigation."

Francisco stopped in his tracks, evidently surprised by the suggestion.

"I don't currently have a job. What if I helped you chase down leads or digitize files or whatever?" It was a bold proposition, putting myself right in the middle of his investigation, but if I was in the middle of it, I could steer it. I could point him away from my own ties to the Schupperts and benefit from his investigative skills.

"I don't know about that."

"Oh, come on," I said, keeping my voice playful. "Let me prove to you I'm not bad luck and help you out."

He hesitated a little longer, then said, "How would you feel about wearing a wire?"

18

The too-small polyester pencil skirt made it hard for me to bend at the waist, so I was half-seated, half-laying across the passenger seat of Francisco's car as he wound through town, grilling me on Hudson's former opponent in the race for his supervisor position.

"Position on installing red light cameras as part of the county's plan to reduce pedestrian fatalities?" he asked without taking his eyes off the road. He swung us into a turn, and I slid across the seat and gripped the handle above the door to pull myself further upright.

"Against," I replied. Francisco opened his mouth to correct me, but I continued, "The first time he ran, when he was a resident of District 5. Last year, in his run against Hudson for District 1 Supervisor, he changed his tune."

I glanced over to see Francisco's lips curl back in a smile. "Good job. College major?"

"Economics, but he started in engineering before he switched."

"Prior public service?"

"Five years as Head Zoning Administrator for the Planning and Development Services Department."

"And before that?"

"Sales rep for a software company." Before Francisco could ask another question, I said, "We've been over it all. You gave me five pages of the guy's background and I've memorized them all. It's all I've done for the past three days. I'm ready."

Francisco frowned. "That's all about Cory. But what about you?"

I rattled off the details on the character we'd invented for me. "My name is Maddy Simmons and I'm making a career change and trying to break into the journalism industry, but I'm currently freelance."

Maddy Simmons. Close enough to my actual name that hopefully I'd remember it. It had felt so exciting, developing a false identity for this operation, but now all I could picture was me blowing the whole thing by forgetting to respond to the fake name.

Francisco looked at me expectantly, waiting for the rest of the information we'd crafted around my persona, and I heaved a tremendous sigh. "It's a press conference, Francisco, not a direct interview. I'm not going to be exchanging my details with him tit for tat."

"But what we care about is *after* the press conference."

"I'm not convinced I'm going to be able to successfully seduce this man, and even if I do, why would he tell me anything about Hudson? Do you go around talking about your former work rival's corruption while trying to get into a woman's pants?"

He took his eyes off the road long enough to give me a look that made me squirm. "You'll be successful. And if a woman who looked like you acted impressed when I talked about my former work rival's corruption, I'd never stop talking."

We pulled into the packed parking lot at the administration building. Francisco pulled into a tiny spot between an Escalade, which was over the line on one side, and an Expedition, which was just barely inside the line on the other.

"Trust me." Francisco gave me one more once-over, making me blush. "He'll talk."

I could only open the car door a few inches without hitting the enormous SUV beside us. Francisco squeezed out of his side and came around to help me. When we'd extricated me from the car, we made our way toward the crowd of people in front of the building's front steps, my walk lopsided with the boot on one foot and a high heel on the other. At the top of the concrete steps was a podium with a microphone, and a horde of people who I assumed were all real journalists, unlike me, waited for Cory Clemens to come and talk about why he should be the next District 1 Supervisor for Pima County now that Hudson had disappeared on the job.

When we were ten yards away from the edge of the crowd, Francisco stopped. "There are journalists here who will recognize me, and if Clemens sees me, he'll put his guard up."

"I don't understand why you think he'll talk to me about any of this. He'll shut down completely if he sees you since you've asked him about Hud—Supervisor Schuppert's corruption in the past, but he's going to open up to me about it no problem just because I'm in a tight skirt?" I looked over to see if Francisco had noticed my near-slip, almost calling Hudson by his first name when, as far as he knew, I had no connection to the guy. But Francisco was casting furtive glances around, his attention barely on me.

He grabbed my upper arm and pulled me closer, then lowered his voice. "It's not just that I brought up Schuppert's corruption. Clemens's letter to the Board of Supervisors asking them to consider him when they appoint a replacement for Schuppert was submitted prior to Schuppert's disappearance becoming public."

I blinked, trying to understand what Francisco was telling me. "Why would he write that letter?"

"I think Clemens knows something about Schuppert's disappearance. And he knows I think that. Hence, his desire to keep his distance."

I felt unbalanced, my boot threatening to slide out from

under me while I teetered on my one high heel. This new piece of information changed everything. I wasn't just trying to lure Clemens into talking with me about corruption at the Board of Supervisors for Francisco's article; I was fishing for information on Hudson's disappearance.

Francisco touched my arm, winked at me, and said, "You've got this."

He disappeared before I could protest, before I could grab him and tell him I absolutely could not do this, but he was gone and the crowd was growing and suddenly I was surrounded on all sides by journalists with little notebooks. Everyone was abuzz, and the volume grew and grew and then suddenly cut out. I turned to see what had made everyone fall silent.

The podium wasn't empty any longer. A tall blond man in a suit was waving at the crowd. "Good morning, everyone. Thank you for coming to this press conference. I'm Cory Clemens, and I'd like to be the next District 1 Supervisor for Pima County."

His mouth kept moving, but I didn't hear what he was saying, because up on the steps of the administration building was the man from the Polaroids. Hudson's election opponent, the man who was now vying for his seat and apparently knew Hudson was missing before that information was public, was the man with whom Christina had been having an affair.

19

The blond Adonis talked for another five or ten minutes, declaring that the District 1 Supervisor's disappearance was horrible, and that he hoped Mr. Schuppert had merely abandoned his constituents to go on an unplanned vacation with his wife and hadn't fallen victim to something more sinister.

"However, as he has not been seen, nor has he responded to attempts at contact in a full week, we must be pragmatic and recognize the likelihood that a tragedy has occurred in our county. And a county needs leadership and direction in a time like this. The Board of Supervisors should have its full membership to make decisions in service of its constituents across all districts."

Clemens frowned and exhaled as if what he was about to say was very difficult for him. The frown tightened the skin on his cheek, and his scar caught the light. There was no room for doubt. He didn't just bear a close resemblance to the man in the photographs. It was him. Christina had slept with the man who ran against her husband in his political campaign. *What else were you hiding?* Every new piece of information felt like peeling back a mask bit by bit until the woman who was revealed looked nothing like the friend I thought I knew.

"If Mr. Schuppert is found," Clemens began, then shook his head. "*When* Mr. Schuppert is found—I believe in the phenomenal first responders and detectives of Pima County, and I believe they will find him. But when Mr. Schuppert is found, even if our merciful God has preserved his life, we must acknowledge that whatever events have transpired to cause him to go missing may leave him with lasting damage. The residents of our fine district and the people of Pima County deserve representation by someone who is fit to perform the job.

"I believe our Board of Supervisors should appoint a replacement for Mr. Schuppert in order to ensure that its constituents are represented across all districts and to ensure that when Mr. Schuppert is found, he can take the time he needs to recover in whatever ways may be necessary without the pressure to return to work immediately. And I believe I'm the right person for the job."

Cory Clemens went on to list his qualifications and vision for the county, then moved on to taking questions. The journalists around me jostled this way and that, eager to be chosen. At first, I backed away, happy to be swallowed by the crowd. But then I remembered why I was there—I wanted to be seen. I wanted Clemens to want to talk to me. I threw my hand into the air alongside all the other reporters.

When Clemens pointed to me and nodded, I felt a zing of triumph followed quickly by the realization that every talking point, every prepared question I'd memorized from Francisco, had vacated my brain the moment I'd laid eyes on my mark. Someone thrust a microphone in front of me, and I hesitated for a moment. "Uh…"

The woman next to me flipped open her tiny notebook and stepped toward me, ready to take the mic from me and ask her own question. I threw my shoulders back and blocked her off, then schooled my lips into a subtle pout, trying to ooze as much sex appeal as I could while wearing an orthopedic boot. If I blew this moment, I'd lose my chance to talk to a man who may have inside knowledge about Hudson's disappearance, and I could kiss any chance of Francisco keeping me in the loop for the rest of his investigation goodbye.

"Maddy Simmons, freelance. You've run for supervisor twice: once in District 5 and more recently in District 1. Between those two campaigns, you changed positions on a number of issues, including red light cameras. How can the people of Pima County know where you stand on the issues they care about when your positions have changed?"

It was a lousy question. I knew Francisco would be cringing in the back seat of his car, where he was listening to me from the microphone we'd carefully hidden in my clothes. But it was better than staying quiet and missing my shot entirely.

Clemens smiled, and I thought I saw his gaze flick down to where Francisco had instructed me to leave one button too many undone on my blouse. "That's a great question. I want the people of this magnificent county to know that I, like everyone, am human, and I learn and grow with time. In the years between those campaigns, I learned a lot. I read studies. I talked with experts. And, as a result of that new knowledge, I changed my position. I think our county, our state, and our nation would be best served if everyone were more willing to admit when they're wrong. The people of Pima County have my word that I will stand up for what is in their best interests while always remaining open to learning more and doing better. Thank you."

He pointed to a man on the other side of the crowd, and just like that, another question was being asked and my moment was over. The session continued, but I stopped listening, only keeping my ears open for mentions of Hudson, though no one directly asked anything about him. Twice while he was responding to other questions, I caught Clemens glancing back over at me. I had a real shot, I realized. He was interested. I just needed to reel him in.

When the Q&A wrapped, Clemens was escorted into the administration building and the crowd around me dispersed quickly. Journalists and reporters disbanded to go back to their desks and type furiously, all eager to be the first to get anything out about the conference. I climbed the steps to follow Clemens.

Just inside the door, stanchions guided entrants to a metal detector alongside a table where a security guard waited with a stack of small trays. He frowned at me, and when I didn't produce a badge, said, "This building isn't open to the public."

Beyond the metal detector, Clemens huddled with a few other people in suits near the elevator. I saw him turn to see what the fuss was about and looked back to the security guard.

"I really need to use the restroom. Is there any way I could—"

"I'm sorry, ma'am." The guard cut off my sob story and shook his head.

I was opening my mouth to give it one more try when Clemens broke off from his conversation partners. "She's with me, Benny. I'll escort her." He stood on the other side of the metal detector and locked eyes with the security guard.

The guard only shrugged; I thought maybe he'd argue with Clemens or bristle at having his power questioned, but once Clemens took over responsibility for me, the guard was satisfied he'd done his job. If I ran off and threatened the security of the employees in this building, it was on Clemens, not him.

My skirt lacked pockets, but I turned over my small purse when the guard handed me a tray. I took one step toward the metal detector and froze. Would the microphone that was secreted away inside my blouse set it off? I wondered if Francisco was listening from his car, frantically praying I wouldn't do something stupid and get us caught.

"Will this set it off?" I asked, motioning to the boot on my left foot. "Maybe you should pat me down instead?"

I laced a hint of seduction through my words, and the security guard's skin flushed under his collar. I didn't actually want him to pat me down—there was a chance the metal detector would give away the wire I was wearing, but it was near certain if he searched me himself. I was banking on the idea he'd be too embarrassed to take me up on the offer.

"No, uh—well, you should—it's all right. Here, just go around. You're good." Clemens smirked as the security guard fumbled his words, opening up one of the retractable belts between the stanchions.

When I had my purse back, Clemens started walking. I followed, unsure where we were going and equally unsure how to start a conversation. He led me down a hallway and paused in front of a set of restroom doors where I pretended to be relieved and not surprised, though I'd already forgotten my pretext for entering the building.

I peed, then grabbed another wad of tissue to dab the shine of sweat and oil off my face in front of the mirror. When I checked my phone, I had a text from Dave, which I deleted without reading, and one from Francisco from several minutes before.

Francisco: Smart thinking. Now make your move.

I whispered into my chest, "Were you listening to me pee?"

My phone lit up with another message.

Francisco: You didn't exactly give me much warning. Now get back out there and make your move!

I rolled my eyes, shoved the phone back into my bag, and tried to find a hint of confidence to step into the role of seductress.

"Thanks," I said, walking back into the hallway with the best strut I could manage in a boot. I stepped right up to Clemens and grabbed his arm with both hands, looking up into his surprised expression and batting my eyelashes. "You really saved me."

Clemens's chest puffed up and his lips curled into a self-satisfied smile. "Any time."

I let go of his arm but stayed close, my chest just inches from his. "You were really great out there." Clemens started to wave me off, but I pressed on. "No, really. Some of those reporters really knew their stuff. They asked hard questions, and you handled them so well. It was really impressive."

He clearly enjoyed being told he was impressive. His chest swelled even more, almost closing the gap between us. "I'm glad I could impress."

"This is, um, this is going to sound a little weird, but I'm new here. New to town and new to reporting. I really want to make a name for myself and cover the local political scene, but I feel like I'm missing so much history and context. You seem to know everyone." I gestured back down the hall to where he had been talking with the group of people near the elevator. "Would you, um..."

I trailed off, staring down at my feet and biting my lip like I was too embarrassed to finish, and when I looked up at him he looked back at me so hungrily I thought he might try to kiss me there in the administration building where any of his would-be colleagues might see.

"Would you maybe get lunch with me and give me a few pointers? Who to watch, what to be on the lookout for, that sort of thing?"

Clemens agreed, and as we turned to leave, I made sure to angle myself so my chest brushed his arm. His eyes flitted down to that extra button I'd left open, and I pretended not to notice and followed him back out of the building, giving the guard a wave on our way out.

"There's a pub just a block away, if you're okay to walk." He looked down at my mismatched footwear.

"That sounds perfect."

The pub was dark. Entering felt like plunging into a cave, and we stood just inside the doorway for a minute waiting for our eyes to adjust.

"Hey, Cory!" the bartender called from behind the enormous oak bar. A man with long, stringy hair was sat at the bar, huddled over his pint glass like it was a fire on a freezing night.

Clemens waved at the bartender, then a host appeared and guided us to a booth near the back of the restaurant, away from the bar and all the other lunchtime patrons.

"Don't be alarmed," Clemens said as soon as the host left us alone with our menus, "but I think someone is following us."

20

"Why would someone be following us?" I asked, turning to peer at the person Clemens pointed out, a young man who had slid into the pub behind us. He was sitting at the bar engrossed in his phone and not looking at us at all. When I turned back to look at him, Cory Clemens had turned a pale green color and looked like he might vomit on the table.

"I don't, uh, I don't know." He patted his pockets and started to stand, but I motioned for him to stay seated.

"He's not even looking at us. What makes you think he's following us?"

"He was at the press conference but didn't try to ask a question. Then I saw him pretending to smoke a cigarette outside the administration building. Now he's here."

I frowned. "Pretending to smoke?"

"And doing a damn bad job of it," Clemens scoffed. "Lifting the wrong end of an unlit cigarette to his mouth."

My stomach sank. I looked back over at the bar.

The man was still scrolling on his phone, not looking our way, but now that Clemens had told me he was there, I could remember seeing him on the very edge of the crowd at the press conference.

"What should we do?"

Clemens looked at me like it was an absurd thing to ask. "You need to leave. I need to go." His eyes flitted back and forth as he worked up a plan in his mind. "If I wait until he orders a drink, he'll have to stay and pay for it. I'll ditch him then."

I felt like I was two steps behind and the path was shifting under my feet. The man who had, just minutes ago, seemed like he was on the hook ready for me to reel him in was now entirely disinterested and telling me to go.

"I don't think I should leave you," I said, trying to save this operation. I needed him to tell me what he knew about Hudson and his disappearance. "You'll be safer if you're not alone."

This was the wrong move. Cory Clemens was not a man who wanted to feel like a woman was keeping him safe; he needed to feel like the protector. The moment the words were off my tongue, I could feel him stiffen, offended.

"I'll be fine," he said sharply, moving to stand again.

"I'm scared," I blurted, peering up at him through my eyelashes. He softened a little, and I said, "I'm so slow in this boot. I don't want to walk back to my car alone. What if something happens to me?"

Clemens frowned, looking from me to the man at the bar and back. "You don't need to be afraid. This has nothing to do with you, I'm sure of it. But if you're scared, I can—"

Clemens was cut off by Francisco swooping into the pub and over to our table. "Hey, baby," he said, sliding in next to me. I turned toward him in shock, and he reached out to cup my head and kissed me possessively. My eyes flew open wide, and I let out a little squeak of surprise.

When Francisco pulled away, my gaze flew immediately back to Clemens, who was frowning at me in stunned disgust. "I should have known," he muttered, and then the man at the bar ordered a beer and Clemens hurried out of the pub without a goodbye.

"What the hell was that?" I demanded.

Francisco wasn't looking at me, though. He was looking at the man at the bar, who was still scrolling on his phone and paying no attention to any of the other patrons, us included.

"Is that the tail?" Francisco asked, with a nod in the man's direction.

"You ruined the operation!" I hissed instead of answering his question.

Francisco's brows rose in amusement. "The operation? We're spies now?"

I gestured to my blouse, then immediately felt self-conscious and did up another button.

"It was going south anyway. He was bolting. You weren't going to get anything from him."

"And now I never will. After your little show, he knows I'm working with you. He'll never talk with me again."

"Good," Francisco muttered. "Let's go."

He stood and turned to leave, and I followed him out. "Good? Francisco, that man knows something. I was *this* close to getting him talking before he spooked. If you hadn't barged in, maybe I wouldn't have gotten the information today, but I'd have gotten it from him eventually."

The early afternoon sun had me blinking furiously while I struggled to keep up with Francisco, and though I continuously tugged at my skirt, I could feel it riding up with every step. Eventually, I couldn't take it anymore and shouted, "Will you slow down?"

He turned to look at me, his eyes going first to the skirt I was yanking down once again and then to the boot on my foot. He waited for me to catch up, then started walking more slowly.

"He's dirty, Mandy. And I didn't like the way he was looking at you. I didn't want you alone with him anymore."

"I'm wearing a microphone, not a camera. You couldn't see the way he was looking at me."

"Was it something like this?" He paused on the sidewalk and puffed himself up, mimicking Clemens's posture, then looked from my chest to my eyes, his gaze finally settling on my lips. He looked like he wanted to devour me. He looked exactly like Clemens had looked on our way out of the administration building.

I swallowed thickly and nodded.

"I thought so," he said, satisfied, and started walking again.

"But I can handle myself. The whole plan was for me to seduce him so he'd talk to me."

"And I changed the plan. That's that."

"He knows something about Hudson's disappearance, and now I'll never be able to get it out of him."

We reached the car, and Francisco eyed me over the top of it while we stood on either side, waiting for him to unlock it.

"He might know something about Supervisor Schuppert's disappearance," he said, and I winced, realizing my mistake. I'd used Hudson's first name. "But you're not going to be the one to uncover it."

He unlocked the car and got inside, and when I'd lowered myself into the passenger seat he said more softly, "You wanted to help me with my story. I thought it was a good idea, but I was wrong. Whatever Clemens is involved in, it's nothing good, and I don't want you anywhere near it."

I didn't have any rebuttal to that. Investigating Hudson's disappearance was supposed to be Francisco's domain, something he was doing for a story so he could make it as a journalist. As far as he knew, I had no connection to the supervisor and no personal interest in his disappearance. And if I pushed too hard to stay involved in the investigation, it would only drive Francisco to look closer at me, which I did not want.

I mumbled a reluctant agreement, then fished the microphone out of my clothes while Francisco started the car. We were halfway home when I noticed in my rearview mirror that the driver of the car behind us looked familiar. It was Clemens's tail from the pub, only he seemed not to be tailing Clemens, but me.

21

"Will you drop me off at Fry's? I'll get an Uber home from there." My eyes were glued to the rearview mirror, watching the old white Nissan match us turn for turn as we drew closer and closer to home. The only thing I could think of was that if this man *was* following me, I didn't want to lead him straight to my house.

Francisco looked over at me in concern. "Look, I know I was harsh, but—"

"I'm not mad. I promise. I just need some groceries, and once I get home and into comfortable clothes I'm not going to want to run out again." I tried to keep my voice light and gave him a sincere look, but it was hard to take my eyes off our tail.

We turned left. So did he. Dread built in my core.

When he dropped me off at the front of the grocery store, Francisco asked, "Are you sure you don't want me to wait for you? Or I could go in with you."

I waved him off. "Don't worry about it. Seriously. Thanks for giving me an adventure today. It really beat the usual drudgery of unemployment." I flashed one more smile to make the point that I wasn't mad at him, and he waved and drove off.

I scanned the parking lot. The white Nissan had circled the lot and was moving back toward me. I watched in horror, expecting someone to leap out of the car and grab me, but the driver put his blinker on, turned in front of the store, and left.

I stood frozen on the sidewalk in front of the store until a wolf whistle from a patron exiting the supermarket brought me back to my surroundings. I flipped the heckler off, but he didn't see me, already halfway to his car.

By the time I was loading my frozen pizza onto the checkout belt, my pulse had returned to normal. Though I'd wound my way through the entire store with unparalleled paranoia, I hadn't seen any signs of the man from the pub, and he didn't make an appearance while I stood on the curb feeling dangerously exposed waiting for my Uber.

My driver didn't give me a second glance, and he was silent for the entire drive. I tipped him extra and tried not to think about my dwindling bank balance.

My street was devoid of a white Nissan or any other sign of my tail. Just the neighbor girl sitting on their stoop again. I waved, then hurried inside and yanked my blinds closed. While I waited for the pizza to cook, pacing from window to window to peek through the slats, I wondered if I'd been wrong and maybe the man hadn't been following me, after all. Could he have been following Francisco and not me? Someone had followed him before, when they stole Maureen's security footage from his car at the gas station. Maybe it was connected? But that didn't explain why this guy followed Clemens and me to the pub after the press conference.

I passed over the plastic table and settled in to eat the pizza in bed instead while watching *How I Met Your Mother* on my laptop. I knew the episode by heart, but instead of the quips and laugh tracks, all I heard was Francisco telling me, "I think Clemens knows something about Schuppert's disappearance." What a way to send me into the press conference.

My fingers moved to my lips when I remembered the way he'd barged into the pub and brought our plan to a screeching halt. Our plan that *he* cooked up and then decided he didn't like after all. I wanted to push back again and ask Francisco if there was anything else I could do to help him with the research and investigation he was doing for his article, but I'd already gotten a little too personally invested in our press conference plot.

As far as Francisco knew, I was just an unemployed neighbor looking to help a friend and have a little adventure. If I kept pressuring Francisco to let me get involved, he'd wonder if I was more than just a neighbor looking for adventure. I'd already slipped up by using Hudson's first name—I didn't need to do anything else to shine a light on my connection to this case. At least not until I was sure that whatever I'd helped Christina bury was benign and not about to make me an accessory after the fact if anyone found out about it.

No, Francisco wasn't going to be my way to the heart of this mystery. But I was pretty sure Clemens was right there at the center, if I could find some other way to get close enough to him to figure out what he knew.

I put the memory of Francisco's lips on mine out of my mind and pulled up Clemens's LinkedIn page. It was weird, seeing that stunning, scarred face smiling out at me from the computer screen when I'd first seen it in a Polaroid smiling up at me from on top of my naked best friend. I knew his professional history like the back of my hand after all the preparation I'd done before the press conference, but I looked anyway. He'd shared a video clip from the press conference. I pressed play, and his voice filled my room, echoing off the hard surfaces without furniture to dampen the sound.

"I believe our Board of Supervisors should appoint a replacement for Mr. Schuppert..."

I stopped the playback and scrolled through the comments.

You are an incredible leading force within our county government. You will make a great supervisor.

I have always loved your energy and passion. Your growth mindset is something Pima County desperately needs in its leadership. Great job, Cory.

Back at the top of the page, Clemens's current role as a zoning administrator for the county was listed in bold. I clicked the link to the Planning and Development Services Department's LinkedIn page and browsed their posted job openings.

The department didn't have a single open position that I was qualified for, but I broadened my search to the county at large and saw that they were looking for a financial analyst. I didn't have an economics degree, but I had a math degree, and I was desperate. It wasn't Clemens's department, and I didn't even know how much longer he'd be in that role if the Board of Supervisors appointed him as Hudson's replacement, but people talked. From what I'd seen after his press conference, Clemens was well-connected within the local government; maybe there would be rumors floating around even outside his department. And even if the job didn't pan out as a lead, the paycheck would certainly be welcome.

Afternoon faded into evening and then night as I updated my resume and worked through the application questions, spinning my math background and grad school grant-writing experience into something resembling the background and expertise Pima County wanted in a financial analyst. I submitted the application through the web portal just after midnight, then fell back against the pillow.

My phone buzzing against the pillow woke me with a start, drool coating the side of my face. I snatched the phone up, some naïve part of me thinking the hiring manager was getting back to me about my job application already. A text had come in from an unknown number, and I blinked at it in my exhausted confusion.

Unknown Number: I'm safe. Don't look for me or the chest. I love you and I'm sorry.

22

I hit "call" before my brain could even form a complete thought, an endless loop of "oh my god, oh my god, oh my god" running in the background of my mind. It went straight to voicemail, a robotic voice instructing me to leave a message. I dialed a second time, just in case.

Christina is alive and she's safe and she's texting me. Thoughts began to solidify, the fog of being thrust from unconsciousness straight into chaos starting to clear. Worries I hadn't dared put into words—that Christina was lying dead in a ditch, having been abducted from her home—evaporated as I stared at her message. *I'm safe.*

I swung my legs over the side of the mattress to sit upright, and my head swam. I took shallow breaths, waiting for it to pass. Three solid knocks on my door sent me leaping up, which then sent me toppling over as I tried to get my balance with the boot on one foot. I caught myself with the wall and held onto it while I waited for my head to stop spinning.

The knocks sounded again, and this time I used the wall to steady myself as I hurried to the door and threw it open. Christina was alive and safe—was she here at my door, ready to explain everything over a bowl-sized mug of coffee?

I blinked in confusion as my eyes adjusted to the light outside.

"Can I come in?" Detective Styles looked at me expectantly.

You're not supposed to let a cop into your house. You're not supposed to tell them anything without a lawyer present, no matter how innocent you may be. You're *really* not supposed to let a cop into your house and talk to them if there's any chance you may have buried your best friend's husband in their backyard, no matter how small that chance may be. But when you've been awake less than five minutes, all five of those minutes consumed with trying to process the new information that your missing best friend is alive but using a new phone number and telling you not to search for them, maybe you're not on top of your game. I certainly wasn't, which is why I said, "Uh, yeah," and stepped back from the door to let Detective Styles stride right into my home.

She took three steps inside and then turned in a slow circle, taking everything in with her cop eyes. This was about when I realized I might have made a mistake inviting her in. *There's nothing here,* I reminded myself. Except that wasn't true. Hudson's laptop might have been safely tucked away inside his nightstand, but his agenda and legal pad full of notes were still on the floor in my bedroom, and pictures of Christina with another man were still tucked beneath my mattress. I felt the blood drain from my face at the realization.

"Are you okay?"

My head jerked toward Detective Styles, who was looking at me quizzically. Was that concern on her face or scrutiny?

I tried to suck in a breath to reply, but it felt like trying to breathe through a straw. I coughed and eventually sputtered out, "I'm fine."

She pointed to my boot and asked, "What happened?"

"I tripped."

Styles raised an eyebrow but didn't object, only walked over to the table and pulled a chair back with a loud scrape. I started to pull out my own chair, then stopped and pointed to the coffee maker. "Actually, do you mind if I...?"

Her expression said that she absolutely did mind, but she said, "Go ahead."

When I was finally seated across from her, the sound of coffee brewing behind me, Styles asked, "What's your connection to Cory Clemens?"

Clemens? Of all the questions she could have asked me, this was perhaps the least expected. "What?"

"What is your connection to Cory Clemens?" she repeated, an edge of bite to each of her words.

"I, uh, don't have a connection to him."

"What were you doing at his press conference yesterday?" She pulled out a tiny notebook not unlike the ones the real reporters had during that press conference. I stared at the pen she held poised above the page as a realization clicked into place.

"Do you have officers following me?" The idea was horrifying. Were they convinced enough that I was involved in the Schupperts' disappearance that they'd put a tail on me? I tried to call up the image of the man from the pub who'd followed Francisco and me after we left. He didn't look like a cop, but that didn't mean much.

Styles didn't answer. She just continued her line of questioning. "How long have you known Mr. Clemens?"

"I don't know him," I insisted.

"You left the press conference with him."

I could feel my cheeks redden under the accusation and stood to pour myself a cup of coffee from the beeping machine. With my back turned to Styles, I said, "I went inside the building after the press conference to use the restroom and Clemens invited me to lunch." As soon as I said it, it occurred to me that if Styles was asking about Clemens, she might question him, too, and he'd have a different story to tell.

"Are you aware of Mr. Clemens's relation to the Schupperts?"

My heart thudded. *More aware than I'd like to be.* "He's vying for Hudson's job," I said. True, though far from the extent of what I knew.

When I turned back to face Styles, she was frowning at me, not taking notes. We locked eyes for what felt like minutes, my thundering pulse melding with the headache blooming behind my eyes. Between the late night last night and the stress I'd felt since Christina's disappearance, my body was at its limit. If I didn't rest, it was likely a short matter of time before I'd be paying the price.

Unable to tolerate the silence, I asked, "What does this have to do with the Schupperts' disappearance?" Did Styles know about Clemens and Christina? Did she know Christina and Hudson's marriage wasn't as solid as it appeared?

Styles's eyes narrowed slightly, a coldness coming over her. "It'll be public information this afternoon. My office now suspects foul play in the disappearance of your friend and her husband."

I tried to swallow around the knot forming at the base of my throat. "And you think...?"

"I think it's always important to consider every angle." Styles pinned me to the spot with her gaze. "What do you know about the freshly turned dirt in the Schupperts' backyard?"

It took every ounce of willpower not to vomit on the spot. I breathed deeply through my nose, my focus entirely on the nausea rolling through my stomach until Styles stood. I expected her to cross the kitchen and slap handcuffs on me. Instead, she moved toward the front door, the heels of her loafers clicking with every step.

She turned the knob and pulled the door open but didn't leave immediately. When I lifted my head to see why she was still there, she asked me, "What is the nature of your relationship with Francisco Como?"

It was as surprising as her first question about Clemens. What did he have to do with any of this?

I clenched my fist at my side to keep from bringing my hand up to my lips, his name bringing the memory of his proprietorial kiss at the pub to the forefront of my mind.

"We're friends," I said.

There was a long pause before she said, "Be careful with that one. We'll talk again soon."

23

The moment Styles swung the door shut behind her, I sank down onto the kitchen floor, the cool tile a balm against my flushing skin. Sweat beaded on my forearms and face, and I could feel my head beginning to go cloudy. Detective Styles thought I had something to do with Christina and Hudson's disappearance. If I'd been at my limit before, I was now firmly over it. And what was with her question about Francisco?

I dragged myself back to the bedroom and reached for my phone, calling back the unfamiliar number Christina had texted me from once again. Just as before, it went straight to the robotic voicemail. Unlike before, this time I left one.

"Wherever you are and whatever is going on, I need you to tell me more than just that you're safe. I need some answers, C."

I stared at the phone long after I hung up, waiting for it to ring even though I knew it wouldn't. The questions multiplied. What was in the chest we buried? Where did it go? And why didn't Christina want me looking for it—or her?

Theories swam through my mind. Styles wanted to know more about Clemens. He was Hudson's rival in the local elections and had slept with his wife. Beyond that, he knew Hudson was missing before the public did. Could Clemens have hurt Hudson? I imagined the blond, muscled man at their home, smacking Hudson over the head with a lamp and then turning to Christina and smiling. "Now we can be together," I pictured him saying as he stood over Hudson's crumpled body. No matter how lost in the affair Christina had gotten, she wouldn't have wanted that. Would she have run to avoid his fury at her rejection?

But then why would Hudson have had a bag packed? And if Hudson was in that chest, why would anyone come and dig it up? *Don't look for me or the chest.* Christina knew the chest was gone. Could she have come back for it?

If she thought a text message warning me off would keep me from searching for her, Christina didn't know me at all. But the tiny voice in the back of my head told me that was the truth of it all. That was the whole point: she didn't actually know me, and I didn't actually know her, either. What had she done before grabbing her things and vanishing into thin air? What had she made me do?

Heat rose in my veins with every unanswered question, and I suddenly wanted Christina to call me not just so that I could get the answers I needed, but so that I could give her a piece of my mind. *How could you pull me into this and then leave? How could you drag me into your mess and then leave me here to have cops knocking on my door and tailing me around town while you hide out somewhere?*

Tears rolled down my cheeks and pooled beside my face on the mattress. Snot bubbled in my nostrils, and I swiped it away with a shirt I grabbed out of the dirty clothes pile, then went to the sink and splashed water on my face.

No. I clenched my jaw and gave a shake of my head. I *did* know Christina. I might not know what situation she'd landed in, but I knew *her*. Christina wouldn't have run unless she was in danger. And she wouldn't leave me in the dark unless she believed it was the only way to keep me safe.

While I wondered what could possibly have made Christina run, I popped two Aleve in my mouth and swallowed them dry, then pulled my hair back in a ponytail, carefully guiding the strands to cover my bald patches as well as I could. Then, I slipped out of my damp pajamas and into my cleanest pair of jeans before slipping a sneaker onto my right foot.

Christina knew the chest was missing. Either she'd come back to the house to take it herself, or someone else had found whatever she'd so desperately wanted to keep hidden. I could only think of one person who might be able to help me find some answers. I needed to go talk to Maureen again.

THE RIGHTSIDE DAUGHTER was on the porch again when I locked the door behind me. When I gave a short wave and started toward my car, she hopped to her feet and hurried toward me.

"Where are you going?"

I turned toward her, once again looking toward the house in the hopes that one of her parents would call her back, but no one was there, and she was looking at me with wide, eager eyes.

"I've got to go visit someone."

"A boyfriend?" She matched me stride for stride as we made our way down the block.

I couldn't help the little laugh that bubbled out of me when I said, "Nope, not a boyfriend."

"Is it because of the police lady?"

I stopped short and turned to face her, her brown eyes innocent and curious behind the curtain of dark hair that kept falling in front of her face.

"I don't have time to talk right now."

"Can I come with you?"

"No." My response was immediate, and her deflation caught me by surprise. I softened and said, "It's a private visit."

She continued to scurry alongside me when I started walking again and said, "Please? I can wait in the car." When she saw me hesitating she doubled down. "Pleeease?"

I sighed. "It's going to be boring. Why do you want to come?"

"It's boring here," she replied with a shrug.

"No," I said again, but then we were at my car, and she pulled open the passenger door and slid in anyway. "Look, uh... What's your name?"

"Ariel." She was beaming at me triumphantly.

"Ariel," I repeated, "you can't come with me."

"Why not?"

"I already told you, it's a private visit!"

"Well, I already told you I'd wait in the car."

I sputtered in exasperation. "Your parents will freak out when they see you're gone."

With a shake of her head, she said, "They're working. And my brother is at his friend Jason's house."

Though I continued to look around for someone to save me from negotiating any further with a preteen, no one came to my rescue.

"I'm home alone," she pressed. "What if I set the house on fire or a maniac breaks in? Isn't it safer if I come with you?"

I stared at her across the console, and she stared right back, the gleam in her eyes saying she knew full well she'd beat me.

"Do you have a phone?" I asked. She nodded and held up a pink phone with a kitten charm dangling from it, and I told her to text her parents. "Tell them you're with me and give them my number in case they want to reach me." I recited the number and watched her send the message, then gripped my key fob carefully to keep it from falling apart when I twisted it in the ignition, muttering, "Lord help me," as we pulled away from the curb.

We hadn't even made it to the end of the street when Ariel frowned and held her hands up to the AC vent. "I don't think your air conditioner is working," she said.

"It's broken." I rolled down the windows, and the air swirled her hair into a little tornado around her face.

Horrified, she cried, "This is Arizona! You can't have a broken air conditioner!"

"Well, when I have the money, I'll fix it."

I turned up the radio to head off any other complaints Ariel might have about my ride, and we made the drive without talking. Just before we arrived at the entrance to Christina's neighborhood, I looked over to see Ariel with her face turned toward the window, eyes closed with the sun on her skin and her hair whipping behind her. My chest tightened. She was almost the age Christina and I were when we met.

"What?" She looked over at me, and I turned away, embarrassed at the moisture pooling in my eyes.

When we pulled onto Christina's street, I immediately noticed the black sedan with tinted windows sitting across the street. My breath hitched, and my eyes fixed on the transponder on the trunk. I slowed down and pulled over several houses away, taking in the sight. I had no doubt it was an unmarked police car and whoever was inside was watching to see if anyone approached the Schupperts' house. Given my interaction with Styles that morning, I figured it was likely they were specifically watching to see if I showed up.

"What's wrong?" Ariel asked, looking around. Her mouth dipped open and she raised her hand and pointed. "Hey, I've been there before. That's the crazy lady's house."

I followed her gesture to see she was pointing right at Christina's place.

24

"The crazy lady?" My voice wobbled, and Ariel shot me a concerned look before turning back to the Schupperts' house, its usually manicured lawn beginning to look scruffy and long next to the neighbors'.

"My mom cleans houses. She used to clean that one and sometimes I would go with her if it was after school. Mom told me they had a game room upstairs, and I went to go play pool. I hadn't even touched anything but the lady came in screaming at me. She said no one was supposed to go in that room. I don't know how we were supposed to know that since she didn't tell us, but she just yelled and then told us to go home and not to come back. She said she didn't need cleaners anymore. She still paid Mom, though. Mom counted the bills when we got to the car and said the lady actually paid her extra."

"When was that?"

"March, I think. It was before Ryder's birthday because Mom was worried about how she could buy him a birthday present if she lost that job, but then after she realized how much the lady gave her she was happy again. She got him a hoverboard, which was totally not fair because I wanted one for *my* birthday but Mom said it was too expensive."

I counted back, trying to figure out how long before Christina and Hudson disappeared that would have been. A month, maybe? It would have been right around the time Christina came to get me from Ann Arbor and move me into her pool house.

A blue Mercedes sped past us and whipped into the driveway a few houses down, drawing my attention back to the unmarked patrol car up ahead.

"Actually, I forgot; my visit was supposed to be tomorrow." I made a tight U-turn in the middle of the wide street and hightailed it out of the neighborhood while Ariel looked perplexed in the passenger seat.

The entire drive home, I waited for that unmarked police car to pull up behind me and flash its lights. My eyes flitted to my rearview mirror so often we had two close calls where I missed that traffic ahead of me had slowed down. But no black sedan with tinted windows ever appeared in those mirrors. I thought I glimpsed a white Nissan once, but it slipped out of view before I could be sure.

When we pulled back onto our street, Ariel pouted slightly. "Now what are you going to do?"

For a moment, I thought she meant about Christina. If I couldn't go talk to Maureen, I'd have to come up with another plan. Before I could make that mistake, she added, "Can I keep hanging out with you?"

Validation surged through my chest, warming me, but I shook my head. I needed to come up with a new plan—a way to figure out what had been in that chest, who had the chest now, and why Christina thought looking for it would put me in danger. Would the chest be the key that led me to Christina herself? And would Hudson be alive and well with her?

"I'm sorry," I said. Ariel deflated immediately, and I scrambled. "Maybe later this week you can come over and we can watch a movie together? Or if your parents agree, maybe I could, uh, take you to the mall or something?" Did kids still like going to the mall?

"Yeah, maybe," she said noncommittally and climbed out of

the car, bounding toward our duplex and taking up her perch on the porch again.

I waved to her as I let myself into my side of the house, then plopped down onto the hideous floral print loveseat. As soon as I laid my head back against the top of the cushion, my body felt heavy. My lids fluttered closed and my breathing deepened. *Maybe just a quick rest before I come up with a kickass plan to find my friend.*

The quick rest turned into a deep sleep, only cut short by the clatter of my phone falling off the cushion and onto the floor. It skittered across the tile, and I crawled to retrieve it from under the folding table, praying it hadn't shattered. Until one of my many job applications produced an actual paycheck, there was no way I could afford to replace it.

It buzzed against the hard floor, then again in my hand when I picked it up. I had three missed calls from Dave just within the hour that I'd been napping, and his messages kept coming.

Dave: Mandy, I'm worried about you. I'm seeing stuff in the news about Christina and her husband. Please at least let me know you're all right.

Dave: Mands, I get it. We're done. But can you at least tell me you're safe?

I started to write back to say I was fine and that he could stop worrying about me, but then I remembered the feeling of coming face-to-face with the police officer he'd sent to my home for a wellness check. The humiliation and fury I'd felt when I realized Dave had tracked my laptop after I'd told him I didn't want any more contact came back to me, and I deleted the half-typed message. He didn't get to keep demanding access to me under the pretext of being concerned.

I had just flicked the conversation away and opened my email when another text from Dave came through. This one was just a link to a news article titled "Clemens Appointed Supervisor While Schuppert Still Missing."

My phone buzzed in my hand again while I processed the news.

Dave: Christina and Hudson are missing. Are you okay? If you don't answer I'm calling the police to look for you.

I dashed off a quick response.

Mandy: I'm fine, Dave. Stop contacting me. I mean it.

Replies rolled in as soon as I sent the text, but I ignored them all, instead opening the article and glancing at the first paragraph. I took a screenshot and sent it to Francisco. His response came through almost immediately.

Francisco: Guess his presser was convincing.

We hadn't spoken since the day before, when he'd dropped me off at the grocery store after ambushing me in the pub with Clemens after the press conference. Not since he'd kissed me. Not since Styles had cryptically warned me away from him.

I typed out three partial replies, but nothing felt right, and I abandoned the effort and instead grabbed my laptop and read every news article I could about the board's decision to appoint Clemens as supervisor.

Every article contained the same few quotes. "While my colleague has been missing, issues are still coming across our desks every day. These issues are important to our constituents, and it is our duty as supervisors to ensure all of our districts have representation." That was District 4 Supervisor, Wendy Washington.

District 2 Supervisor, Elias Holtz, said, "If the Board of Supervisors failed to appoint a replacement for Supervisor Schuppert, the seat would sit empty until eventually a judge would set a date for an election. Cory Clemens is a highly qualified candidate who will represent District 1 well."

The articles all speculated about whether Hudson would be

found and, if he was, what his condition might be. Some predicted that he would be located and would challenge the appointment of Clemens in his place. Legal experts weighed in on the validity of the appointment, were that to happen.

I scrolled through the articles, scanning them quickly, then opened a new tab. Hudson had been up to something at the Board of Supervisors, and now he was missing. Clemens knew he'd gone missing before the rest of the public. What else did he know? And could the rest of the board know more than they were letting on?

I browsed the webpage for the Board of Supervisors, and my attention lit on a header in the navigation bar. *Employment Opportunities.* I clicked it, and my eyes darted across the page, searching for anything I was remotely qualified for. Desperation snowballed inside of me. I suddenly needed more than anything to find an in at the board. If I couldn't go to Maureen to find out more about the chest, I'd find out anything I could about Hudson's activities in his political role and hope that held the key to his—and Christina's—whereabouts.

When I saw a posting titled "Administrative Assistant," I held my breath, scanning the description at record speed. The job posting began, "Independently performs a variety of administrative duties for a member of the Pima County Board of Supervisors." Which member, I wanted to know.

The listed duties included providing administrative support to professional staff, researching and organizing legislative materials for board members, and drafting written materials including information for public dissemination. All sufficiently vague. I filled out the application immediately.

Could this be an opening to work with Clemens? My heart sank when I realized he'd never hire me once he saw me; he knew I was connected to Francisco and Francisco suspected him of something to do with Hudson going missing. But there were four other supervisors—there could still be a chance.

I submitted the application and said a silent prayer: *Please let me get this job. Please let this job help me figure out what happened to my best friend and her husband. And please don't let her have murdered him and buried his body in the backyard.*

25

The next day passed in a blur of constantly staring at screens, either searching online for any new articles, blog posts, or forum discussions about Hudson's disappearance and Clemens's subsequent appointment to his spot on the Board of Supervisors, or checking my email for a response to my job application. I no longer cared about the financial analyst role for the county at large; suddenly it felt as if everything depended on my securing the administrative assistant job at the board. Though it was the weekend and I'd submitted the application less than twenty-four hours ago, I couldn't stop picking up my phone to check for a response.

Monday morning, when I finally gave up on sleep and sat upright on my mattress before dawn, I was more tired than I'd been when I'd lain down the night before. In the moments of sleep I'd managed to get, I'd been tormented by more vivid dreams, this time of Hudson coming after me with a pickaxe while I tunneled into the ground with a shovel. It seemed like every night my brain worked to create new horror shows to play for me when I was supposed to be resting. And in the moments of wakefulness between the nightmares, the constant throbbing of my joints was little reprieve.

I dragged one of my plastic chairs into the shower and sat under the hot stream of water, letting it pelt my back and soothe the aches. When the hot water ran out, I reluctantly toweled off and pulled on the outfit I'd worn for the job interview at the insurance company. In the night, I'd decided I wasn't going to sit around waiting any longer. A week and a half ago, I'd been trying to convince a stern-faced Carol that I wanted to be an actuary. Now, I was going to go convince a county supervisor that I, an early-thirties former math professor, would be a good fit for an entry-level administrative assistant role.

Clouds loomed overhead as I climbed the concrete stairs of the administration building, casting an ominous shadow over the day. I forced a smile and smoothed the front of my blouse. If Christina ever found out I was interviewing for jobs in the same outfit I'd worn for my doctoral dissertation defense six years ago, she would have a fit. I took a deep breath and tried to infuse some pep into my lopsided step.

"Good morning." I stepped up to the metal detector in front of the security guard with confidence. Then I lied through my teeth. "I have a job interview upstairs. Do I need a visitor badge?" I plopped my bag on the table and proceeded toward the metal detector without waiting for his answer, like it was a given that I'd be going upstairs. If I could just get myself in front of the hiring manager, I knew I could talk myself into this job. I pointed to my boot. "Do you have a wand or something? I think this will set off the machine."

The boot jogged his memory, and he blinked at me in surprise. "Didn't you—?"

"I was here last Friday at Supervisor Clemens's press conference," I said with a nod, hoping he might let me through if he remembered how Clemens vouched for me before. When he didn't immediately move to wave me through, I continued with my lie. "I'm interviewing for an administrative position with the Board of Supervisors. How should I...?" Trailing off, I gestured to the metal detector and my boot again.

The security guard's brow furrowed, and he picked up a clipboard. "They don't have anything on here about an interview candidate. Let me just call up and have one of them come and escort you."

Shit. "Oh, uh, you don't—"

"Good morning, Benny!" A singsong voice sounded behind me as a petite woman in a lavender pantsuit hurried into the building and flashed her badge. She was halfway across the lobby toward the elevator when the guard called out to her.

"Wendy, wait up. We've got a visitor here to interview for some, uh,"—he looked at me with raised brows as he tried to recall what I'd told him—"administrative role with the Board of Supervisors. I don't have her on the Visitor Log, though." He shifted uncomfortably.

Wendy Washington, District 4 Supervisor, turned, her face lighting up when she saw me. "Dana got a candidate lined up to interview already? Oh, that's fabulous news! I'll bring her up, Benny."

Benny seemed relieved that, once again, if I was going into the building against his better judgment, someone else was taking on the responsibility for me. He pulled out a metal detector wand and gave it a half-assed wave in my direction before handing me a sticker that said "Visitor" on it.

"I'm Wendy," the tiny purple-clad woman said, extending her hand. "I'm the supervisor you'll be reporting to. Assuming the interviews go well, that is. I'm really going to have to have a word with Dana. She didn't even tell me I had an interview today."

The elevator chugged slowly before delivering us to the fourth floor. I squirmed, then admitted, "I don't actually have an interview scheduled. I only just filled out the application Saturday afternoon."

Supervisor Washington's face dropped. Where she'd previously looked at me like some sort of savior, now she regarded me with suspicion. I hurried to add, "I think I'm a fantastic fit for the role, and I'm eager to get started as soon as possible. I wanted to come in and show that I'm serious about this job." I threw my shoulders back and my chin up and tried to give off an air of confidence instead of desperation.

Wendy's frown tempered. Sensing an opportunity, I said, "I can start today if you'll have me."

"Why do you want this job?"

I rattled off the speech I'd rehearsed on the drive over. "The work you do is so important, and I don't think most people understand the magnitude of what goes on in this office. It's vital to the county that the office of the Board of Supervisors is fully staffed and running efficiently. I'm excited by the prospect of contributing to such meaningful work and seeing my efforts directly result in things like increased access of local organizations to their representatives and faster approvals for important conservation projects."

To my surprise, Supervisor Washington rolled her eyes. "Why do you want this job *now?*" When I hesitated, she smirked. "You submitted the application less than forty-eight hours ago. It's barely eight o'clock on a Monday morning. You saw the job posting, applied, and then rushed over to try to talk your way into the role immediately. You're desperate to get this job, and I want to know why. I can't have someone working for me if I don't know their motives."

She was good.

My mouth flapped open, and I shifted my weight while trying to decide what to say. The shift sent a particularly piercing pain up my leg, and I flinched. Then I told the truth, because keeping any more lies straight would have required more mental capacity than I had right then.

"I realized recently that I was living a life I was not happy in, so I decided to change it. I quit my job and left my husband and moved across the country to someplace warm because I had spent too many years telling myself that my desire to live someplace warm wasn't important. And now I want to have a job serving my community instead of publishing papers on dispersive partial differential equations. And I want it *now* because my landlord wants me to pay the rent next week." The "serving my community" bit was a stretch, but the rest was true.

Wendy looked up at me with an inscrutable expression. Just when I was about to apologize for the brazen act of showing up uninvited, she broke into a grin. "Work for me today, and if I like you, you're hired and we'll pay you for the day's work."

For a moment I was sure I'd heard her wrong. Then, the elation of a triumph rushed through me and I mirrored her grin. I'd done it—I had an in.

But the elation didn't last, as Supervisor Washington turned and walked from the elevator bay toward a small room full of cubicles, and I realized I had no idea what I was supposed to do. I scurried after her as she passed through the bullpen and turned right down the hallway running along the back of the room. The hallway was lined with offices, each one's door hanging open to reveal they were empty, though a few people flitted from cubicles in the open office into the private offices to drop papers off on the desks inside. When a young woman with striking red hair emerged from one of the offices with an armful of folders, I nearly collided with her, mumbling apologies after she'd already hurried past me.

Supervisor Washington gestured to an office on the left. "This one's mine." Then she pointed back down the hall toward the open office we'd entered through. "The admins sit over there in the cubicles. One of them will show you the ropes." With a swish of lavender fabric, she turned into her office and shut the door behind her.

Surprised at the lack of introduction, I turned back. Though the offices were all empty this early in the morning, the cubicles were mostly occupied. Two of them seemed to have been converted into printer and copier stations, and three more were piled high with papers, folders, and spiral-bound notebooks that made me assume no one worked at those desks. But four of the other five hosted a set of employees who all looked at least ten years my junior. I wondered if they had even graduated yet or if some of them might be interns still in school.

"I'm Mandy," I said when one of them looked up at me. "I'm new. Um, I'm not sure if I actually have a job yet, but Supervisor Washington said I could work for her today. She didn't actually tell me what I'm supposed to do, though…"

The young woman with red hair looked at me sympathetically. "Washington's desk is there." She pointed to the empty cubicle. By then, the other three admins were watching us.

"Washington's got an admin again?" One of them asked. He wore his blond hair gelled to the side, and his dress shirt hung loosely over his lanky form. "Hell yeah!" He walked over to the desk the redhead had just pointed me to and dumped a stack of papers on it.

When I looked up at him in shock, the first girl said, "Jake, she doesn't know anything yet! You can't just dump that on her."

"If it's not for District 1, it's not for me. If Washington has an admin now, I'm not doing any more of her work." He swiveled his chair around and picked up the desk phone that had just begun to ring. District 1—so this was Clemens's assistant.

"You guys seem busy," I remarked, and the last two admins who hadn't acknowledged me yet both snickered.

"You think?" one of them asked, gesturing to the overflowing organizers crammed with papers and his desk phone, which, like Jake's, was now ringing.

The first woman looked back at her own work, then at me, deciding whether to help me. She sighed and stood up, and I breathed a sigh of relief. "I'm Eliza. I'm Supervisor Tucker's admin." Brandon Tucker represented District 3, a fact I'd learned when speed reading about the potential supervisors I might have been supporting in this role. I'd seen quite a few pictures of him playing golf with Clemens.

"How much does the supervisor you work for impact the job?"

"It's basically the same for all of us." She winced, then said, "But Washington's the only one who's had an admin quit."

Hearing our conversation, Clemens's assistant piped up, "This job is purgatory for all of us, but if you work for Washington it's hell."

"Jake!" Eliza hissed at the same time I said, "Sounds like I made a great career move."

One of the other admins chuckled and introduced himself. "I'm Johan." He was tall like Jake, but broader. His jet-black hair was buzzed close to his skull.

"And the one who's too busy to introduce himself is Peter," Eliza said.

Peter lifted his head just enough to give me a nod of acknowledgment before returning to furiously typing at his keyboard.

The others returned to their work, and I turned to Eliza. "Um, I'm sorry to ask this, but Supervisor Washington didn't tell me much. What exactly do we do?"

The papers Jake had plopped onto my desk seemed to be printouts of zoning proposals and meeting minutes from past Board of Supervisors meetings. I had no idea what to do with any of them.

"Oh!" Eliza seemed surprised that I knew so little about the job. I'd read the job description a dozen times, but it didn't exactly translate to the real world. "Essentially, we handle all the scheduling and coordination for everyone who wants to meet with the county supervisors, and we research all the requests that come in and prep memos so our supervisors know which way they want to vote when they meet."

"We do all the work so they can do their jobs in a quarter of the time," Jake grumbled. "That way they can keep whatever high-paying gigs they had before they got elected supervisor and bring home two salaries."

I looked around nervously, worried Supervisor Washington would hear and I'd be fired for this conversation before I was even officially hired. But Washington didn't emerge from her closed office, and none of the other supervisors were around. When I asked about it, Jake made another joke about how the supervisors show up when they feel like it thanks to all the hard work of their assistants, and Eliza diplomatically said they're frequently out of the office visiting with their constituents or important local organizations.

Eliza rolled her chair up next to mine and pulled out the list of topics to be voted on in the upcoming Board of Supervisors meeting. She pointed to a few items that Supervisor Washington would be concerned about—items pertaining to District 4 or items she'd made a major piece of her election campaign and was on public record as caring about.

"You'll want to prep her for these," she said, drawing asterisks next to the items, then flipped through until she found an environmental study related to one of the zoning requests. "She'll want copies of all the relevant studies. She likes to walk around with big stacks of paper and make a show of having done all this research, but you'll need to give her a half-page brief summarizing everything. Let me see if I can find one that Deb put together..."

Eliza dug through file folders until she found examples of memos from Supervisor Washington's previous administrative assistant, and I took that guidance and ran with it. When the other admins left for lunch, I stayed at my desk and ignored my stomach's grumbling. Wendy came out of her office then and gave an approving nod to my presence, then left for the rest of the day. It was after seven in the evening when I finally packed up to leave, almost twelve hours after I'd arrived. I put the pages I'd prepared on Wendy's desk, then slipped out of the office, unsure whether or not I should come back the next day.

The parking lot was dark. It was just past dusk, but the streetlights hadn't turned on yet, and I had my head down fumbling in my bag for my keys as I walked toward my junker of a car. It was one of only a few left in the lot. My hands touched upon the keys and I grabbed them, careful not to bust the fob open when I pressed the unlock button. I'd never find the pieces in this darkness.

The sound of footsteps behind me startled me and I spun around, brandishing my useless car keys, but there was no one there. Still, my pulse hammered as I closed the distance between me and the car and climbed inside. I took a deep breath. *You're imagining things. You're on edge with everything going on. Calm down.*

I turned the key in the ignition and my headlights kicked on, shining at one of the few other cars still there. Lit up, I could see that it was a familiar white sedan, and my blood turned cold. Illuminated in the driver's seat was a young man with dark, shaggy hair. A man I'd seen before, first in the pub with Clemens and then driving that little white Nissan behind Francisco and me. Something in me knew without a doubt that this man was not a police officer. He wasn't following me on behalf of Detective Styles, but he was most definitely following me.

26

The tail matched me turn for turn until we were a mere three blocks from home. Unwilling to let him see where I lived, I took a sharp right turn without using my blinker, then turned left onto the next block over. I made it four blocks and was considering whether to risk going home when his headlights appeared in my rearview mirror. I turned again, and we wound circles around the neighborhoods near mine for fifteen minutes until he suddenly turned off behind me and left me alone.

It took me another ten minutes of driving alone before I accepted that he'd left and started back toward my house, and I drove down the street twice before parking, on the lookout for his car parked anywhere nearby. My heart beat wildly as I raced as quickly as I could to my front door and threw it closed behind me, breathing hard when I leaned against it. I dragged one of my plastic chairs in front of the door; it seemed unlikely to hold if someone really wanted in, but my only other option was to drag the loveseat across the room, and that seemed beyond my capabilities after working almost twelve hours and skipping lunch.

I shoveled cereal into my mouth for dinner, the quickest thing I could grab. Once my pulse had slowed and the shaky hunger was fading, I stripped off my slacks and blouse and tossed them both on the floor. A stalker had followed me home from my unofficial first day of work. After that, it was hard to imagine going back for an official first day even if Supervisor

Williams decided to hire me. It was hard to imagine leaving my house, period.

I filled a wine glass nearly to the brim from the box in my fridge, then double-checked that all the windows were locked and blinds all the way shut. Then I sat down on my loveseat with the glass of wine and my phone and read Christina's text again and again.

I couldn't try to convince myself anymore that the man in the Nissan was following Clemens or Francisco—I was being followed. I knew that for sure.

But why?

Did someone know I'd helped Christina bury the chest? Did they think I knew what was inside, or where the chest had ended up?

Did they just know I was poking around looking for answers —looking for Christina exactly like she told me not to do? Was that why she'd warned me? To keep me safe? If Christina was in some sort of hot water and ran because people were after her, she'd try to shield me from getting involved. She'd try to protect me.

I took another long sip from my glass of wine. I didn't want to think of what sort of hot water Christina could have been in that would lead her to disappear, that would put me in danger for even trying to figure out where she was. Her husband had disappeared without taking his things. She'd left with her bag and her car after enlisting me to help bury a chest large enough to conceal an adult man. And their marriage had been on the fritz, no matter how much she tried to hide it.

But if Christina had killed Hudson and I'd helped her bury him, who would she be running from?

Christina clearly had secrets; I'd uncovered photographic evidence of that. Still, I couldn't imagine any of her secrets could be big enough to send her on the run. But there was *something* she'd needed to hide. Something had been in that chest. Something that would motivate people to come after her, to come after me.

Francisco's words floated to the top of my mind. *I've been working on a piece about a corrupt local politician.* If Christina didn't have secrets dark enough to send her on the run, maybe Hudson did. Bribes, money laundering... What sort of corruption was Hudson involved in?

I was carrying my empty wine glass into the kitchen when I heard it—a rustling in the bushes outside my back door. I froze in place, willing my heart to stop beating so loud as I strained my ears to hear any more noise. I had almost convinced myself I'd imagined it when I heard another rustle followed by the unmistakable sound of footsteps on the small concrete patio just outside the back door. I held my breath for what felt like an eternity, listening closely but hearing nothing.

When I couldn't stand waiting any longer, I walked the rest of the way into the kitchen as quietly as I could. Then I pulled the curtain over the sink back just an inch, hoping I'd see a coyote or a skunk and be able to rest easy. Instead, I found myself face to face with another human standing directly outside my window.

27

I screamed, stumbling backward and dropping the wine glass, sending shards of glass skittering over the tile. I landed hard on my ass and slammed my elbow into the ground, the impact eliciting a second scream. I crab-walked backward away from the window, desperate to put as much distance as possible between me and the person in my backyard, when I realized the face peering into my house was familiar.

I shoved myself upright, inspecting the floor carefully before planting my palms to avoid embedding a piece of glass into my flesh, then marched to the back door and yanked it open.

"What the fuck?" I shouted at the now-cowering figure beside my house. My pulse was still thundering, adrenaline coursing through me with every heartbeat. I drew in a ragged breath and yelled, "What are you doing?"

Ariel straightened up and took a few steps back. The glisten in her wide eyes slipped out of view as she moved away from the window into the darkness of the yard. Her outline was barely visible, hands raised in surrender. "I'm sorry. I wasn't trying to scare you."

"What were you trying to do, then?"

Ariel flinched at my shrill voice, and I turned my face skyward, breathing in deeply and waiting for the adrenaline in my blood to dissipate. Shouting would only draw attention, and if I was really unlucky, maybe a call to the police. Another officer on my doorstep was the last thing I needed tonight.

When I'd calmed down enough, I asked, "Why were you looking into my house?"

Though she didn't flinch this time, Ariel was still half-crouched like a prey animal ready to run. She looked from me to the back door of her family's side of the duplex, then back to me. "Are you going to tell my parents?"

I heaved a sigh. She'd made me think I was about to be murdered in my home, and she was worried about her parents being mad. "No," I said, softening as I saw her relax in relief. "As long as you promise not to do it again."

She smiled and straightened up. "Can I come hang out with you?"

With another enormous sigh, I agreed and waved her inside. She bounded across the threshold, saying, "I was looking inside to see if you were awake to ask if I could—" She stopped short at the sight of the shattered glass, then gave me a sheepish look.

"I've got it. Go sit over there."

I swept the broken glass up while Ariel recounted her day at school. She'd had choir because it was Monday, but then Kaylie passed her a note in the hallway reminding her that if she didn't quit, Kaylie wouldn't be friends with her anymore. I opened my mouth to remind her that that wasn't how friends behaved, but she breezed past the subject and was already onto the next thing.

"Then Mom made entomatadas, but Ryder whined because he wanted meat. Mom said we don't have enough money right now because my dad's hours got cut, but then he got mad because he said she was blaming him. Then everyone was yelling at everyone. That sucked, so I decided to come over here. You cry a lot, but that's better than yelling." She looked down at her feet as she said, "Turns out you yell, too, if you get scared."

I dumped the swept-up glass from the dustpan into a cardboard box I'd grabbed out of the recycling bin, then leveled a glare at her.

Ignoring my look, Ariel kicked her feet and asked, "Where were you today?"

"What do you mean?"

"Usually you're at home when I get off the bus."

I blinked, processing how much this girl had been watching my every move. When she just kept looking at me expectantly, I told her, "I was interviewing for a job."

Ariel gave me a quick nod of approval, then launched into a rundown of the latest episode of a show I'd never heard of. As she spoke, aches crept into my limbs. The adrenaline from the shock had entirely worn off, and the pain from where I'd fallen in the kitchen grew in intensity until I could barely hear what she was saying. Finally, I stood up, knuckles white where I clutched the arm of the loveseat.

"Okay, time for bed," I said, herding her toward the door. I watched as she walked from my back door to her own. When she was halfway across the yard, I called out to her. "Ariel? Have you seen a white car driving up our street?" If she was so aware of my comings and goings, maybe she saw more than I realized.

"A white car?"

I nodded. "One that you didn't use to see but maybe has been driving by recently?"

In the dark, I could see her cock her head to the side but couldn't see her expression. "I don't think so," she said.

I shook off my disappointment and said, "That's all right. If you do see one, will you let me know?"

MY HAIR WAS PLASTERED to my cheek with drool when I awoke to the sound of my phone vibrating against the tile beside my mattress. When I blinked the sleep from my eyes and brought the screen into focus, I saw an unfamiliar number, not the name of a contact in my phone. *Christina.* I jerked it to my ear.

"Hello?" Desperate, frantic hope dripped from the single word.

"Ms. Perkins, you're hired. I want you here in an hour."

I was so disoriented by the voice not being Christina's, I couldn't place it. "Who is this?"

"Wendy Washington. Dana got your official application and gave me your information. Now, get over here. I've got a meeting with Green Heart Housing Developers later and I need talking points."

She ended the call, and I washed my face with cold water and tried to adjust to the idea that she actually wanted me to work for her. I had a job if I wanted it. If I could bring myself to go back there after being followed home the day before.

But it would be a paycheck—something more than zero flowing into my bank account—and if someone was following me because of my connection to the Schupperts, turning down this job wasn't going to keep me any safer. And it would be a means of getting close to Clemens and the people who worked the closest with him. Whatever corruption Hudson had been involved in, it had taken place right there at the board, and now Clemens was taking his seat. Clemens, who had known Hudson was missing before anyone else. Clemens, who had pursued Hudson's wife alongside his job. I couldn't pass up this opportunity.

I grabbed the outfit I'd worn yesterday off the floor and hung it in the bathroom, then turned the shower on extra hot to try to steam out the wrinkles. I regretted not buying another decent outfit. I'd just assumed I'd have enough notice of getting a job that I'd have time to go buy a few other work-appropriate articles of clothing before I had to actually start work.

I was running out the door, or getting as close as I could to a run with my orthopedic boot, thirty minutes after the phone call with Wendy ended. Unless traffic was crazy, I'd make it to the administration building on time.

"Hey!"

I turned, key still in the lock, to see Francisco in his running attire standing at the end of my front path.

"You're dressed up," he remarked.

"I got a job!" As I said the words out loud, an unexpected feeling of pride bubbled up inside me. I hadn't really wanted this job—not for the job itself, at least. It was just a means to information. But as I told Francisco I'd landed it, I found myself feeling gratified.

Francisco lit up and wrapped me in a hug. It was the first physical contact we'd had since he kissed me in the pub, a show of possession put on for Clemens's benefit. I stiffened at first, then relaxed into his embrace. When he pulled away and I saw his eyes full of genuine excitement for me and my accomplishment, I felt heat color my cheeks.

"That's incredible," he said. "Where at?"

The heat intensified as I considered what to say. "Oh, just filing papers in some boring office. It's nothing long-term, but it'll keep a roof over my head for now."

He gestured to the lime-green duplex. "That roof in particular is really something special. Wouldn't want to lose that."

I threw my head back in a laugh.

"Look," Francisco said, bringing his hand up to rub the back of his neck. "I'm really sorry about the other day. The press conference, and after... I shouldn't have kissed you like that. It was a dick move, and I'm really sorry."

I swallowed thickly, looking away from the earnest expression in his espresso-brown eyes. "It's fine," I mumbled toward my feet.

"It isn't." The intensity of his words pulled my eyes back to his. "I put you in a bad situation, sending you to seduce a sleazeball for my own purposes, and then when I realized what a shit idea it was I made a complete ass of myself."

I shook my head, cutting him off. "I appreciate your apology, but really, it's—" I cut myself off before I could say "fine" again. "I forgive you," I said instead.

He cleared his throat and stepped back. "Anyway, I know I made a big deal about how important it was to get information out of Clemens. For me to then blow the whole thing, it made perfect sense for you to be upset, and I'm sorry about that, too.

"But look, don't worry too much about that. I got a new lead yesterday that more than makes up for anything we might have lost on the press conference operation." He said it in a slightly lowered voice, like he shouldn't really be telling me and wanted to make sure no one else heard. And I almost didn't hear him myself, because as he said it, an old white Nissan drove down our block, the driver's head turning to look as he passed us.

28

My pursuer followed me to work, then parked across the parking lot. My hands grew sweaty on the steering wheel, my thoughts spiraling out of control. He knew where I lived. He knew where I worked. I would never get away from him, and soon I'd disappear and Detective Styles would either decide I was on the run for my horrible crimes or regret that she ever suspected me.

I sucked in shallow breaths and searched for someone I could ask for help, or at least someone else to be present while I crossed the parking lot so I wasn't all alone. But there were only a half-dozen other cars in the lot, and only mine and the menacing little white sedan were occupied. Where was everyone?

I eyed the distance from my car to the front door. Whoever was following me already knew where I lived; what use would it be to turn around and run home now? With one last breath, I jumped out of the car and ran across the parking lot, then hurried up the concrete stairs.

I tugged on the door handle, remembering Benny the security guard and realizing I didn't have a badge yet. He'd have to call Wendy downstairs again to let me up, but at least I wouldn't be alone while I waited. None of that mattered, though, because the door was locked. I spun wildly, checking for someone closing in on me, but the shaggy-haired man hadn't emerged from the Nissan. Heart pounding, I ran over to the second of the three doors. It had a sign in the window that read "Use Other

Door" with an arrow pointing to the main door, the one I'd just found to be locked. It, too, was shut fast. The third door was the same.

I ran back over to the main door and started knocking on it, but when I cupped my hand to peer in through the glass insert, the lobby was empty. No security guard.

I whirled back around, pressing my back to the door so I could look out onto the parking lot. A small tree, listing to one side despite the wooden stakes strapped to its thin trunk, partially concealed my pursuer. My chest heaved with every breath, and I pressed myself harder against the door to steady myself, its metal hot already despite the early hour. There was nothing else to do. I couldn't very well pick the lock to a government building, and even if I did, there didn't seem to be anyone inside. Had I imagined the phone call this morning?

I flattened both palms against the door and prepared to push off and run back to my car. I had no idea where I'd go, but anywhere would be better than standing vulnerable out in the open. Before I could bring my legs to move, my phone rang, and I answered it without checking to see who was calling. If I was about to be dragged down the stairs and stuffed into the trunk of someone's car, at least there would be someone on the other end of the line who knew I was in trouble.

"Where are you?" my new boss demanded. "I told you to be here in an hour. It's been an hour. Did I make a mistake hiring you?"

I turned back to face the doors, trying to make sense of the situation. In a trembling voice I said, "The doors are locked."

Supervisor Washington made a frustrated sound. "I'll be right down to let you in."

I wanted to stay on the line while I waited for her, but she hung up immediately, leaving me alone. I put my back to the building again, watching the parking lot while the wait for

Wendy to arrive dragged on. I heard a noise behind me, inside the building, but when I turned and looked through the glass again, I didn't see anything. When I turned back around, a man was coming up the stairs. He had dark hair, but I couldn't tell whether it was the same man. My throat tightened and my hands began to sweat. I inched away, but he kept coming, his head down so I couldn't see his face. I opened my mouth, but nothing came out. What was I going to say, anyway?

Before I could find my voice, the door swung open and Wendy Washington filled the frame, five feet tall but exuding a don't-mess-with-me energy in today's pastel pantsuit and shoulder pads. "There you are," she grumbled.

I scampered inside, then cast a quick glance backward. The man had taken the top off the trash can at the top of the stairs and was removing the bag inside. The relief felt overwhelming. A sanitation worker, not a murderer.

"Sorry," I mumbled in the elevator. "Why is the door locked?" It was eight in the morning—early, but not so early the building should be empty and locked.

"The building's closed. It's election day. Gubernatorial primaries. It's technically a holiday, but some of us still have work to do. We'll get you a key tomorrow when we get you a badge. Not everyone gets keys. Benny's always on about safety and not giving too many people access, but it's important to me that my admin have access to the building at all hours."

Great, I thought. *This bodes really well for my work-life balance.* Lucky for Supervisor Washington, I didn't actually have a life to balance against this job.

"I read through your memo from yesterday," she said, standing in the open office next to my desk. "Make me another one of those today for my meeting with Green Heart. I need it by eleven."

My eyes bugged out of my head, but Washington was

already walking to her office. I had three hours to do a full day's worth of work.

All thoughts of the man following me evaporated. The nagging desire to know what it felt like when Francisco kissed me for real and not for show disappeared. Ideas of how I could leverage this role to get information on Clemens faded. Suddenly and surprisingly, my brain narrowed in on the task at hand. I felt an unexpected desire to do a good job, to please my new boss.

I worked feverishly until 10:55, then knocked on Wendy's door with the memo. She glanced at it and gave a sharp nod, then waved me out of her office. The dismissal was disorienting, but it soon became clear that was how Wendy operated. She had extremely high expectations and she did not do praise. If she dipped her chin in that small nod, it was to be recognized as a compliment of the highest order.

I learned that the next day when, after getting my badge and the key Supervisor Washington insisted I needed, I put together more notes that earned the same nod and saw the shocked faces of my peers.

"What?" I asked, sure I'd made some major misstep.

"Washington does not do that," Eliza said in a low voice.

"Do what?"

"Nod," Eliza said at the same time Jake said, "Show any sign of approval."

"The last admin cried almost every day. She worked her ass off, and then Washington would take the memos or notes or whatever and wave her out of her office without any acknowledgment."

My cheeks flushed and the corners of my mouth twitched upward. Washington might not have said it out loud, but I was doing a good job. Somehow, I was excelling at this thing I had no reason to be good at.

All week, work continued in the same way. I arrived early in the ill-fitting clothes I'd thrifted Tuesday afternoon to last me until I got paid and could afford new work clothes. The other administrative assistants flooded in alongside me. We took phone calls, prepared schedules, gathered research, and armed our supervisors with the information they needed to do their jobs efficiently. The supervisors did their jobs at a level of "efficiency" that surprised me—one to three hours a day seemed to be the average. They came and went throughout the day. Supervisors Washington, Holtz, and Clemens seemed to be in the office the most. Sometimes local business owners or the heads of local organizations came to meet with the supervisors in their offices.

But we admins were in the office all day, every day, and by Friday I was feeling some camaraderie with the others. They invited me to lunch with them, and though I was surprised by the gesture and not sure what we'd talk about outside of the office, I was about to accept when Supervisor Clemens stepped off the elevator with another person.

As they stepped into the open office, Clemens glared at me the way he had every day since he'd come in on Monday to find me there. He'd cornered me that afternoon to say he knew what I was up to and that I'd regret it; I'd made doe eyes and acted like I didn't know what he was talking about, and ever since then I'd been too busy to try to snoop around his office or grill his admin for information.

Today, his glare hardly registered because my eyes, along with every other pair of eyes in the room, were on the visitor he was escorting. Her heels clicked with every step of her long, long legs, and my heartbeat fell into sync with her rhythm. She was the most beautiful woman I'd ever seen, and I'd seen her once before. Clemens was escorting Diamond from the Heaven on Earth gentlemen's club into his office.

29

All four of the other admins laughed as Eliza grabbed my arm and spun me toward the elevator.

"You were staring," she whispered at me, then giggled.

"Don't worry, you'll see her again," Jake said. "She's in here once or twice a month."

"Why?" Why was a dancer Hudson had been sleeping with visiting him—and now his successor—at work?

Jake shrugged. "Schuppert always took her meetings. He wasn't about to pawn a woman who looked like that off on his admin. Then Clemens took over, and it's the same. Clemens takes all his own meetings, though. He's the only supervisor who doesn't have another job on top of this one."

"You're so lucky," Johan groaned. "Holtz's philosophy is, 'Why would I do any part of my job if someone else can do it for me?'"

"Life certainly is better now that Schuppert's out," Jake said. "I have time to date again, guys. My niece has a birthday party this weekend and I actually got to RSVP 'yes.'"

"Stop bragging that you get to have a life," Eliza pouted.

My mind was still on Jake's remark about the supervisors all having other jobs. He'd mentioned it on my first day, but it hadn't stuck with me then. "The supervisors don't have to quit their other jobs when they're elected?"

Jake snorted a laugh, and Eliza's lips pulled into a taut line.

"No, they don't," she said.

Jake elaborated, "They usually cut back to part time, but

until someone passes a law against it, they're not about to give up the opportunity to draw two paychecks at the same time."

Had Hudson still been drawing a check from the law firm while working here? Could that have rubbed someone at the firm the wrong way? My thoughts snagged on another bit of information and I asked, "What's Washington's other job?" but the others didn't hear me, already having moved on. I followed them across the parking lot and crammed myself into the back of Eliza's car with Johan and Peter.

I'd wondered what we would talk about outside of work, and the answer was work. I didn't need to worry about being a decade older than the others and starting over in my life rather than embarking on my first career. It didn't matter that they were dating outside of college for the first time whereas I was recently separated from my husband of almost eight years. We were all in the same trench now, responding to ridiculous inquiries from constituents and learning more about zoning requirements and local conservation efforts and the merits of different traffic calming measures than we ever expected to.

When we were halfway through our burritos in the tiny hole-in-the-wall restaurant I never would have found if my new coworkers hadn't shown me but now wanted to patronize every single day for the rest of my life, I tried to broach the subject of Diamond again.

"So, that woman Clemens was meeting with—do you know what organization she's with?"

Jake guffawed. "You've got it bad!"

"I'm just curious."

"Uh-huh," Peter, who had been mostly quiet through the meal, muttered. Then the subject changed and my moment to press any further was lost.

When we returned to the office, Clemens's door was still closed. I pulled a proposal for a grant for a new women's shelter in front of me, but my eyes passed over the words without absorbing them, and I kept finding myself peeking at Clemens's office door. When Supervisor Washington left for the day without giving me any new assignments, it was a relief because I wouldn't have been able to focus on them. I was on my fifth read-through of the grant proposal when Clemens's door finally opened. Instead of walking her out, Clemens shook Diamond's hand in the doorway and she turned to leave by herself while he retreated back into his office and closed the door again.

I stood up without realizing I was doing it. The other admins looked at me with either smirks or surprised expressions. I could still sit back down and let it go, get back to my work and eventually figure out a way to get Clemens to talk. But that wouldn't work. I knew it wouldn't. Clemens was a brick wall. He knew I had a connection to Francisco, and he knew Francisco suspected his involvement in Hudson's disappearance. He'd never talk to me.

But Diamond didn't know me. I'd talked to two other dancers outside the club, but Diamond hadn't seen me. She knew Hudson, and now it seemed she knew his successor, the man who'd been sleeping with Hudson's wife and had inside knowledge into his disappearance. I couldn't miss this opportunity; I had to talk to her.

I hurried toward the elevator after her, praying I wouldn't be too late. When I burst out into the lobby, she was already gone. I cursed under my breath and took off toward the parking lot. In the far corner was the white Nissan. He'd followed me twice since Tuesday, and I set more elaborate booby traps each night when I got home, but so far he'd made no move to approach me. He just terrorized me from behind the wheel, appearing out of nowhere when I thought I was alone.

A car beeped as it unlocked. Diamond was pulling open the door of a stunning emerald-green BMW in the first spot next to the front steps. I looked back to the Nissan. The driver was eating a burrito, and I wondered if he'd followed me to lunch. I hadn't seen him this morning. I took off toward my car. If Diamond noticed me, she didn't think anything of my rush across the parking lot. My tail, on the other hand, was panicking in his seat, rushing to set down his burrito and turn the car on.

Diamond pulled out of the parking lot. I followed her. The Nissan followed me. The three of us drove down Congress Street caravan-style, then merged onto the interstate and headed north. Just as when I'd followed Francisco, I tried to stay far enough back that Diamond wouldn't notice she had a tail. My own tail did nothing of the sort; he stayed directly behind me the entire time.

We passed exit after exit, continuing north, and it occurred to me that maybe Diamond was leaving town. With no warning, Diamond turned into the exit lane without using her blinker, and I turned the wheel hard. Horns blared behind me as I cut over two lanes to follow her. I reached the stop sign just as she was turning left in front of a torrent of traffic blocking me from following her. I waited, then peeled out in a right turn, much to the surprise of my tail, who'd been sitting behind me with his left blinker on to match my own. He was still blocked in by the heavy traffic when I did a U-turn and sped off in the direction Diamond had turned.

I drove like an asshole, cutting people off without mercy and ignoring the indignant honks that sounded in my wake. Diamond was gone—whether she'd realized she was being followed or gotten lucky, she'd left us in the dust. I drove several more miles on that road with my eyes peeled for her car before accepting that I'd blown it and giving up.

With a sinking sensation in my stomach, I began to make my way back toward the interstate. I was at a stoplight, scanning the road behind me for the Nissan—still nowhere to be seen—

when a shimmer of dark green caught my eye. I made another U-turn when the light turned green and pulled into the parking lot to get a closer look.

It was Diamond's car, all right. My hand clenched into a fist and I gave the air a tiny victory punch. I'd found her. I turned to see where we were. We were in front of a white stucco building with brick accents around the windows and roofline. Desert shrubs framed the door, and huge gold lettering spelled out the name of the business above the entrance. *Warner & Loeb Law Offices.* I stared open-mouthed as Diamond walked up the front walkway and disappeared into Hudson's law firm.

30

No white Nissan materialized behind me during my drive home. I considered going back to the office to finish out the day, but I knew that the moment I walked back into that bullpen I'd get picked on by the other admins for taking off after Diamond. With no new asks from Wendy, I could get away with taking the rest of the day off, and avoiding my colleagues for the rest of the day and getting an early start on the weekend sounded infinitely more appealing than showing back up to be the target of their jokes.

Instead, I wound my way home, head spinning with possible reasons an exotic dancer would be visiting Hudson's law office after meeting with his successor at the board. Dancers needed lawyers just like anyone else, but it seemed a wild coincidence that hers would belong to that firm.

I drove up my street twice before parking, checking for my pursuer. When I'd checked the entire length twice, I forced myself to park and hurry inside, though I still looked over my shoulder for the entire short walk. I was feeling more on edge with every day that I waited for him to make a move.

I was in the middle of pushing the chair in front of my locked door when my phone chimed with a text.

Francisco: saw you pull up. want to come over later for dinner?

My stomach fluttered and I bit my lip. I instinctively looked toward my kitchen, where cereal and frozen TV dinners were the two options I'd be picking between tonight if I stayed home, but it wasn't the prospect of a home-cooked meal that had me eager to accept Francisco's invitation.

I typed out a series of responses, deleting each one in turn.

Yes!
You bet!
Sounds good!

Finally, I typed out a fourth response and hit send.

Mandy: I would, but I've got a hot date with a frozen lasagna and a Sandra Bullock movie.

Francisco: damn, I can't compete with that! all I have to offer is pork chops and my own company.

Mandy: Well, when you put it that way, you sound awfully lonely. I'll tell my lasagna and Netflix that I need to reschedule.

Francisco: ;)

I looked up from my phone. I was standing in the middle of my dining room grinning down at the screen, and everything from my throat to my toes was tingling beneath my clothes. This wasn't the plan. I was supposed to be single for a while and figure out what I wanted after leaving my entire life behind. I was *not* supposed to get the hots for my neighbor. I was doubly not supposed to get the hots for a journalist circling Hudson's case when I wasn't entirely sure what my involvement in that case comprised. And yet here I was, smiling like a fool at my phone while my heart tap-danced behind my ribs.

When it was time to get ready, I surveyed my closet with a new lens and hated everything I owned. I pulled on the last clean pair of jeans and held up every top I owned in succession, ruling each one out as too matronly, too frumpy, or in the case of the half-dozen math department t-shirts I'd previously worn without a second thought, too dorky.

I pulled a plain black t-shirt out of the dirty laundry basket and gave it a sniff. Not bad, and as it was the only piece of clothing I had that felt casual while still hugging my body just right, I was inclined to let it slide. I reapplied deodorant and tugged the shirt over my head, then swiped on mascara and slid the chair out of the way before heading out the door.

Francisco's curls hung wet in front of his forehead when he swung back the door, the smell of his shampoo greeting me alongside a big, goofy grin. "Glad you could reschedule with the lasagna."

"It took it pretty hard, but you have to show up for your friends when they're all alone."

He led me to the kitchen, where I was hit by the savory smells of meat, spices, and butter. I was salivating instantly.

Francisco offered me a glass of wine or a beer, and I took the beer because I wanted to look cool and easygoing. Francisco poured himself a glass of wine, and I regretted my choice.

"How's the new job going?"

I took a sip of my drink while deciding what to say. "It's fine. My boss is a bit much, but my coworkers are pretty cool. It's been a long time since I had a job like this, working on small tasks given to me by someone else. In my previous life as a professor, I was the one giving out the tasks, and the pressure to publish is enormous but those papers take ages. I forgot how good it feels to be assigned a task and complete it in the same day."

"That sounds pretty good for a job you were pretty sure was temporary."

"Oh, it's definitely still temporary. But it's a confidence boost, you know? Racking up little wins."

Francisco plated the food, and we ate and flirted. We avoided the topics of my former life and husband, Hudson Schuppert's disappearance, and our joint attempt to get Clemens to reveal what he knew. Instead, we talked about our most mortifying memories from high school—I changed Christina's name in the story where I laughed so hard at a sleepover I peed my pants and had to ask to borrow a pair of underwear to change into—and the first bands we ever saw live. By the time we cleared the dishes, I'd finished my beer and my abs ached from laughing.

"Do you want to stay and watch a movie?" Francisco asked. "I know you had big plans with Sandra Bullock tonight."

My body was sagging with the fatigue of the week bearing down on me, and what I really wanted was to crawl into bed and sleep for twelve solid hours, but as we flirted, I felt the warm buzz of possibility, and I didn't want to leave that feeling behind.

"Yes, but I get to pick the movie, and it's going to be *Two Weeks Notice*."

"Hugh Grant is the worst," Francisco groaned, but he was still smiling.

I sat on the end of the tan leather couch, and when Francisco joined me he took the other end. The space between us felt charged, and even after he turned on the movie, the only thing I was thinking about was the air between his skin and mine and the electricity that seemed to be thrumming in it. He paused the movie abruptly, and I looked over at him, worried I'd somehow made him uncomfortable.

"I'm going to go get another drink. Do you want anything?"

I shook my head.

When he returned, Francisco sat in the middle of the couch, straddling the break between cushions so his arm just barely brushed against mine. My breathing went shallow and I wondered if he could hear my heart beating. The hairs on my arm stood up where he'd brushed against it. I wanted to lean against him to close that tiny gap, but I couldn't bring myself to do it. Every part of my body was telling me I definitely wanted him in a way I hadn't wanted anyone in a very long time, but what if he didn't want me back? What if I was misreading the signals?

Francisco resumed the movie, then shifted his glass of wine from his right hand to his left. With that motion, he pressed his body just a half inch closer to me, closing the last of the space between us. I inhaled sharply, and my thigh involuntarily moved closer to his, pressing against him and opening the space between my legs slightly. He looked over at me and there was a question written plainly on his face, one that I was sure mirrored my own. *Do you want me?*

My lips parted on a shaking inhale, and I let my chest rotate toward him, my thigh pushing harder into his. Francisco leaned in, and my chin raised, tipping my mouth toward him. The smell of his tea tree shampoo mixed with the leftover faint smoky smell from cooking wrapped around me as his lips met mine. He pressed them gently against my own, but I was suddenly ravenous. I kissed him back once, then again, harder, then opened my mouth and ran my tongue along his lip.

A soft grunt of surprise escaped him, and he pulled away to put his glass down, then cupped one hand behind my head and the other behind my shoulder blades, pulling me tighter to him so our chests pressed together. My arms wrapped around him, and I leaned back against the arm of the sofa, rotating my hips to bring more of our bodies in contact. He reached down and grabbed my leg, pulling it up onto the sofa so he could roll on top of me.

He kissed me hungrily, lips and tongue a blur as I rolled my hips against him. "Do you...?" I breathed when he moved his attention to my neck, freeing my mouth.

He pulled back, swollen lips hovering over me and eyes darting rapidly from my lips to my eyes to my chest and back.

"Do you have—?" I started to ask again, but he pushed himself off me and tugged his twisted shirt back into place.

"I'm sorry," he muttered, staring at the floor and pointedly not at me. "I got carried away."

I pulled myself up and brought my knees in front of my chest, my face hot with embarrassment. When he saw my expression, he reached for me.

"Mandy, no. I didn't mean—"

"I think I should go." I couldn't meet his eyes.

"Don't." He reached for me, but I was already standing.

The movie played on, casting moving light over us as I straightened my own shirt, the space between my thighs still throbbing. He rose and reached for me again, but I moved away, letting his hand brush along my forearm and trying not to feel the way my skin heated beneath his touch.

I hurried out of the living room and into the dining room he used as an office to grab my bag. File folders were stacked on the table next to his keyboard, and when I leaned over to pick up my purse from where I'd left it on the chair, my arm brushed his computer mouse and the monitor lit up.

A neighborhood website was open on the screen, one of the ones people go to to complain about neighbors not cleaning up after their pets or letting their grass get too long. The name of the neighborhood was spelled out in block letters on the banner at the top of the page: Sunrise Canyon Estates. Christina's neighborhood.

Francisco had one post pulled up—a post by a user named mliddel1984 sharing a screenshot from a security camera recording.

We have rules for a reason. We don't allow yard sales or similar because it invites criminals to come case all our homes. If you have *goods to get rid of, the rule is you take it to a consignment shop or the dump yourself, NOT that you have outsiders come to our neighborhood and put us all at risk in the process. It seems some of our neighbors disagree with this rule, so much so that they'd invite potential criminals into our neighborhood <u>after dark</u> to avoid getting caught! This is unacceptable!*

Under the text, the picture was of a coyote running through the yard, but mliddel1984 had drawn a red circle around something in the background, several houses over. They'd also shared a cropped, zoomed-in version of the photo. It was blurry at that range, but it was clear that the image was of two men—one bald, his head reflecting the glare from the streetlight, and one with dark hair buzzed close to his skull—carrying something between them. I leaned in closer. I recognized the house in the background of the image. The two men were in front of Christina's house, and they were carrying a large wooden blanket chest between them.

31

I leaned in close to the monitor as if proximity would improve the resolution of the grainy screenshot. Despite the low resolution, a few things were clear: it was definitely two men carrying the chest I'd helped Christina bury, neither of them was Cory Clemens or anyone else I'd ever seen before, and they were hauling the chest toward a big, black SUV.

Judging by the angle of the recording, and based on Maureen's assertion that no one else in the neighborhood had any doorbell or security cameras, the picture had to have been taken from Maureen's. She'd told me she'd deleted the security footage after putting it on a flash drive for Francisco, but this post was from days after that. Maureen had lied to me about deleting the footage.

"Mandy." Francisco startled me when he came into the room, and I jumped and spun to face him, my hand over my heart. He saw the monitor on and crossed the room quickly, then locked the screen before turning back to me. If he was suspicious of me looking at this screen, he didn't show it. Contrition and desperation clouded his eyes when he peered into mine. "I'm really sorry."

"You don't have to say that."

"I'm not just saying it." He stepped closer, and I started to back away. My back bumped into the wall, and he took another step toward me. "I didn't pull back because I didn't want you."

My throat constricted and, to my eternal humiliation, tears

stung my eyes. I bit my tongue and tried to keep them from falling.

"I wanted to kiss you the first time I saw you, when you fell face-first into the grass and we had to crawl around finding each individual piece of your broken key fob."

I leaned harder against the wall, wishing I could just fall through it. The first tear dripped down my cheek, more accumulating and blurring Francisco's sharp features in my vision. He took another step closer.

"And now that I've kissed you..." He broke off with a sigh and looked up at the ceiling. "Mandy, I didn't want to stop."

"Well, you did," I said bitingly, then pushed off from the wall. When my arm brushed across his chest as I shoved past him, he raised an arm like he might grab me, and every cell of my body screamed for me to stop and turn back around.

But he didn't grab me, and I didn't turn back around. I squeezed my purse to my chest and hurried through the entryway before yanking the door open and walking straight into the man standing on the stoop, a six-pack of beer in one hand and the other raised as if to knock.

The man stepped back in surprise just as Francisco walked up behind me and said, "Eric, I didn't know you were coming over tonight."

Eric was tall and broad, his chest and arms straining at the long-sleeved t-shirt he wore with the sleeves pushed up to his elbows. He had short red hair, and russet stubble covered his jaw. "I was nearby for work and thought I'd stop by in case you were free. It's been a while. It looks like you already have company, though, so I'll just—"

"I'm on my way out," I interrupted.

"Give us just a minute?" Francisco asked, and Eric nodded before taking a few steps back onto the path in front of Francisco's home, but I stepped forward away from Francisco.

"I'll see you around," I said, turning away to avoid his hurt expression and then striding past Eric, who looked equal parts uncomfortable and entertained by the scene he'd stumbled upon.

I kept my head down as I started the short walk home, but a swath of color in my periphery caught my attention, and I looked up to see a bright red car, low-slung and nicer than anything anyone on this street owned. It looked familiar, but I couldn't place it. It wasn't until I'd gotten home, shoved the chair in front of the door, and stepped into the shower that I realized where I'd seen it before: it was the car the hooded figure had emerged from to steal Francisco's bag after I'd followed him to Maureen's.

———

MY HAIR DRIPPED water down the front of my pajama top as I pulled my laptop toward me and entered Christina's address into the neighborhood website, Good Neighbors, to create a new account. Maureen had had another copy of that footage all along, and was posting screenshots from it for anyone to see. And Francisco was two steps ahead of me with access to those screenshots and whatever else Christina's neighbors might have shared in the wake of her and Hudson's disappearance.

I glanced toward my window, the blinds drawn tight so I couldn't see whether his friend Eric's red car was still out there. Once I'd placed it, there was no doubt in my mind that it was the car I'd seen at that gas station. Had it been Eric, hooded and shrouded in darkness, who had taken Francisco's bag and Maureen's security footage along with it? Or could someone else have borrowed his car? Why would Francisco's own friend steal from him?

I turned back to the laptop screen and cursed. Red text

headed the page. *An account already exists for this address.* I tried again with the next house number, then went one by one incrementing digits until I came to one that didn't already have an account created. *Bingo.*

A spinning wheel indicated the page was loading, and then it filled with text. Where I expected to see a stream of posts, instead there was a welcome message. *Thank you for joining Good Neighbors. To verify your address, please upload an image of a piece of mail containing your name and address.*

My head fell back and I let out a groan. I was already behind Francisco, and now I needed to somehow get a piece of mail addressed to the fake name I'd entered at an address I didn't have access to.

A call from Dave came in and I declined it, then padded to the section of the kitchen counter where the first electric bill in my name sat waiting to be paid until I received my first paycheck from my new job. A knot formed in my stomach as I stared at it.

I was not above dishonesty. I'd followed Francisco and then Diamond just like the man who had been terrorizing me. I'd lied to Maureen about who I was and taken a job I didn't care about just so I could snoop on Clemens. And worse, I'd lied directly to Francisco, a man I liked more than I was prepared to like anyone this soon after leaving my marriage, and hidden my connection to the case he was investigating.

But picking up the envelope felt different. It felt like a turning point in how low I was willing to go—how deceitful I was willing to be if it would help me find my friend. I hesitated. Then I remembered Francisco had clearly done the same thing in the pursuit of his big break, the investigative piece that would put him on the map as a journalist. *If he can do it, so can I*, I thought, then snapped a picture of the envelope.

Detective Styles's remark about Francisco came back to me —*be careful with that one*—but I put her warning out of my mind. I opened a photo editing tool and carefully erased the text from the image, replacing it with the name and address I'd given the Good Neighbors site.

I was finishing up when Dave called again. I declined the call and uploaded the doctored image. Just as the check mark popped up on the screen to indicate it had been received and now needed to be verified, my phone chimed three times in quick succession as Dave sent text after text.

Dave: Please answer your phone, Mandy. I need to know you're okay.

Dave: It was one thing not to tell me you'd moved out of Christina's, but I had to find out from a news article last week that she was missing, and now this?? You need to call me!!

The final text contained a link to a news article. The link preview included a headshot of Hudson and the headline "Pima County Supervisor Found Dead."

32

Adrenaline shot through me and I leaped up from the chair, but there was nowhere to run. There was nothing to do. There was only Hudson's photo smiling at me through my phone screen, the words beneath it unable to sink in as my brain refused to accept them.

Hudson's body was found north of the city, dumped close enough to a hiking trail that a young couple taking their dog for a hike got the shock of their lives when the dog came running up to them with a human tibia in its mouth. Thanks to the desert climate, parts of him were mummified, but thanks to animal activity in the area, those parts weren't all found in the same spot. Dental records confirmed the body was Hudson's.

I read the article again, then searched for others, but none of them had any more information. None of them mentioned a large wooden chest. His remains being scattered by animals and the lack of any reference to a chest supported my theory that Hudson hadn't been in the chest. Whatever I'd helped Christina hide, it wasn't her husband's body.

But now that his body had turned up partially mummified in the desert, any hope I had of reuniting with the two of them to hear some great tale of how they'd had to run away together to escape whatever trouble they were in was gone. All I could hope for now was that Christina's body wouldn't turn up next.

Headlights cast thin beams of light through the tiny openings in my blinds, and my pulse increased at the sound of a passing car. Was it just Eric leaving Francisco's? Another neighbor coming or going? Or was it someone else?

The image of my shaggy-haired stalker behind the wheel of his old white sedan forced itself to the front of my mind, his face more sinister in this new conception. I knew from the short glance at the screenshot I'd gotten from Francisco's computer that the man who'd been following me hadn't been one of the two men who had taken the chest from Christina's house—nor had Cory Clemens—but that didn't make him less dangerous.

If Hudson had landed himself in trouble and Christina had needed to hide something to protect them, I had no idea how many people might be after whatever it was she'd been so determined to hide.

As my mind spiraled, my breathing became quick and shallow. I tried to breathe a slow, steady stream out through pursed lips, but it didn't work. Just as soon as I tried to breathe out, I was gasping in again, the panic increasing and only making it harder to breathe. Soon I found myself wheezing, my chest tightening with every inhale while I struggled to get air into my lungs.

I stood and staggered to the window, pulling the blinds open. I was met with my own reflection and stumbled closer, cupping my hands to see out into the darkness. If I could just prove to myself no one was out there, maybe I could calm myself. Instead, each exhale clouded the glass, further obscuring my view, and the thought that if he was out there, my hunter could be watching me descend into a panic attack just made it worse.

I bent over, hands on my knees, trying to get air, then moved away from the window. When dizziness began to cloud my vision, I realized I needed help. Ariel would be awake; if her parents were home, they could call someone. I kicked the chair away from the door and threw it open. The moment I stepped outside and felt the chill air hit my flushed skin and saw the quiet street laid out before me, relief began to unfurl in my chest, each breath marginally deeper than the last. I remained hunched over, gasping but slowly recovering myself as the dizziness subsided.

I stayed on the porch for several minutes until I felt almost normal, able to breathe in for multiple heartbeats instead of the short, sharp intakes. My eyes traced up and down the street, and its emptiness helped calm me. There was no white Nissan. No one was watching me. I was safe. With each breath, I repeated it like a mantra. *I'm safe. No one is watching me. I'm safe.*

It was the crunch of gravel that first caught my attention and made me jerk my head to the side. It came from several houses down, and I wrapped my arms around myself as if for protection even while I stepped out further onto the path to try to see. Gravel crunched again, and I strained my eyes to make out a figure crouched beside Francisco's house just in front of his fence.

"Hey!" I shouted, and the figure sprang from their crouch into a run, sneakers beating the pavement with every stride.

I took off after them before I even knew what I was doing, consumed in an instant with rage. I'd been stalked and terrorized all week. I was exhausted. I was tired of setting booby traps and wondering each morning whether that would be the day the mysterious man stopped following me and instead made a move to hurt me. And all of that weariness transmuted into an anger that fueled me as I chased the fleeing figure. This blur of dark clothes thought he could lurk around Francisco's home. He became a symbol of the man who'd been lurking around my own, and I chased him down with a fury I hadn't felt before.

"Argh!" I leapt forward, the gap widening between me and my target.

At the sound of my cry, the figure turned. With their head turned, they missed the patch of uneven pavement in front of them and stumbled, landing hard. I pumped my legs harder, gritting my teeth through the burning sensation, and closed the distance. Just as the figure had pushed themselves upright, ready to take off again, I threw myself forward on top of them, both of us grunting as we hit the concrete together.

"Get off me." The stranger's hood had flown up over the back of his head, obscuring his hair, but his voice was undeniably male. He tried to push himself up again, nearly bringing himself onto all fours before I threw my weight against him again, forcing him back down onto the ground. Instead of pressing back up, the man rolled onto his back beneath me, revealing his face.

I leapt back in surprise, a scream caught in my lungs, then lunged forward and punched the man who had been following me since the press conference in the face.

33

"Ow! God damn it!" I shook out my throbbing hand.

My stalker grabbed at his face, glaring at me over his hands with hatred. He'd been following me unrelentingly, filling my days with fear, and he had the gall to look at me like I was a monster? I let out a battle cry and dove at his face again, ready to throttle him.

"Wait!" he cried.

I didn't wait but wrapped my hands around his neck and leaned as much of my weight against them as I could. "Stop fucking following me!"

The man squirmed beneath me but looked largely unaffected by my attempt to choke him. Blood dripped from his nose, but no matter how hard I tried to force my fingers around his throat, he seemed to breathe normally.

"Whatever was in that chest, I didn't see it. I don't know what it is, or even where it is now. So you can leave me the fuck alone now." I thrust my arms forward, fingers digging into the man's neck as I pressed his head into the hard concrete beneath him.

The man opened his mouth to respond but let out a rasping cough instead.

I shifted my weight further forward, pressing harder into his throat. "Is Christina still alive?" The man's brows knit together, and I shook his head in my grasp, demanding again, "Is she?"

The man gasped between my hands, then raised both arms, catching me completely off guard and knocking my arms away from him. In a flash, our positions were reversed. I was laid out flat on the concrete with an aching head, and the man was above me, his hands gripping my wrists to pin them by my side.

The streetlight illuminated his face, and I realized for the first time how young he was. He looked barely out of high school, with soft, young features poking out from behind long, wavy brown hair. I was entirely vulnerable, unable to move my legs beneath his body weight or my arms beneath his grip, but I felt more surprised than afraid of him.

"You're a kid," I said incredulously.

"I am not!"

"Why are you doing this?" He should be doing homework or trying to impress girls, not abducting corrupt politicians and their wives and hunting down anyone connected to them.

"Your asshole husband hired me."

It felt like the sidewalk began to spin beneath me. I lost all sense of orientation and closed my eyes to try to stop the dizziness. Dave was behind this?

"Why would—?" I stopped abruptly, trying to tug my arms away from the boy on top of me so I could grab at the ground. I was going to throw up.

He let go and in a panicked voice, asked, "Are you okay? I didn't mean to hurt you."

I spread my fingers wide and pressed them into the concrete, trying to still the spinning sensation. "Why would Dave want to kill Hudson? Why would he want to hurt my best friend?"

Christina and Dave hadn't ever clicked, but there'd never been any open animosity between them, just an underlying tension. But for Dave to want them dead? For him to hire some kid to abduct them and then chase down anyone who might have seen something? It didn't make sense.

The boy reared back, scrambling off of me and shaking his head. "I don't know what you're talking about. I was just supposed to follow you and report back."

I propped myself up on my elbows, ignoring the sting of the concrete biting into them. "Explain."

"I—your husband—well, I started doing some private investigating work to make some extra money. You know, if a guy thinks his girlfriend is off with some other dude, he can hire me and I'll follow her around. If he pays extra, I'll take pictures for proof."

I leaned over and vomited into the grass.

"My husband and I are separated," I told him. "I couldn't be cheating on him because I already broke up with him." That didn't stop him from tracking my location, sending police to my house, and now hiring this kid to follow me around.

"Well, he didn't hire me to catch you cheating."

"I don't understand. You said that's why people hire you."

"Your, uh, husband said you'd had some sort of breakdown. He wanted me to get proof that you weren't in your right mind—erratic behavior, putting yourself in dangerous situations, that kind of thing."

I stared at him, trying to think of one good reason Dave could possibly want that. "Like, he wanted you to assure him I was actually doing okay?"

The boy shook his head. "That's what I thought at first, but when I told him you were doing okay—crying and normal breakup stuff but not, like, buying drugs or doing anything reckless—he doubled down. He said he knew you weren't in your right mind and he wanted proof."

I turned and vomited again, and the boy inched closer like he wanted to give me a comforting touch but was afraid I'd try to choke him again.

"What the fuck was he going to do with that?" Even if I had been having some sort of breakdown, Dave couldn't just put me in a straitjacket and force me to move back home because he thought I was suffering from hysteria, could he? My inhales came shorter and faster, and I closed my eyes, trying to control them.

"Well, I didn't get anything," the boy said quickly. "Like I said, I told him you seemed stable to me. He said to keep watching you, and he paid in advance."

"How long have you been following me?"

"Uh, like three weeks? A month? I don't know."

"How long?" I pressed.

The boy thought back. "He hired me for the first time almost six weeks ago, and I told him you were staying with a friend and that everything seemed normal. I got a different job and told your, uh—"

"Ex," I interrupted. "Please don't call him my husband again."

"Okay, I told your ex I couldn't watch you for him anymore because I had this other job. A few weeks later, he reached back out and said you'd moved and asked me to follow you for him again. I didn't have another job lined up, and I needed the money, so..."

"So, you've been following me for a *month*?" The entire time I'd been in my duplex?

The kid only shrugged, a vaguely apologetic look on his face.

"You've been reporting my every move to Dave this entire time?"

"Well, there weren't a lot of movements to report at first," he said, and I reached out and swatted him. "It's true! You just stayed inside alone. By the time you started going out more, like a couple weeks ago when you went back to your friend's house and stayed overnight, I'd stopped telling your ex much. The more I talked with him, the more I got the sense that he's kind of a dick."

"Anyone who would hire you to stalk someone is a dick," I told him, but the bite was gone from my voice. I was thinking about the visit to Christina's he had mentioned. This kid had followed me the night I'd helped her bury the chest. "What did you tell Dave about that visit?"

"Just that you went to see your friend. I think you also had a job interview that day? I'm pretty sure I just told him you were doing better and seemed to be settling in."

"Well, he must not have thought you were doing a good enough job checking on me, because he sent the police to my house a few days later."

The boy's eyes bugged out, and he had the decency to look guilty.

"If you've been following me for weeks, how come I only started seeing you a week ago, starting with the press conference?"

"I got sloppy at the press conference," he said, "and then I told Dave I'd messed up and that you'd seen me. I was a little relieved, actually, thinking he'd fire me so I could stop following you."

"Instead, he had you openly stalk me in order to terrorize me?"

Again, the boy gave me a guilty look. "He actually did fire me, but then he called me back last weekend to hire me back on. He seemed different. More worried."

That was when Dave had seen the news article about Clemens being appointed supervisor and realized Hudson and Christina were missing.

"I thought eventually you'd confront me, and then I'd have to tell him the jig was up."

I gestured around us. "Well, I finally confronted you."

He reached up and tenderly touched his nose where I'd punched him, then raised his gaze to look back down the street where we'd come from.

Reminded of what started this encounter, I asked him, "Why

were you by Francisco's house? Did Dave ask you to spy on him, too?"

The kid nodded. "I told him you'd been flirting with him and that I thought you might start dating him. That's usually what my clients want to know. He asked me to tail the guy, and when I told him about Francisco visiting his brother in prison, he wanted me to find out more."

A porch light clicked on and a door swung open. "Everything okay out here?" A man in a tank top and sweatpants peered out from his front porch at us.

I pushed myself up and waved at him. "All good, thanks!" I turned to the boy, who looked ready to sprint in the opposite direction, and grabbed the front of his shirt. "We're going to go to my house, and you're going to tell me everything."

34

"First off, what's your name?" I asked the young man shifting nervously in my dining room. He looked from the small loveseat, the lone piece of furniture in the small living room, to the plastic table and chairs, but remained standing instead of moving to sit at either option. I grabbed one of the chairs to shove against the door, but realized the person I'd been trying to keep out was standing in front of me, taking in the sight of the cans stacked beneath the window.

"Ethan," he said. His assessing gaze went from the stacked cans to the open door into my bedroom, where my laptop still sat on top of my unmade bed, the mattress directly on the tile floor with no frame. I wondered if I'd made a mistake in bringing him inside, not because I thought he would hurt me, but because he might report back to Dave about my living situation. Could Dave use my lack of a bed frame and the generally dismal conditions of my barely furnished space to try to force me to move back with him? Even if he couldn't compel me to go back where I didn't want to be, I didn't want him knowing the intimate details of my current living arrangements. It was meager and dim, but it was mine, and the space was growing on me.

"Ethan." I turned his name over on my tongue. I finally had a name for the person who had filled my recent days with terror, but I found myself feeling a little sorry for him now that I could see him in full relief. His dark, shaggy hair fell greasy and limp over the very pale skin of his forehead. His fingers twitched at his side, his discomfort at being here obvious.

"I'm actually going to go," he said and turned toward the door.

I slid between him and the door and crossed my arms over my chest. "Nope. You're going to tell me what you know about Francisco first. You owe me."

"I don't owe you anything," he retorted, and any sympathy I had for the young kid caught up in a job he didn't really want to do for my asshole ex disappeared. "You're not the one who paid me to find that information, so you're not the one who gets it."

I hadn't expected him to protest; he'd said he'd wanted Dave to fire him, so I assumed he'd happily give up whatever information he'd found for Dave to me instead. Now dollar signs were practically gleaming in his defiant eyes, and with the first paycheck from my new job still almost a week away, I had little to offer.

"You said it yourself, Dave's a dick. Don't you want to get back at him?"

Ethan shrugged. "Not really. I mean, I'm not the one he was a dick to. He's paid me pretty well."

It wasn't the first time he'd mentioned Dave paying him. "How much?" I asked.

"What?"

"How much did Dave pay you to follow me and dig up information on Francisco?"

"A hundred dollars a day."

My eyes bulged as I tried to reconcile Dave's generally responsible nature with his forking over what must amount to several thousand dollars to have a kid spy on me.

At my reaction, Ethan asserted, "It was basically a full-time job. That's a competitive rate for private investigators. It's not like I was fleecing the guy!"

"Yeah, I'm aware it was basically a full-time job. I've been full-time living with you following me around, asshole." An idea came to me, and I decided to try a new tactic. "Are you even a licensed private investigator? I could have you arrested for stalking."

"You could have called the cops on me days ago, but you didn't. For whatever reason, you don't want the cops involved in this."

Damn. He was young, but he wasn't a fool. Detective Styles was pretty sure I was involved in Hudson's disappearance—now murder—and I didn't want Ethan giving her a detailed rundown on my whereabouts lately. If he wanted to, he could stalk me indefinitely, reporting my every move back to Dave, and I couldn't do anything about it.

"Fine," I sighed. "How much will it cost me for you to tell me everything you've found out about Francisco?" He'd said Francisco's brother was in prison, and I knew he and Styles had some weird connection. Now that I knew Ethan had that information, I wanted it badly.

"A grand." Ethan spouted the number immediately.

"That's insane!"

"One thousand dollars, and I'll tell you everything I know about your new boy toy and stop working for your ex."

I hadn't even considered that he might keep working for Dave after everything he'd told me. "You said earlier you *wanted* him to fire you! He's an asshole, you said it yourself."

"If I stop working for him, it's going to take me some time to find new work. I need that money to get me through until I can find something else."

I had a feeling he could find some other jerk ready to hire him to follow their girlfriend around more quickly than he was letting on. But I also had an idea.

"I don't have that kind of money," I said, and Ethan started toward me like he was going to walk around me and right out the door. "Wait! I do have a rich friend. Well, a reasonably successful artist friend with a rich husband. Well, a recently deceased rich husband. But that means all his money is hers now. She's missing, and I want to find her. If you can help me do that, I'll pay you the thousand, plus two hundred dollars a day for every day between now and then. Well, she'll pay you."

My offer was met with a skeptical frown, and Ethan wasn't wrong to doubt it. Christina's husband's money wasn't hers yet, and there was no guarantee it ever would be. If I was wrong and she'd had something to do with his death, or if I was right but Detective Styles and her team convinced a jury otherwise, that money wouldn't go to Christina.

"If she's missing, why should I believe she'll be alive to pay me when we find her?"

There it was, the piece of this I didn't want to think about. It had been a week since Christina had texted me that she was safe. While I pushed away the idea that whoever had gotten to Hudson could have also gotten to Christina between that text message and now, one piece of Ethan's counter stuck out. He'd said "when" we find her—not "if".

"You think we can find her," I said.

"I think you stand a lot better of a chance with me helping you."

"Christina's alive. She texted me last week from a burner phone."

His eyebrows rose. He raised a finger in the air. "One: last week isn't now." He raised a second finger. "And two: it sounds like she's not missing. She's on the run."

"Does that make a difference?"

Ethan's lips curved upward in a dark smile. "People on the run don't hide themselves as well as the people who make other people go missing hide them." When I didn't give any indication of following his logic, he said, "They get tired of being on the run. They do stupid things like text their friends. They make mistakes. Yeah, I think we can find her."

"So you'll help me?"

Ethan pursed his lips and tilted his head as if he were considering the pros and cons, trying to decide if it was worth his time. I scoffed at the display.

"Oh, come on. You want to do this. I can see it. You follow people's wives and girlfriends around all day because you want to be some sort of secret agent or undercover investigator. But at the end of the day, you're just sitting in a parking lot hoping to snap a picture of some woman kissing someone she shouldn't be, when what you *really* want to be doing is exactly what I'm offering you."

"What I really want to be doing is getting paid."

"I told you, she'll pay you."

"You got a job. You get paid on the first and the fifteenth. And guess what's next week? The first." Ethan pulled his gangly frame up straight and puffed his chest out while I glared at him. He continued listing his demands. "Your friend will pay me the thousand, plus the two hundred a day. And you'll pay me another two hundred per week, up front."

"One hundred per week," I countered. It was the absolute most I could afford.

Ethan looked like he was going to counter me, but then he held out his hand. I stared down at it, then took his thin, bony hand in my own and gave it the firmest squeeze I could manage, determined to show some strength after basically agreeing to hand over every penny I had for his help. I might be eating peanut butter for every meal from here on out, but we were going to find Christina.

35

When I woke feeling refreshed, my first thought was that something was wrong. I lifted myself up, patting around for my phone and rubbing the sleep from my eyes, worried I must have missed my alarm or forgotten something important if I'd slept long enough to feel this good. But I hadn't missed anything—it was Saturday and Wendy hadn't asked me to do any work over the weekend. I'd simply underestimated how good sleep could feel when I wasn't subconsciously waiting for a stranger to break into my home and murder me. Now I knew Ethan wasn't a murderer, just a creep-for-hire, and he wasn't going to kidnap me but instead would be on my side helping me find Christina. Without the threat of him looming over me, parts of me I hadn't even realized were tense relaxed.

I stretched my arms overhead, my elbows and shoulders stiff but not painful. Then I strapped my boot onto my left ankle and rose, the same stiffness creaking in my knees and hips. Stiff, I could handle. The marked lack of pain was such a relief I didn't trust it, waiting for one of my joints to send a surprise bolt of pain through my limbs.

I padded slowly into the bathroom with my eyes down, checking the messages on my phone. I had a missed call and a voicemail from Francisco from early that morning. I set the phone on the counter and hit "play," and the tinny recording bounced off the hard surfaces, echoing slightly in the close room.

"Hey, uh, Mandy, it's me. Francisco. I can't stop thinking

about you, and I wanted to say again that I'm really, really sorry. I had a great time with you last night before, uh... Anyway, I think you're probably still asleep, which is good since you've got that new job and I'm sure it's been a long week. I hope you have a really great day tomorrow, and I hope I can see you soon."

Fresh tears sprang up in my eyes, and I splashed my face with water. "Nope," I said to myself in the mirror. "We're not doing this today."

One cup of coffee later, I was feeling restless. I wasn't used to having energy, my body feeling ready to take on whatever I might want to get up to with my time. I checked my watch and scowled; Ethan was supposed to be here by now. We'd agreed he'd come over first thing in the morning so I could give him more details on Christina's case and we could start plotting how to find her, and after a lengthy debate over what "first thing in the morning" meant, we'd settled on nine thirty. It was now ten minutes to ten.

I opened the blinds, relishing in the sun spilling into my space, filling it with natural light. Since I'd first seen Ethan following me, I'd kept the blinds shut tight and barricaded myself inside as much as possible. Now, after opening the blinds, I even opened a window, birdsong filtering inside with the light.

Without Ethan, I was as stuck as ever when it came to Christina. I'd been wrong when I thought I was being stalked by someone who either wanted whatever Christina and I had buried or wanted to eliminate anyone who might know about it. The same people going after Christina weren't coming after me. No one was coming after me. I was safe, and I luxuriated in that knowledge.

But if no one was coming after me, were there actually people going after Christina? There had to be. Why else would she warn me off of looking for her, if not to protect me?

Ethan knocked at my door and I checked the time again. "Finally," I called out on my way to the door. "What happened to 'first thing in the morning?'"

I swung the door open and then reeled back when I was met not with Ethan but Detective Styles standing on my doorstep.

"Expecting someone?" she asked, taking half a step toward me.

My natural inclination was to step back and wave her into the house, but after our last encounter, I held my ground. She pursed her lips in displeasure.

"Nope," I lied. "How can I help you?"

"Can I come inside?" She took another half step toward me, practically forcing me backward into the entryway, but I stood still and gripped the doorframe to keep from toppling backward.

"Nope," I said again and waited. Despite the nonchalance I forced myself to project, my pulse was fluttering, and the second cup of coffee I'd just downed roiled in my stomach. Hudson was dead, and there was a detective on my doorstep.

After a beat, Styles said, "I have some questions I'd like to ask you. It would be more comfortable inside."

"We can talk here," I said, my grip on the doorframe tightening as I fought to remain upright and keep from visibly cowering. It wasn't so much that I was worried about what Styles might see in my house, but I was sick of her showing up out of the blue and intimidating me, and I didn't want to give her a single win.

The detective's nostrils flared around her irritated exhale. "Fine. I'm here to talk with you about Hudson and Christina Schuppert."

I only nodded. I'd expected nothing else—Hudson's body had just turned up the previous day, and Styles had made it clear before that she thought, based on my relationship with Christina, I knew something about their disappearance.

When I didn't respond, Styles continued, "Hudson Schuppert's body was found in the desert yesterday."

"I saw that in the news."

"The medical examiner is still working with the body, but it seems he'd been dead for a while. Likely weeks."

That, I hadn't seen in the news.

"When was the last time you saw Christina Schuppert?"

"You asked me that last time you were here."

"And you didn't answer me then."

"I talked with her on the phone two weeks ago, on the Friday before she and Hudson went missing."

Detective Styles was silent. I hadn't answered her question; I hadn't told her I'd *seen* Christina that day, that I'd been to her home and helped her bury a large chest. Did Styles notice the omission?

If she did, she didn't comment on it, and I didn't let her, instead asking, "Was there a second body?"

I didn't think there was. Some part of me believed I'd feel it if Christina was dead, that I'd just instinctively know. But I had to ask.

Instead of answering me, Styles raised an eyebrow and let me stew for a minute. As the seconds ticked on, I felt the urge to break the silence, but I knew anything I said or asked would just be giving Styles ammunition.

"Can you tell me about the Schupperts' marriage?" she asked eventually.

I felt my face pale. I didn't want to answer. I couldn't tell an antagonistic detective that my missing best friend and her dead husband had a fractured marriage and were both sleeping with other people.

"I thought you were looking at Cory Clemens," I said instead.

"We're looking at all our options. Again, can you tell me about the Schupperts' marriage?"

"It was—"

"Sorry I'm late!" Ethan bounded up the sidewalk with a fast food bag in his hands and leapt up the path onto the small porch next to Styles. "Ready to find your—"

"Ethan!" I cut him off and yanked him toward me by his arm. He yelped in surprise, and Styles watched us, her hawk eyes taking in his confused expression.

"Sorry," I told her, "but it looks like I'll have to talk with you another time."

I stepped back, pulling Ethan into the house with me, and shut the door and locked it, leaving Styles on the porch alone.

"What the hell?" Ethan demanded as I tugged him further into the house away from the door.

"That's a cop," I hissed at him.

"Why is a cop on your doorstep?"

I heaved an enormous sigh and said, "Because of my missing friend's dead husband. I think she thinks my friend killed him and I know something about it."

"Did she?"

"No! God, you're annoying." I looked down at the greasy paper bag in his hand and added, "At least you brought food."

Ethan scrunched his face and pulled the bag close to his chest. "I brought food for me. I just quit my job and am working under the assumption of future payment. I can't afford to be buying you breakfast right now." He walked over to the table and dumped out the contents of the bag, and I glared at him when three breakfast sandwiches rolled out. "Now, catch me up."

36

While Ethan devoured the three breakfast sandwiches one by one, I told him the entire story, starting with Christina's phone call the day we buried the chest. His expression never once changed. He reacted so little, I wondered if he was even listening, but when I finished the story he pinned me with his gaze and said, "So your friend asked you to hide a body and you went over there and buried a gigantic box without asking questions?"

"I told you, it was our secret code!"

"You still could have asked a few questions."

"Well, I went back to ask her those questions after the fact, but she was gone."

"You said she was rich because she's inheriting her recently deceased husband's money. You can't inherit money from someone you killed and then tried to bury in the backyard."

"She didn't kill him! I already told you, Hudson wasn't in that box. Whoever killed him dumped him in the desert, and whatever secret Christina wanted hidden so badly is something else. Not a dead husband."

While looking wistfully down at the final empty sandwich wrapper, Ethan said, "She cheated on her husband with the person running against him for political office. He was cheating on her with a stripper. She found out about this and threatened to kill him." He looked up from the table to meet my eyes. "Just because his final resting place wasn't in the box doesn't mean he wasn't ever in there."

"She told me not to look for her or the chest, Ethan. She's in danger, and she believes that looking for her or whatever she tried to hide will put me in danger, too. If she was the one who killed him, that wouldn't make any sense. There wouldn't be anyone else to run from."

Ethan's unruly eyebrows raised in amusement. "So now not only do I have to hope your friend who asked you to bury a body didn't actually kill her husband or else I won't get paid, but there's also danger waiting for me if I help you look for her? Is there anything else you neglected to mention when you begged me to take this job?"

I groaned. "Ethan, you'll get your money. If somehow Christina can't pay you, I will sell a goddamn kidney to get you your money."

"And the danger?"

I looked back at this kid, clad in a t-shirt for a band I didn't recognize and loose black jeans. He was so young, and behind the eyebrow he raised in challenge there was a pent-up energy. I could see his brain already working.

"The danger makes you want to take this job even more," I said, and he smiled before holding his hands up in surrender. I went into the kitchen and poured yet another cup of coffee from the cheapest coffee maker I could find into the only mug I owned—a cheerful yellow cup the size of my head that said "Good Vibes Only."

"So," I asked when I sat back down, "who should we follow first?" Clemens may not have been one of the men who dug up and took the chest, but I still had a bad feeling about him. And I was eager to find out more about Diamond. It was a Saturday, so she'd be dancing for sure. I wondered how Ethan might clean up. If I brought him to Heaven on Earth, did he stand a chance of getting backstage to talk with her?

"No one," Ethan said.

I balked at him.

"You think whoever killed your friend's husband is the person she's running from, right?"

"Yeah, them or an accomplice."

"For suspect number one, you've got a political opponent who is wary of a possible tail following him around and knows you're onto him. If we try to follow Clemens, he'll spot us immediately. And suspect number two is a woman we know almost nothing about. If we follow Diamond, we're going to waste a whole lot of time because we don't know what we're looking for." He cocked his head and added, "But maybe it would be prudent to check out her place of employment tonight, just in case…"

"Don't be a creep." He had a point that following Clemens and Diamond around might not be the best use of our time, but the only other idea I had was continuously refreshing Good Neighbors until my account was verified.

Like he could read my mind, Ethan asked, "You said you saw your boy toy's computer and there was a screenshot from security footage showing the people who unburied the chest—the one you insist did not have a body in it—on the neighborhood website?"

I held up my hand. "First of all, stop calling him my boy toy. And while we're on the subject, you never told me what you found out about him. Did you say his brother's in prison?"

"What's your priority here, getting the dirt on your male plaything—"

"That's worse."

"—or coming up with a plan to find your friend?"

"The latter, obviously, but your taking five minutes to tell me about Francisco isn't going to jeopardize that plan."

With a sigh so dramatic you'd think I'd just insisted he read the latest journal from the American Mathematical Society cover to cover, Ethan rattled off the facts of Francisco's life like he was reciting a grocery list.

"Francisco Eduardo Como, thirty years old, born and raised outside Dallas, Texas. He has one sibling, an older brother who had some substance abuse problems in high school and went to rehab twice before the age of eighteen. He moved to Arizona to go to U of A where his brother, who had apparently turned his life around, was in medical school.

"The brother finished med school while Francisco was in undergrad but wound up stealing prescription painkillers from work. Francisco got him into rehab again and started writing a long-form article about addiction in doctors. Francisco's then-girlfriend, Farrah Styles of the Pima County Sheriff's Office, got her hands on his list of sources for the piece. She passed along the intel and there was a big round of arrests, including Francisco's brother. Cue breakup.

"Styles was promoted twice shortly thereafter, and your man Francisco dropped out of school in his last semester and started writing puff pieces for local papers. The brother still has two years to go on his sentence, and Francisco visits roughly every two weeks. Their mother died about a year after the brother's sentencing, and their father's been dead fifteen years. No other family. Not a lot of hobbies to speak of besides running, although I didn't follow him for long so there's plenty I could have missed."

By the end of his recitation, my jaw was hanging open.

"That's horrible! How did you even find all that?"

He shrugged. "It wasn't hard."

I closed my eyes and shook my head, trying to get past his complete indifference to Francisco's pain. Styles had acted like Francisco was the one with secrets when she'd exploited his work for her own professional advancement and landed his brother in prison in the process. I wished she would knock on my door again so I could slam it in her face even harder.

"Can we get back to the important stuff?" Ethan asked, and I glared at him. Undeterred, he said, "Your tragic male plaything—"

"Just say 'boy toy.'"

"—had that neighborhood website up on his screen when you were over there yesterday. Someone posted a screenshot from security cameras pointing at your friend's house?"

"Yeah, but I don't have access to the website yet."

He waved the protest away. "That's fine. We want more than that screenshot, anyway. We need to get the whole footage."

"I told you, I tried that. Francisco had it, but it was stolen by his friend, which I don't understand. And Maureen—the woman with the doorbell camera—lied to me and told me she'd deleted it. She'll never hand it over."

"I wasn't going to ask her for it."

I stared, waiting for him to explain.

"All of that footage is stored on a cloud server somewhere, waiting for someone like me to break in and take it." When I looked aghast, he said, "I was a computer science major before I dropped out. People don't understand how vulnerable they are."

The sensation I'd experienced when I realized Dave had tracked my location from my laptop came back. I'd felt violated and unsafe in my own home. It felt like everything I thought was safe was secretly a mirage, like I'd just discovered the walls of my house were actually one-way mirrors and anyone might be looking in at any time.

"Okay, so you're going to, what, exploit her vulnerability and get the security footage?" I felt queasy at the idea, but the prospect of seeing that footage was too enticing to say no. It could hold the answers I was looking for. And I thought it was only a matter of time before Detective Styles tracked down

Maureen and got the video recording for herself. I wanted to know what sort of trouble I might be in when she did.

"That's right," Ethan said. "And while I'm figuring that out, you're going to find out more about Diamond."

"I thought you said following her would be a waste of time."

"It will be, if we don't know what we're looking for. You're going to see what you can find online. Figure out her real name. She's bound to have an online presence, and if she's like most people, she puts more on there than she should."

It felt obvious once he said it. "Diamond isn't her real name! But how am I supposed to figure out what it is?"

Ethan pushed the folding chair back and stood. "You hired me to help you, not to figure out every single thing for you." He started toward the door. "Give me a few days for the footage."

I started to tell him to wait, but he was gone before I could. I leaned my head back and groaned up at the ceiling in frustration. I had no clue where to start.

I pulled up the social media pages for Heaven on Earth, but none of them had anything besides Diamond's stage name, and Diamond herself didn't seem to have a profile. I scrolled past photo after photo of scantily clad dancers and bright, colorful cocktails, but found absolutely nothing to hint at who Diamond was behind the character she presented on stage.

Then an email came through from the county's HR department letting me know I'd left a field blank by mistake on one of my new hire forms and needed to correct it. With a sympathetic murmur for the poor assistant working the weekend, I pulled up the form and filled in the missing information, and then it hit me. Even the sleaziest of businesses had to keep some sort of records.

Heaven on Earth probably had paperwork listing Diamond's real name. If I could find that, I could figure out who she really was and what she was up to with Clemens and Hudson's law firm. All I had to do was find the office at the club, sneak in, dig through their paperwork until I found what I was looking for, and sneak back out without getting caught.

I opened up the text from Christina and read it again to give me a boost. *I'm safe.* My fingers tightened around the phone as I read and re-read the message. *I'm going to find you,* I thought, imagining the message beaming from my head into Christina's, wherever she was. *And when I do, you're going to owe me big time.*

37

Heads turned as I walked through the pulsing crowd inside the gentlemen's club. I cursed silently. This is exactly what I wanted to avoid. Having surveyed my closet and found absolutely nothing that stood a chance at blending in here, I'd made a quick trip to the mall and put a tight, short dress on Dave's and my joint credit card. I hadn't used the card or paid anything toward the bill since I'd left—I'd taken nothing out of the joint bank account, subsisting only on what I knew was unquestionably mine to avoid conflict later. But if he could spend a hundred dollars a day to track me down, he could pay the credit card bill for this cheap black dress.

On my previous visit, I hadn't given a second thought to my clothes. I was there to ask questions, not to blend in, and I thought nothing of showing up in jeans and a t-shirt. But tonight, I wanted to slip through unnoticed. Somewhere in the club was an office, and I planned to find it. I didn't need all eyes on me when I was trying to sneak into a part of the club where I didn't belong.

I realized when I stepped inside that I'd miscalculated. A woman in jeans and a t-shirt was there looking for someone, and no one wanted any part in whatever was going on between her and the man she was looking for. But a woman in a skimpy dress was a different story, and even my orthopedic boot didn't compel people to lose interest and look away. Instead, the combination of the dress and the boot seemed to make people look harder. I walked to the bar, flushed with color at the eyes on me.

"Can I get a vodka soda, please?"

With a drink in hand, I perched at one of the high tables along the outer edge of the room, above the sunken main floor with the larger tables, booths, and stools along the stage. As I sat by myself, sipping my drink and watching the activities around me but being careful not to make eye contact, gradually the eyes of the other patrons stopped looking my way and I found relative privacy from which to concoct the rest of my plan.

To the right of the bar was a velvet curtain covering the entrance to a hallway, and judging by the traffic, I guessed that's where the restrooms were. I watched as men came and went, trying to get a glimpse down the hallway when they pushed the drape back on their ways in and out. It was fruitless; all I could see was a short stretch of wall, and then the heavy curtain fell back into place each time.

The only other exits were the main doors through which I had entered and the curtained-off portal from the stage into the private backstage area where only dancers—and, apparently, Hudson—were allowed. With no chance of getting backstage, I decided I might as well check the hall with the restrooms. I downed the rest of my drink in one quick gulp, feeling an instant warmth in my stomach from the alcohol, and slipped off the stool to head for the curtain.

Heads turned again as I pushed past groups of people on my way, but then I pulled back the velvet curtain and stepped into the hallway and found myself alone in the small space. It was lit by a pink fluorescent light overhead, staining the walls, floor, and ceiling a rose hue. The music from the club was still audible behind the heavy curtain, but muffled enough that I could hear my steps click with each stride.

One wall was solid and uninterrupted, but the other had four doors spaced along it. The first three had unisex restroom signs on them. The fourth was unmarked. *That has to be the office.* I hesitated in the hallway. What if I pushed open the door and there was someone in there? The curtain behind me swung open, letting in the loud thump of the music. A man in a crumpled suit that looked like he'd been wearing it for three straight days gave me a lecherous look.

"Lost?" He stepped toward me with a drunken sway, then slurred, "I can help you find your way."

Revulsion and fear swirled together, and I lunged for the bathroom door nearest me. Mercifully, the door swung open, and I hurried inside and locked it behind me. The drunk man pounded on the door a few times, groaned that I was a tease, and then apparently remembered what had brought him there in the first place. I heard the door to the restroom next door open and slam shut, then the flush of a urinal shortly thereafter, followed by the door opening and closing again. No sound of a faucet. *Gross.*

I waited, hovering near the door and listening for any sound of motion outside. I counted to one hundred and then, when I still hadn't heard any noise, decided to go for it. I swung the door open, glanced quickly up and down the short hallway, and then reached for the handle of the fourth door.

The door flew open before I even grabbed the handle, and a short man in a black tank top barreled out of it. I immediately pivoted, reaching for the restroom door to feign confusion, but he pushed past me without seeming to register my presence.

"Camille!" he hollered as he burst through the curtain into the main room. "What's this about Leslie calling out again?" Before the fabric swished back into place behind him, I saw him marching toward the bar.

A squeak behind me made me whirl. The man had thrown the door so wide in his surge toward the bar, it was still swinging shut even when he was long gone. On instinct, I stuck my foot out and blocked the door a second before it would have latched closed, then scurried inside.

Where I expected to find a small office, instead I found myself in another hallway. This one led down the full length of the club and around a corner. "Ethan, you'd better be right about this," I breathed as I started down the hallway, aware that at any moment, the man could return. I could have just waited in the parking lot for Diamond to leave after her shift, then followed her home. Instead, I was trying my best to walk on tiptoes with an enormous rigid boot on one ankle to keep the sound of my footsteps as quiet as possible.

When I was inches from the corner, I paused and listened. The way he'd talked to the bartender, I figured Mr. Tank Top had to be the club owner, and he'd come from this hallway. That meant I had to be in the right spot; the office had to be down here. Still, I couldn't stop my hands from sweating as I prepared to turn the corner. All I could hear was the low thump of the club music—no voices, no footsteps. Finally, I let out a breath and rounded the corner to find myself chest-to-chest with the tallest man I'd ever seen. Behind him was the man in the tank top, his arms crossed in front of his chest.

38

"You want to explain what exactly you're doing, sneaking around my club?" the man asked from behind the wall of flesh separating us. Behind him, a television monitor hung suspended from the ceiling. The screen was split into four video feeds, one of which showed the hallway I'd just come from.

Shit.

"I was looking for the bathroom," I squeaked out.

The enormous muscled man took a step forward, his body nearly touching my own, and I had to tilt my head all the way back to look him in the eye.

"Don't worry, boss. I'll help her find it." He reached for my arm, and I jerked away. He reached out again, grabbing me tight around the bicep and making me wince.

As he stepped to the side, I registered for the first time that we were in the backstage area I'd tried to glimpse through the curtains at the back of the stage on my previous visit. It looked like a small office break room but less well lit, with a round table in the center of the room and a vending machine in the corner next to a door with a lit exit sign above it. Off one wall, beneath the monitor displaying the surveillance camera footage, was the office I'd been looking for. The only other door in the room was cracked, and I could hear women's voices and laughter coming from the other side. I figured it must lead to a changing room for the dancers.

The club owner left me in the mountain man's grip and went into the office, closing the door behind him. I was being pulled toward the exit when applause roared from the other side of the curtain, and then the woman I'd been trying to name stepped through the curtain and into the room.

"What's the matter, Snake?" Diamond asked, looking me up and down. "Another woman here looking for her husband?" She started toward the changing room without another look, and I surmised I wouldn't be the first woman to sneak around searching for her unfaithful husband.

"I'm here to talk to you," I blurted before she could leave.

Diamond laughed. "I don't do autographs. I'm flattered, though."

"It's about Hudson Schuppert."

At the mention of Hudson's name, Diamond froze.

"You gotta look for your cheat of a man somewhere else, honey," Snake said with another tug toward the exit.

"She's fine, Snake." Snake and I both looked at Diamond in surprise—his laced with frustration, mine with sheer relief. "I want to talk to her." She turned to me and said, "I'm done working for the night. Can you wait five minutes for me to change?"

I nodded. Snake waited until Diamond disappeared into the changing room and shut the door behind her to let go of me with a disapproving grunt.

"That girl is too trusting," he grumbled as he moved back into position just inside the curtain, ready to stop anyone who tried to slip backstage. He'd dropped all the macho aggression from his voice, and sounded more like a concerned father than a bouncer about to toss me into the street and maybe give me a quick kick in the ribs for good measure.

"What do you mean?"

Snake frowned at the closed changing room door. "She thinks she's invincible. She thinks anyone who means her harm is too stupid to actually get to her. She lets people back here, for one thing, and the boss man wants her happy, so I'm not allowed to tell her no. Like you, for example—someone comes back here and they should get tossed out on their ass. But no, Diamond says you can stay, so I just have to let it go."

"I'm not going to hurt her."

"No, but the more she lets people get close to her, the easier it'll be for the one who actually tries to."

Diamond emerged from the changing room, her twists pulled back into a massive bun and a sweatsuit replacing the skimpy sparkling set she'd worn to perform. "Come on," she gestured to me. "See you tomorrow, Snake." She shoved the exit door open, greeted Snake's counterpart on the other side, and stepped outside. I followed.

When we were halfway across the parking lot toward the group of cars in the back, I asked, "Uh, where are we going?"

"I don't want to talk about Hudson in there."

I was struggling to keep up with her pace in my boot, and she hadn't answered my question. "So, should I get my car and follow you somewhere, or...?"

Diamond stopped and turned around, rolling her eyes at me. "We can talk in my car. I'll give you five minutes."

I hustled after her as she beeped her car unlocked. She climbed into the driver's seat. I pulled open the passenger-side door and hesitated. This woman might be connected to a murder, and I was about to willingly get into her car.

"Five minutes," she reminded me, tapping her wrist, and I lowered myself into the seat against my better judgment. With narrowed eyes, she asked, "Why do you want to talk to me about Hudson?"

I hadn't been planning to have this conversation. I'd been planning to dig through paperwork until I found Diamond's name, then hurry home to see what I could turn up that might explain her connection to the Board of Supervisors and Hudson's law firm.

Diamond tapped her wrist again, and I said, "He went missing two weeks ago, and last night the news broke that his body turned up in the desert."

"So?"

"So, he came here a lot."

"Why do you care? Are you a girlfriend of his?" She was being cagey, trying to feel me out. Trying to see how much of a threat I posed and how much I already knew.

"I'm just interested in finding out what happened to him."

Diamond's guarded expression changed, and she laughed. "Oh, you're one of those true crime nuts who thinks they're going to solve a case before the police and become internet famous. Listen, I don't know shit about what happened to Hudson. He came here to watch me dance. Then he stopped coming. It seems like now we know why." She dragged a finger across her neck.

The flippant gesture turned my stomach, and I raised my voice. "I don't think you're telling me the truth. I think you *do* know what happened to him. You saw Hudson the night before he disappeared. What's the story? Exotic dancer and patron fall in love, but when he won't leave his wife for her, she kills him in a fit of rage?"

"Whoa! I don't—"

I cut her off, spinning out a theory. "You had an affair with a married man. You got tired of only seeing him backstage in a changing room or in his office. He strung you along, saying he'd leave his wife so you could be a real couple. The night before he disappeared, you met with him and gave him an ultimatum. And then, when he didn't choose you, you waited until he was home alone and you killed him, then dumped his body in the desert."

Wide-eyed and looking like she deeply regretted letting me into her car, Diamond shook her head. "You don't know what you're talking about. I didn't kill Hudson. I wasn't in love with him. You've got it all wrong."

"So you just brought him backstage to toy with him? Were you just milking him for expensive gifts? Money?"

"Hudson was helping me study for the bar!" she blurted.

I recoiled. "The what?"

"The bar exam. It's a test lawyers have to take before they can—"

"I know what the bar exam is."

"Then why'd you ask?"

"I don't understand why you're studying for it."

Diamond's eyebrows reached for her hairline and her mouth dropped open as she leaned back and shook her head. "Oh, because I'm a dancer at a gentlemen's club I can't also be competent in other fields?"

Shame colored my cheeks. "I didn't mean—"

"You did," she interrupted. "I'm used to it. You see me dance on a pole and assume that's all I can do. Meanwhile, I'm the best damn paralegal my law firm has ever seen, and I'll be a damn good lawyer once I pass the bar in July." Diamond reveled in my surprise and embarrassment. "I didn't kill Hudson. In fact, his disappearance was a real inconvenience for me, seeing as now I'm on my own to prepare."

"When you say 'my law firm,' would that happen to be Warner & Loeb?"

Diamond looked at me like I was stupid and gave me a nod-and-eye-roll combo that screamed "Duh." I squirmed uncomfortably, and Diamond gestured to the car door behind me. "Now, if you'll excuse me, I need to get home and do another set of practice questions."

I reached for the door handle, then turned back to her. "If

you work at Hudson's law firm, does that mean you saw him the day he disappeared?"

She nodded, then said more quietly, "Yeah. I saw him come in for the partner meeting."

"How did he seem that morning? Was he out of sorts at all? Any change from when you saw him the night before?"

Diamond's lips pursed and creases formed between her brows. "I didn't see him the night before. We never met up on Thursdays. I didn't notice anything different about him at work on Friday, but he'd been stressed out for a while."

"How long?"

After a moment's consideration, she said, "A month, maybe?"

I filed that information away, along with the detail that according to Diamond, she and Hudson never met up on Thursdays, but according to Hudson's agenda, he'd planned to see her that night. Someone was lying, but I didn't know who.

"Did you and Hudson ever meet anywhere else?"

Diamond shook her head.

"What about in his office at the Board of Supervisors?"

Shock flooded her features, and Diamond sputtered, "How did you know that?" So she hadn't seen me during her visit to Clemens at work yesterday.

"Why did you visit him there? It doesn't seem like prime study time, the middle of the workday."

She shifted in her seat, eyes calculating, then said, "I really can't tell you that."

I huffed a breath of air out of my nose and raised a brow at her. "Really? Because I really *can* tell everyone at your law firm what you do after work." I instantly regretted the threat as surprise and hurt washed over her.

Bitterly, Diamond said, "I'll tell you, but only if you swear not to tell my work about the club and not to put any of this in your little YouTube video when you're telling all your followers how you're going to solve the case."

"There's no YouTube video. I just want to figure out what happened to Hudson." I didn't tell her I was investigating Hudson's death to try to figure out why my best friend went on the run and where she was hiding.

She studied me carefully, then dipped her chin. "I was visiting Hudson at his job at the board in a professional capacity. Mr. Warner thinks it's important for the firm to maintain a close relationship to the Board of Supervisors, especially our district supervisor." Warner, as in the named partner from Hudson's law firm? I kept my face as neutral as possible, though my head was spinning. "He wants to make sure Warner & Loeb clients' interests are...known to the supervisors."

"So the clients who work with your law firm can count on what? Zoning decisions being decided in their favor?"

"Zoning decisions, county ordinances, funding appropriations..." She nodded.

"But why did you have to visit him for that? Hudson already knew the clients and their, uh, interests."

"Hudson didn't like the arrangement at all. He thought if he just voted in the interests of his law firm's clients all the time, people would notice. His decisions would be contradictory or inconsistent. Mr. Warner sent me in as a concerned citizen to try and placate him. I would visit Hudson—sometimes the other supervisors, too, but mostly Hudson—and pretend just to be a politically inclined citizen. I'd advocate for the positions Warner wanted Hudson to vote for in the board meetings. Having a citizen come in and voice my concerns gave Hudson a reason to vote in ways that might otherwise seem suspicious."

So, corruption. Plain and simple corruption—a supervisor using his position to favor the people and businesses who paid his other place of work, where he was still employed and still drew a salary. Was this what Francisco had been digging into?

"Has anyone else confronted you about this? Have you talked to anyone else about it?"

Diamond shook her head. Francisco might have uncovered a connection between Hudson's actions as supervisor and his clients at the firm, but he didn't know about Diamond's involvement. Or if he did, he hadn't tried to question her yet.

Diamond eyed the car door behind me again, clearly past ready to be done with this conversation, but I was still trying to figure out what this all meant for Hudson and Christina. Hudson had been using his political position to further his own ends—rather, those of the people who paid the law firm where he was a partner—but would someone kill him for that? Could evidence of this scheme be what Christina had buried before going in the wind?

Hudson's law firm clearly comprised at least one partner willing to play dirty if Warner was willing to fake civic engagement to make Hudson play his game. If Diamond was right and Hudson didn't like the arrangement, could Warner have seen Hudson as a threat? But Hudson was an asset to the firm in his position. They wouldn't want him dead. Hudson's death would sever the tie between the firm and the Board of Supervisors, unless...

"You've been visiting Clemens since he was appointed after Hudson's disappearance," I said, and Diamond nodded. "Is he in on it too?"

She shrugged. "Probably. I never talked to him about it. I just showed up playing my part, acting like a rich lady with too much time on her hands who had opinions on some upcoming matters the board would be voting on. I imagine he got the lowdown from Warner, but maybe not. Maybe I'm just convincing." She smiled as if the idea amused her.

"Does he ever visit the law firm? Have you seen him talking with Warner?"

"Just once, that I've seen. A few weeks ago, I left the office but had to go back for my wallet. Clemens was in Warner's office then."

"A few weeks ago—was that before or after Hudson disappeared?"

"Before." Her response was lightning fast. She was sure.

I thanked Diamond for the information and promised her that her secrets were safe with me before reaching for the door handle. I had plenty to puzzle on, but I could do it from the comfort of my mattress on the floor and not the passenger seat of Diamond's car.

I was halfway out the door when Diamond called, "There's one more thing!" I stuck my head back in the car, and she said, "I saw Hudson arguing with Warner once. It was about a month before he went missing, around the time he started acting stressed. They were arguing over a case, though, I'm pretty sure. Not the supervisor stuff. Mr. Loeb went in and settled it, and I didn't see them arguing again. I don't know if it's relevant, but I thought you might want to know."

I thanked her again and turned toward my car, taking care to hold the fob just right to avoid breaking it open and spilling its contents on the asphalt again while unlocking it. I raised my gaze when it beeped unlocked and shuffled the rest of the way across the lot. The growl of another engine starting sounded behind me, and I turned to see Diamond backing out, then peeling off into the night. In the corner of the lot, visible now that Diamond's car was gone, an inconspicuous black sedan was idling in a spot, and behind the wheel Detective Styles had her eyes trained on me.

39

I faltered, and the detective lifted a hand and wiggled her fingers in a tiny wave.

"Shit," I cursed. I hurried the rest of the way to my car and climbed inside. The engine cranked ineffectually when I turned the key. "Come on..." On the third try, it turned over, and I breathed a sigh of relief and then rotated my torso in my seat to look back at where Detective Styles was still sitting in her unmarked police car.

Had she been following me? Or was she here, like I was, for Diamond? If the police were investigating Diamond, they weren't far from uncovering Hudson's corruption scheme with his law firm. The idea sent a frisson of hope through me. While I wasn't sure how the pieces all fit together, any leads the police might be investigating that weren't part of the "Christina killed her husband and Mandy helped bury him in the yard before someone dug him up and moved him to the desert" theory sounded good to me.

Styles followed me out of the Heaven on Earth parking lot, and I felt the familiar tightness in my gut at being followed. Three turns later, she pulled up in the lane beside me at a stoplight, gave me the same tiny finger wave, then abruptly turned right and sped off.

Though I was alone the rest of the drive home, I couldn't stop my eyes flitting to the rearview mirror every few seconds. I hadn't even enjoyed twenty-four hours of peace after unmasking Ethan before I felt like I was being hunted again, except this time I wasn't worried my pursuer would snatch me up and murder me. Instead, I thought she'd slap a pair of cuffs on me and throw me in a cell.

I reached for the living room light switch while I pulled the door shut behind me, and the overhead light flicked to life, casting the room in stark relief.

"You're home."

I shrieked and backed into the door I'd just shut behind me, my head smacking into it with a thud.

"Whoa, it's me!"

I blinked through my panic and saw Ariel emerge from my bedroom with her hands up. "What are you doing here?" My chest heaved under my hand, my heart beating fast beneath my palm.

She lowered her hands slowly and guiltily said, "You got scared when I was looking in your window on Monday, so I just thought…"

"You just thought, why not one-up yourself and break in to scare me even more?"

She tugged at the skirt of her dress and squirmed. "There was a light on in your bedroom, so I thought you were home. I knocked, but you didn't answer."

"So you let yourself in? How'd you even get in, anyway?"

Sheepishly, Ariel held up a small pouch of lock-picking tools. "I found these in my brother's room."

I breathed out slowly, forcing myself to count to ten.

"Are you mad?" Ariel asked, and I breathed out another long exhale, repeating my count before I felt calm enough to answer.

"Just don't do it again," I said. When my pulse had leveled out, I dropped my purse on the loveseat, went into the bedroom to flick off the light I'd thoughtlessly left on earlier, then filled a glass with boxed wine and drank deeply.

Evidently satisfied by my forgiveness, Ariel bounded over to the loveseat and plopped herself down before tucking her Converse-clad feet under her black-and-white striped dress.

I opened my mouth to ask her to keep her shoes off the furniture, but she cut me off with an abrupt question.

"Do you have a new boyfriend?"

My cheeks flushed with the memory of Francisco pulling away from me. "No."

"Then who was that guy you brought inside last night?"

"He, uh, knows my ex."

She screwed up her face in confusion. "Why was he here?" Instead of waiting for an answer, however, she jumped up and exclaimed, "Oh! I saw a white car parked on our street earlier this week when I was walking to the bus stop. You told me to look for one."

"Thanks."

Before I could say anything else, she frowned at me and asked, "Are you a snitch?"

"What?"

"I saw the police lady talking to you this morning. Mom and Dad said you had to be in trouble, but Ryder said he thinks you're a snitch for the police."

I assured her that the visit from the officer was nothing, but she didn't seem overly concerned with my response, eager instead to continue telling me every thought that popped into her head. When I finally ushered her out of the house, the silence felt like sinking into a pool of cool water on a hot day.

I washed the lingering smell of Heaven on Earth from my hair and then crawled into bed. Lying on my side, I held my phone inches from my face and searched Hudson's name again. No new information about the discovery of his body appeared in any of the articles I found. I searched for his law firm and clicked through images of the two men who must be the Warner and Loeb the firm was named after.

I tried to guess which one was Warner—the rotund man with a red face and the air of a bulldog or the skinny string bean of a man with a prominent nose and the air of a shark. Both looked capable of dreaming up the scheme they were running with Hudson at the Board of Supervisors. But did either look capable of murder?

I continued to scroll through the images until I came to a picture that seemed to be from some charity gala. The picture captured a table of ten men and women in suits and gowns all holding up their drinks in a toast. The two named partners from Hudson's law firm were present, and beside them Cory Clemens grinned, toasting with a glass of champagne.

———

THE DREAMS WERE BACK, this time featuring Warner, Loeb, and Clemens standing above me laughing as I dug a hole chasing after Hudson, who burrowed deeper every time I was nearly upon him. By the time Monday morning rolled around, I gave up on sleep long before dawn and dabbed extra concealer under my eyes before heading to work. After leaving early Friday to go chasing after Diamond, it was probably for the best I'd get in early today. I needed a moment to get my bearings and remember what I was supposed to be working on before I could dive back in.

My brain lagged at every step; I put my dirty cereal bowl in the fridge instead of the sink and left the house without my keys before finding myself on the stoop unable to lock the door. I made another cup of coffee when I went back inside for the keys, hoping it could somehow turn the pile of mush inside my skull back into a functioning cerebrum.

On my second exit from the house, Francisco was passing in his running gear just as I was crossing the front yard, making for my car. *Please keep walking, please keep walking.* I turned my head and looked up the street, trying to look deeply interested in something far away and avoid making eye contact with Francisco. The last time I'd seen him, he'd humiliated me. Though I now knew, thanks to Ethan, that his relationship with Styles and her betrayal of his trust probably left him with some damage, it did little to dull the sting.

"Mandy!" he called, stopping where the path across my lawn met the sidewalk. I turned and did my best to look surprised to find him standing there. "I was hoping I'd run into you soon. I wanted to talk about—"

"I'm actually late for work." The words flew out of my mouth so quickly they surprised even me, and Francisco leaned back, stunned.

"With a... mug?" He pointed to the full mug of coffee in my hand, then said, "It's barely 6 a.m."

I looked down at my coffee and took a sip to buy me a minute. "I guess I should put a travel mug on my list of things to buy. And things are crazy this week." Francisco opened his mouth to respond, but I cut him off and said, "See you later!" before hurrying past him.

As it turned out, I really did need to put a travel mug on the list of things worth parting with a little of my hard-earned cash for. I'd spilled coffee on myself before I was even out of the neighborhood. When I arrived at the administration building, I made a pit stop at the bathroom and dabbed at the spill with a wet paper towel before standing under the hand dryer until my blouse was dry.

While it blew hot air on my soaked shirt, my thoughts wandered back to Francisco and Friday night. Besides the humiliation at feeling unwanted and rejected, there was another reason I'd been unready to see him. I hadn't yet made sense of his friend stealing his bag after Francisco had gotten Maureen's security footage, and I didn't know whether to tell him or not. What was I supposed to say? *You know that good friend of yours? Well, I saw him steal your bag when you went to go get security footage for your story. How did I come to see that? Oh, I was following you, but don't worry about that.* I didn't see that going over well.

The coffee stain was no better for my efforts. I headed for the bullpen and wondered whether any of the other admins might have a stain remover pen in their desks.

"Look who's back," Jake said from his desk, glancing up at me for half a second before turning back to his work.

"Clemens has you working early today." Jake and the others always got to work early—the expectation was that the administrative assistants got to work before their supervisors and left later—but not before seven.

He looked over at me with a haggard expression. "You picked the wrong day to dip out early."

"What do you mean?"

"Not thirty minutes after you left, the police showed up. They wanted to talk to Clemens."

My eyes sprang wide. "Here?"

Jake nodded. "It must have been about Supervisor Schuppert. It was only a few hours before the reports broke about his body being found."

"What happened?"

"Three cops came in and went straight up to Clemens's door to ask if he would speak with them. He invited them in, and they were in there maybe ten or fifteen minutes. Then they left, and then Clemens told me to start getting ready for another press conference."

"A press conference? When?"

"This afternoon. He wants to"—he looked down at his notes and read from them—"'reaffirm his commitment to his constituents while paying tribute to his predecessor.' I have no idea what to write for him."

I gave him a sympathetic smile. "You'll figure it out." I could see the disappointment in his eyes when I didn't offer to help him, but I had my own work to do, and he hadn't exactly been eager to help me when I'd started this job with no clue what I was doing.

The office picked up, bustling with a frenetic energy as the morning progressed. Every one of the supervisors was in the office, a rarity owed to Clemens's press conference. Though my mind wandered to Clemens and the cops, furiously trying to piece everything together, Wendy had a long list of requests for me when she arrived, and I soon found myself occupied by the work. Along with the other admins, I worked through lunch, and then we all filed down to the lobby just before one. I could see through the glass doors that someone had rolled a podium out to the top of the stairs, and reporters and journalists were all milling about. I began to follow the other admins out the door, but then a familiar shock of dark, curly hair caught my eye and I recoiled.

"You okay?" Eliza asked worriedly.

"Fine," I said, still moving away from the door. "I just remembered something upstairs."

She studied me for a moment before nodding and hurrying out to meet the rest of our colleagues, and I headed for the elevators, wanting to be safely outside of Francisco's field of vision. I didn't want him to know I'd gone and gotten a job working with Clemens after our failed operation at his last press conference. My mad dash for the elevators earned me a quizzical look from Benny, the security guard, but I flashed my badge and he didn't stop me.

Upstairs, I immediately ran to Supervisor Washington's office and pressed myself up against her window. Clemens and the podium were obscured, but I could see the crowd of reporters. My eyes instantly lit on Francisco's head, and I was surprised at the shot of emotion I felt when I saw that he was talking to a woman. I leaned in even further, my entire forehead pressed against the glass, to watch as the two of them laughed. Suddenly, the crowd turned en masse.

"Good afternoon." Clemens's unmistakable voice carried up to me, amplified by a microphone. "As I'm sure you all know, Pima County received the tragic news on Friday that Hudson Schuppert has been found dead. When I made the case to the Board of Supervisors to appoint me following Supervisor Schuppert's disappearance, I had every hope he would be found alive, if not in a fit state to resume his duties as supervisor. I have never been so sad to be wrong."

Clemens continued to wax poetic about his predecessor, then launched into a speech about how he'd carry on Hudson's legacy by working hard for the people of his district. "In my role as supervisor, I am going to work with my colleagues to explore every possible avenue to increase the budget for the Pima County Sheriff's Office. Our excellent police officers and detectives are doing great work, and I have every confidence that they will get justice for our former colleague."

He made no mention of the fact that their pursuit of justice had led the officers straight to his own office door, of course. Applause went up in the crowd, along with a smattering of hands. I couldn't hear the questions the reporters asked, so as Clemens called on them one by one, I slipped down the hall and into his office. Everyone would be downstairs for at least another ten minutes. It was the best chance I would get to poke around.

Clemens's desk was a mess of papers. Memos from Jake on the items to be voted on during the next Board of Supervisors meeting comprised most of the pages. I flipped through them, trying not to leave anything visibly disturbed. Near the bottom of the stack, one of the pages caught my eye. Someone had drawn a star in the top right corner of the page. It was the only one I'd seen so far that had any handwriting on it, so I pulled it from the stack to read it.

The memo detailed a proposal to create a new grant to encourage pharmaceutical innovation and bring new jobs to Pima County. The grant would funnel millions of dollars to any pharmaceutical company that made a large capital investment in the county and created over one hundred new jobs. Below the high-level summary, Jake had included an analysis of the likely impacts if the grant was approved.

Jake's ultimate conclusion was that the grant was unlikely to grow the local economy by enough to offset the amount of the grant, and his recommendation was that Supervisor Clemens vote against the grant creation. But where Jake had typed "Recommendation: No," Clemens had crossed it out in blue ink pen and written "YES."

The elevator chimed, and I shoved the paper back to the bottom of the stack and rushed out of Clemens's office. I was back at my desk, slightly out of breath, when my colleagues filed out of the elevator and back into the office.

"Are you sure you're okay?" Eliza asked as she slid into her chair.

"Yeah, I just remembered Supervisor Washington asked for this report by the end of the day." I gestured to my computer, but the screen was dark, and I nudged the mouse to wake it up. Eliza regarded me suspiciously but turned back to her own work without questioning me any further.

At three o'clock, Supervisor Washington gathered her bags and waved at me on her way out of the office. I tried to focus on the brief I was writing, but my brain kept returning to the one in Clemens's office. It had to be connected to one of Warner and

Loeb's clients. It was the first bit of evidence I'd seen of the arrangement Diamond had told me about, and it made me wonder how many of the votes were skewed by this firm's influence.

After nearly an hour of failed attempts to focus, I pushed my chair back and grabbed my bag.

"Leaving early again?" Jake asked.

"What's got you rushing to get out of here?" Johan chimed in.

I stuttered, then found my voice. "I've got a meeting with a divorce attorney."

40

I didn't have an appointment, of course, and I didn't think high-end law firms like the one where Hudson worked took walk-ins. I wasn't even sure if they handled divorces at all, but I suddenly couldn't stand the thought of putting off a visit any longer. I tried to think up a plan on the way there. What was I looking for? A bloody knife sitting in plain sight in the middle of the office? Written evidence of the arrangement with Hudson and now Clemens? In all likelihood, there would be nothing to find, but maybe I could drop Hudson's name and see if it elicited any reaction.

I pulled into the parking lot and swerved into a space across the lot from the white stucco building emblazoned with *Warner & Loeb Law Offices* in gold. Diamond had only talked about Warner's involvement in the scheme with the Board of Supervisors. Was Loeb in on it, too? Was he just as corrupt as his partner? I wondered for a moment whether I was stepping into a tank full of sharks or a tank full of tropical fish with one rogue shark swimming around.

Outside my car, I smoothed the front of my black and white polka dot blouse and pulled up my slacks as high as I could, tucking the blouse into the waistband to cover up the coffee stain. I gave myself a once-over in the rearview mirror and frowned. From the way Christina had talked about Hudson's colleagues and his work events, I got the sense that this firm took on a certain clientele, and the sales-rack blouse that had felt perfectly adequate for my desk job suddenly felt anything but.

My fears were confirmed the moment I stepped into the firm's entryway. Marble floors gleamed in the sunlight streaming in from the massive windows, and large potted trees adorned the space. Interspersed between the trees were a series of chairs I would have wagered had never supported an actual human person; the thin back and seat were made of slim concrete slabs, and bronze-colored rods curved around the back and then down to form the cold arms and legs of the chair.

The sound of someone clearing their throat took my attention off the bizarre, spartan furniture, and I turned to my right to find a tiny, birdlike woman almost entirely hidden behind a large, sleep reception desk. She stood from her chair, and though she couldn't have been even five feet tall, I felt pinned by her unwavering gaze.

"Can I help you?" she asked, though the sneering tone of her voice suggested she had no actual interest in helping me.

"Um, I'm looking for..." I trailed off, flustered, any script I'd rehearsed in my car lost from memory. Finally, I squeaked out, "I'm getting divorced?"

"Is that a statement or a question?" Her mouth twisted into a mocking smirk.

"I'm—I'm getting divorced," I repeated more firmly.

"And do you have an appointment?"

"No, I, uh—"

The receptionist opened her mouth to cut me off and chide me for daring to set foot on these premises without an appointment, but she herself was cut off when the door opened and the boisterous sound of laughter flooded the atrium, rebounding off the hard surfaces.

"And that's why you're the best, Will!" one of the men said, clapping the other on the back.

The second man laughed again, and I recognized him as one of the named partners, the rotund one with the ruddy complexion. Rings adorned several of his fingers and flashed in the sun as he put an arm around his companion. He turned and dipped his head in greeting toward the receptionist, then spotted me and frowned, his eyes traveling from my unwashed hair to my stained polyester blouse, the coffee stain poking out of my pants waistband, then finally to my orthopedic boot.

"Who's this?" he asked the receptionist as if I weren't there to tell him myself who I was.

"She says she's getting divorced, Mr. Warner," the receptionist answered, her lips pulled down into a tight expression of disapproval. "She doesn't have an appointment."

So this was Mr. Warner. He continued to look me over with a cold stare, an air of wealth and power and ruthlessness rolling off of him. I could immediately envision him mercilessly firing a low-performing associate or tearing an opponent apart in court without emotion.

I shifted uncomfortably, and as I avoided meeting his piercing gaze, my eyes flitted to the man beside him humming with slight impatience. Like Warner, this man oozed wealth from every stitch of his impeccably tailored suit. Unlike Warner, this man was trim, and smack dab in the middle of his tie was a clip adorned with the largest diamond I'd ever seen.

"Yes, well—" Mr. Warner started, but I interrupted.

"I was hoping to make an appointment with Hudson Schuppert."

It was impulsive, but it seemed like even if I managed to get an appointment with a lawyer here, I'd never get an appointment with Mr. Warner himself. This might be my only chance to see how he reacted to Hudson's name. Warner had cooked up a scheme and forced Hudson to go along, and now Hudson was dead—and no longer drawing a salary from the firm while spending more of his time on another job—and replaced by a man Diamond had seen in Warner's office shortly before Hudson disappeared.

If I was hoping my mention of Hudson's name would elicit some grand reaction and prove I was on the right track, that wasn't what I got. His companion stiffened, but Warner didn't give anything away. He only said, "Unfortunately, Mr. Schuppert recently passed away. Our other lawyers are all exceptionally competent, and we can see about getting you an appointment, but we're very busy, and our retainer fee might be outside your price range. Sandy here can help get you sorted."

He took off, striding through the open reception area toward the rest of the office. His companion followed, turning back once to look at me. They were nearly at the doorway when Mr. Warner's booming voice called out, "Diana!" Another figure hurried from deeper within the office to meet Warner in the doorway, and I gasped. It was Diamond. Warner made some request of her that I couldn't hear, then disappeared out of sight. Diamond turned to follow him but caught sight of me and froze, eyes wide with panic as she stared at me from the doorway.

The receptionist cleared her throat again, and I broke eye contact with Diamond—or, I now knew, Diana—and turned back around to face her.

Ten minutes later, I was back in my car, no closer to the truth. The receptionist had offered to schedule a consultation with one of the firm's attorneys, but the consultation would be billed at their hourly rate of $450 charged in six-minute intervals. I had respectfully declined the offer, ignoring her faintly smug look at the way my jaw dropped when she quoted that figure.

I threw my head back against the headrest and blew out a long breath. Before I left, I flipped through my phone and checked my emails, deleting junk message after junk message until an email from Good Neighbors caught my eye. I saw the bold subject line, "Your account has been verified," and immediately clicked the link.

41

The website loaded agonizingly slowly. When it finally materialized, my eyes darted across the page and my thumb swiped across the screen, bringing up post after post. I came across the post with the screenshot of the men carrying the chest from Christina's yard and took another look at it, then continued, wondering what else the neighbors might have said about Christina and Hudson.

Very little, it seemed. They had lots to say about grass length, trash collection and how quickly their fellow neighbors brought their bins in from the curb, and where it was acceptable to allow your dog to urinate on a walk, but as I scrolled and scrolled, no one had shared anything about the disappearance of their neighbors, even after one of them turned up dead. I was ready to give up and write off Good Neighbors as a bad lead when I saw it: buried beneath a request for recommendations for landscaping companies was a tribute post to Hudson.

A tribute to Hudson Brian Schuppert, friend and neighbor to us all. Though he was a member of our neighborhood for less than two years, he touched many lives. Please share any stories or memories you have for all of us to enjoy as we remember him.

Alongside the text was a close-up picture of tea lights. I looked to see who created the post, but the username was unidentifying—sunbum27—and the profile was private.

Beneath the post, comments included vague niceties about Hudson, how he kept his yard looking very nice and always waved when he saw neighbors walking around, and Christina, how she came around the entire neighborhood with baked goods when they'd moved in. A few comments expressed hope that she was okay. Not one of the comments shed any light on why Maureen might have thought she was under investigation, nor did they speculate on what might have led to Hudson's murder. I supposed it would have been shockingly rude if they had, but I was more interested in theories than decorum since I was holding out hope Christina was still out there and safe for me to find.

I took a screenshot and sent it to Ethan.

Mandy: Got access to Good Neighbors! Someone posted this tribute of Hudson, but no good info from it. Come over later to look at the site together?

My phone chimed with a response just as I was pulling up to the administration building.

Ethan: Can't. Busy tonight.

I let out a frustrated grunt. I was paying this kid every dollar I could afford and then some to help me crack this case, and now he was "busy?"

I stayed at work later than the other admins, no longer afraid of being ambushed in the parking lot. The other admins may not have been my superiors, but they gossiped, and I didn't want the supervisors hearing rumors I was constantly ducking out early. It was full dark by the time I arrived home to peel off my work clothes and microwave a lasagna.

With wine and my half-frozen, half-molten lasagna, I pulled the website up on my laptop to get a better view than I'd had on my phone earlier. Someone had pinned Hudson's tribute post to the top of the page, and the number of replies had grown slightly, but none of the new replies were anything more than the same surface-level niceties as the ones I'd already seen. Only one comment mentioned Christina.

A terrible tragedy. I only hope his sweet wife is found safe. She is very nice and genuine, and her art is lovely. Does anyone know if there will be a fundraiser we can donate to for their families?

My throat constricted as I read. Christina had bitten back tears when she told me they were leaving their vibrant community to move to the foothills for Hudson's political career. He wanted to run for supervisor, and the supervisor from District 1 was retiring, so it was the sensible thing, she'd told me, like she was trying to convince herself she wasn't upset. After the move, she'd been unable to keep from crying when she told me how isolated she felt there. And it didn't get better over time—no matter how much she reached out, Christina had felt rejected and unwelcome and alone. Now, those same neighbors who had barely acknowledged her when she tried to connect with them were asking where they could donate money to feel like they'd done something good.

Feeling the warmth of the wine spread through my midsection and the loosening of inhibitions that came with it, I added my own comment.

Maybe if we all made more of an effort to really get to know each other and look out for one another, this would never have happened. How can none of us have seen anything suspicious?

Someone *had* to have seen something. Maybe this would draw them out, or maybe it would just sting a little.

I hit "Enter" before I had a chance to talk myself out of it, then took another sip of wine. My palms were sweaty with the feeling of doing something reckless, and when my phone rang I jumped.

"I thought you were busy," I said to Ethan.

"I *am* busy."

"You're supposed to be helping me."

"I am helping you," Ethan replied, sounding as annoyed with me as I was with him. "You didn't exactly cover up your visit to your friend's place."

"What are you talking about?"

"Was it or was it not you who pushed a pool chair up to the wall to exit the backyard?" When I was silent, too confused and stunned to think up a reply, he added, "There was a clear footprint that, if police came back and discovered it, I'd bet all the money you're paying me would match your sneakers."

Finally, I blurted, "You went to Christina's house?"

"You said she acted weird about the neighbor kid going into the game room. I wanted to check it out."

"And?"

"Nothing there that I could find. I took care of any hints you'd been there, and I also took a look at the house with the doorbell cam."

"Maureen's?"

"Is there another house on the street with a doorbell camera?"

I rolled my eyes. "Why'd you go there? I thought you were going to hack into the system or whatever, not try to talk her into giving you the footage from her camera."

"I didn't try to talk to her. I just wanted to look around. Whoever the lady is, she's not just run-of-the-mill concerned about security. She's got hidden cameras all over her house."

"What?" I shook my head. Maureen had told me she only had a doorbell camera, no other security cameras.

"They're well hidden—not the cheap cameras that are obvious, like fake rocks that look nothing like rocks—but if you have any experience, they're pretty easy to spot. I don't know what she's worried about, but it's the second-most security cameras I've seen at one house."

"What was the most?"

"About a year ago, a guy hired me to find out if his girlfriend was cheating, but it turns out he was a high-level drug dealer and she was informing on him. The bust was in the news. They found guns and dirty money and an obscene amount of drugs in the house. He'll be in jail for at least another decade, and I never got paid. Pretty shitty gig."

I HAD A POUNDING headache and my entire body felt stiff when I rolled into work the next morning, but I wasn't sure if it was from lack of sleep—I'd stayed up well into the night browsing Good Neighbors—or from the wine I'd drunk while scrolling and reading post after post. The office energy was tense in the wake of Clemens's press conference the previous day and Styles's visit last Friday; everyone was on edge.

Washington had given me a long list of briefs she needed me to prepare, but between the jackhammering sensation between my eyes and the way my mind kept going back to the events of the day before to try to tease them out, I was working slowly and making mistakes.

Clemens was in on the corruption scheme with Warner and planned to vote against his admin's advice on a grant for pharmaceutical companies. Warner certainly felt dangerous, although I had nothing else on him. Diamond's real name was Diana. Maureen was drug lord-level concerned about her home security. Disjointed thoughts cropped up one after the other.

My text tone chirped.

Ethan: What's your GN login?

I glared at the message. The last thing I'd seen on Good Neighbors before I'd fallen asleep at the folding table was a flyer for a cookout the next weekend. *Come celebrate our grads before they leave the nest!* An illustration of baby birds wearing mortarboards and holding hot dogs accompanied the big bubble letters. I'd sent a screenshot to Ethan only to receive a thumbs-up reaction. I'd expected more—it was a perfect opportunity to peek around Christina's neighborhood without arousing suspicion—and now I wanted to ice Ethan out a little in return.

When my phone buzzed again ten minutes later, I expected another message from Ethan, but instead I had a notification from the Good Neighbors app I'd installed. Next to the app logo were the words "New Message."

I tapped the notification and revealed a message from sunbum27, the user who had created Hudson's tribute post.

Sunbum27: I agree with your comment. It's hard to believe none of us saw anything that night. This neighborhood is full of people who drive in and out of their garages and never take a look up or down the street.

My pulse raced beneath my skin and my palms began to tingle. Before I could type out a reply, the phone buzzed again in my hand.

Sunbum27: Can you think of anyone in our neighborhood who might be hiding something?

My fingers hovered over the screen as I tried to come up with a response. That's exactly the information I was on Good Neighbors to find out.

"New boyfriend?" Jake's question made me look up from the phone.

"Jake," Eliza chided.

Jake kept his eyes on me while addressing Eliza. "She makes the rest of us look bad, coming at going as she pleases and spending the morning texting when we're all swamped with work."

The other admins looked on and I felt the blood rush to my cheeks, painting my face bright red. I opened my mouth and mumbled an apology, but Jake just rolled his eyes and said, "Whatever," before turning back to his computer.

My phone felt like a magnet, pulling my attention to it while I tried to focus on my work, hyperaware of my colleagues' presence. When Jake got up to use the restroom, I grabbed it up, but instead of another message from sunbum27 on Good Neighbors, it was a follow-up text from Ethan asking again for my login information.

Ethan: I want to see if I can find anything you haven't.

I pursed my lips in irritation. Of course Ethan thought he'd do a better job than I had at combing through the site for helpful information. I fired off the information and went back to my work, but it wasn't long before Ethan texted again.

Ethan: You're messaging with someone on here?

Mandy: The person who created Hudson's tribute post messaged me. If they care enough about Hudson to make a tribute post, they must be close to the Schupperts. They seem to think someone might know more than they're letting on.

Ethan didn't respond, and it took all my effort to turn my focus back to my work. Though the daylight lingered longer as summer drew near, it was dark by the time I left the building to cross the parking lot. I was exhausted and fully intended to crawl straight into bed the moment I got home.

When my phone vibrated, I paused in the middle of the lot and pulled it from my back pocket. Every time my phone rang, some piece of me thought it might be Christina, and every time I was disappointed.

"Are you calling to tell me I did a great job combing the Good Neighbors website for relevant posts and you have nothing new to add?" I asked Ethan.

"Hello to you, too," he said. "And no, not exactly."

I groaned. "Fine, what did I miss?"

"It's not that you missed something. It's the user who posted the tribute to Hudson, the one who messaged you."

"What about them?"

"I was curious, as you were, about whether they might know your friend and her husband. And a neighborhood message board is a lot less secure than, say, a doorbell security camera company. Easier to get into via a back door."

"Ethan, I'm exhausted. You're going to need to come right out and tell me whatever it is you called to tell me."

He huffed a breath and then quickly said, "I hacked into Good Neighbors to see if I could find out who posted Hudson's tribute. Francisco is sunbum27."

42

Francisco was on Good Neighbors masquerading as a concerned neighbor who wanted to honor Hudson. The news shouldn't have struck me as hard as it did. I already knew Francisco was on Good Neighbors; if I knew he'd lied in order to create an account, why was it a surprise that he would then use that account to try to get information exactly like I was? Still, it rattled me.

When I got home, I ate a handful of dry cereal and then crawled into bed early as planned. By some miracle, I fell asleep almost immediately, but I wasn't spared from the vivid nightmares. This time, I was watching Christina chase Hudson with a shovel. I tried to stop her, but then she turned on me and, in a maneuver straight out of Scooby Doo, pulled her face off to reveal it was a mask and she was actually Francisco. For the rest of the dream, Francisco chased me while calling out, "I know the truth!"

When I woke before my alarm, I didn't even try to go back to sleep. My body felt marginally better than the day before, and it wasn't worth risking plunging myself back into that dream to try to get another hour's rest. Instead, I brewed the coffee extra strong.

A reminder on my phone notified me I could go boot-free today, two weeks since I'd jumped the fence into Christina's yard to replace Hudson's laptop in their home. I moved gingerly around the house, feeling it out. It twinged slightly when I flexed my foot, but otherwise felt no worse than my joints usually did, so I called that a win.

I was fully dressed and pouring myself a third cup of coffee before heading to work when there was a knock at the door. I immediately dismissed the idea that Ethan might show up at my house so early. It seemed early even for Detective Styles, and I wondered if that was part of her plan—if I was still half-asleep when she came to talk to me, maybe I'd slip up and tell her more than I meant to.

I crossed the room and pulled open the door, ready to tell her I wasn't answering any more of her questions. Instead, I found Francisco standing in the doorway wearing running clothes and an expression that was both nervous and hopeful.

"Sorry to come over so early, but I was heading out for a run and your light was on, and—" He looked down at the keys in my hand. "Did I catch you at a bad time?"

I hesitated. "No, come in."

Francisco followed me inside and paused in the mostly empty living room. He reached up and scratched the back of his neck, letting his fingers rake through his dark curls before dropping his hand. "No boot," he said, pointing to my foot.

"Nope," I said, picking up my foot and wiggling it back and forth. "I'm a free woman."

He smiled and cleared his throat. "I was hoping to talk with you about last week."

A flashback to his lips on my collarbone set my blood rushing, but the sting of his rebuff combined with the embarrassment that I had spent the previous day fishing for information from him while he was doing the same to me tamped down my desire.

"Look, I get it," I said in an attempt to avoid a conversation I really, really did not want to be having.

"You don't." He shook his head vehemently and crossed the room to lean against the plastic folding table, his hands gripping the table beside his hips. "I haven't stopped thinking about you for five days, Mandy, and I haven't stopped kicking myself, either. I like you. I like spending time with you. I think you're funny. You're clearly smart, and you're brave, and my god you are hot."

I swallowed loudly and took a gulp of coffee. Francisco took a step toward me, and for a moment I thought he was going to grab my hips and pull me to him, but he stopped short.

"You are beyond sexy, and I don't know if I've ever wanted anyone as much as I wanted you last week. As much as I've wanted you every time I let myself think about that night."

My throat constricted and my skin burned, and I squirmed at the glowing warmth pooling beneath the waistband of my pants. I wanted to take that single step forward to put my body against his, but I also wanted to pull back and put as much space between us as possible. I wanted to keep myself safe. So I stood still while he kept talking.

"I haven't dated in a while. Years. And the last person I was with... I thought I could trust her, and I couldn't. It wrecked me."

Detective Styles. She'd betrayed him by stealing his journalistic sources and using them to put his brother and a slew of other doctors behind bars, earning herself a promotion for it.

"And now," Francisco continued, "I'm elbows-deep in this investigation into people who are anything but trustworthy, and it has me seeing the world through a cynical lens."

"I understand," I choked out, but Francisco was shaking his head and stepping forward, wrapping his arms around my waist. I held my coffee cup with two hands, clutched to my chest to keep some space between our bodies.

"I don't want to look at you through that lens. I don't want to go around looking for the worst in people, waiting to catch them in a lie and expecting to find skeletons in every closet." His dark brown eyes searched mine, pleading. "I want to just let things be good. Let people be good."

I couldn't find the words for a response, and then his mouth was on mine and I couldn't speak even if I had the words. The kiss was deep but sweet, without the desperate intensity of last week. When he pulled away, it felt like the promise of more, and any truths I wanted to tell him died on my tongue.

Francisco released his hold on my waist. "I'll let you get to work, but would you like to come over for dinner again sometime?"

I took a dizzy half-step back and nodded, internally screaming at myself. I was no better than Styles; I'd followed him and lied to him and tried to use him for information. And, for all his talk about not being able to trust anyone, Francisco clearly wasn't above lying and using others for information, either. It was a bad idea and I knew it, but my cheesy grin only spread wider as I bobbed my head.

Francisco gave me one more brief kiss, then turned and opened the door. Before he could step over the threshold, he was stopped in his tracks by the person blocking the way, fist raised as if about to knock.

"Mandy Perkins," Detective Styles said as her eyes skipped between us. "Got a minute to talk?"

"About what?" Francisco challenged, stepping sideways to position himself between Detective Styles and me.

"About the d—" she started, but I hastily shoved him out of the way and said, "It's fine."

Francisco looked at me in surprise, but I turned to Styles and said, "Yes, I've got time. Just give us one minute."

With one more assessing look, Styles agreed and retreated from the stoop, leaving me to look back at Francisco's now-furious face.

"You don't have to talk to the police," he said. "In fact, you shouldn't. What's this about, anyway? If your ex is still using the police to harass you, you should—"

"It's fine," I interrupted. "I know I don't have to talk to her, but I'm going to see what she wants. I'm sure it's just Dave. I'll explain the situation again, and if it keeps happening, I'll look into what I can do."

Francisco glowered toward where Styles waited on my front path. He let out a huff, then grabbed my hand and gave it a quick squeeze before shooting Styles an icy look and turning back toward his own house.

"Do you want to come in?" I asked, much preferring to have this conversation—which I knew was *not* going to be about Dave—outside the range of other listening ears.

Styles cast one last look over her shoulder toward where Francisco had disappeared, then stepped inside. Just as she did last time I'd let her into my home, she spun in a slow circle, eyes narrowed as she scrutinized her surroundings.

Turning to me, she started, "I'm here to talk with you about—"

"The Schupperts," I interrupted. "We've been through this before."

Styles drew in a deep breath through her nose as if to calm herself. I forced myself to take a sip of coffee and tried hard to continue projecting an air of being unconcerned. Frowning at me, Styles asked, "How'd you like Heaven on Earth last weekend?"

I choked on my coffee, and she smirked at me.

"Why were you there?" she asked. I didn't say anything, but she didn't seem deterred. "I'm wondering if your friend, like me, saw the charges on their bank statements that showed Hudson Schuppert spent quite a lot of time at that club. Did she tell you that?"

"No," I answered truthfully.

"Interesting. Did she tell you she was withdrawing a huge pile of cash from their bank account on the day she and Hudson disappeared?"

My hand trembled, and I had to set my mug down. No, Christina had certainly not told me she was pulling cash out of the bank. She hadn't told me anything besides "We need to bury this chest *now*."

"When was the last time you heard from Christina?" Styles had asked me this before. I'd only told her I'd talked with Christina on the phone on that Friday, the day she'd apparently made preparations to disappear without telling me.

"Do you think she's still alive?" I asked. "If you think I might have heard from her, that must mean you don't think she's dead."

"Do *you* have reason to believe Christina is dead?" Styles challenged.

"Hudson's body was found in the desert almost a week ago. When both members of a couple go missing, and then one of their bodies turns up..." I trailed off, implying that I expected Christina's to be in the desert, too, waiting to be dug up by another unsuspecting hiker's dog.

"If Christina were to leave town, can you think of anyplace she would go?"

"You think she's alive and on the run?" I asked again.

"Her family is in Charlotte, correct?"

Finally, a question I could answer with no trouble. "She hasn't been close to her family in years. Her parents divorced when she was a kid. Her dad was pretty much absent, and she hated her stepdad. It basically destroyed her relationship with her mom, and once she left for college she never went back. If Christina's alive, she's not with her family."

"To your knowledge, has Christina ever gone by any other name? Used another name for her art, for example?"

I scrunched my face. "No. You think she's alive and going by a fake name?"

Styles raised an eyebrow and took a step toward the door before turning back around. "I think you know more than you're telling me. I think that if you really thought your friend was dead in the desert with her husband, you wouldn't be shacking up with the neighbor like everything was hunky-dory."

I flinched at the jab.

"I'll tell you what else I think. I think your friend killed her husband. I think she tried to bury his body in the backyard, possibly with your help, and when that didn't go to plan she dumped his body in the desert as Plan B. I think you're keeping her secrets now so she can get away with it, and I think I'm going to find enough evidence to prove it."

My blood chilled at the threat. I hoped like hell she wasn't right, that Christina was still the person I knew and loved and not a killer. Hudson was never in that chest buried in the yard, and Christina hadn't been the one to put him in the desert. That *had* to be true. It had to be.

Styles started to leave, then pulled out a notebook and said, "Why are you working for the Board of Supervisors?"

"What?" I asked, trying to keep up with the change in direction. She didn't repeat herself, content to wait through the uncomfortable silence, and I eventually answered, "Um, I saw a job opening. I needed work and they hired me fast."

She pursed her lips and lowered her brows. "And why did you leave when I arrived to question everyone last Friday?"

I drew myself up straight and said, with as steady a voice as I could manage, "You're all over the place. You've come here asking all about Cory Clemens. Then you show up and accuse me of helping my friend get away with murder. Now you want to know about my job. You've got nothing."

"Heaven forbid a detective consider all possible suspects and motives," Styles said sarcastically. She pulled the door open and, on her way out, said, "Enjoy your fun with Francisco while your best friend is 'missing.' With all your secrets, you two deserve each other."

43

When Detective Styles left, my hands were shaking so hard I couldn't hold my coffee mug steady. I'd known she suspected me of involvement in the Schupperts' disappearance, and I'd known she had questions about Christina and had seen the filled-in hole in the Schupperts' yard. Still, it unsettled me deeply to hear her come straight out and say she thought Christina killed Hudson and I helped her do it.

I called Ethan on the way to work.

"Do you know what time it is?" he answered on the fifth ring, his voice thick with sleep.

"Styles just came to pay me another visit."

"Styles?"

"The cop," I snapped.

"Oh." In the background I heard a pop top opening.

I groaned, "She literally told me she thinks I helped Christina cover up the murder of her husband."

"Well, you didn't, so at least there's that."

"What good is that if a police officer is dead set on putting us behind bars?" I cried.

"Presumably, your friend could use some of her money to hire a good lawyer for you two."

My free hand came off the steering wheel to gesture madly in the air. "I don't want to need a lawyer! I don't want to be in this situation at all!"

Ethan was quiet on the other end, the only sound a shuffling as he moved around his apartment.

"If I can prove someone else killed Hudson—if I can figure out what happened—Styles can't arrest Christina and me for it, can she?"

"Do you want a lesson on wrongful convictions or do you want me to hype you up?"

I ignored his comment. "They're looking for her, Ethan. They were asking me about her family and any other names she might be using."

"That's not really news, though, is it? The cop's been asking you about Christina for a while."

"This feels different," I said, my stomach churning. Sitting in the parking lot of the administration building, I watched people get out of their cars and shuffle inside to work. "She's been asking about Christina, but now it feels like they're going after her for real."

"That could be good though," Ethan said, and I wished we were on a video call so I could level him with a glare.

"How exactly could it be *good* that the cops are dedicating resources to chasing down my friend to try to put her—and probably me, too—behind bars?"

"We figure out who killed her husband and we let the cops do the work of finding her. They've got people and money and experience, and it takes half our work off our plate. As long as we can prove she's innocent when your cop finds her, we're golden. Probably."

Ethan hung up abruptly, but his words lingered. Could Styles turning her resources to finding Christina be a good thing? I wasn't so sure.

The week passed slowly, creeping toward Saturday and the neighborhood cookout. I needed to get close to Maureen's cameras to pass Ethan the information he'd need to work his technology magic and steal their footage. He'd seen the cameras at night; my job was to take surreptitious photos of them during daylight.

"Not every brand does fake stone owls," he'd said when we went over the plan. "But was that garden ornament an owl or an eagle? Was that rock more of a dome shape or flat? I need you to get me some clear pictures in the daytime so I can figure out what security company we're dealing with."

I'd wanted to go sooner instead of waiting for the cookout, but Ethan had been adamant I wait. It wouldn't help our investigation if I got arrested for trespassing or harassment or whatever else they might charge me with if Maureen caught me. The cookout would provide some cover, and it would be an opportunity to feel out the other neighbors. That is, unless Francisco showed up.

I'd considered messaging him on Good Neighbors to see if he was planning to attend but didn't. I kept my eyes peeled for his blue Corolla as I entered Christina's neighborhood. Signs with balloons tied to their stakes were planted at the edges of the yards, pointing people in the direction of the cookout. The HOA-owned park butted up against Christina's street on the east side and spanned three blocks. Not wanting to draw attention with my car's squealing belts and dilapidated appearance, I parked several blocks away and walked toward the cookout.

My brain was firing off reasons this was a bad idea. What if Maureen recognized me? How was I going to explain my presence since I didn't know anyone there? But my legs carried me forward, and as I stepped into the park, I tried to remember to keep my shoulders back and chin up and act like I belonged there.

"Congrats," I said, waving at a girl with long blond curls hanging down from beneath her mortarboard. I strolled over to one of the coolers full of beer and soda and grabbed a seltzer out of the ice. I popped the tab and took a sip. No one pointed and shouted that I was a snooping interloper and told me to leave.

"Hard to believe it's summer," I said when a nearby group broke up, leaving one woman alone. She gave me a polite smile and a small nod. "Do you have a kid graduating this year?"

Eyes still wary, she nodded and pointed to where three boys in gowns were throwing cheese puffs for each other to catch in their mouths. "You?" she asked.

I shook my head. "I'm a friend of Maureen's." The lie just fell out, and I was almost proud of how smooth it sounded. "She invited me. 'The more the merrier.'"

The woman's eyes narrowed, but the wariness had faded and her mouth was pulling back into a smirk. "That doesn't sound like Maureen."

In a conspiratorial tone, I said, "I was as surprised as anyone. I get the sense she's trying to be…" I trailed off, searching for a way to broach Maureen's obvious distrust of her neighbors.

"Less of a bitch?" the woman asked, laughing.

"More friendly," I said.

"She's got some work to do." The woman sipped her can of white wine.

This was my chance; I could feel it. "I think what happened with your neighbors might have something to do with it." I cast a sidelong glance to gauge her reaction and kept going. "Maybe it made her think about how everything can change on a dime. She's right across the street from them. For something like that to happen so close to her home, and in such a safe neighborhood…"

"It's horrible," the woman agreed, although her eyes danced with an eagerness to gossip about it and she leaned in ever so slightly closer to me.

"Maybe not entirely surprising, though." I watched her expression carefully as I said, "Not surprising that it was *them*, I mean. From what Maureen's told me, it sounds like that couple had been, well… Maybe we shouldn't gossip."

"Maureen's been mad since they moved here," the woman said. "She's your friend, so I don't want to talk badly about her, but there were all sorts of rumors that she was having an affair with the man who lived in that house before. People said his wife found out and that's why they moved. Maureen was bound to hate anyone who moved into that house just because they weren't him, but she was truly furious at all the traffic from that woman's art classes. She tried to get them shut down, saying it was against the bylaws to run a business out of your home, but the HOA had actually voted to remove that bylaw just last year. One of the board members' wives wanted to sell sourdough out of her house or something. Maureen was *furious*."

"She told me about that," I lied. I took one step closer and said, "But it wasn't just the art classes, right?" When I'd turned up on Maureen's doorstep after following Francisco, she'd seemed certain that the person in her neighborhood most likely to be the subject of a journalistic investigation was Christina. Running art classes out of her home didn't seem like enough to warrant that sort of attention, no matter how much traffic it brought to the neighborhood.

The woman rolled her eyes. "Maureen was convinced the wife was doing more than just teaching art classes. She tried telling the neighborhood she was selling drugs, but everyone pretty much wrote her off."

"Drugs?" I whispered.

The woman shrugged dismissively. "She said she saw some man come over late a handful of times. Apparently when he left, the wife—Christine?—handed him cash."

"That sounds more like an affair to me." The words felt sour on my tongue. Even if Christina had been having an affair, I didn't want to gossip about it with her neighbors. But I needed to get every bit of information I could. Anything could end up being the clue that would lead me to Christina.

The woman shrugged again and took another sip of her drink, and I could tell with a sinking heart that this line of conversation was over. Her attention turned to where her son and his friends had moved from tossing cheese balls to catch in their mouths to seeing who could fit the most in their mouths, and I strolled along the edge of the park, making my way toward Christina's street.

I lingered at the end of the street, trying to look casual as I surveyed the area. There were a few people walking up the street toward the park to join the party, but there was no Maureen. I started down the street toward her house, eyes fixed on her yard as I searched for any sign of hidden cameras. Ethan had mentioned a stone lawn ornament of an owl. As I got closer, I saw the decoration he was talking about, but it didn't look suspicious at all to me. I squinted, trying to guess where the camera could possibly be hidden, and pulled my phone out of my pocket to take pictures.

I zoomed in and snapped several photos, unsure of what area on the stone ornament I should focus on. I turned my attention to the landscaping rocks that stood artfully in several areas of the yard. Were all of these fake? With no clue what I was looking for, I decided to take pictures of all of them. I was zooming in on one when the squeal of tires startled me, and I looked up to see a red sports car hurtling toward me.

The car came to an abrupt stop just in front of Maureen's house, and I shoved my phone back into my pocket and started walking, trying not to look suspicious. I kept my head down, but my skin prickled with recognition as the car's engine turned off and the driver's door opened. With a gasp, I turned to confirm my suspicions. I looked just in time to see Francisco's ginger-haired friend Eric climb out and shuffle toward Maureen's front door.

44

My mouth opened involuntarily as I watched Eric jog up the path. Maureen's door opened before he knocked, and I only realized I was still rooted to the sidewalk staring openmouthed at the door when Maureen's figure filled the doorway, her Chihuahua in her arms.

"What are you doing here?" she hissed.

I turned around and took several hurried steps away, desperate to listen but even more desperate to avoid being recognized.

"Relax," Eric said. He used the unbothered voice Dave used to use when I was melting down over something going wrong in my lab, and I felt a visceral rage spread up my body. "No one followed me. No one knows who you are."

The slam of a door punctuated his remark, and I turned to see Maureen's stark white door closed, Maureen and Eric inside. I crept back toward the house. My eyes roved over the exterior, searching for open windows or any other way I might hear what Eric and Maureen were discussing. *No one knows who you are.* What did that mean?

Ethan's story about his failed surveillance job for a drug kingpin came back to my mind, and I wondered if all Maureen's protestations against Christina were projection, her attempt to throw her neighbors' scents off so they didn't look too hard at Maureen herself.

The hedges between Maureen's and her neighbors' houses

stood roughly four feet tall, and I crouched behind one, trying to tuck myself away so that a tree in the neighbor's yard obscured me from view from that direction. I squinted, trying to peer through the hedge, but it was too dense, and I had to raise my head and look over the top to see anything. My thighs burned as I scanned the house.

Every window was shut tight with curtains blocking the view into the home. I edged my way along the hedge. I needed to get a view of the back of the house. I tipped my head back and scanned the soffit, checking for any other cameras that might capture me creeping along the edge of Maureen's property. If there were any, they were hidden well enough that I couldn't make them out.

When I reached the edge of the privacy hedge and couldn't go any further without climbing a fence, I pulled out my phone to text Ethan.

Mandy: Francisco's friend is here!! He knows Maureen!
Ethan: What friend?

I muttered a curse.

Mandy: The one who broke into his car!! The one who stole the footage Maureen gave him!

Francisco's friend stealing from him didn't make any sense, but if Eric knew Maureen, I wondered if he was stealing it back for her. If she gave Francisco her doorbell camera footage, she looked cooperative, but then she got Eric to steal it back so no one actually watched it.

Ethan: Get his plates.

My thighs burned and sweat broke out along my forehead as I tried to stay crouched while moving back toward the street and Eric's car. I squatted down at the end, resting on my heels, and zoomed in as far as my phone camera would go.

"Hey!"

The shout startled me, and I jumped and dropped my phone

into the grass. I shot up from my crouch, an involuntary cry loosing itself as pain seared through my knees.

"What are you doing in my yard?"

I whirled to find the source of the voice and saw a man leaning out of the front door of the house next to Maureen's. I opened my mouth to respond but couldn't come up with any reasonable explanation. My eyes darted from the man back to Maureen's house and then up the road toward the park, and when they landed on a figure walking with a familiar gait, I found myself backing up until the branches of the hedge poked me through my clothes.

Francisco was here.

I grabbed my phone from the grass, then turned and ran.

"You ran?" Ariel asked me with a skeptical look.

I'd left Christina's neighborhood as quickly as possible, hoping like hell that Francisco hadn't seen my car when he'd arrived and that he didn't happen to look down that particular street just as I was frantically running in the opposite direction.

When I'd returned home, I'd been surprised to find both Ethan and Ariel on my front stoop.

"Ethan told me you were spying on a lady," Ariel had said, eyes wide in amazement.

"I wasn't spying," I responded. "What are you doing here?"

"I was in the neighborhood and I wanted to see if you got anything useful," Ethan had said.

"And I'm bored," Ariel had added.

They had both followed me inside without waiting for an invitation and now looked at me doubtfully as I finished telling them about the cookout.

"You don't run," Ethan said, and Ariel nodded emphatically.

"Yes, I ran. Since *you* made me wait until the cookout to go check out Maureen's"—I stabbed my finger in Ethan's direction—"instead of going earlier in the week like I wanted, there were people everywhere."

"Did Francisco see you?" Ethan crossed the room and opened my fridge, peering inside instead of looking at me.

Ariel asked, "Is Francisco your boyfriend?"

"No," I said to Ariel, "and no," I said to Ethan, snapping the fridge shut and putting myself between him and the appliance. "At least, I don't think so. I had my back turned during the running part."

"Well, you need to find out if he saw you," Ethan said, frowning as I preemptively blocked him from the pantry.

"What I need to find out," I said, herding him back toward the living room, "is what his friend is up to with Maureen."

"Did you get his license plate?"

I winced and pulled out my phone. I'd snapped a photo just as the neighbor startled me, but instead of capturing the license plates, I'd captured a blurry image of the grass.

With a sigh, Ethan scrolled through the rest of my pictures. He paused on some of them, zooming in to look at specific parts of the rocks I'd photographed.

"Why did you take a bunch of pictures of rocks?" Ariel asked, peering over his shoulder with her face scrunched up.

"They're hidden cameras," Ethan said, and her reservations disappeared.

"Really?" she gushed.

"Can you tell what security company they're from?" I asked.

"How can you tell they're cameras?" Ariel leaned in closer, squinting at the screen.

Ethan pointed out the features he said gave it away, zooming in and pointing to the screen, but I interrupted.

"Do you know what company?"

Ariel turned her disgruntled face on me, but Ethan didn't even look my way as he said gravely, "Spiderfang Security. They won't be easy to break into."

"Break in?" Ariel asked.

Ethan clarified, "Hack. I'm not physically breaking into anyplace."

"I want to learn to hack!" she said with enthusiasm.

I shook my head and said, "Absolutely not," and at the same time Ethan said, "Hell yeah, kid!"

"No," I repeated.

Ethan and Ariel looked at each other conspiratorially, and I yanked my phone from Ethan's hand and gave them both a stern look. When I'd taught my first class, I'd spent an hour in the mirror perfecting the look. The first time I'd leveled it on students, they'd laughed at me. Neither Ariel nor Ethan looked particularly chastened, but they didn't laugh at me either, so I considered it a win.

"What if you *did* break in?" I asked Ethan. "Instead of trying to hack into an impenetrable fortress, what if you follow Francisco's friend and then break into his apartment when he's out? You can steal back the flash drive with the footage Maureen gave Francisco."

"I don't break into people's houses, Mandy," Ethan said.

"Well, I'm paying you a lot of money, Ethan."

"It's risky and messy. Spiderfang may be a fortress, but I'm up for the challenge. I'll get into their systems and—"

"There might not be anything on their systems anymore!" I interrupted. "What if Maureen deleted it all? Once a journalist came around, maybe she deleted everything just to make sure no one actually saw it. If she got Eric to steal back the flash drive, maybe she wiped everything out at the source, too."

"And Eric might have brought the flash drive back to her

place instead of keeping it for himself, or he might have deleted the footage off the flash drive. There's no guarantee either way."

Maureen had posted the screenshot to Good Neighbors days after she gave the drive to Francisco and then lied to me that she'd deleted it and couldn't make any more copies. In all likelihood, Ethan was right and the footage from her cameras did still reside on Spiderfang's servers. But after my afternoon hiding in the bushes and then running from Francisco, my knees and ankles were swelling up and I was tired of doing what Ethan told me to.

I crossed my arms over my chest. "I'm paying you, so I'm calling the shots. Do your stalker thing and follow Eric. Get into his house. Find that flash drive."

45

When Ethan left my house, Ariel stalked out after him, turning her sullen face on me before slamming the door in their wake. For the entire next day, I contemplated texting Ethan to tell him I'd changed my mind, but I stopped myself every time. I'd listened to Ethan when he told me to get into Heaven on Earth to find out more about Diamond, and that led to me almost being thrown out on my ass by a man named Snake. I listened to him and waited until the cookout to go check out Maureen's cameras and then had to run for my life to avoid being spotted by Francisco. For once, I wanted him to do things my way.

From my desk at work on Monday, I texted him asking for an update.

Ethan: Outside his place.

I swallowed my guilt when I read the terse reply. This was the logical way of doing things, I reminded myself. So much more efficient than spinning our wheels trying to get the footage off Spiderfang's servers.

And while Ethan was staking out his home, I considered other ways to find out what Eric was up to. Why did Francisco's friend steal his bag out of his car? Did it all come back to Maureen? Had she put him up to it so she could appear helpful without actually giving a journalist anything useful? Or did Eric have his own reasons for wanting to keep Francisco from finding out what Maureen's cameras might show?

Mandy: Do you have plans tonight?

I fired the message off to Francisco before I could stop myself. The play-it-safe Mandy inside me was yelling at me to cancel immediately and keep my distance. Francisco was tenacious, and he wouldn't stop digging into Hudson's case for his article. If he found out I knew Christina and had been lying to him about my connection to the Schupperts this whole time, he'd be crushed, and until I had proof that whatever Christina and I had buried was not Hudson's body, I didn't want anyone looking too closely at me.

Despite all that, my cheeks flushed, and I fought the reflexive smile that spread across my face when he replied.

Francisco: dinner with my hot neighbor, if I'm lucky

I tried to remind myself that I was on an information-gathering mission. I was there to find out what I could about his friend. Francisco, for all his talk about wanting to be able to trust other people, was not trustworthy. I needed to stay guarded.

No matter how much I told myself that, I still found my mind drifting throughout the day, daydreaming about Francisco's lips and wondering if he might kiss me again.

I pulled myself out of the daydreams for long enough to write a memo for Supervisor Washington that earned me the almost imperceptible chin bob that signified she was impressed. As distracted as I'd been lately, I'd worried my quality at work was slipping, and though I now had my sights elsewhere, I didn't want to lose the proximity to Clemens, nor could I afford to lose the income.

Ethan: He's leaving. Going in.

The text from Ethan came shortly after I'd scarfed down a peanut butter sandwich at my desk, and it buoyed me for the rest of the day. I was going to have dinner with my hot neighbor who called me his hot neighbor, and Ethan was going to get

Francisco's flash drive back from Eric's place. Everything was going my way.

Everything went my way until I'd left with the other administrative assistants and waved goodbye in the parking lot, at which point my phone rang with a call from an unknown number. I answered, expecting spam but hoping it was Christina from a new number.

A robotic voice came over the line. "This is a collect call from an inmate at the Pima County Adult Detention Complex. To accept this call, press one."

My heart sank, and I scrambled to press the button. Had Styles found Christina already? If she had, I had nothing that could help, and it was only a matter of time before she came for me, too.

"Mandy?"

"Ethan?"

"I, uh, need you to come get me from the jail."

I cranked the ignition. "Why are you at the jail? Is Christina with you?"

Ethan huffed a frustrated sigh. "No, Mandy. I got arrested. I need you to talk to a bondsman and come get me out."

As my brain caught up with the facts, guilt drained the air from my lungs. "Is this because you broke—"

"Stop!" Ethan cut me off forcefully, then in a lower voice said, "This call is being recorded. Just come and get me, please."

Ethan gave me the name of a bond company and told me the bail amount that had been set, and I balked.

"Twenty-five thousand dollars? Ethan, I don't have that kind of money!"

"That's the point of the bond company. They pay it. You'll need to pay them ten percent, and I'll pay you back, but—"

I interrupted him again. "Ethan, I don't have two thousand

dollars. I don't even know if I have two *hundred* dollars. I can't pay that!"

Ethan cursed, then went silent for so long that I thought the call had disconnected. Finally, he said, "I'll call someone else for the bail, but will you still come pick me up?"

I dashed off a text to Francisco cancelling dinner. When I arrived at the jail, Ethan was standing out front, rubbing the back of his neck and talking to a heavily tattooed man with a shaved head.

"Seriously, thank you," he was saying as I approached. "I'll pay you back by Friday."

The other man said nothing, only tipped his chin back in a sort of reverse nod of acknowledgement. When he turned to walk away from Ethan, his face became visible and I recoiled automatically. A giant tattoo of a spider filled his entire neck. He gave me the same upward nod, and I forced my mouth into a tight smile.

"Thanks for coming," Ethan said, sidling up next to me.

"Who is that guy?" I whispered to him.

With a shrug, Ethan just said, "A colleague."

"He posted your bail?"

Ethan nodded.

"So, what happened?" I asked when we were safely ensconced in my car, outside the listening ears of anyone else at the jail.

"I waited until your guy left his place, then let myself in. I was only inside for maybe five minutes when sirens started up outside."

My head fell back against the headrest. I'd insisted on Ethan breaking into Eric's place, and it had landed him in jail before he'd even had time to look around.

"I did find this, though," he said, and I looked over to see him holding a flash drive between two fingers, wiggling it back and forth.

I reached out and grabbed it from him, then peered at it to see the worn writing spelling out Francisco's name in Sharpie on the side of the drive.

46

"Stop breathing into my ear," Ethan grumbled, and I took a step back from where I'd been looking over his shoulder as he slid the flash drive into the port on my laptop.

"What if it's a trap and it's filled with a bunch of viruses?"

He spun to face me. "Then your computer will be filled with viruses."

He returned to clicking around on my laptop, and I turned my focus toward breathing deeply and slowing my racing heart. After three weeks of wondering what was on that drive, I was about to find out. I wiped my sweaty palms down my thighs. I suddenly felt too hot. What were we about to see?

I wanted to see footage of Hudson leaving the house—proof he hadn't died there. Proof he hadn't been in that chest. And I wanted to see Christina leaving, too. Had she been alone?

And, of a whole different concern, I wanted to see if I appeared on the recording. Maureen's house was across the street and two doors down, and I wanted to know whether, if the police got their hands on this footage, they'd be able to recognize me arriving at the Schupperts' house the day Hudson disappeared—the day Styles said he'd died, though he wasn't discovered until weeks later—and leaving covered in dirt. Would they recognize me letting myself in two days later and emerging with Hudson's laptop? I kicked myself again for how stupid I'd been.

"Here we go," Ethan said, then double-clicked the mouse. A video player opened, and the video started playing.

The recording started with a video of an Amazon driver leaving a package at Maureen's doorstep. The timestamp in the bottom right corroborated Maureen's story that she'd given Francisco footage from the last month.

"Doorbell cameras only record when motion activates them, and then they record for a minute or two and stop," Ethan said. "You'll only be able to see what's going on over at your friend's house during the moments when there was movement at Maureen's."

I frowned and leaned in close to the screen. Only a sliver of Christina's house was visible—just the garage and half of the front door. The other two-thirds of their house and front yard were entirely out of frame.

"Wishing you'd agreed to let me hack into Spiderfang instead?" Ethan taunted. "Whatever camera she pulled that screenshot of the men with the chest from is going to have way more information than this will."

I groaned and jerked the laptop toward myself, turning my side to box out Ethan. He sat there while I watched the footage progress, jumping from clip to clip. They showed package deliveries, Maureen's car pulling in and out of the driveway, and Maureen tending to her garden in the front. Occasionally, a coyote or other animal ran through the yard and activated the camera.

In every clip, I looked to see what was going on at the Schupperts', but there was nothing.

The only video clips where there wasn't obvious activity in Maureen's yard triggering the motion-activated camera were a few night clips. At a certain angle, a car's headlights could trigger it, and the camera would capture the bright lights of the car driving up the road toward Maureen's house.

Ethan pulled out his phone while I continued to scrutinize the footage, clinging to the hope that in one of these clips, something would happen in the background that made everything else make sense.

The timestamps in the corner progressed, closer and closer to the date of Hudson's disappearance. Twice, car headlights triggered the camera and it turned out to be Hudson's car pulling into his garage late at night. I wondered if he was returning from Heaven on Earth and winced.

I held my breath when the first clip from that Friday started up. It was Maureen who triggered it, crossing her lawn to tend to her flowers, although when I looked closer I realized she was inspecting her stone owl. After giving it a good look, she rotated it slightly, turning it so its face pointed directly at the Schupperts' house. In the background, just before the clip ended, the Schupperts' garage opened and both cars pulled out.

I jumped up, the chair scraping the tile floor beneath me, and Ethan looked to see what had triggered that reaction.

"It's not really anything," I said. "But Hudson and Christina both left the house that Friday morning."

The garage door closed behind them, and Hudson and Christina drove off. There was another clip of a package delivery, and then nothing until my own headlights triggered the camera that night.

"Fuck," I muttered, and Ethan looked over to see what was the matter. "I'm on this."

He squinted at where I'd paused the video. "Not recognizably," he said. "No one would know that was you."

He was probably right, but I couldn't help but picture myself in a courtroom under oath, Detective Styles producing a blown-up still from the footage in order to convince a jury that I'd helped a murderer bury her husband.

We watched the clip together as my car stopped right in the camera's field of view and I ran across the street to the front door. My face never turned to the camera, and as soon as I crossed the threshold I was out of view of the camera, but that didn't stop my stomach from churning with the fear that this could somehow be my undoing.

The next clip was another recording triggered by headlights, showing another car speed past me before my car passed right through the video frame. I flinched at the memory of the brilliant lights flicking on, blinding me just as I'd been about to leave Christina's after burying the chest.

"Was that you?" I cried, pointing at the blurry white vehicle where I'd paused the video.

Ethan nodded, not an ounce of contrition on his face. I thanked my lucky stars he'd been staking us out on behalf of my ex and not on behalf of whoever was after Christina. I let out a long sigh and pressed "play" again.

The video jumped to another night clip, the timestamp showing it was that same night, or rather the early hours of the next morning. I had to rewind the video and rewatch it to confirm.

"That's Christina leaving," I breathed. Ethan looked up to where I'd paused it again, Christina's SUV clearly visible.

"Her car, at least," he said, and I zoomed in. He was right that the driver was entirely unrecognizable, but I knew it was her. I'd helped her bury the chest, and then she'd run barely an hour after I'd left.

The next video clips were innocuous, neighbors with their dogs or the mail carrier, and it was hard for me to watch life in the neighborhood go on like normal when I knew I'd just seen my friend drive away before disappearing entirely.

"So they both left that morning," I said, stopping the recording, "and then Christina calls me that afternoon to come over. Then I go over after dark and bury the chest, and then she leaves almost immediately after."

I shut my eyes, closing out all distractions to let my mind

wander, hoping it might connect some dots. "What if," I began, keeping my eyes closed to avoid the skeptical look I knew Ethan would give me, "Hudson never came home that day? What if he never made it home from the partner meeting?"

Ethan frowned at me, but I barreled forward.

"Everyone saw him at the firm that morning, but no one has come forward saying they saw him after that. Ethan, what if he never came back?"

With a sigh, he said, "His car is there, Mandy. I saw it when I went to look around."

My heart sank. He was right.

I resumed the video. When a coyote ran through the yard during a clip timestamped from the following night, I paused it. This was the clip Maureen had taken the screenshot from to post on Good Neighbors. The coyote paused, turning his head one way and then the other, and in the background two men walked toward a big, black SUV with a large chest between them. The clip ended before they loaded the chest into the vehicle, but I still felt a twinge of excitement.

"They were barely struggling with that chest," I said. "Like it weighed nothing. It's big, sure, but if it was heavy they would have been waddling or something. There's no way there was a body in that thing."

I resumed the video, desperate for another clue, but there was nothing. When the timestamps approached the morning I'd gone back and taken Hudson's laptop and agenda, I leaned in and watched closely, but there weren't any clips capturing me then. There was no evidence on the recording that I'd ever gone back.

Unfortunately, there was also no evidence on the recording that anyone else had visited the Schupperts' house—no alternative suspects exonerating Christina.

I leaned back, letting my head hang back and staring up at the ceiling while the last few seconds of the video played.

"Who's that?" Ethan asked.

On the screen, another night clip was playing, triggered again by headlights entering the frame. I waited for the car to drive past like in most of the other clips, but I gasped when the Schupperts' garage door opened and Christina's car pulled in.

47

"That's her!" I shouted, pointing at the screen.

Ethan leaned in, his head blocking the screen, and I shoved him out of the way so I could see.

"Her car, at least," I said, heading off Ethan's rebuttal before he had the chance to make it.

It was undeniably Christina's SUV heading up the road and turning in to her garage. The garage door closed, and then the footage skipped to a clip from the next morning, the day Francisco and I had paid Maureen a visit and she'd given him this footage. I rewound and watched Christina pull into her driveway again and again. There was no recording of her leaving, but I chalked it up to the headlights not facing Maureen's house on her way out the way they did on her way in. I'd been back to her house to replace Hudson's laptop, and Ethan had been there even more recently. She definitely hadn't stuck around.

But she'd been back.

As if to make myself believe it, I whispered aloud, "She came back."

Ethan eyed me but didn't remind me that we didn't know it was her.

I recounted the timeline. "We know that both Hudson and Christina left the house Friday morning. We know she came back because I saw her. That night, she and I destroyed our bodies burying that god awful chest, and it was near dawn Saturday morning when I left. She left shortly after I did.

"Sometime between Friday morning and Sunday morning,

Hudson's car returns to the house. With or without him, we don't know. On Saturday night, two men came and dug up the chest, but without the footage from the rest of Maureen's cameras, we just have this grainy recording where we can hardly tell anything."

Ethan lifted a brow but didn't bring up Spiderfang again. The truth was that he was right—I never should have pushed him to break into Eric's place. Now he had an arrest on his record and all we had was this doorbell camera footage, when Maureen had other cameras pointing directly at the Schupperts' place running around the clock.

I shoved down my guilt and continued my timeline. "Then, Sunday night, Christina came back. Presumably, she saw my poor handiwork refilling the hole. She left...sometime. We don't know when. And then the next weekend is when she sent me that text. 'I'm safe. Don't look for me or the chest.'"

When Ethan still said nothing, I cleared my throat and forced out the question. "Do you, uh, still think you can get into Spiderfang?"

He broke into a smirk.

"I know I said—"

"Yes," he said, cutting me off. "I'll do it, but I'm tacking on an extra fee for getting me arrested."

———

THE NEXT MORNING, I looked toward Francisco's house on my way out the door and frowned. Before I pulled my car away from the curb, I sent him a text asking to reschedule the dinner I'd cancelled.

Francisco: how's tomorrow? everything all right?

I wanted to tell him everything, partially to avoid the guilt of keeping secrets from him when I knew he'd been hurt by that before, and partially for the relief that was sharing your problems with another person.

Mandy: All good. Will be a lot better tomorrow! ;)

I checked my phone impulsively all day but Francisco didn't respond, and when I finished compiling research on women's healthcare costs in Pima County for a memo I needed to give to Supervisor Washington the next day, I packed up and left the office before the other admins.

My phone buzzed in my back pocket while I was unlocking my front door, and I turned to look toward Francisco's again as I pulled it out. My face fell when it wasn't from Francisco, but Dave.

Dave: Mandy, I've been trying to give you space, but I'm going crazy here. Seriously. Please call me.

I swiped it away and filled a glass of wine to the rim, then downed half of it before digging through the freezer and pulling out a tray of enchiladas to pop in the oven.

By the time I'd finished my plate, I'd also finished the glass of wine and was working my way through a second. A roar outside made me jerk my head up, and I peered out the window to see a familiar red-haired man climb out of a red sports car.

Eric bounded toward Francisco's while I watched, open-mouthed. Francisco was his *friend*. Eric had broken into his friend's car and stolen his work, and now he could come around and act like nothing had happened?

I quietly seethed, and when I'd finished my wine, I found myself slipping out the front door and hurrying across the street toward Eric's car. I sank down onto the sidewalk and positioned myself low so he wouldn't see me. I tipped my head back and looked up at the sky, a deep orange streaked with blue and purple clouds, while a warm breeze indicating we'd tipped into summer brushed my skin.

I'd almost forgotten what I was there for until I was startled by Eric's "Whoa!"

I pushed myself up to face him.

"What are you doing here?"

I looked behind him at Francisco's house to see if his friend's shouts would cause a commotion. I could still play it off, pretend I'd just gotten tired on a walk and sat down and didn't mean to scare him. But when I didn't see Francisco or anyone else watching us, I turned back to Eric and met his gaze, channeling the anger I'd felt earlier. This was a man willing to hurt his friend, and I wanted to know why.

I held up Francisco's flash drive, waiting for Eric to recognize it. I could tell when he did by the way the color drained from his already pale face, turning it pure white.

"Recognize this?" I taunted.

"You—!"

I shook my head. "I didn't break into your house. But I do want to know what this was doing there."

Eric's mouth flapped open, but he just looked from me to the drive and back, unable to form a response.

I dug deep, channeling the energy of someone confident and in control, something I had rarely felt outside of a classroom.

"I saw you take this. And don't try to tell me it's yours. It's got his name on it, and like I said, I was there when you hopped out of that shiny red car of yours and took his whole messenger bag. What I want to know is why you did it."

Eric's color was returning in the form of a ruby red flush. He clenched his fists, and I swallowed, forcing myself to keep my spine straight in the face of his growing anger.

"Was it Maureen who put you up to it?"

At the mention of her name, Eric's eyes flew wide and his fists released, hands flying up toward his chest in a gesture of surrender. He shook his head wildly and opened his mouth again but still said nothing.

"I saw you together. And I know the camera that produced the footage on this flash drive is far from her only one. Why'd she give it to him if she was just going to have you go retrieve it for her?"

"She's got nothing to do with this."

Eric took a step toward me, and I lifted the drive up higher. I could feel my own cheeks draining of blood but didn't let my feet budge. He was close enough that he could reach out and snatch the drive from me if he wanted, but I wasn't going to back down.

"The best I can figure is that Maureen hated her neighbors. *Hated* them. There was gossip in the neighborhood about her affair with the man who lived there before him, and the wife's art classes were drawing traffic into the neighborhood. That's more people on her street who might find out what she was up to—what it was that was prompting her to deck her house out in drug kingpin levels of security cameras.

"So, what? She makes the neighbors go missing, then when a journalist comes around she hands over her doorbell camera footage to seem cooperative, then calls her trusty friend Eric to go steal it back so that journalist never actually gets to see what's on the recording?"

"That's not what happened!"

I raised an eyebrow at Eric in challenge. *Then tell me what happened*, I wanted to say.

"Are you two together? She's a bit old for you, but you never know what people are into." I wiggled my brows suggestively, and Eric scrunched his face in disgust. *Not lovers, then,* I thought.

With a gesture toward his still-wrinkled nose, I said, "Then why? The only other thing I can figure is that you're involved in whatever it is Maureen's trying to hide, and—"

"Stop saying her name," Eric said, his voice low and urgent. He took another step toward me, looking up and down the sidewalk. Instead of anger or disgust, fear dripped from his words, and I finally let myself take a step back so I could look at his face without having to crane my neck.

"I didn't take that because of M—" He shook his head. "I didn't do it for her." Eric looked behind him, then said even more quietly, "I did it to keep Francisco from moving forward with his article."

My brows came together and I frowned. "I don't understand."

Eric sighed deeply. "Francisco and I were in school together. He was always good. Like, top of the class good. Some people can be trained to be good, but Francisco just *was*. He had that seed of talent that can't be trained.

"When he dropped out, it was a shock. All of our classmates were devastated for him, but it also meant all the newspapers and magazines that had extended him job offers rescinded them. I only got my job because they took their offer back from Francisco."

Dread gathered in my stomach as Eric spoke. Ethan had already told me Francisco had dropped out after Styles had busted his brother based on Francisco's work-in-progress on addiction in doctors. I didn't realize what a rising star he'd been before that, though.

Eric broke my gaze and looked down at his feet. "He's been doing online classes to get his degree, and when he told me about the piece he's been working on… It's going to catapult him back into the spotlight. Journalism is dying and no employer has any budget, but they'd all be willing to ditch anyone in their employ in order to get Francisco."

"You'd destroy your own friend's career?" My shoulders sagged with disgust and disbelief.

Immediately defensive, Eric said, "Not destroy! He'll still get the piece finished. But when he told me he had a source in the neighborhood with security footage, I knew it had to be her. I couldn't let anything about her make its way into that article, and if it delays his piece and means I don't have to fight to keep my job quite yet, I can't deny that it feels like a bonus."

"But why did it matter if Maureen's footage"—Eric waved his arms at my mention of her name—"was mentioned in Francisco's article? She gave it to him herself."

Eric shook his hands by his side. "She has no idea how far his piece is going to go. He reached out and she looked him up and saw nothing but puff pieces. She figured it was perfectly safe to hand over her doorbell footage. But I've read some of it, and this article he's working on isn't some puff piece. It's going to be picked up and talked about nationally."

"It's not right." I shook my head firmly. "I'm going to Francisco's tomorrow night, and I'm going to plant this drive somewhere he'll find it. It's his, and he deserves to have it returned."

"No!"

Eric lunged at me and caught me off guard. His hand closed around mine, snatching the drive in one quick motion before we both tumbled to the ground.

"Argh!" I cried out, clutching my side.

Eric climbed off of me, looking behind him to see if anyone was watching us.

"Why?" I asked again.

Eric turned away, and I yelled out, "I'll tell him!" When he looked back to me I said, "You can take the drive, but I'll tell him everything you told me."

"Please," Eric begged, stepping back toward me. "Please don't. You don't understand. It's life and death."

I looked at him with disgust. "Losing a job is not life and death."

"Not me. *Her*."

"Mauree—?"

"Shh!" Eric extended a hand and pulled me up with one final look over his shoulder. He breathed out a sigh of resignation and then said, "She's my aunt."

I looked at him and tried to place any resemblance to Maureen but couldn't.

"When I was a kid, she was dating a cop back in—well, back where we're from. He was dirty and she turned him in, then testified against him at his trial. The boyfriend went to prison, but there were plenty of people in town who were angry at my aunt. The night after the boyfriend's sentencing, there was a drive-by shooting at her house. She and her brother—my dad—were watching TV. I was upstairs playing. She was hit in the arm. My dad... My dad was hit in the head."

Eric pursed his lips and paused. I wanted to tell him he didn't have to finish the story, but I couldn't bring myself to.

"I heard the noise and ran downstairs. My aunt was covered in blood but trying to help my dad. She yelled for me to call 911 and I did, but my dad was dead before the ambulance arrived."

"Eric, I'm so sorry."

"She ran. Changed her name, moved across the country. My mom and I moved, too. She wouldn't ever tell me what name my aunt had assumed or where she was living, but when I picked U of A for school she was against it. I didn't know why. She tried to forbid it, which of course just made me dig in harder. Finally, she told me that my aunt was here.

"My mom had a 'for emergencies only' number to call her, and she did. To our surprise, my aunt encouraged me to come to school here, and she welcomed the chance to get to know me as an adult. I've been careful never to say anything that could reveal her identity or raise the attention of anyone from back home."

With a pleading look he asked, "Do you see why I had to do what I did?"

I nodded.

The security cameras. Maureen's aversion to increased traffic in her quiet neighborhood and her hatred of Christina for bringing more people to their street with her art classes—more people that could recognize her and spoil her quiet, undercover life. It was all coming together.

"Please don't tell him," Eric said, and I nodded again.

"I won't, but I want the drive." I was on that footage, however unrecognizably, and I didn't want it floating around where anyone with access to Eric might get hold of it.

He started to object, but I said quickly, "It's a trade. My silence for that flash drive."

After another moment's hesitation, he dipped his chin and extended his hand to me. I seized the drive before he could change his mind, curling my fingers tight around it. I slid it into my pocket as Eric peeled off in his car, leaving me alone on the sidewalk with blood trickling from my skinned palms.

48

The alcohol stung as I cleaned my scrapes. The whole time I spent bandaging my hands, my mind was on Francisco. He'd lost so much—his brother, to drugs and then prison, and his parents to death. He'd been betrayed by a woman he loved and trusted, and now by a friend. And I'd deceived him, too.

When he pulled back his front door and his mouth opened in surprise, I was just as shocked as he was to find myself standing there, fist still raised from knocking.

"Is everything okay?" He looked me over with concern, eyes dropping from my face to the ripped elbow of my blouse to the dirt-smeared slacks and bandages on my palms.

"I need to talk to you."

I pushed inside and he spun to follow me. When I turned back to look at him, his face was drawn. His eyes still roved over me searching for injuries, and I wanted to make him stop, to tell him I didn't deserve his care. I wanted to tell him everything—how I knew the Schupperts and was looking for them, how I was trying to figure out what had happened to Hudson just like he was.

I couldn't, though. The words were blocked by a lump in my throat. He looked entirely vulnerable and open, and I couldn't bring myself to hurt him.

Instead, I let another secret tumble out.

"I'm sick."

Francisco took a step toward me and started to respond, but I shook my head and cut him off.

"I haven't told anyone. When I was in school, I started having problems with fatigue. I'd fall asleep at my desk. My hair was falling out. Dave thought the PhD program was just too much for me, that I couldn't hack it, and I believed him. I made it through, but things didn't get better when I got my professorship. I was exhausted all the time, and my whole body hurt. Every day I woke up as tired as I'd been when I fell asleep, and I felt like I'd been punched by a professional boxer all over.

"I went to the doctor. He told me to manage my stress. I started meditating. I went to another doctor, and she told me the same thing. It was the third doctor who gave me a referral to a rheumatologist, but the wait was seven months."

It wasn't until Francisco took another step to close the space between us and brushed his thumb over my cheek that I realized they were wet with tears.

"I wasn't just tired or incapable. I was sick. But I didn't tell Dave, and when it was time to submit my application for tenure, I looked around and realized I didn't want it. I didn't want that career, and I didn't want to be married to someone who made me think I was the problem. That's why I ran.

"I ran away from the life I didn't want, but it didn't take away my illness or magically bring me clarity, and I am avoiding reckoning with the fact that I have to actually decide what I *do* want in order to build that life. I can't just keep running away. But I don't want to think about that yet, and I didn't want to be alone right now, and—"

His lips were on mine before I'd even finished speaking. The hand that had been stroking my cheek moved to cup the back of my head, and the other one rose to my neck. Mine climbed his chest, clutching the front of his shirt. The cotton fabric bunched between my fingers as I pulled him closer.

Part of me still expected him to pull away, waiting for his rejection, but instead he slid one hand down my back, his fingers leaving a trail of goosebumps in their wake until they settled just above my hip. His fingertips brushed under the hem of my blouse, barely making contact with my bare skin and yet setting it ablaze.

I sucked in a gasp, pressing my body into his and forcing him to step backward until he rested against the wall. My hands dropped his shirt and rose to his hair, fingers twining in his curls as he reached beneath my top. He traced my back delicately, fingers almost hovering against the skin, and when I shivered and moaned into his lips, he grabbed at the flesh above my hips and tugged me closer so the whole of my body pressed against his and I could feel his desire matching mine.

Francisco's lips moved from my mouth to my neck, and I tipped my head back, breathing in jagged breaths. With my arms around his neck, he gripped my hips with both hands and lifted me so I cried out in surprise, spinning me around so I was the one with my back pressed against the wall. He lowered me so one foot was on the ground, but kept the other leg lifted, his hand hooked behind my knee, and pressed against me.

"Please," I whispered, my whole body shaking as he nipped at my neck.

He pulled back to look at me, his deep brown eyes molten.

I twisted my fingers into his hair again and brought his face so close to mine our lips brushed when I said, "I want this."

He crushed my lips with his again, tongue sweeping inside my mouth, and I arched my back off the wall.

"Hold on," he whispered into my ear, and the sensation of his breath made me moan again, my body quaking.

He lifted me, and I wrapped both legs around him. When he carried me into the bedroom and laid me down on his bed, he stared hungrily at me laid out beneath him. I reached for him to drag him down on top of me, but he hesitated.

"Mandy..."

"Please," I growled again, tugging harder at his shirt. I couldn't take it if he pulled away now. I couldn't handle another rejection.

He raised his t-shirt over his head, baring his chest, then swooped down over me, his mouth and hands and all of him taking me in the furthest thing from a rejection.

49

The rustling of papers roused me from sleep, and I blinked open my heavy eyelids to find Francisco smiling at me, bathed in the orange glow of his bedside lamp. His bare chest rose from the flannel sheets, and I raked my eyes over the planes of his muscles before looking up at his face and flushing.

I'd shown up uninvited and practically thrown myself at him. Shame clawed at me and made me wish I could teleport back to my own bed, but Francisco set the pages he'd been reading down on his nightstand and slid back beneath the sheets to pull me toward him.

"I'm glad you came over," he whispered, and goosebumps broke out again all over my body. At the sight of them, Francisco laughed, and his breath on my neck only intensified my reaction.

With one hand, he tipped my chin to bring my lips to his, and with the other he wrapped around my thigh and pulled my body flush with his.

I could feel him hard against my stomach, and my body moved closer of its own volition.

Francisco deepened the kiss, rolling onto his back and pulling me on top of him, but I made myself break away.

"I should sleep at my own place tonight," I said, though everything in me wanted to move closer and keep going.

Francisco frowned but nodded and glanced at the clock. "Probably the smart choice," he said when I rolled off of him and looked around for my clothes.

He ducked into the bathroom while I stepped into my slacks and grabbed my blouse from where it lay in a pile on the floor with his own clothes. I held it up under the bedside lamp, trying to determine whether the rip in the elbow was small enough that I could mend it or whether I'd need to buy a new one. As I turned it under the light, the papers Francisco had set aside caught my attention.

In the Superior Court of the State of Arizona in and for the County of Pima

Court transcripts. I leaned in, intrigued first by the unfamiliarity of the documents' layout, then by what I read.

Diamond Pharmaceuticals, Plaintiff v. Trevor Hall, Defendant

The name Hall felt vaguely familiar, but I couldn't place it. I glanced over my shoulder at the closed bathroom door, then leaned in closer.

Beneath the title, a block of text indicated it was a transcript from a court hearing dated earlier in the year, but what caught my breath in my throat was the bold line listing the attorneys for each side.

For the plaintiff: William Warner, Esq.
For the defendant: Trevor Hall, Pro Se

I grabbed my phone and snapped a picture as quickly as I could. Warner wasn't an especially uncommon name, but I thought it had to be Hudson's boss, the same Warner responsible for devising the scheme between his firm and the Board of Supervisors. Francisco's article was on corruption in Pima County politics and now Hudson's disappearance and death. This wasn't just casual reading material; it had to be connected.

I'd just flipped the first page over and taken a picture of the next page when I heard running water in the bathroom. I replaced the pages and was straightening, sliding my phone into my back pocket, when Francisco entered the room.

He looked from me to the nightstand and back, but then broke into an easy smile.

"Everything okay?" He asked.

I nodded and started toward the door, but he caught me around the waist with both arms and spun me to face him. He leaned in and kissed me thoroughly before releasing me to stumble dizzily into the doorframe.

"I'll still see you for dinner tomorrow?"

I nodded again, then hurried home as quickly as my woozy legs would carry me.

I TYPED "Pima County court transcript request" into my search engine and skimmed the results. When I'd zoomed in on the photos I'd taken hastily at Francisco's, I'd been disappointed to find that those two pages only covered the table of contents and nothing useful. I needed to get my hands on the full thing. If Francisco was reading court transcripts from a hearing Hudson's boss had participated in, I wanted to know why.

I opened up the court's website to make my request for the full transcript but stopped when I was met with the instruction to contact the court reporter directly with my request.

If you do not know who the reporter was, call the managing reporter's office for help finding that information.

I groaned.

Unwilling to accept total defeat, I typed in "Diamond Pharmaceuticals" to see what I could find.

A full page of headlines popped up.

Disgraced Pharma Lab Tech Dies by Suicide

At the first headline, I gasped. On the day I'd seen the news that Hudson was missing, the next story had been about protests outside a pharmaceutical company by Trevor Hall's family. That's why the name felt familiar to me.

I read more, my eyes bulging wider with each headline I took in.

Tucson Pharma Company Says Accusations 'Absurd'
Pharma Technician Ordered to Pay $20 Million For False Claims
Promising New Heart Med Under FDA Review

I opened tab after tab.

I read about the new medication Diamond Pharmaceuticals had developed for preventing heart disease, one that was currently under FDA review and was touted by many as being world-changing. I read the claims by a former lab technician, Trevor Hall, that the data Diamond Pharmaceuticals had submitted to the FDA for their review was fabricated. I read the articles exposing Hall as a disgruntled former employee who had complained to his colleagues when Diamond Pharmaceuticals denied him a pay raise.

Diamond Pharmaceuticals took Hall to court for defamation —the hearing from which Francisco had been reading the transcript—and won. Trevor Hall had been disgraced and ordered to pay a mind-boggling eight-figure sum in restitution, and three months later he took his own life.

My throat tightened as I read.

I played a video where Hall gave an interview from the courthouse steps after the trial, tears streaming down his face as he spoke. "What they showed in there was not the truth. And because they have money, they're getting away with it. Millions of people could die because of their lies."

In the background of the interview, two familiar figures exited the courthouse and descended the stairs. The first was Warner; he had a triumphant gleam in his eyes when he turned to face the camera over the technician's shoulder. The second I'd seen with Warner once before in the lobby of the law firm.

The camera kept rolling after Hall finished speaking, and over the chaotic noise of reporters I could hear when Warner clapped his companion on the back and said, "Great job today, Chuck."

Chuck. I frowned and returned to one of the articles I'd just read. It featured a quote from the Diamond Pharmaceuticals CEO, Chuck Tourney: "My father died of heart disease when I was in college. I changed my major the next week, from history to chemistry. I knew right then that I had a new mission in life: to create a world where heart disease is no longer a leading cause of death. And with this new drug Qorlexin out in the world, I believe I will have done that."

I made one more search, an image search for "Chuck Tourney" just to be sure.

Staring at pictures of the man I'd seen with Warner in the lobby of Warner & Loeb Law Offices, I sent Ethan a text

Mandy: You need to come over here right now.

50

I brewed a pot of coffee while I waited for Ethan, even though it was nearing midnight. I knew I wouldn't sleep anyway, and I needed to do something with my hands while my brain worked to process how this new information fit with what I already knew.

Hudson's law firm had represented a major pharmaceutical company in a lawsuit that led to the defendant's suicide. Every single report described the attorney for Diamond Pharmaceuticals—Will Warner—as ruthless. And after ruthlessly tearing down his opponent in the courtroom, Warner was trying to use his inside man at the Board of Supervisors to push through a grant that would funnel money to pharmaceutical companies.

That grant I'd seen on Clemens's desk was Warner's work—I was sure of it. Jake had done the research and concluded that the grant would be bad for the county. The investment required by pharmaceutical companies to secure the funding wouldn't grow the local economy by enough to offset the cost. And despite his assistant's thorough analysis, Clemens was prepared to vote in favor of the grant.

Was Hudson?

The front door opened, and I spun, hand flying to my heart, to find Ethan coming inside.

"It was unlocked," he said when he saw me, a gruff irritation in his voice that I hadn't heard from him before.

I waved it off and told him, "I think I know why Hudson's boss might have killed him."

"Straight to the point. I like it."

Ethan helped himself to the pot of coffee, filling a pint glass since I was using the only mug. While he sipped, I told him about the transcripts I'd seen Francisco reading and what I'd learned about Diamond Pharmaceuticals and the trial.

He frowned at the end of my spiel, but I barely noticed. Hearing the word "Diamond" out loud in my own voice had triggered a connection in my brain that I was trying to tease out.

"What if... What if the 'Diamond' in Hudson's agenda really wasn't about an affair?"

At Heaven on Earth, Diamond—or rather, Diana—had insisted she hadn't met with Hudson at the times he'd written "Diamond" in his agenda. I'd assumed she was lying, but maybe...

"What if it was about this pharmaceutical company?" I suggested.

Diana had also told me Hudson and Warner had argued about a month before he went missing. She'd been sure it was about a case. Could it have been *this* case?

Ethan crossed his arms over his chest. "You think your guy was what? Going to meet with a client of his law firm who he didn't actually represent?"

I glared at him. "I don't know! Maybe he was meeting with his boss to talk about how the case went. Or maybe he was on the fence about the grant proposal and wanted to talk with its biggest beneficiary first."

I thought about the time Christina and Hudson had been supposed to come visit Dave and me one spring break. At the last minute, Hudson had backed out to spend more time preparing for a trial. She and I were on FaceTime with Dave and Hudson in the background.

"I told him to file a motion to move the trial, but he won't."

Christina looked over her shoulder to where Hudson was at his desk, papers strewn all over.

"It wouldn't be right," he insisted.

"Other lawyers do it all the time," Christina pouted.

"I told my client I'd be ready for the hearing in two weeks, so I'm going to be ready. I'm not going to make him sit in limbo for an extra week just because I want to go on vacation instead of reading through these files."

I frowned at the memory. Hudson had never been my favorite person, but he had been *good*.

And then he'd become corrupt.

"Earth to Mandy." Ethan snapped his fingers in the air to get my attention. "What are you thinking?"

"I'm thinking Diamond, err, Diana already told me Hudson didn't like the arrangement he had with his boss when he became a county supervisor. And I'm thinking Hudson would have been uncomfortable with the fact that his firm and its client went after a lab technician so viciously that he killed himself."

"From what you've told me, his boss was just doing his job. He's a good litigator and—"

"I'm not saying Warner was wrong for fighting for his client. I just think the outcome might have made Hudson uncomfortable. And I don't get the impression Warner would have been happy if Hudson was hesitant on that grant proposal."

Ethan's brows were creased in skepticism, but I knew I was onto something.

"Warner met with Clemens before Hudson disappeared, and Clemens knew about the disappearance before the public did." And based on Clemens's writing across the top of that grant proposal, he planned on passing it against the recommendation of his assistant.

"You're saying Hudson's boss killed him to install a more

loyal supervisor in his place?" Ethan asked, but the challenge had leaked from his voice.

"I don't know!" I said again. "I need to find out whether Warner left the law firm after the partner meeting."

Ethan had already pointed out that my theory that Hudson never made it home didn't hold water since his car was there.

I glanced at the clock. "I'm probably too late for her shift, but I'm going back to Heaven on Earth to see if I can find Diana. I need to ask her—"

"No!"

I looked at Ethan in surprise.

He swallowed and said, "I just don't think that's the best plan. I'm getting close with Spiderfang. When I'm in, we'll have 24/7 footage of the Schupperts' house that you can take to the police."

He stood and reached for his bag to leave, his hand knocking into the pint glass and sending it flying.

"Oh!" I shouted, rushing for the roll of paper towels while Ethan grabbed his bag out of the path of coffee streaming across the tabletop. He tossed the bag across the room onto the loveseat to help me mop up the mess.

When the spill was cleared, he crossed the room toward his bag, and I noticed some of his things had fallen out of it when he'd thrown it.

I reached down to pick them up. "Here you g—"

I froze, surveying what I thought were pieces of paper when I'd reached for them but what I was now realizing were photographs. The face staring up at me from the top photo was one I'd seen earlier that night when I'd searched for information on Diamond Pharmaceuticals. It was Trevor Hall, the lab technician they'd sued for defamation.

Beneath it was a photo of another familiar face—Diana's.

I flipped to the third and final photograph.
Christina's face stared up at me.

51

"Ethan, what the fuck is this?"

I looked up at him from where I was crouched over the photographs. When he saw what I had, his already pale skin lost the last of its color, becoming stark white against the dark hair falling over his forehead.

He lunged for the photos, but I jerked them away, toppling over backwards and then using my feet to push me along the floor away from Ethan until one of my plastic chairs stood between us. My chest heaved with every breath as I tried to put distance between us.

"I can explain," he said.

"You'd better."

"It's not what it looks like."

I didn't even know what it looked like. Only that it felt wrong. Before my human brain could even guess at why he had these, my animal instincts were screaming at me that I was in danger.

"Why do you have these?" Photographs of a dead lab technician, a paralegal at the law firm that opposed him, and my missing best friend.

Ethan stepped back, covering his eyes with his hands and turning his head skyward. "Someone gave them to me."

"Who?"

"I don't know."

"Why did they give them to you?"

Avoiding eye contact with me, Ethan said quietly, "So I could follow them."

My stomach felt like it would sink all the way through my body. My throat tightened, and I couldn't have spoken if I'd had the words.

"I haven't hurt anyone," he insisted.

"You need to leave." I forced the shaky words out, slowly scooting backwards to try to get to the back door. If I could reach it, then I could run.

Yeah, right. The bitter voice inside me reminded me I couldn't outrun anyone. My joints were constantly on fire, and if Ethan wanted to catch me, he'd be on me before I made it a full block.

Urgently, Ethan pleaded, "I'm on your side."

"Leave," I said again.

Ethan backed toward the front door, but instead of leaving, he said, "I didn't mean to become a private investigator. I mean, obviously, I made a website and everything, but it's not what I set out to do when I dropped out of school. I left to move with my girlfriend when she wanted a change of scenery."

He sighed deeply, eyes going to his shoes. "My buddy texted me one day that he was pretty sure she was cheating on me. The whole PI thing started because I was trying to get proof for myself. Then his girlfriend started acting weird a few months later, so I helped him out. Then our friend Jace... You see where this is going."

I nodded, almost to the back door.

"After your ex hired me and I told him you were staying with a friend and seemed mentally stable, I got another inquiry. Someone reached out through my website with a meeting time and location. It seemed kind of weird, but I was trying to quit working for your ex and I didn't want to turn down other jobs, so I went.

"We met on a park bench at night like something out of the movies. Some dude in a hat and a trench coat with the collar turned up handed me that picture of the guy"—he gestured to the photographs in my hands—"and told me he wanted twenty-four seven surveillance on him.

"He handed me a paper bag of cash, more than I'd seen in a long time, and gave me an address where he thought the guy lived."

Ethan blew out a breath and wiped his hands up his face as if wrestling with what he was going to say next.

"I put a tracker on the guy's car. He didn't leave his apartment much. He had a job waiting tables, but he was awful at it. I told all this to the client."

"Who was it?" I interrupted. By the time I'd moved to Arizona, the trial was over. The lab technician had lost and been disgraced. Why did someone want surveillance on him then?

Ethan shrugged. "I told you, we met at night. He kept his face hidden."

"Could he have been Warner?"

He shook his head. "The build isn't right for Warner."

"What about Chuck Tourney?" I pulled up the interview with Trevor Hall where Chuck and Warner left the courthouse together in the background.

Ethan shook his head again. "I don't think so."

I groaned in frustration. "Some stranger taking lengths to keep his identity hidden asks for twenty-four-hour surveillance and you just go along with it? You don't ask any questions?"

"Mandy, the amount of cash in that bag was staggering."

I scoffed.

"I didn't know the guy was going to wind up dead! I told the guy about his job, and he just said to keep watching. He handed me another bag.

"A few days later, the target left his apartment to go somewhere other than work for the first time. He paid a visit to your friend in the foothills."

The target. I cringed.

"Christina?" I tried to make sense of why a lab technician would visit the Schupperts' house. "Was he there to talk to Hudson about the case?"

"No clue. I told my client where the target had gone. He handed me a third bag of cash and said the job was over, and that was that. When I saw the news that he'd—well—that he was dead, I told myself it had nothing to do with the job I'd done. Trevor was obviously troubled. And then your husband called me again to tell me that you'd moved and he wanted me to watch you at your new place. I agreed, and then I put the previous job behind me."

I looked over at the pictures beside me on the tile floor. Trevor smiled up at me through the photo, sitting on a picnic blanket. Someone outside the frame had their arm draped over his shoulders.

"That man died after you told your fucking mystery client where he'd been," I spat. He'd died after Ethan had told his client that Trevor had visited the Schupperts.

"I didn't kill that man!" Ethan shouted, backing further away until his back pressed against the door. A flicker of uncertainty shone in his eyes.

I needed to decipher the connection, figure out why this technician had paid them a visit, how it all fit together, but my brain was fixed on something else.

"You said the man gave you Trevor's photo, and after he died you put the job behind you." I gathered the pictures and held them up in a shaking hand. "Why do you have two more photographs, Ethan?"

When he looked at me, his eyes were red and his face beseeching. "I tried to turn him down. I really did. He called and said he had another job for me. When I told him I wasn't interested, he said it wasn't an offer. He knows where I live."

Ethan was shaking, terrified, as he described the events of the evening. "He told me to meet him where we'd met before. He gave me the two photos and Diana's address. She's the one he wanted surveillance on, but he said she might have visitors, and if the woman from the other photograph—Christina—showed up, I had to tell him immediately."

A flash of hope speared through the devastation settling around me. Someone was after Christina, yes, but they believed she was still alive and well. And while they suspected she might visit Diana, they didn't know where she was hiding.

"Ethan, when was this?"

"Earlier tonight."

I pushed myself up off the floor and held up Diana's picture. "We have to tell her. She's in danger, and—"

"We don't know for sure that she's in danger," Ethan said, and I gawked at him. "Trevor's death was ruled a suicide," he stressed.

My mouth dropped open in disgust. "Trevor turned up dead after he paid a visit to Hudson's house. After you told your client about it. Now Hudson's dead and his wife is missing, and that same client wants you to follow Diana around and keep an eye out for Christina. If you want to cling to the idea that Trevor killed himself and pretend your client had nothing to do with it, fine, but I'm going to warn Diana because she *is* in danger, Ethan. This is all connected."

I grabbed my keys off the counter. Ethan gave me a sheepish look and then recited the address he'd been given for Diana. With one last disappointed glance, I opened the door and marched out into the night, where I ran straight into the woman I'd just been going to find.

"Diana?"

She looked up at me, eyes swollen and makeup streaked down her face. She clutched a small duffel bag under her arm.

"I think I need your help."

52

When I brought Diana into the house, Ethan shrank away, pressing himself into the corner of the kitchen. I watched him while I led Diana to the loveseat, but he made no move to pull out his phone. If he was going to tell his client that Diana was here, he wasn't doing it yet.

"What's going on?" My eyes kept flitting to Ethan even as I faced Diana, and he shoved himself off the counter in frustration before sitting at the table, making a show of putting his phone on the tabletop where I could see it.

Diana looked between the two of us, her mascara-smeared face pulled into a taut expression of caution.

Finally, she turned to me and raised her chin, something of her normal confidence shining through. "I didn't realize this was your address."

My brows knit together. "Then why are you here?"

"You came to the club to ask me about Hudson," Diana said. "I found this address in his house. The pool house, to be more exact."

I'd been living in that pool house when I'd searched the classifieds and found this place. I'd circled it in the paper, and I could easily have left that behind when I moved out.

"I knew I couldn't stay there, so when I found this address, I decided to try it."

"What do you mean you couldn't stay there?" I asked. "Why were you in his pool house?"

Diana's lips pressed together as she weighed whether to tell me more. She swallowed deeply and then said, "His wife came to see me at my apartment."

"Christina?" I leapt up from the loveseat, the sudden redistribution of weight leaving Diana sinking deeply into the worn cushion. "You've seen her?"

Surprised by my reaction, Diana nodded.

"When?" I looked over to Ethan to see whether he mirrored my excitement, but his brows were furrowed with concern.

"Two days ago. She was waiting outside my door when I got home from the club. I recognized her from when she showed up at the club railing at her husband. I got scared because I thought she'd killed him—I've seen the speculation online—and was at my place to kill me because she still believed I'd been having an affair with him. Instead, she said she needed my help.

"I let her inside. She told me she needed me to get all the files at the firm related to the Diamond Pharmaceuticals case so she could avenge Hudson's death."

I leaned against the wall, head in my hands. Christina was alive. She'd been at Diana's apartment two days ago. The relief at knowing she was still alive warred with my jealousy that she hadn't come to see me, and I forced myself to push that down.

"What did she mean, 'avenge Hudson's death?'"

Diana shook her head. "She didn't say." She clutched her duffel bag in her lap, arms wrapped tight against it. "Why was your address at their house?"

I dropped my hands and slid down the wall until I was seated on the tile directly opposite the room from her. "Christina's my best friend. She helped move me here when I broke up with my ex, and I was living in her pool house until a couple weeks before Hudson disappeared."

"That's why you came to ask me about Hudson," Diana said, understanding clicking in her voice.

I nodded.

Ethan spoke, surprising both Diana and me. "You still haven't answered Mandy's question. Why were you in the pool house tonight?"

"I'm in trouble. I was doing what she asked and making copies of everything I could find related to the Diamond Pharma case." Her voice broke and she sniffled before continuing. "I told her there was no way I could get those files without getting caught, and I didn't want to lose my job. She threatened me, said she'd tell my whole office what I do for my second job."

She leveled a glare at me and said, "It's fitting you're best friends. Two peas in a pod."

Guilt immediately pulled at my chest. I'd made the same threat when I'd gone to Diana thinking she was the "Diamond" in Hudson's agenda.

Diana sniffled again and said, "If I did what she asked, I figured there was an eighty percent chance I'd get caught and lose my job. If I didn't, she'd tell everyone I'm a stripper, and there was a one hundred percent chance Warner would fire me if she did that. So yesterday when I was making other copies for a few of the partners, I grabbed the first of the Diamond files to copy those, too.

"I was almost finished when Warner came into the copy room. I've never seen him in there—he doesn't make his own copies. He was in a bad mood, agitated and on edge, and he yelled at me that he had been looking for me everywhere and he needed me to get something for him. Then he saw what I was copying and..."

Diana sobbed, unable to finish.

I felt the blood draining from my face. Everything I'd uncovered pointed to Warner. His law firm represented Diamond Pharmaceuticals and then he had Hudson draw up a grant proposal to benefit Diamond Pharmaceuticals as a kickback. Hudson fought with him and then wound up dead, replaced at the Board of Supervisors with a friend of Warner's who knew Hudson was missing before anyone else did.

Now, the same man who hired Ethan to tail the lab technician who accused Diamond Pharmaceuticals of fabricating data for the FDA wanted him to watch Diana, and they knew Christina was likely to pay her a visit. Based on the fate of that lab technician, I thought the terror on Diana's face was appropriate.

"He saw you looking into that case and now he's coming after you," I said, but to my surprise, Diana shook her head.

"No, he's not the one who's coming after me."

I looked over at Ethan in confusion and found his expression mirroring my own.

"Warner was angry," Diana allowed. "He fired me on the spot, but I pleaded. I told him Hudson's wife had put me up to it and tried to get him to let me stay. He—god, I'm so fucked—he made me clean out my desk and walked me out in front of everyone. Clients, coworkers, everyone!"

"But you don't think he's coming after you now?" I probed.

"No. He called me yesterday and told me I needed to leave town. He told me to put as much distance between the firm and myself as I could."

"He threatened you?"

She shook her head fervently. "It wasn't threatening. He sounded scared, like he was afraid of someone else.

"Either way, I ignored him. I've got my job at the club; that pays enough for me to have some time to figure out what to do to try to save my chance at being a lawyer. But today, when I got home I could tell someone had been in my apartment."

I looked at Ethan again. Maybe he wasn't the only PI his client had hired to keep an eye on Diana.

"I ran," she said. "I didn't know where to go, but since Hudson's wife is the one who got me into this, I went to her place. I figured she owed me a place to crash. When she didn't answer the door, I hopped the gate. I tried looking through the glass door, then checked the pool house. When I found this address, I thought maybe I'd find Christina here. Instead, I found you." She gestured at me.

"Did you—?" I asked, whirling on Ethan. He'd been tasked with following Diamond, and he'd broken into places before.

But he was already shaking his head emphatically.

"Whoever did," I started, flying to the windows and drawing the blinds tight. "Could they have followed her here?" Panic plunged through me, narrowing my field of vision.

"What's going on?" Diana asked in a voice that mirrored my own fear. She looked from me to Ethan, her wild gaze eventually landing on the photographs I'd left on the floor. She bent and picked up the picture of herself. "What is this?"

Ethan tugged at his hair and paced in a small circle, breathing out slowly the whole time. Then he said, "I'm a private investigator. A while back, someone hired me to watch this man." He picked up Trevor's photo and held it out to Diana.

In a whisper, she identified him. "That's the guy from the pharmaceutical company. The one who…"

Ethan scrunched his eyes closed and massaged the space between them. "After I reported back on his location, he turned up dead."

"But I thought he killed himself," she said. "How could…?" She trailed off as understanding sunk in, then pointed to the other two photographs. "What about those?"

For a long time, Ethan was silent, and I wondered if he was going to tell her or if I would have to.

"Ethan," I prodded, but he waved me off.

"The same man contacted me earlier today," she said in a shaking voice. "He hired me to watch you. He wanted me to tell him about your movements. He also said it was possible

Christina would be with you, and if I saw her I was to let him know."

Diana stepped backward toward the door, abject horror in her eyes.

Ethan quickly added, "I haven't told him anything, and I won't. I took the job because he threatened me, but we're going to find a way out of this."

But I wasn't sure how.

Diana was convinced Warner wasn't the one who was after her.

"The timing of all this," I started. "Whoever is chasing you is doing it because you were looking at the Diamond Pharma files. They have to be."

Diana nodded. Ethan remained stone-faced.

"Who else besides Warner could have found out?"

When Diana only shook her head, Ethan prompted, "Maybe someone else at the firm? Was there anyone besides Warner working on that case?"

"No." She scrunched up her face. "It was weird, actually. Normally, paralegals and assistants would be pretty heavily involved in the prep work, but Warner didn't want anyone else working that case with him."

I took a step toward the loveseat and cried out when a searing pain shot through my leg.

Diana and Ethan looked at me with alarm.

"I'm fine. I just need to rest." As if there was any chance I could sleep with everything running through my head. Christina was alive, and she was probably close.

Diana looked around, craning her neck to look inside my bedroom and see the sad mattress on the floor.

"You can stay at my place," Ethan said. When Diana hesitated, he said, "I've got a spare bedroom." Whoever was after Diana also knew where Ethan lived, but at least there she wouldn't be alone.

She nodded and swiped at a tear that had rolled down her cheek.

"Tomorrow you need to follow Warner," I ordered. She looked at me with surprise, but Ethan nodded like he'd been thinking the same thing.

"He has to have told someone," he said. "Maybe he'll meet with them again."

"Can you get me a bug? Like a little microphone?"

Ethan frowned at my request.

"Clemens," I explained.

Warner wouldn't visit Clemens at the board. He wouldn't risk being seen mixing his business with local politics. But if Clemens was involved in any of this, maybe I could catch his half of a phone conversation.

Diana's full lips pulled into a frown, but she didn't say anything, instead gathering her bag to leave with Ethan.

"I'll bring one by tomorrow morning." At my raised eyebrow, Ethan said, "I can get up before noon under special circumstances. I think these count."

"Six-thirty," I said. "I need to be the first one at the office if I'm going to bug it."

"Six-thirty," he echoed.

They left, and I shoved the whole table in front of the front door and both plastic chairs in front of the back door. Someone besides Ethan had been in Diana's apartment tonight, and the thought of them following her here made it hard to breathe.

Lying in bed practically vibrating with energy, I tried to tell myself it was almost over. Tomorrow I'd bug Clemens's office. Ethan and Diana would tail Warner. One way or another, we'd figure this out.

53

At first I thought the pounding on my door was Ethan. I checked the time on my phone as I pulled myself out of bed. It was five minutes before my alarm; Ethan was early.

"Just a minute!"

I don't know what possessed me to peek out through my bedroom blinds before answering the door. Instinct, intuition, a message from Hudson's spirit. Whatever the motivation, I pullet the slats apart just enough to see a cop car idling at the curb and felt my stomach sink. I muttered a curse and moved as quickly as I could, nearly tripping as I tried to leap into my jeans.

Three more raps at the door shook the walls, and I took one last look outside. A uniformed officer was walking across my yard with his hands on his hips, heading to where Styles was leaning against the squad car with a pair of handcuffs dangling from her hands.

I grabbed my phone, slipped on my sneakers without bothering with socks, and ran out the back door.

"Going somewhere?"

The voice froze me so quickly I had to flail my arms to remain upright. I spun to find Francisco leaning against the wall of my house, arms crossed over his chest.

"Wha—?"

He slipped a hand into his pocket and pulled out a small object, holding it up so I could see it.

The flash drive.

"This fell out of your pocket when you were leaving my place last night."

I shook my head, thinking as fast as I could about how to explain.

"You lied to me, Mandy." The surprise in Francisco's voice, the hurt in his eyes, felt like a knife to the gut.

"I didn't mean to—"

"You did," he interrupted. "I always felt like you were keeping something from me, but I told myself I was being paranoid. I was letting my experience with Farrah color every new experience.

"When I found this, at first I thought it was a mistake. I thought I must have somehow dropped the drive myself and never realized it, but I know that's not true. You stole this out of my car.

"Once I wrapped my head around that, I wanted to know why. I watched the footage, Mandy. You're on this."

"No." I took a step toward him, shaking my head harder.

Around the house, I heard voices getting louder. Styles and her team were heading our way.

When I looked from the direction of the voices back to Francisco, the hurt on his expression was now laced with triumph.

"You called Styles?" My question came out as a hoarse whisper of disbelief.

Francisco dipped his head in a nod, his hard eyes showing not a sliver of remorse.

"You don't understand, I—"

But then Styles's voice sounded even closer, and I knew I was out of time. I held Francisco's gaze for as long as I could, hoping somehow my pleading expression would convince him, and then I took off as fast as I could in the other direction.

54

I stumbled over myself almost immediately, hitting the ground and then scrambling back to my feet, my brain's only directive to run. I had no plan. Nowhere to go.

I'd made it three houses down, cutting through backyards and thanking god this neighborhood wasn't full of six-foot perimeter walls around every property like Christina's. Behind me, shouts started up.

"You go that way!"

"I'll take the north!"

A whistle blew.

I knew I couldn't keep running. I needed to hide.

I would never outrun Styles's crew. My thundering heart pumped adrenaline through my blood, but I was dangerously close to getting sensation back in my body, and when it came, I knew I'd be in trouble.

At the end of the block, a neighbor had a low three-foot stucco wall around their property and a large carport in the front housing two oversized pickup trucks and a small car up on blocks swallowed by a dark gray car cover. I hopped the wall, hissing as I landed, and made my way around the side of their house to the front, eyes peeled for police. I wedged myself between the covered sedan and the pickup, keeping as close to the wall as possible, and then slowly slid myself up under the cover.

The air under the car cover felt thick and heavy as I breathed, and I blinked quickly, waiting for my eyes to adjust to the darkness. It was barely dawn, and little of the orangey-pink morning light penetrated the fabric of my shelter.

Footsteps and voices grew closer as the police officers worked their way down the street. I held my breath, certain that I was about to be caught and arrested. I sent up a silent prayer of thanks that Ethan and Diana were elsewhere. They would drive by my house and see it crawling with cops, and then they'd book it and follow Warner like we agreed.

But while I'd be sitting in a cell waiting for them to come to Detective Styles with proof I didn't kill Hudson, Christina was still on the run, and until we brought down whoever was after her, she was in danger.

I squeezed my arms tighter around my legs, making myself even smaller.

After a long stretch of silence, when more light was filtering through the cover, slow, tentative footsteps sounded from nearby. I held my breath as they approached, trying to triangulate their location.

The steps were definitely inside the perimeter wall. Was it the homeowner coming to find out what I was doing hiding in his carport?

They crept closer, slow and soft, almost drowned out by the sound of my own heartbeat.

I put a hand over my mouth and closed my eyes, praying that they'd change direction and walk away, but then the cover was yanked back and the world was orange behind my eyelids. When they flew open, I was greeted not by a uniformed officer and not by the angry face of the homeowner discovering a miscreant on his property, but by a wide-eyed Ariel holding a finger up to her lips.

"What are—?"

She shushed me, pressing the finger harder to the front of

her mouth. Then she turned and looked over her shoulder and waved for me to follow her.

My legs screamed in agony as I straightened. I opened my mouth wide and breathed a silent scream. Ariel slipped along ahead, and I forced one leg after the other to bend and follow her, whimpering softly with each step.

We reached the back wall and she gestured for me to wait, then stuck her head out. With a wave, she summoned me, and I followed as quickly as I could. We crossed the back alley and hurried down the next block before making a left turn. When we were even with our shared duplex, she pointed to a large black trash bin sitting up against the sun-bleached brick of a house.

"Get in there," she whispered. When I hesitated, she waved her hand impatiently, looking fearfully down the driveway and across the alley that separated this house from ours.

I lifted the lid of the bin and turned my head away at the odor that rose up out of it. When I moved to close it again, she grabbed my hand.

"You have to," she urged me.

I looked back at this twelve-year-old girl, black choker encircling the smooth skin of her neck and dark, glossy hair falling in front of her face. Her dark eyes shone with moisture as she looked from me toward our duplex and back, and I felt a surge of guilt. Instead of an innocent youth, she was helping me evade capture by the police.

I swallowed the feeling down, then nodded and grabbed the rim of the bin. She held it steady as I climbed in, immediately gagging on the foul air.

Without another word, she slammed the lid closed and then carted me away.

My shoulder slammed against the plastic side when she tilted it up onto its wheels, and the uneven pavement of the driveway and then the alley made my teeth rattle in my head. I pulled the neck of my shirt up over my mouth and nose to filter the air and kept my breathing shallow.

We came to a stop and I waited, but she didn't open the lid, and I didn't dare open it myself. I counted my heartbeats to try to get some sense of the passage of time. I counted three-hundred before the commotion.

A door slammed open and banged against the side of the house.

"Officer!" Ariel shouted. "Someone just ran through my front yard!"

The thwap of her footsteps sounded close, then farther, then disappeared entirely.

I didn't have long. If there was a police officer stationed in the backyard, there was bound to be one out front, too. She'd lure the officer from the back to the front, but then they'd all realize I wasn't actually out front and they'd come back around.

I lifted the lid an inch, then two inches, breathing the fresh air eagerly. The trash bin was up against the lime-green painted walls of our duplex, right beside the back door to her family's side. She'd left the door hanging open for me.

I put one hand on the wall and one hand on the rim of the trash can as I tried to climb out, but it was unsteady and I tipped it too far. With an enormous clatter, the bin was on its side on the ground with me still inside it.

I crawled out and ran through the open door into the Rightsides' home.

It felt immediately familiar, almost a mirror image of my own. At first I paused, waiting to see if anyone else was home and would be alarmed to find me there, but when I heard no one moving inside I hurried down the hall away from the doors.

As expected, the officer and Ariel returned to the backyard only minutes later. I heard only tiny fragments of their words.

"...raccoons...careful..." Then there was the clatter of plastic on plastic as Ariel righted the bin and closed the lid, and then she slammed the back door closed. Safe at last, I let out a long breath and was surprised when a sob escaped me along with it.

Ariel burst into the bathroom where I'd hidden myself, brown eyes wide with excitement and a brilliant smile on her face. "That was so c— What's the matter?" She frowned at me.

Once I'd started crying, I found I couldn't stop, and when she realized it might be a minute she left me, returning with a handkerchief with what I assumed were her dad's initials embroidered on it and a can of Coke.

I smiled weakly and thanked her, pressing the cool metal of the can against the skin of my face before sipping the drink.

The moment I took a full breath in and out without crying, Ariel asked, "So why are the police looking for you?" Her eager eyes were dancing with curiosity, and she sat on the bathroom floor so close that her folded legs touched mine where I sat on the edge of the tub.

I hesitated.

"Is this because of the hacking? They did a lesson on cyber crimes and internet safety at school."

I closed my eyes and pressed the cold metal of the soda can against them. "Kind of. My friend is missing, and someone killed her husband. The police think that she did it and I helped her."

Her expression of curiosity intensified.

"When you and Ethan were at my house, we were trying to figure out if we could get footage from security cameras that overlook my friend's house to help us figure out what happened."

"The hacking," she said again, and I nodded.

Ariel stood. "I have to go to school soon, but you can stay here to hide. Ryder slept over with his friend Jason last night so he won't be here until after school, and both my parents have double shifts today."

I couldn't stay. I could have a rest, maybe nab some Ibuprofen from the medicine cabinet, and figure out my next steps, but I couldn't hide out in a stranger's house just because their twelve-year-old daughter said I could.

Ariel bounded out the front door and toward the bus stop. I pulled back the sheer yellow curtain that hung in the kitchen window to see whether police were still outside looking for me. The officer who'd been stationed out front was still there, though his attention was on the phone in his hand.

I walked to the back door and did the same, pulling the curtain in the door's small window back just an inch to look outside. I couldn't see an officer at the back of the house, but it was possible he was just around the corner out of sight but would catch me if I tried to leave.

My stomach grumbled, but I didn't dare take food from the kitchen. Instead, I filled a glass with water and downed it, then returned to the bathroom where I'd hidden and curled up inside the tub.

I hadn't asked any questions when Christina invoked our secret code and called me over there. Lying in the neighbors' bathtub, I thought of all the ways I'd fucked up in the last four weeks. Styles had said Hudson had likely died the day he went missing and just wasn't found until two weeks later; had he been dead by the time I was at Christina's? I still felt sure he'd never been in the blanket chest, but was he dead somewhere else, or if I'd acted differently could Christina and I have still saved him?

And Francisco.

I wiped fresh tears from my face, thinking of the hurt on his when he'd held up that flash drive. He hadn't been wrong that I'd betrayed him. He had the specifics wrong—I hadn't stolen that drive from him—but on the whole he was right. I deserved his anger.

It was his hard face I saw when I closed my eyes, his ice-cold voice still ringing in my ears.

I KNEW something was wrong the moment I opened my eyes. The light wasn't right.

My nose was the next clue. Cooking smells filled the air, the aromas of meat and spices making me salivate.

Shit. I was still at the Rightsides', and I wasn't alone anymore.

I scrambled to a seated position and looked around. The bathroom door was wide open to the hallway. I grabbed the edge of the shower curtain and pulled it slowly closed, holding my breath until it was fully extended.

Breathe, I reminded myself.

A loud sizzling sound started up, and then Ariel's mother, the woman I'd thought of us Mrs. Rightside, yelled something in Spanish. I caught the name "Ryder," and then he yelled something back before the stomping footsteps of a teen boy echoed through the small home. I gasped, then slammed my hand over my mouth when he entered the bathroom.

The faucet turned on, then off, and then he left, wandering toward the kitchen.

I had to get out.

The bathroom had a small window, but it opened onto the front of the house, so even if I managed to squeeze myself through it I thought there was a good chance I'd be depositing myself right into Styles's lap. I could wait until the family was eating dinner, then try to sneak out the window of the back bedroom, but someone was sure to see me cross the hallway if I tried that.

I was thinking that I was well and truly stuck when the front door opened and slammed closed again. The TV turned on, filling the home with the sound of *Days of Our Lives* layered over the sizzling from the kitchen. Mr. Rightside said something to his wife, and I waited with bated breath for him to walk down the hall and discover me, but he must have planted himself in front of the TV instead.

Then another voice joined the chorus, and I felt hope. Ariel was home, saying something to her parents. She could help get me out.

For half a second I cursed myself for relying on a pre-teen girl to get me out of a mess I'd made, but then the bathroom door closed and she peeked her head around the shower curtain and my relief washed away every other emotion.

"What are you still doing here?" she hissed.

"I fell asleep," I whispered back. "I need your help."

"The window," she suggested, but I shook my head.

"There's police that way. I need to go out the back."

But Ariel was already shimmying the window open. "They're gone. I saw them drive away when the bus was pulling up."

I could have cried happy tears at the news. I was going to get out of here, and while I still had no clue where I was going to go, it wouldn't be straight to a cell.

"Here," she said, cupping her hands beneath the window.

I whispered a thanks, then let her boost me up.

My head and shoulders made it through without issue. It was the hips where things got dicey.

"Push," I hissed, trying to bend and straighten to wiggle my way free.

"I am pushing," Ariel hissed right back.

I winced as the window frame dug into my flesh but didn't let up.

I was nearly home free when I heard a crunch on the gravel

stretch between the two front porches of the duplex. I twisted, looking toward my half of our lime-green abode.

"Mandy?"

Familiar blue Adidas came into my field of vision first. As I rotated, I took in the pair of jeans with the rip in the side that I'd recognize anywhere, then the t-shirt I'd bought and wrapped and placed under the Christmas tree three years ago.

"What are you doing?" Dave asked me.

55

The combination of being upside down and seeing a man I used to see every single day but hadn't seen in almost two months made it hard for me to work out what I was actually seeing.

"Dave?"

He rushed toward me, overdressed in a long-sleeved shirt that strained at his biceps and a brown puffy vest over it.

"Here," he said, grabbing me under the shoulders and pulling while Ariel pushed on my feet from inside the bathroom.

The moment I was freed from the window frame, I ducked down low, whispered a thanks to Ariel for the help, and then hissed at Dave, "We have to go."

I hurried to my front door, ducking the whole time to avoid being seen by the Rightsides as I passed their front windows, and then rushed into my apartment.

"What's going on?" he asked.

"I could ask you the same thing!" I was already throwing clothes from the dresser drawer onto the mattress. I needed to run, and I needed to run now. Styles and her officers were gone for now, but I didn't know how long I had until they returned, and I wanted to be long gone when they did.

When I'd stuffed my most treasured clothes into a backpack, I moved on to the bathroom and started gathering my toiletries.

"Mandy, slow down," Dave said, stepping behind me and

reaching around to grab my hand as I reached for the toothpaste.

I whirled on him and said, "Don't tell me what to do!"

Hurt and shock bloomed across his face when I yanked my hand away from him.

"I came to see you because you wouldn't respond to my messages and I was worried about you. A month ago you were living with Christina and Hudson, and now he's dead and she's the prime suspect. That's scary, Mands! And then I show up to find you dangling out of a window. You have to see my concern."

I shoved the toiletries into a clear plastic pouch. "Was it concern that made you hire a private investigator to follow me around?"

I turned to watch his reaction to learning that I knew about Ethan. His mouth turned downward, his face seeming to sag, and his eyes twitched back and forth while he fished around for words to explain.

"He told me that when he told you I was fine, you pressed him to find proof that I was having a breakdown and wasn't in my right state of mind," I told him. "What was that about, Dave?"

I'd nearly finished packing my backpack, taking only the essentials.

"I'm sorry," Dave finally said. The pain slicing through his voice made me look, and he pulled out one of the plastic chairs and sat down, hanging his head in his hands. "I didn't know what to do. I was broken without you, Mandy. I needed...I needed to find something to try to get you back."

"Well, I'm not broken without you, Dave." It wasn't entirely true. I was broken—my body was fighting itself every day, and I had no clue what I wanted out of life beyond securing Christina's safety and my own freedom—but it wasn't because I'd left him.

Dave wiped the heels of both hands across his cheeks and sniffed. Then he looked at me, really taking in the scene for the first time.

"Why are you packing?" he asked. "I don't get the feeling you're going to agree to come home with me."

I weighed how much to tell him, mind racing to come up with an explanation that would send him on his way and leave me free to go. As far as I knew, Styles didn't know anything about Ethan. His apartment would be a safe place to hide out.

"Are you in trouble?" Dave asked.

I shook my head, started to tell him I was fine. But Dave reached out and touched me, gently this time, not to grab and hold me but to let me know I wasn't alone, and I found myself sobbing before I knew what was happening.

"Christina's in trouble," I eventually got out. "Hudson's boss is corrupt and a bully, and I think Hudson pushed back too hard. Christina's on the run. She hid something in their backyard before running, but it's gone, and she's—she's—"

Dave pulled me to him, and I let him, the sobs wracking my body.

"Shh," he said, tucking my head into his chest and rubbing his hand over my back. How many times had he done this for me before?

When I finally collected myself, I pulled away. My snot and tears left dark splotches on his shirt. I wiped at my face and then said, "I had nothing to do with Hudson's death, and—"

"Whoa," Dave cut me off, but I shook my head and kept talking.

"—neither did Christina, but there's a detective on the case who believes otherwise, and we need to get out of here before she gleefully drags me away before that private investigator you hired has a chance to prove our innocence."

Dave looked horrified at the idea.

"I'll explain more when we're out of here," I promised him. I grabbed my phone to text Ethan to let him know what happened this morning and ask for his address.

"Come back to my hotel room," Dave said, pulling me toward him again before I could send the message. It was strange to feel my body automatically give in to him. His touch instantly soothed me, the familiarity of a decade together woven through every brush of his skin.

"You can text your friends an update from there," he said when I hesitated. "And you can tell me the rest of the story. We can make a plan."

A hotel bed sounded a lot better than whatever the sleeping arrangements would be at Ethan's. I nodded and grabbed my bag, and when Dave grabbed my hand on the way out of the house, I didn't stop him.

THE MOMENT the heavy hotel room door closed behind me, I felt like my chest expanded and I could breathe again. I sent Ethan a text.

Mandy: Styles is coming for me. Had to run. Are you and Diana still on Warner?

Dave turned on the shower and gestured for me to get in, making a show of turning away. I stepped into the bathroom and shut the door, then stood under the water until my skin turned pink all over. As adrenaline seeped from my bloodstream, every muscle I had reminded me that I was asking too much of my body. I leaned against the cold wall of the shower, letting it support me while the hot water sluiced over me.

When I emerged from the bathroom in my holey pajamas, Dave was seated on the edge of the bed looking grim.

"You need to come back with me, Mandy," he said.

I frowned. This wasn't what we'd talked about before.

"Hudson was involved in something dirty. If it got him killed, it must have been truly bad. And I know you said Christina is on the run, but the most logical reason to go on the run is—"

"Don't!" I held up my hands, and he looked at me with sympathy.

"You're in trouble here. If you come with me, we can make it go away. I can make it go away. And besides being in trouble, you're clearly sick or injured. You're limping all over the place, and your skin is so pale it's practically translucent. You need rest. You need to see a doctor. You—"

"Dave," I interrupted him again, this time more forcefully. "I've seen a doctor." All the times I lamented that my body felt wrong, that it wasn't working properly, that something had to be wrong for me to be as exhausted as I was, and all the times he responded by telling me I just needed to rest came flooding back.

"Remember when I fell asleep at the dinner table last spring?" I asked him.

His eyes lit up with amusement. He'd joked about my course load and that I wasn't built for the life of a research professor; I was delicate and needed my precious sleep.

That had been the prompting event that finally led to the referral to a rheumatologist and ultimately a diagnosis after the seven-month wait to be seen.

"I'm sick, Dave. I'm not lazy, and I'm not a delicate princess who can't handle the realities of life or a difficult career. My immune system is attacking my own body every single day, and I know the disease isn't currently under control and I need to see another doctor, but I don't have it in me to jump through all those hoops again right now."

Dave's mouth opened in horror. "I'm so sorry," he whispered, and I could tell he meant it.

We looked at each other for a long minute before he slapped his palms on his thighs and said, "I'll call my old roommate, Dylan. He'll have contacts. We'll work this out. We'll get you seen as soon as we get back."

Instantly, he was in "fix it" mode, and once again I felt a part of me relax at the familiarity of him. Though I wanted to be able to let someone else take care of me, to make the calls and handle the legwork, I shook my head.

"I can't go back with you, Dave."

"If you need an attorney, I'll call—"

I stopped him. "It's not that. I mean, it is that, but it's not only that. Someone is trying to hurt Christina and I am so close to uncovering the truth."

Dave gave me a pitying look, and all the relaxed familiarity slipped away into the familiar fury of not being taken seriously.

"Mandy, I know you said Hudson was taken in by a corrupt boss and that's what sparked this whole thing for them, but you should read some of what they're saying online. People are reporting seeing him out at strip clubs. Their marriage wasn't what it seemed."

I wanted to throttle the people speculating about my friend's marriage on the internet. And I wanted to throttle Christina and Hudson for setting this stage. No, he wasn't cheating at Heaven on Earth, but he had to know he'd be seen, and as far as I knew, Christina had actually cheated.

"Even if she didn't kill him," Dave said in a voice that made me think he felt that was unlikely, "they made this mess themselves. Between their marriage and his involvement in whatever corrupt racket he was into, they created this situation. If you stay here, you'll end up going down for it."

I shook my head, swiping tears away. What he said was true, and I'd been angry at Christina for exactly that—setting me up to land in the mess she and Hudson had left. Still, I didn't want to hear it coming from Dave.

He raked a hand through his blond hair, longer and shaggier than it had been when we were together. "You've got to come back, Mandy. You need medical care. It sounds like you need a lawyer since there's a detective gunning for you. Come with me, Mands. Come with me and I'll protect you. I'll help you."

"I can't," I whispered.

"You can," he urged. "You have to. Stay here and go down for something you didn't do, or come back with me and live. You'll get the help you need. You'll be happy again."

Happy.

I hadn't been happy in Michigan. I hated the cold, I was busting my ass in a job that didn't light me up, and I was married to a man whose first thought when I couldn't hold my head upright was that I just wasn't cut out for such a challenging field and not that there might be something medically wrong with me.

But I wasn't exactly happy here either.

My best friend pulled me into a mess that got her husband killed and left her on the run. A detective was determined to put me behind bars, and I'd become a dishonest person in trying to evade her, lying and hiding things from a neighbor I'd come to care about. I lived in a tiny duplex with almost no furniture, and I still didn't know what sort of career I might actually find fulfilling.

Dave reached for my hand.

"Come back with me, Mandy," he urged again.

I looked into his blue eyes and saw the yearning in them. I couldn't help it; I nodded.

He stood from the bed and pulled me to him, wrapping my body in his. My limbs relaxed and I melted into him, my heartbeat slowing as my body felt safe. Saying yes to Dave was easy. It was comfortable.

"I already bought a ticket for you just in case," he said, moving quickly to logistics. "Is there anything else from your place here that we need to get? The flight's not until noon tomorrow, so we've got a little time."

I let him talk through the plans while I crawled into the bed, a groan of pleasure escaping me as I sank down into the mattress. The sun was still up, but my eyelids fluttered closed immediately.

Dave pulled the covers up over me and tucked me in, and I sank into a dreamless sleep for the first time in weeks.

———

A LOUD THUD WOKE ME, and I opened my eyes to see Dave walking into the room with two coffees in his hands. For a moment, I was confused about where I was and why he was there. Then I remembered—I was going back to Michigan.

I can be happy. I repeated the refrain in my head. *I'll be safe.*

"Here you go." He handed me the cup and I took a sip, then screwed up my face.

"What is it?"

"Caramel latte," he said, then took a long sip of his own. "They only had that and vanilla."

"They didn't just have plain coffee?"

He frowned. "I forgot you have the coffee taste of my elderly father." He reached out for the drink. "If you don't want it, I'll drink it. We can get you something at the airport."

Happy, I thought again. *Safe.*

I checked my phone and saw multiple missed calls from Wendy. I'd missed work the previous day, and—I glanced at the clock—was officially late for work today.

I deleted the voicemails without listening to them. I was leaving. What my boss had to say about my missing work because I was hiding from the cops in my neighbor's bathtub didn't matter, and if I called her back to let her know I was leaving, she'd just relay that to Detective Styles when Styles inevitably went to my workplace looking for answers.

I pulled on the pair of jeans I'd worn yesterday and one of the three shirts I'd packed in my backpack, then shoved my pajamas back inside. When I looked up, Dave was cringing.

"Those are dirty," he said, pointing to where I was zipping the bag closed around the pajamas.

"So are these jeans," I told him.

His expression traveled down to my pants. "But now everything in the bag is going to be dirty."

"It's fine, Dave," I said. "We'll do laundry when we get back."

Happy. Safe.

My head pounded from the lack of caffeine, and I wished I hadn't handed over the syrupy sweet latte.

"Can we swing by a Starbucks on the way to the airport?" I asked.

"They have those all over the airport. Let's just go once we're through security."

I nodded. Tucson was small. Security would be quick. It would be fine.

Happy. Safe.

Dave called us an Uber, and I shifted my weight from one foot to the other while we waited, certain that at any moment the police would jump out from behind the pillars of the hotel carport and I'd have to run again.

When we slid into the back seat of the Uber, I was still so anxious my foot was tapping out a rhythm on the floorboard beneath me. Dave put a hand on my knee to steady it, and I gave him a forced smile.

I pulled out my phone, wondering idly if I'd need to get a different phone, or if I should leave it behind to avoid being tracked. I was scrolling through images of my college friends and their babies when it vibrated in my hand. A message from Ethan.

Ethan: SOS

My throat tightened, my fingers going white as they gripped the phone harder. It buzzed again with another text.

Ethan: I NEED YOU TO HELP ME HIDE A BODY

56

"You okay?" Dave asked, leaning toward me to peek at my phone screen.

I tilted it away from him. "Yep. Just work," I lied.

When the Uber driver dropped us off at the terminal, I told Dave I needed to use the restroom and slipped away before he could tell me to wait until we were past security. I dialed Ethan's number and pulled the stall door closed behind me.

"Where are you?" Ethan demanded. He sounded panicked.

I flushed the toilet to cover the sound of my voice. "I'm, uh, I had to go. I assume you saw the welcome reception at my house when you came by yesterday morning?"

"Yes, but I've been searching arrest records and you're not on them."

"No, I got away, but now I can't come back. At least not until this is all over."

"Are you in a bathroom?"

I flushed the toilet again and kept my voice low. "I'm in public. I don't have long. What's going on?"

"Good news: I got into Spiderfang."

My heart leaped in my chest. Ethan got it. He actually got it. This might all be over. I thought about Dave, waiting for me by the check-in counters, and what I'd tell him.

"What does the footage show?" I asked, lifting my foot to flush the toilet a third time.

"That's the bad news. My mystery client, the one who gave

me the photographs and the cash... He went to your friend's house that Friday and walked Hudson out before Christina came home. It's not one-hundred percent clear on the video, but it looks like he had a gun to his back."

Video proof that someone else killed Hudson, or at least that they marched him out of his home at gunpoint.

"How do you know?" I pressed. "I thought you said he wore disguises when you met up."

"His gait."

"And you're confident?"

"Positive."

"From just his gait?"

Ethan huffed exasperatedly. "Yes, Mandy! I recognized his gait and I am confident the person who hired me to watch Trevor and Diana is the person who marched Hudson out of his own home the day he went missing. He's also one of the two men who went back and stole the chest."

My stomach fluttered, and I paced a tiny, excited circle in the stall. "We've got to show Styles."

"Already on it," he said immediately. "I've made copies of copies and emailed the clip to the police department."

"Ethan, just take it there. Go there. Give it to her. This is important," I urged. Emailing video clips was fine, but who knew how regularly anyone was monitoring the tip line email address?

"I can't go there. That's the other bad news." He paused, then said, "I got a call. I know where Christina is, or at least where she will be this evening."

"Ethan, what—where—" I blurted half-formed questions.

"I'm supposed to go there and kill her."

The toilet tank quieted and the silence rang in my ears, my brain trying to make sense of what I'd just heard.

When I didn't reply, Ethan added, "My client, the same one I'm now pretty sure either killed Hudson or helped Warner do it, called me. He said he had another job. Christina is going to be at some park this evening, and I'm supposed to go there and kill her."

"Ethan, what the fuck?" I demanded.

"I don't know what to do!" he shouted back.

"You have to go to the police!"

"I can't!" His breathing got heavier. "If I go to the cops, I'm dead. If Diana leaves my apartment and goes to the cops, she's dead, and then I'll be dead later. He's watching me, Mandy. He's watching my apartment and will shoot me if I step one single toe out of line."

"Why ask you to kill Christina if he's just going to follow you around? Why make you kill her if he's so willing to do the shooting himself?"

"I don't know what kind of sick game he's playing, Mandy." Ethan's tone grew increasingly stressed, and there was an edge to his words like he was trying not to cry. "I don't know if it's because I never reported back on Diana and he's trying to punish me. I have no clue why he's doing this, but I'm stuck and I need a way out.

"There's a gun waiting for me taped to the underside of a park bench. I'm supposed to use that to kill Christina when she shows up at the park, then go to an address outside of town to collect my payment, although I'm pretty sure the only thing that will be waiting for me there is another person with a gun ready to shoot me."

I breathed out slowly, then tried to assume an air of confidence I didn't actually possess as I said, "You need to go talk to Maureen."

"What?"

"She knows how to disappear. She can help you."

"But I'm being followed," Ethan said louder, as if I hadn't heard him the first time.

I pinched the bridge of my nose. "You can be watched sitting in your apartment all day, or you can be watched visiting Maureen. In one of these scenarios, someone who has managed to disappear for decades might actually be able to help you get out of this.

"Then you go to the park. Make Christina go with you, and then disappear."

"But—"

"You said you sent the police the video footage. You've set the machine in motion and now you need to get out of there. You can go back when it's over."

"What about you?"

I flushed again. "I'm on my way out of town."

"What if Christina doesn't want to come with me? If you could meet us there—"

"I can't, Ethan."

He exhaled, then grunted an acceptance and hung up.

Outside this room, a plane was taxiing toward my gate, ready to get me out of here. Ready to take me to safety.

And only a few miles away, Christina was walking into what was supposed to be an ambush. I tried to reason out why this man who hired Ethan would know where she was going to be—why she would be meeting anyone in some park when she was supposed to be in hiding. Had he promised her something? And instead, he was sending Ethan to kill her.

I reminded myself that Ethan was a private investigator; he had experience going unnoticed on the job, and if Christina went with him, he'd be able to keep her safe.

If she went with him.

Whatever she was going to the park to get, Ethan wouldn't be able to offer her, and she was stubborn. She would protest when he tried to get her to go with him, I knew it.

I shook my head and opened the stall, heading back into the crowded airport terminal. She would go with him. She had to. Just like I had to get on this plane.

57

Everything made me jumpy after that call. Every noise sounded like a threat, and when I emerged from the bathroom I half-expected someone to jump out and grab me.

"You seem anxious," Dave observed after I nearly jumped out of my skin when the person behind me in the security line bumped into me.

"I'm fine."

I tucked my shoes into the bin alongside my backpack and walked through the scanner.

"Let's just get some coffee and get to our gate," I told him. I'd made it through the check-in and security process without officers descending upon me the moment my ID was scanned. Now we just needed to get on the plane and then I could breathe properly for the first time in a month.

Dave browsed the bookstore while I waited in line at Starbucks, then sidled up to me just as I placed my order. "Add a sausage, egg, and cheese breakfast sandwich to that order," he said, and swiped his card.

I turned, miffed even though he'd paid, and he handed me a book. "I got this for you."

I looked down at the glossy cover of a biography I'd had on my to-read list for months. *See,* I told myself. *He does know you. You can be happy. This is the right decision.*

At our gate, he pulled out his laptop to work, and I couldn't stop myself from remembering how he'd tracked my location on my laptop, his old one. I tried to put the memory aside and opened up the book he'd given me.

My eyes read the words on the page, but my brain didn't take any of them in. As I scanned the same paragraph over and over, my thoughts turned to Ethan and Christina every time I tried to focus.

What if she doesn't want to come with me? Ethan hadn't been wrong to ask that. If Christina was going to that park, she had a reason, and I didn't think she'd run off with a stranger without getting whatever she was going there for, even if he told her someone was coming to kill her.

The intercom sounded, paging a late passenger for another flight, and I surveyed the crowd gathered at our gate. We were less than half an hour out from boarding. Men in suits with briefcases were already lined up in the priority boarding lane, several of them on their phones. A toddler was having a meltdown in the next row over from us, throwing herself on the floor while her dad tried to wrangle her and her older brother, who seemed intent on escaping the gate. A man in a golf shirt had a newspaper unfolded in his lap, though like me, he was ignoring his reading materials in favor of people watching. Something about his face looked familiar, but I couldn't place him.

I watched a couple pull a Tupperware container of boiled eggs out of one of their backpacks and hoped I wouldn't be seated next to them on the flight, then abruptly jerked my head back toward the man with the newspaper.

I knew him. I'd seen him once before. It was the first police officer who'd come to my house, the one who came after Dave called in a wellness check for me.

I reached over and laid my hand on Dave's forearm, stopping him from typing.

"What are you doing?" He lifted his elbow to shake my hand off, but I gripped him harder and whispered, "We have to go."

"We're not until boarding group four," he said without looking up.

"No, *now*."

My urgent whisper caught his attention, and he looked up to see what was the matter.

"The man with the newspaper," I hissed. "He's a cop. I've seen him before."

"That's just a coincidence. He's not here for you. Listen, it's all going to be—"

At that moment, the man dipped his chin and seemed to speak to the collar of his shirt.

"Okay, we have to go," Dave said, slipping his laptop into his backpack and zipping it in one fluid motion.

"Where?"

"Out of here." He was already up and walking away from the gate.

I took a few quick strides to catch up with him. The sudden movement sent a sharp pain through my legs, but I kept on. One glance behind me confirmed that we weren't overreacting; the man in the golf shirt had set his newspaper aside and was walking after us.

"He's following us," I warned.

Dave sped up and I matched his pace. The policeman did, too. When we'd speed-walked half the length of the terminal, the policeman broke into a run.

"I guess we're running," Dave said. Without another word, he reached over and grabbed my backpack off my back, slinging the straps around his own arms so it hung at his front. He grabbed my hand and pulled me forward, and I focused all my energy on keeping up.

As we ran, some travelers leapt out of our way. Others glared. One woman stepped directly into my path, and I glanced off of her, falling forward. Dave turned and caught me before I could hit the ground, then tugged my arm, urging me to run faster.

I gasped for breath, unable to get enough air into my lungs. I couldn't run anymore.

We passed a long restaurant line, and Dave grabbed a rolling suitcase from one of the patrons standing in line.

"Hey!" the man shouted, but Dave had already given the suitcase a hard shove behind us, forcing the officer pursuing us to run around it and costing him a second.

Dave repeated the maneuver once more, and then we rounded a corner and burst through the door to the main terminal, slamming into the push bar.

"Go!" Dave shouted. I ran past him into the bustling atrium, and he shoved the door closed behind us. It would hardly slow our tail, but anything to buy us a fraction of a second was helpful while I was pushed so far past my limit the edges of my vision were starting to cloud.

Dave caught up to me and grabbed me once again. My mouth hung open in an agonized cry. "Almost there," he assured me. He hardly sounded out of breath at all.

I didn't know where "there" was, only that we were running. As if he read my mind, Dave pointed to the door and said, "The taxi line."

I could see a few taxis lined up, doors open and drivers waiting beside them, through the glass walls of the terminal. They were so close. We were less than twenty yards from the doors. We were going to make it.

"Mandy Perkins, you're under arrest!" The voice behind me sounded much closer than I expected. I didn't turn to see how close he was. I just pumped my arms harder at my sides, forcing myself forward. "Stop!" he cried again, and then there was a loud clatter and a shout as someone hit the ground.

"Stop her!" the officer cried.

I chanced a look back to see the officer on the ground, an empty stroller on its side beside him and a woman wearing a baby in a sling on her chest looking stunned.

Dave stopped ahead of me and waved his arms for me to hurry. I turned my back on the scene and dashed for the door. It opened for Dave, and he swung to the right, closing the gap between him and the first taxi in the line.

"Taxi!" he called, waving his arm. The driver of the first car snapped to attention, preparing to welcome us. Dave ran around the front of the car, giving me the quicker entry via the door facing the sidewalk. He slid into the car and pulled his door shut. The driver followed him around to the other side of the car.

"Taxi!" I waved to the driver of the second car, then threw myself into the back seat.

The astonished driver hurried around and climbed into the car, and I gasped out, "Drive. As fast as you can."

58

The driver peeled out from the curb, tires squealing, my heart thundering loud over the engine.

"Which direction?" he called back to me.

"Uh, toward Lakeside Park," I replied, pulling out my phone to text Ethan at the same time.

Mandy: What's your address?

I fired off the message, then added another.

Mandy: I'm heading your way.

I looked around, my pulse settling and brain calming enough to take in my surroundings for the first time, and realized with a sinking feeling that I had nothing. Dave had my backpack. I had the phone in my pocket and nothing else. No charger, no wallet. No cash to pay the driver.

Mandy: When I get there, can I borrow cash to pay the cab?

I felt guilt instinctively, hating to ask for anything but especially money, but then remembered that Ethan was taking practically my entire paycheck for helping me solve this case. I could ask him for a small fraction of it back to help him evade a murderous client.

Dave: Mandy, what the fuck?

Dave's texts started pouring in. Message after message asking what I was doing and where I was going and telling me to be smart and come back to him so we could make a new plan.

I blocked his number.

I had some explaining to do, sure, but now was not the time. Now, I needed to be focused on finishing this. I had to meet up with Ethan, and we had to get Christina out of danger until Styles and her team identified the man in the Spiderfang footage Ethan sent them and arrested him.

Ethan had said "this evening" when talking about meeting Christina at the park. It wasn't even noon yet. We had time to figure this out.

My phone lit up in my palm, and for a moment I worried it would be Dave texting from a new number, but it wasn't. I read Ethan's reply.

Ethan: Don't come to my place. I'm not home, and someone may be watching it.

Great. I breathed out slowly, trying to quell the alarm stewing in my gut.

Mandy: Okay, where are you? I'm in a cab and need to give the driver a location.

Ethan: Just meet me outside the park at 5:30. Job's supposed to be at 6.

Along with the message, he'd sent the address of a park northwest of town.

I wanted to throw my phone. I wanted Ethan to appear so I could throw it at his head. I had no money to pay this driver, and now I had no destination to give him.

I cast a net around my mind for all the places I could go, all the people I knew in Tucson who might be able to help me.

"Uh, Miss," the driver said. I met his eyes in the rearview mirror, and he said with mild concern, "The other cab is following us."

I turned in my seat, wincing at a flash of pain in my shoulder. Sure enough, Dave's cab had joined us on the highway.

"Shake them," I told him. "I don't care where we go. I'll pay you double the fare if you get away from them."

Dave couldn't follow me. There would already be too many of us at the park—Diana would probably be there, unsafe staying at Ethan's alone and wanted by the same man who had just hired Ethan to kill Christina, so there would be four of us trying to get out of town before Ethan's client realized he hadn't done the job. I didn't need Dave trying to get me to go with him again while the rest of us tried to get Christina to go with us.

Would she go with us? The question popped unbidden into my mind, and I let my brain try to puzzle it out while the taxi driver took quick turns without a blinker in an effort to evade Dave's taxi driver.

Christina had shown up at Diana's demanding the files from Hudson's law firm related to the Diamond Pharmaceuticals case. Something in those files would avenge Hudson's death, or at least that's what she'd told Diana. But the person who had hired Ethan to follow the lab technician involved in that court case wasn't Warner, and he wasn't Chuck Tourney.

When Ethan had that first job, to follow the lab tech and report back on his movements, he said Trevor went to visit the Schupperts' house. Hudson had been upset about the case; I wondered if Trevor had information that Hudson would have used to try to get the verdict overturned or otherwise upset things. And now Hudson was dead, and the man responsible was after Christina and Diana, the two people who were working together to get the court case records out of the law firm.

Ethan's client might not be Warner or Chuck, but I had no doubt one of them was pulling the strings, or maybe both of them together. They already had a mutually beneficial agreement, after all, with Chuck bringing money to the law firm and the law firm funneling money back to Chuck via the Board of Supervisors.

"They are gone." The driver's voice startled me out of my speculations, and I looked behind him to double-check.

He was right. No Dave.

My sigh of relief was interrupted by the driver asking, "Now where to?"

I deliberated for a moment, but I knew I had no other choice. My circle in Tucson was small, and almost everyone in it was on the run or under surveillance. He wouldn't be happy to see me, but he was my only option. I gave the driver Francisco's address.

We'd wound our way east of Tucson in our chase with Dave, and the desert flew past outside the car window as we headed back toward town and my street. An endless expanse of beige sand, almost white in the noon sun and hard to look at as it reflected the sun back at my eyes, stretched out from the highway, dotted with low trees and brush.

An RV park appeared on the left side of the road, the first sign we were coming back into town. Billboards popped up, followed by a small strip mall, and soon we were in a neighborhood surrounded by stucco homes and people in their cars running errands on their lunch breaks, unaware of the police manhunt and murder-for-hire plot unfolding around them.

Francisco was not happy to see me. I'd asked the taxi driver to make two passes of the street, not trusting the first pass when I'd seen no police, and then I had him idle by the curb while I ran up to the door.

"Before you say anything," I blurted before Francisco could say anything, "can I borrow some money to pay the taxi fare?"

"What are you doing here?" he asked, leaning forward to look past me up and down the street.

"I won't stay long," I assured him. "You weren't wrong to call Styles, and you're not wrong to be mad at me, but please hear me out before you call her again. If after everything I tell you, you still want to call her, be my guest. I'll wait on your porch for her to haul me away. But please let me explain first."

He frowned but didn't immediately slam the door in my face, which I considered a win.

"And, uh, the cab fare?" I asked, pointing over my shoulder.

Francisco stood still so long I opened my mouth to beg him further, but then he shoved off the doorframe and walked back into his home. He left the door hanging open in his wake. I waited awkwardly on the step until, sure enough, Francisco returned a moment later, wallet in hand.

When the taxi drove off, Francisco demanded, "Do you know how much that man just asked me for?"

I winced. "We had a situation and I, uh, said I'd pay him double."

"And yet *I* was the one stuck with the bill somehow."

"Thank you," I said, trailing him inside.

The moment the door was shut behind me, I launched into the story. For all I knew, Francisco had called Styles while he was inside getting his wallet, and I might not have much time. If she showed up to arrest me, I could tell her about the footage sitting in her department's email inbox, but that didn't guarantee she wouldn't haul me off just for good measure.

"I was at the Schupperts' home that night because Christina is my best friend," I confessed. "I kept that from you because at first I thought there was a possibility she'd done something horrible and roped me into helping."

"When you were covered in dirt the day after Hudson Schuppert went missing?" There was a bite to Francisco's question.

I nodded, then told him about the security footage Ethan found. "Hudson was gone long before I went over there, and he never returned. A man marched him out of the house at gunpoint. We sent video footage of it to the police, but I don't know if they've seen it yet."

Frowning, Francisco said, "That's not on the footage. You left it behind; I watched it."

"Not the doorbell footage. Maureen—the Schupperts' neighbor—has other cameras. Hidden ones. And I didn't steal the flash drive from you. E—" I stopped myself just before blurting out Eric's name. I didn't want this to come back onto Maureen. I was standing in the home of a journalist, and I couldn't risk anything that might put her in danger making it into an article.

"I found it," I lied. "I followed you that night, and I am so sorry. It was a massive invasion of privacy. But my friend had just gone missing, and I'd learned you were investigating her husband. I had to know if you'd found anything. I didn't take the flash drive, but I did see someone else take your bag out of your car when you went inside the gas station. When you left, I went to look around. They dropped the flash drive. I found it on the ground."

The lie tasted sour coming out of my mouth, and judging by Francisco's narrowed eyes and pursed lips, he didn't believe it anyway.

Before he could challenge me, I launched into the rest of the story. I told him everything I'd learned about the scheme between Hudson's law firm and the Board of Supervisors, the Diamond Pharmaceuticals case, and Ethan's mystery client.

As I spoke, my body grew heavier, and by the end I was leaning heavily on the back of one of the carved wooden chairs around the dining room table Francisco used as an office desk.

Instead of something about Hudson, Warner, or Diamond Pharmaceuticals, the first thing Francisco asked was, "Are you okay?"

I looked at him quizzically. I'd lied to him and kept things from him and now I'd turned up at his house and made him pay an astronomical cab fare before launching into a story of all the ways I'd snuck around and played detective while he was an actual investigative journalist. He wasn't supposed to be concerned with how I was feeling.

"You said you're sick. Last time you were here, you told me about your diagnosis. You're clearly struggling now." He gestured with his hand up and down, from my face to my legs.

I could feel how hot my skin was, sticky with sweat, though I was lightly shivering, and my legs wobbled at even the reduced weight they were supporting while I leaned on the chair. I didn't want to know how bad I looked.

"Sit down, and I'll get—"

"We have to get to that park," I said. I relayed my conversation with Ethan, how the person who killed Hudson wanted Ethan to be at that park when Christina arrived. "We have to get her out of town."

Francisco nodded as he took my hand and guided me to the living room, then lowered me onto the couch. "We will, but we still have hours. Rest first."

I crashed hard, asleep almost as soon as my body hit the leather upholstery. When I woke, I launched immediately into a panic.

"What time is it?" I demanded, pushing myself up and feeling like my insides had all been replaced with lead. How was I so heavy? Why was moving so hard? "We have to go!"

"It's okay," Francisco said softly, hurrying into the room. He was dressed all in black. "We have twenty minutes. I was just getting ready."

I managed to get myself upright and into the bathroom to splash water on my face. If anything, I felt worse than I had when I'd laid down. I was so cold my teeth were chattering, though my skin was hot to the touch; definitely a fever. And every movement of my limbs took triple the usual effort.

I pawed through Francisco's medicine cabinet and took two

Ibuprofen, then gave it a moment's consideration and took a third. In the mirror, I saw how swollen the bags beneath my eyes had gotten and why Dave had been so alarmed at my appearance. My pale skin looked thin and yellow-tinged except for the flushed areas of my face that were a vibrant red. My hair hung stringy and limp, and I had a near-constant grimace on my face when I moved around.

I pulled my hair into a ponytail, going through the familiar motion of moving strands around to try to cover the visible patches of scalp. Francisco appeared in the doorway and made me jump.

"Ready?" he asked.

I nodded. "Thank you for taking me." He could have turned me away from his doorstep, but instead he was helping.

"I'm happy to. Selfishly, this is a first-hand account that I'll put in my article."

I wondered if he'd focus at all on Styles and the police investigation in his article or if he'd stick to the facts and his own digging to uncover them. Would he take the opportunity to paint the woman who had so wronged him as a bumbling detective fixated on the wrong person while a killer was out there hiring college dropout private eyes and breaking into paralegals' apartments?

Francisco led me toward the door, stopping to grab something out of the refrigerator on the way. I looked into the plastic grocery bag he was holding and saw two tall cylindrical plastic containers filled with a dark red, almost-black substance.

"Is that...?" I looked closer.

Francisco replied, "Pork blood," and I swallowed a gag.

"Why do...you...have...that?" Each word was punctuated by a swallow and a deep breath as I tried to tamp down the nausea that swirled in my gut at the thought of the half-gallon of blood.

Francisco pulled the front door open and stuck his head out, then ushered me out in front of him so he could lock the door behind us. "I went to the butcher while you were napping."

"But why?"

I pressed my lips tight together to stop myself from groaning as I lowered myself into his car. No part of me felt rested or recovered from that nap.

Francisco slid into the driver's seat and turned the ignition.

"I don't think there's a world in which the man who killed Schuppert and hired your friend to take out his wife is going to believe this job went to plan and never come after you guys."

He was right, of course. We would convince Christina to run with us, and then there would be four of us trying to skip town and hide out until the police took care of things here.

"But I do think we can buy you some time." Francisco nodded to the bag. "Instead of just running, you stage a murder."

I looked from him to the containers of blood, understanding clicking into place.

"We make it look like Ethan did the job," I said.

Francisco nodded and stepped on the gas.

59

I saw her hair before anything else. The bright blonde strands swung back and forth, catching the evening sunlight and glowing gold while she argued with Ethan at the edge of a wood, shaking her head vigorously.

I could have keeled over at the sight of her. I ripped the door handle hard, opening the door and falling out of the car before Francisco had brought it to a full stop.

"Christina!" I scrambled toward them on hands and knees.

Behind me, Francisco parked the car next to Ethan's. I saw Diana waiting in the passenger seat, anxiously looking around, phone to her ear. When I got closer to Ethan and Christina, I could see that he had a wireless earbud in, and I guessed that she was supposed to warn him if she saw anyone approaching. If she warned him about Francisco and me pulling up, he wasn't concerned. He didn't look my way.

"You're in danger," he warned Christina. "You need to come with me."

"He's right," I wheezed when I reached them, pulling air into my burning lungs in quick, shallow breaths.

Christina's horrified face turned to mine, and Ethan gestured to me. "See? It's not a trap. Well, being here is a trap. *I'm* not trying to trap you. We need to go."

Christina shook her head again, blond bob swaying. From where I was leaning over my knees, I saw her familiar red sneakers, a line of pale skin visible above them before her black leggings covered the rest of her legs. The bottom of a white t-shirt stuck out from beneath an old Harvard sweatshirt with holes in it. The college I'd wanted to go to, where she'd gone instead. We'd never had a fight as bad as the one we had when she got into Harvard and I didn't, but if she didn't agree to come with us now, we were going to.

"Please," I said, pushing myself upright. "I can explain it all when we're on the road."

"I can't," she said to me now, ignoring Ethan. "He killed Hudson, Mandy. I can't let him get away with it."

"If you stay, he's going to kill you, too."

Light, quick footsteps approached from behind, and then Francisco joined us with the grocery bag holding the containers of blood.

He held it up. "Ready to fake a murder?"

No one laughed. Ethan's mouth dropped open. Christina went green, and I wondered if she was going to be sick.

Tearing her gaze from the bag, she swallowed and thrust her chin up. "We're not faking my murder, and I'm not going with you." She pulled on the front of her sweatshirt, widening one of the holes near the armpit, and I saw a tiny lens protruding.

"You're recording," I whispered.

She nodded. "Hudson had a recording of Chuck admitting everything on his laptop, but when I went back to the house, the laptop was gone. Chuck must have taken it just like he took the chest." Her voice broke, and when she spoke again it was shrill. "But I'm going to get him to admit it. He won't get away with it this time!"

Chuck. Chuck Tourney. Christina was expecting to meet the CEO of Diamond Pharmaceuticals. Whoever Ethan's mystery client was, he had to be operating on Chuck's behalf.

Ethan said, "Chuck isn't coming."

Christina looked puzzled. "He's meeting me here in"—she checked her watch—"five minutes."

"No, he's not. I was hired to meet you here in five minutes to kill you."

"But he's not going to!" I said quickly, seeing fear flicker across her face.

"I guess hired isn't quite the right word," Ethan considered. "Extorted, maybe? But yeah, she's right, I'm not actually going to kill you."

Francisco held up the bag again and said, "We're going to make it look like he did to buy you guys some time while you get out of town."

Christina shook her head. "I don't understand. Chuck told me to meet him here. I was going to goad him into admitting everything, then take the recording to the police."

"It's a setup," I said. "He told you to meet him here, then got someone to hire Ethan to ambush you instead."

Christina stomped her foot and huffed. "Chuck is coming! He has to."

"He's not," I said gently. "But if he gets wind that Ethan hasn't actually killed you, then we'll be in real trouble. That's why we need to get out of here."

"He can't get away with this," Christina repeated.

"He won't. Ethan already sent a video of—"

"You need to go," she pressed, stomping her foot again. "Let me handle this."

Somewhere behind us, a shriek split the air—children playing on the playground on the other side of the woods. To my right, running alongside the small wood and the playground, was a pond reflecting the brilliant orange sunset. Another child let out a gleeful scream, and it echoed across the water.

"No," I said, throwing my shoulders back and swaying a little on the spot. I clenched my jaw to keep from shivering as my body tried to shut down on me. "You dragged me into this. You brought me over to your house to bury what might have been a goddamn body—"

"It wasn't—"

"—and then you ran. You left me to be hounded by the police for helping my best friend murder her husband, and all this time I've been trying to prove you didn't do it. You ran off and *I* was the one facing the consequences, and all the while I didn't even know what we buried! You don't get to bring me into this and then tell me to leave. You don't get to leave me in the dark and then try to order me around."

Christina wiped a tear from her face. Ethan and Francisco had both taken steps back, looking around while Christina and I faced off.

"You know I didn't kill Hudson," she said.

"Do I?" I threw my hands up in the air. "Because it didn't look great, burying a wooden chest the night your husband went missing and then having you disappear off the face of the Earth. I was pretty sure you wouldn't do that, but then what do I know about what you would and wouldn't do? I never thought you'd cheat on him either, but then I found the Polaroids."

Christina stepped back, aghast.

"You hid your affair from me. You hid your marital issues. And whatever it is that ignited all of this,"—I waved my arms, gesturing at the entire situation—"you hid that, too. Why didn't you tell me what was going on with Hudson? I'm supposed to be your best friend."

Christina's open-mouthed horror morphed into anger that matched my own.

"When was I supposed to tell you any of that? Every time we talk on the phone, it's like you're not even there. It's like I'm talking to myself, getting only the occasional 'wow that's great' or 'oh that's awful' in reply. You haven't been present for almost a year!"

"I've been sick!" I blurted. "I spent months bouncing from doctor to doctor while my body was fighting itself, and every time I think I'm getting better, I take a new turn. It's hard to be present on the phone when I'm literally pinching myself to stay awake, and it's hard to be cheerful when my hair is falling out and I don't know if I'm going to be able to stand up for the duration of the class I'm supposed to teach next semester."

"Then why didn't you fucking tell me that?" she screamed.

"I don't know!" I screamed back, both of us furious and desperate, both of us with tears streaming down our faces.

We locked eyes and then she pulled me into a hug, my shoulders rising and falling with each sob. I breathed in the smell of her and dug my fingers into the folds of the sweatshirt, clinging to it. When she pulled away, I gripped harder.

"You have to leave," she whispered.

I shook my head again, vision blurred by tears and fever. "I can't. Not without you."

"This is all very touching."

We gasped in unison and spun to see a tall, bald man in a leather jacket step out from a dense group of trees. A strangled noise came from Ethan, and I turned to see him wide-eyed and open-mouthed, terror written all over his face where he stared at the man. This was his client, the man who'd marched Hudson out of his home and forced Ethan into coming here.

The man sneered and said, "But I'm afraid your reunion is over."

Christina squared her shoulders at him, her defiance making my stomach clench. "You're not Chuck," she told him.

"No, I'm not," he said, and then he raised his arm, the gun in his hand glinting as it reflected the orange-and-red sunset, and shot her.

60

"Christina!" I bellowed, rushing to her side.

"No!" Ethan and Francisco shouted in unison.

The grocery bag dropped from Francisco's hand, a thud and splatter sounding as the containers burst and blood drenched the grass and leaves beneath his feet.

Christina gasped and bent at the waist, clutching her thigh.

Ethan and Francisco both ran to her side. I remained frozen to the spot.

The smell of the blood triggered my gag reflex, but I choked it down, forcing myself to keep it together. Francisco had already removed his shirt and was pressing it to Christina's leg, murmuring something in her ear as a bright red spot grew beneath his fingers.

"You... you..." Ethan looked up at his client, horror and disbelief choking off his words.

"It's nice to see you again, too," the man replied. Light danced in his eyes, fixed on Christina. He was enjoying this. "I can't say I'm surprised you couldn't do the job I gave you, but I am disappointed." He pointed his gun at Christina again, and for a heart-stopping second I thought he would pull the trigger a second time.

"No!" we all screamed, and the man lowered the weapon to his side, a sinister laugh bubbling up from his round belly.

My muscles contracted, my limbs all shaking beyond my control. I fought to make my arm bend, a trembling hand reaching into my back pocket for my phone. I had to call the police.

"I wouldn't do that if I were you." Another unfamiliar male voice made me jump, but when I looked behind me, the man stepping out from behind another group of trees wasn't unfamiliar at all. I'd seen him in person once before, and in pictures far more than that.

Chuck Tourney stood before us, his suit traded in for a pair of black sweatpants that tapered close to his ankles and a grey-and-black camouflage patterned hoodie.

An ambush. A trap. Chuck and his crony, hiding in the woods waiting for us all.

We'd walked right into it.

My phone slipped between my fingers, landing in the dirt.

I looked around for something to hold onto to keep me upright, anything I could use to hold my weight, but found my knees buckling before I could reach for anything.

"Giving up so soon?" Chuck asked me, amused. "I thought you'd put up more of a fight." He looked around at the group of us and said, "Let's see who we've got here. It's more of a crowd than I was expecting…"

I followed his gaze from Christina, face scarily pale in contrast to the sweatshirt whose wrists were now drenched in blood where she was putting pressure on her wound, to Francisco, to Ethan, and finally to the stranger. To my surprise, Ethan's client didn't look smug to see his partner arrive. He looked horrified.

Chuck frowned at Ethan's client. "Dominic, you've given me more work than I was expecting today."

Dominic shook his head and stammered unintelligibly.

"I was expecting to find you, your little PI, and the wife." He gestured with his hand from Dominic to Ethan and then to Christina, and I saw a ring flash on his pinky finger with a diamond even bigger than the one I'd seen on his tie clip in the lobby of the law firm. "But now the body count has doubled." He looked from Francisco to me and then turned toward the cars.

I gasped. Diana. Was she still on the phone with Ethan? Had she called the police? I tried to push myself up but my fingers raked uselessly through the dirt, my consciousness swaying.

"Dead," Chuck said to me, cocking his head toward the cars.

He reached into the waistband of his sweatpants and pulled out a small gun. The sunset glinted off the metal, and I noticed specks of red on his hand where he gripped the weapon.

I choked back my cry. I'd sent Diana to Ethan's; I was the reason she'd come with him here.

Chuck had already moved on and was surveying the rest of us with a frown. I watched Dominic edging away from the wood slowly and wondered if I could somehow get his gun.

"You shouldn't outsource what you're supposed to be doing yourself," Chuck said slowly, lazily.

Dominic stammered out, "I understand, Chuck. I was just about to sh—"

"Too late," Chuck said, and lifted his own gun.

I flinched when the shot rang out, loud as a clap of thunder.

"We don't have long now," he said, looking around.

I looked back toward the cars. I hadn't heard a gunshot earlier, and I wondered if he'd been bluffing about Diana. But the blood on his hand... I swallowed another cry.

Chuck moved to stand over Dominic's body. Chuck was a much better shot than the other man; he'd shot Dominic square in the chest, and Dominic didn't make a sound when his body landed in the dirt.

"Pity." Chuck muttered the word to himself, his focus entirely on Dominic's still face.

Without taking his eyes off the body beneath him, Chuck spoke to the rest of us. "When I told Dominic I had a plan for the wife"—he waved his gun in Christina's direction but still didn't look up—"I also told him to take out his little PI. No more loose ends. No one else would be left to spoil this for me...except for him.

"It was his idea, you know. Hudson's meddling wife would come here expecting me, but instead of multiple shootings in multiple places, Dominic came up with a plan to bring the PI here and stage some sort of murder-suicide. Cleaner. Less chance that anyone would push for an investigation."

While Chuck stood over Dominic, his apparent sidekick, I shifted onto my hands and knees and crawled as quietly as I could over to the others. As I neared Ethan, I saw that his wireless earbud had fallen out and was lying stark white against the dirt.

"I liked Dominic's idea so much," Chuck continued, "I decided to take it for myself. When I told him he should do his own dirty work, well, it was also a bit of a reminder for myself. When you bring someone else in to do all the kidnapping and surveilling and murdering, you keep your hands clean, sure, but you also create witnesses."

I reached for the earbud and shoved it into my ear.

"Diana?" I whispered, holding onto a shred of hope, but no answer came through. "Diana?" I whispered one more time, now clawing my way across the ground toward Christina.

"It's a true shame Dominic had to go. Diamond Pharmaceuticals wouldn't have become what it is without him. I couldn't have asked for a better second in command." He stuck out his foot, nudging the man's midsection. "I'll have to do better next time. Not delegate what I ought to be doing myself."

"Run," Christina whispered the second I got close enough. "Get this footage off my body and get it to the police."

She started trying to fiddle with her sweatshirt, reaching underneath to remove the camera she'd hidden in her clothes, but I shook my head. I'd already run so many times. I couldn't keep running, and I couldn't abandon her while she lay bleeding out on a pile of leaves.

"Please," she begged, her whisper so soft it was lost on the wind, only the shape of her lips conveying her message.

I shook my head again, my refusal absolute.

Before Christina could press any further, and before I could run if I'd wanted to, Chuck turned away from his dead lackey and looked from Christina to me and then over to Ethan and Francisco.

"I didn't expect quite so many people, but that'll be fine. The paralegal's already taken care of. Her body will need to be moved, of course, but that's no trouble. And nice of you to bring her here," he said, looking at Ethan. "It saved me a trip. Warner tried to hide it from me, you know—that she'd been poking around in the case files. I stopped in on him and he was all out of sorts. Once I got it out of him, I knew she'd have to go. He begged me not to, but needs must. I have to say, I didn't expect her to be handed to me so easily.

"Anyway..." He pulled several folded-up sheets of paper from his pocket and leafed through them. He looked at Christina from beneath his lashes. "Since you've already been shot in the leg, someone else will need to be the killer."

Flip. Flip.

"Ah, here we go." He extended his arm and handed me one of the pages.

By the time this is found, it will all be over. I couldn't live with myself anymore after what I did. I helped Christina Schuppert kill her husband and dispose of his body. Now I and everyone involved in such a horrible act must die. May we never cause pain to anyone else.

Mandy Perkins

I squinted at the note. It didn't make sense.

"I wasn't sure you'd come on this little jaunt," Chuck said, "but it's always better to be prepared for all possibilities. And since the police already think you two did it, I don't see anyone looking too hard at the details. Of course, when I wrote 'everyone involved,' I didn't expect there to be so many others." With a shrug, he said, "Life's full of surprises, isn't it. Now, who's first?"

He raised his gun, and the four of us—Ethan, Francisco, Christina, and I—all shouted in unison. "Wait!"

"They'll investigate," I said, then nodded toward Dominic's body. "The police already have evidence that he's the one who kidnapped Hudson."

Chuck threw his head back in an icy laugh. "The little video you sent? That's already been deleted."

A chill went down my spine, and I turned my head a fraction of a degree to lock eyes with Ethan.

"It helps to have a cop in your pocket," Chuck added. "You'd be surprised what a young officer's willing to do. A wife, a couple kids, and an entry-level salary—the boy took little convincing. With an officer on my payroll and a note admitting guilt in your pocket, no, I don't think they will investigate."

Ethan crashed to his knees, defeat written across his face. Chuck laughed again.

"You've made me realize, though," Chuck said, "that Dominic's body will need to go. No need to have anyone from Diamond Pharmaceuticals anywhere near this crime scene. The rest of you, though, will be victims of a"—he paused to count us theatrically—"quadruple murder-suicide. A small price to pay for Diamond Pharmaceuticals to get Qorlexin on the market. The lives this new drug will save...you five don't even tip the scales."

He lifted his gun again. The opportunity to run was past. I doubted I'd even be fully on my feet before he shot me.

"Wait!" Christina said again.

Chuck didn't lower his pistol but raised an eyebrow at Christina, indicating for her to go on.

"There's another copy."

Chuck growled, stabbing the gun in her direction. "You're bluffing! There is no other copy."

"Let's recount them all, shall we?" Christina kept her voice level, a hint of teasing at the edge of her words. "First, there's the one Trevor had. The one that started it all. Someone smuggled those records from the drug trials out of the company for him after you and Warner perjured yourselves in order to destroy him in court."

Francisco shifted his body until he was positioned in front of me. I looked up at him and saw him turn his head just enough that I could see the outline of his lips mouth the word "run."

Christina continued her slow, taunting speech. "You got that copy, sure, after you—or was it the sidekick over there who did your dirty work?—murdered Trevor.

"There's the copy Hudson was supposed to give to our journalist Francisco, here. That meetup must not have gone to plan, though, or your deceit would already be public knowledge and Diamond Pharmaceuticals would be crumbling at your feet."

With another growl, Chuck lurched a step closer to Christina, moving diagonally away from me. Francisco took another step to the side, his body now fully separating me from Chuck.

"You really thought you could go to a journalist and I wouldn't find out?" Chuck ground out. "Of course that meeting didn't go to plan. Dominic got to Francisco before he'd even left the parking lot and traded him a shiner for the envelope full of those records."

I looked up at the back of Francisco's head, where sweat gleamed on his caramel-colored skin. He'd been supposed to meet Hudson before all of this started? How much had he known this whole time?

"And then there's the copy I buried in the backyard," Christina said. "My plan was to keep it safe until I could come back for it. That didn't work either."

"No, it didn't," Chuck said, flashing his gun again. He was hanging on her every word, his full attention on Christina. And with his back to me and Francisco separating us... "Get to the point," he demanded.

"Did you know I have my own lawyer? Everyone thought it was ridiculous I'd have a lawyer other than my husband when he was so good, but I thought it was safer. And speaking of safes, he received a package of documents from me with instructions to open it in the event of my death. I included a handy list of organizations with large publicity footprints who would be *very* interested in fabricated test data from one of the largest pharmaceutical companies in the nation."

"You're lying." Chuck waved his gun with his accusation, stepping closer to Christina.

"Maybe," she shrugged. I could see the effort in her movement. "But you could give him a call to find out. I think you have his number."

Chuck stepped back as if she'd hit him.

"Robert Loeb," she said. "You know him, right? The other named partner at Warner & Loeb?"

Chuck set his jaw. "He wouldn't. He couldn't publicize those documents without implicating his firm, telling the whole world how his law firm helped me fabricate records and lie on the stand."

Christina stayed silent, and I watched Chuck's face cycle through smug confidence, uncertainty, and finally anger.

Francisco took a half step back, forcing me to crawl backward to avoid being stepped on. Smoothly and silently, he reached into his pocket. When he removed his hand, it was balled into a fist, and he coughed loudly just as he unfurled his fingers, the sound covering the metallic clink of his keys hitting the ground. I looked up just in time to see him mouth "run" again.

"You're lying to me," Chuck said again, though he had his phone in his hand.

While Chuck dialed the law offices of Warner & Loeb to call Christina's bluff, I closed my fist around Francisco's keys and, for what I hoped was the last time in my life, I ran.

61

Behind me, over the sound of my own gasping breaths and my feet on the dirt, I heard Chuck shout. "Hey! Come b— hello, Bob?"

As Chuck began to interrogate the attorney, I skidded to a halt as I reached the sandy gravel parking lot. I ran around Francisco's Corolla to Ethan's little white Nissan, light brown with the dirt from the drive into the park.

"Diana," I breathed, still panting heavily. Her braids were hanging in front of her face, obscuring it from view, but it didn't look like a murder scene. If Chuck had shot her, there'd be blood and brains spattered across the window, I told myself. He was bluffing.

I tried the handle and was surprised when the door opened easily, then further surprised when Diana's body lolled toward me. Her head fell backward at an unnatural angle and the side of it was entirely covered in blood.

I leaned over and threw up on my shoes.

Behind me in the woods, I heard shouting.

"I am so sorry," I said, straightening Diana's body. My hands came away slick with her blood, and I fought to reflex to vomit again.

Keys sliding in my blood-covered hands, I unlocked Francisco's car and cranked the engine. As I pulled away, shots fired once again. I screamed when one made contact with the back windscreen, shattering it, and slid down in my seat while I floored it down the dirt road out of the park.

The moment I was out of firing range, I reached for my phone. My hands met nothing but flat empty pockets, and I cursed myself for leaving my phone lying in the dirt.

At the first gas station I passed, I pulled in and left the car running right outside the door.

"I need to use your phone!" I shouted, rushing the counter.

The attendant behind the counter, a teen working what might have been his first job, took one look at me and backed up until he bumped into the wall of cigarettes behind him. I thrust my arms behind my back, but it was too late; he'd seen the blood on me.

"Hit the silent alarm," I told him. "Call 911. If you don't want to let me use your phone, fine. But you need to call the police. Send them to Daniel Gordon Park, the small parking lot on the west side of the park. Please!"

The teen nodded, eyes wide and horrified. The bell clanged discordantly when I shoved the door open and returned to Francisco's car.

The police were on their way, or would be shortly. I'd seen how terrified that kid was; he'd call them. I felt sure of that.

I looked back toward the park, to where my best friend was lying on the ground losing blood, to where she might already be dead. Then I drove in the opposite direction.

When I pulled into Christina's driveway, it was all I could do to keep my eyes open. I swerved halfway onto their lawn before I managed to bring the car to a stop and clamber out onto legs that burned and buckled.

I didn't have my purse, which meant I didn't have my spare key, but this time I didn't care who saw me. Let them call the police. I slipped off one sneaker and smashed it into the window. If Detective Styles wanted to bring me in on charges of breaking and entering, I could live with that.

A broken piece of glass slid across my bicep as I climbed

inside. I hissed and looked away from where the warm blood slid down my arm. I was hanging on by a thread as it was, and the sight of more blood threatened to push me over the edge. I needed to remain conscious long enough to get upstairs.

The climb up to the second floor was arduous. I crawled up the second half of the flight of stairs, leaving a trail of dirt and blood in my wake.

Every time my brain and body pleaded with me to just close my eyes for a minute, to lie down and rest just for a second, I thought of Diana, the legal career that had been ahead of her and the blood that caked her head now. I thought of Christina, with Francisco and Ethan trying desperately to slow the bleeding while Chuck waved his gun at them.

The unbidden image of Chuck firing, then stripping the camera from Christina's body before fleeing on foot popped into my mind. I told myself it wasn't true. I told myself Styles would be fast enough. And if Chuck left with that recording, that wouldn't be the end of this.

"Argh!" I stretched out my arm and pulled open the drawer to Hudson's nightstand. My head fell back and tears streamed openly down my face. My chest shook, and I crumpled to the floor.

It was the most profound relief I'd ever felt.

Hudson's laptop was right where I'd left it.

I pulled it out, even its light weight almost too much for me, and set it on the carpet before me. When I lifted the lid, I was greeted by the familiar picture of Hudson and Christina smiling from Mykonos. They were leaning against a white wall, Christina's hand up shading her eyes, and a brilliant blue sea dotted with boats stretched out behind them. I stared at the password entry box.

If I couldn't guess the password and got myself locked out of the laptop, I could still take it to the police, but with someone on the force taking money from Chuck, I didn't think I could count on whatever recording lived on this laptop not getting mysteriously deleted. And I didn't have anything left to lose.

I tried the password "Christina." No dice. "ChristinaAndHudson" was another miss. I switched over to numbers and put in his birthday, and when that didn't work I tried Christina's. The message "Incorrect Password" flashed again.

I threw my head back with a groan. My brain automatically began calculating how many possible combinations there were, too many years in the math department having left their mark. Just as I was accepting defeat, preparing myself to take this with me to the police station and pray no crooked cop got his hands on it, I caught sight of the lone photo on Hudson's nightstand.

A thin black frame surrounded the wedding photo. It was taken just after the first kiss, when they'd clasped hands and started to walk back down the aisle together, officially man and wife. Christina was smiling directly at the camera, mouth open wide, bouquet held up above her head in the hand that wasn't intertwined with Hudson's. Instead of looking at the camera, Hudson was focused only on his new wife, eyes gleaming with adoration and joy.

I turned back to the laptop and put in their wedding date.

The lock screen dissolved, replaced by the default Windows background studded with application shortcuts and file folders.

I let out a breathy victory cry, which turned almost immediately into a pained yelp when I tried to clench my hands into fists to pump in celebration. My heart pumped fast in my chest, fatigue and pain pushed aside by the new wave of adrenaline as I searched the screen.

I liked my computer desktops organized, with only the bare minimum displayed. A few shortcuts to my most-used applications lived in the top right corner, but otherwise I hated the clutter. Hudson, on the other hand, seemed to like for every single file he'd ever opened to live on his desktop. The Google Chrome logo lived next to a folder labeled "Taxes," and right below that was an image file whose name was just "IMG_0514.jpg." From the minuscule preview, I guessed that it was a picture of his childhood dog. Either that or their Christmas card photo from the year before; it was hard to tell.

I pored over the page, opening up files I wasn't sure about. There was an audio file named with a date, the day before Hudson went missing.

I held my breath and opened the file, and Hudson's voice filled the room.

62

"You killed Trevor Hall."

Hudson's voice was breathy and his words were obscured by the movement of fabric. The audio recording had been taken secretly, and I guessed that his phone had been stashed in a pocket.

"I didn't kill anyone." Chuck Tourney's reply was harder to make out, dampened by the fabric of Hudson's pocket but still audible.

There was another loud rustle of cloth over the microphone. Then, Hudson: "—could die because you manipulated the data."

"Like this drug hasn't been through half a dozen trials since then. Phase I hardly matters at this point. Qorlexin is safe, and it is going to save millions of lives."

My eyebrows shot up at Chuck's admission. The Phase I data Trevor accused him of fabricating really was phony.

"Oh, Chuck the hero, Chuck who cares about saving lives," Hudson taunted in a high voice. Then, in a serious tone I'd only heard him use once before when I'd gone to watch him during his first court appearance, he said, "How can you pretend to care about saving lives when you've just taken an innocent one?"

"One or two lives sacrificed to revolutionize medicine and prevent heart disease in hundreds of millions more seems a worthy trade to me."

I flinched as another loud rustle covered whatever Hudson said next. His voice cut in at the tail end of a sentence. "—what Trevor didn't get the chance to."

"Oh, I don't think so," Chuck replied, venom in his voice. "Those records are long gone."

"That copy, maybe," Hudson said triumphantly. "But I have another. The whole world is going to see what you did. You'll get what you deserve, Chuck."

I opened a web browser and logged onto my email, then sent the recording to myself. Then I sent it to the police tip address and to Dave, just in case. The more copies of this recording in the world, the better. The more likely it was that Chuck wouldn't get away with this.

Then I closed the laptop and tried to stand.

As if my body understood that my primary mission had been accomplished, that my friends' fates depended on whether police had already gotten to them or not but that I couldn't help them by rushing to the park now, it collapsed. I'd managed to bend my shaking limbs and digits to my will until now, but no longer. I tried to move my arm to push myself up, but it just twitched beneath me. My skin felt searing hot where my forehead lay on one forearm, fever deepening.

I let my eyelids flutter closed, darkness swirling with the gray-beige of the carpet in front of my face. Somewhere, I thought I heard sirens. Then they faded. Through the broken window at the bottom of the stairs, I heard car doors close somewhere outside. I wondered if they would notice the window and call someone to investigate, if that person would find me and take me to a hospital or at least bring me some water. My mouth was so dry.

In the distance, wailing noises started up. They grew louder, and I wondered if they were coming from me. Was I crying? I tried to reach a hand to my face to feel for wet cheeks; I couldn't even tell whether my mouth was open or closed. The connection between my brain and body seemed to have snapped.

The wailing grew continually louder, now accompanied by a

rhythmic metallic clanking I was fairly certain wasn't coming from me, and then it stopped.

I let my eyes close again. My consciousness grew thinner, the blurring at the edges now overtaking everything. I let the darkness encroach. When the darkness spread, the pain faded, and that was good.

"Mandy," a voice said. Was it my own voice? Was it God?

I felt my body being turned over. Without control over my limbs, I couldn't move my arm out of the way and instead rolled over on top of it, pinning it beneath my back. The pain returned, white-hot in my shoulder, but when my eyelids opened, there was an angel standing over me.

"Mandy, oh God."

When the angel reached toward me, I tried to arch my back and meet him halfway. If this was death, it certainly wasn't painless.

The angel reached beneath my knees and shoulders and gathered me to his chest. Up close, I thought he might be human. He had a glowing gold halo around him, but so did everything else in my field of vision, and he felt much more solid than I expected of a heavenly being. He also smelled good, familiar somehow, and I wondered if angels had smells.

I reached out to poke him to determine his solidity, but my arm didn't actually reach out.

"Shh," the angel commanded. "I've got you. You're okay."

The comfort of his words wrapped around me. I let my eyes close, and the pain finally evaporated as oblivion closed in.

63

If I had died, I had not gone to heaven. Heaven didn't have incessant beeping sounds and bright lights and, most especially, pain. But wherever I was sure did.

My eyes blinked open and then closed again, scrunching at the brightness of my surroundings.

"Mandy!" I turned toward the voice and blinked again. Dave was standing over me.

"Dave?" The sound of my own voice, hoarse and feeble, surprised me. I looked down at my body to see that I was covered in a thin blanket, and where my hands rested atop the blanket, they were half-covered in tape holding needles in place with tubes running from them.

I turned my head and found the source of the beeping, a monitor displaying my vitals.

I hadn't died after all. I was in a hospital.

"I thought I'd lost you, Mandy." Dave lowered himself to his knees, hands grasping the railing of my hospital bed so hard his knuckles were white. His face was red and his swollen eyes were wet with fresh tears.

The scent of his favorite cologne—warm, peppery woods with a ginger note—hit me, and understanding clicked into place.

"The angel," I whispered.

He looked at me, confused, then toward the door like he might need to flag down a nurse.

I quickly clarified, "You found me at Christina's."

He nodded. "I did. Mandy, what the hell? I tried to follow you in the cab, but we lost you. I looked everywhere. By the time I decided to try Christina's place..." His voice broke and he trailed off. "I tried your place. I went back to the airport. I called hospitals. Mandy, I thought you were gone."

The pain in his voice stirred up something like guilt in me, but as my mind began to work again, I had too many other questions to dwell on that feeling.

"Christina," I started. "Is she okay?"

Dave looked at me, baffled. He clearly didn't know what I'd been doing between ditching him at the airport and being found mostly unconscious in Christina's bedroom.

"Do the police know I'm here?" I pressed. They would be able to tell me. I needed them to tell me.

His face grave with concern, Dave said, "If they do, I'll get you out—"

"Oh, we know."

Both Dave and I jumped, then turned to see a woman in a suit walk into the room. She held her hand out to him.

"Detective Farrah Styles," she said. "Pleasure to meet you."

Dave gripped her hand uncertainly and shot me a nervous look.

"Good to know you'd smuggle a fugitive out of the state, sir," Styles said, and Dave's pale expression blanched further.

"The park," I blurted, pulling their attention back to me. "Daniel Gordon Park. Chuck Tourney is—"

"In custody," Styles said, and I laid my head back with relief.

"The gas station clerk," I breathed, heart overflowing with gratitude. "I worried it was too late by the time I told him to call."

She frowned. "It was. If we'd waited until his call came in to send officers to the park, it would have been a very different situation by the time they arrived."

"Then how...?"

"Diana Jeffreys."

The memory of discovering her body in Ethan's car flooded my senses, and I closed my eyes, willing the nausea away. I could feel the slick of her blood all over again, the shock when her body had slumped lifelessly toward me.

Styles explained, "A 911 call came in from a caller who was silent on the other end. The dispatcher thought it was a prank until he heard a gunshot in the background. He made the call to send officers to the location. Those officers came upon a murder scene and immediately called for backup before successfully apprehending the suspect."

My brows knit together.

"The caller was identified as Diana Jeffreys. She was found with massive trauma to the head, likely struck with the butt of a gun, and her phone was on the floorboard of the car where she was discovered."

My gut clenched. Diana should never have been at that park. She should still be alive. She should still be preparing for the bar exam, a brilliant career ahead of her, but I'd sent her with Ethan for her own safety, and now she was dead, after using her last moment to hail rescuers for everyone else.

"She—and everyone else—is very lucky responders arrived when they did," Styles said.

I turned the words over in my brain, trying to make them fit together.

Styles saw my confusion and said, "She's alive. She's in critical condition, but my understanding is that her doctors are hopeful."

"But..." I trailed off. *She had a hole in her head. There was so much blood.* I shook my head. She was alive, and if she stayed that way, I owed her everything.

I looked back at Styles. I almost couldn't bring myself to ask, but I had to know. "What about...everyone else?"

"One man was found deceased at the scene. He has been identified as Dominic Jones, an associate of Tourney's. Christina Schuppert, Ethan Howard, and Francisco Como were also at the scene. All three are alive."

They'd made it in time.

All the fear I'd been holding in my body exited by way of my tear ducts, fat droplets streaming down my face and wetting the pillow under my head.

The beeping coming from my monitor sped up, and a nurse entered the room to check on me. She frowned disapprovingly at Styles and Dave for working me up but didn't tell them to leave. She studied the monitor, lips pursed, then left the room.

"Hudson had—" I started, but the nurse returned almost immediately, pushing a wheeled cart.

While she drew something up out of a small vial and injected it into the port at the base of my IV bag, I told Styles what I'd found on Hudson's laptop.

"He had a recording. I have it. Chuck admitted it all." The words flew out in short, desperate sentences. I needed Styles to see that recording. Christina was alive, and neither she nor I were going to jail; with those concerns sorted, my next biggest worry was that Chuck would somehow get away with it.

I tried to slow down and elaborate. "Hudson confronted Chuck about the lab tech—"

"You need to rest," the nurse admonished me. She turned to Styles and asked her, "Can you continue this later?"

I remembered, "Chuck said he had a cop in his pocket. Someone who could delete tips sent by email. He said he was young, new to the force."

Styles's face immediately went stony. She drew her phone and fired off a message before looking back up at me.

"I'll need to get an official statement from you later. You can share the recording with me then. We also recovered a recording Mrs. Schuppert took during the altercation." She looked to the nurse and then told me, "For now, rest up."

Satisfied, the nurse left the room, Styles on her heels. Before Styles followed her out the door, another question floated to the top of my mind.

"Wait!" I called, and she turned to face me, clearly impatient to get back to work. "What about Clemens? You asked me about him once, and he wrote a letter to the board asking them to make him supervisor in Hudson's absence before the public knew Hudson was even missing."

She waved her hand, dismissing my question as if it were unimportant. "We were looking at him for accepting bribes. He had his own little racket going on outside his deal with the lawyer. But no, he had nothing to do with Mr. Schuppert's death. From what we've gathered so far, it seems Mr. Warner had been seeking to install Mr. Clemens as Schuppert's replacement as soon as he could. Clemens was more willing than Schuppert to go along with his schemes. When Mr. Warner learned of Mr. Tourney's actions, he tapped Clemens to put himself forward. Clemens didn't know anything about Hudson's disappearance or murder."

I frowned, trying hard to clear the fog in my mind so I could see the picture more clearly. Styles turned without another word and slipped through the door, letting it shut quietly behind her.

A baffled Dave was by my side the moment she was gone. "What was she talking about, Mandy?" He looked me over with renewed concern. "Who is this Diana woman who—?"

"Shh." I held up a hand. The fog in my head was intensifying, amplified by whatever the nurse had added to my IV. My body felt heavy and my mouth fuzzy, and I knew I couldn't retell the story now. "Later."

He frowned but didn't argue, instead sitting in the blue plastic chair beside my bed. Later, I would have to tell him I wasn't moving back to Michigan with him. There would be another argument. He wasn't wrong that giving up a career and a marriage to someone who cared for me was crazy, but he wasn't right that it was wrong. I may not have known what the life I wanted looked like, but I'd take the time to figure that out. For now, I knew the life I'd been living wasn't what I wanted. And I knew I wouldn't be alone in whatever I chose moving forward.

Christina was alive, and for the first time since we'd buried that stupid chest, I knew she was safe. Chuck was in police custody and I had Hudson's recording to make sure he stayed that way.

CHRISTINA'S HAIR was the first thing I noticed when I saw her lying in her hospital bed, just like when I saw her standing in the woods at that park. The blond was bright against the blue pillow, splayed out behind her head like a halo.

I rushed to her side, leaving Dave to wait in the hallway. The moment I was discharged, I'd urged him to bring me to the hospital across town where Christina was. He'd insisted on stopping for food first but otherwise acquiesced, and now he squirmed uncomfortably while I let tears of both relief and terrible sadness streak unchecked down my face.

"You're alive," I said, still trying to make myself believe it. The last time I'd seen her, she'd been covered in blood, pale as a ghost, lying in the dirt with a homicidal man waving a gun at her. Now, her cheeks were rosy and her eyes were bright.

"Thanks to you, the paramedics, and the half-dozen donors whose blood is now pumping through these veins." She gestured to her body. "Not to mention your hot neighbor. Everyone who gets shot should have a hot guy take his shirt off to help them. I highly recommend it."

I grimaced. "Not thanks to me, as it turns out." I'd been too late. "Thanks to Diana."

She made a sour face.

"You know she and Hudson weren't sleeping together, right?" I asked.

"Yes, but it's hard to undo an association after thinking one thing for so long."

I squeezed onto the bed beside her and we looped our arms together and intertwined our fingers.

"Do you want to talk about it?" I asked.

"No," she said immediately, then gave me a wry smile. "But seeing as you almost died because of me, I think you deserve to know everything."

I didn't bother pretending I was happy to let her keep it to herself. She was right—I could have died trying to find her, trying to uncover what happened to Hudson so she could be safe. She'd kept me in the dark when she'd handed me a children's shovel, and now I wanted the truth. All of it.

"I didn't kill Hudson, obviously—"

"Obviously."

"But we weren't exactly doing well. Right before you called me to come get you when you were leaving Dave, we had a blow-up fight. Things had been simmering for a while; he was always at work, and getting the supervisor position just made everything worse. He wanted us to have kids, but I told him I wasn't going to be a married single mom. He wouldn't step back from any of his work.

"When I found out he'd been spending time at a strip club, I lost it. I saw a charge on our joint account and I immediately looked up Cory Clemens's phone number."

Regret clouded her features, and instead of meeting my gaze, she stared down at her hands when she spoke. "It was stupid. I wanted to hurt him. I took those photographs so I could leave them somewhere he'd find them. I wanted him to confront me so I could tell him I knew all about Heaven on Earth." With a heavy sigh, she said, "But he wasn't cheating on me. He was helping a goddamn paralegal prepare for her exam."

Christina turned away and wiped at her face. I gently squeezed her hand.

"Then I had this student come to one of my art classes. Trevor. He said he'd lost his job and needed to do something with his time. He saw some pen or piece of paper or something with Hudson's firm's logo on it and freaked out. I mean, he flipped his shit, Mandy. And then he told me that firm had helped his employer doctor emails and make a fool out of him in some court case.

"I didn't know what he was talking about. Hudson doesn't talk to me about work, but Trevor swore the CEO of the place where he worked was a liar and someone at the law firm helped him get away with it."

Diamond Pharmaceuticals. The lab technician had been one of Christina's students.

"What did you do?" I asked.

"I told him I'd tell Hudson. Hudson said it couldn't be true. He believed the best in his colleagues, and Will really took him under his wing when Hudson was just starting out."

I tried to picture William Warner, bulldog attorney, as a fatherly mentor, but all I could see was the way he and Chuck clapped each other on the back, good old boys who were used to getting what they wanted.

"Trevor wasn't lying, though. He brought me proof."

"That's what we buried," I breathed, the puzzle piece snapping into place.

"Yes. Trevor brought me the original test data from the first round of clinical trials on Diamond's new drug, along with the submission they'd made to the FDA with the altered data. I gave it to Hudson and he confronted Will. Will told him to stay out of it, but Hudson couldn't do that.

"During the trial, Warner and Chuck presented evidence that Trevor was a disgruntled former employee who had asked for a raise and been denied one and then started threatening the company. They forged damning emails. Not only was Warner helping a man get away with lying in his company's application for FDA review of this drug, but he was making up false communications to do it."

"And Hudson wasn't okay with that," I said.

"Not at all," she agreed. "But he still didn't want to bring backlash onto the firm. Instead of going public, he met with Chuck privately. I wanted to help make things right for Trevor. Hudson agreed that we'd give him some cash, and then he tried to convince Chuck to say he'd uncovered a mistake and would rerun the trial. He asked Chuck to re-hire Trevor. He came up with this whole proposal at the Board of Supervisors to bribe him, basically. It would have funneled obscene amounts of money to Diamond Pharmaceuticals in return for making this right."

So, the grant proposal to funnel money into pharmaceutical companies that added new jobs within the county wasn't Warner's idea. It was Hudson's attempt to cajole Chuck into doing the right thing.

Christina continued, "Things were getting worse at home. If things felt tense while you were living in the pool house, this is why. Earlier, I'd hidden the records Trevor gave me. I wrapped them in a bag and taped it to the underside of the pool table, and then our cleaner's daughter nearly discovered them in the game room. I couldn't stand it, having them in the house, but Hudson kept saying it would all be fine."

Her face clouded. In a lowered voice, she said, "Chuck didn't go for the bribe, so then Hudson threatened to go back to his source and get him to agree to publish the records."

Dread creeping in, I whispered, "Trevor was his source."

She pursed her lips and nodded again. "And Chuck knew he had to be. A friend of Trevor's from work smuggled the documents out after seeing how the trial went. He said he hoped Trevor could use them to get the case overturned."

He didn't get that chance. As we both knew, Chuck and his associate, Ethan's mystery client, had made sure of that.

"The thing is, Hudson told Chuck he'd *seen* the proof Chuck had faked that data. He didn't tell Chuck that he had a copy himself. Chuck killed Trevor—or had someone else do it, I guess—and took the documents out of his apartment, but we still had them. Having them in our home became even more unbearable then.

"I wanted to go to the police. A man was dead. Hudson wanted to go to the press instead. He was worried about crooked cops, and as it turns out, he wasn't wrong.

"He recorded his last conversation with Chuck. When he came home that night he said we had to leave town. He'd let it slip that he had a copy, and he was pretty sure Chuck was going to kill him just like he killed Trevor.

"He put the recording and the scans of the clinical trials data on his laptop and emailed a dozen local reporters to see if they wanted to do a story on corruption in the pharmaceutical industry. Francisco Como was the first to respond, so Hudson set up a meeting to give him a copy of the records and tell him everything." With a whisper of a smile, she said, "Small world, I guess."

"Did you really send a copy to Bob Loeb?" I asked.

"No," she laughed, then immediately cleared her throat and pulled her lips back into a thin line. "I'm glad my lie could buy you time, though."

Once again wearing the cold, blank expression, Christina continued to explain. "We packed bags. That Friday, I went to the bank to get cash while he went to his partner meeting and then his meeting with Francisco. We were going to leave town until Francisco got his article out. The hope was that once the information went public, Chuck would be arrested and we could come home.

"When I got home, Hudson's car was there but he wasn't. The documents were still there, so I thought he was coming back. If something bad had happened to him, they'd have turned the place upside down looking for those documents."

"Ethan—he's the other one who was at the park—has video footage of Chuck's henchman walking Hudson out of the house. As it turns out, Maureen has approximately six million hidden security cameras around her house." When she looked at me questioningly, I added, "I'll tell you later."

"I thought about it a lot," Christina said, halting when her voice broke. "When I was hiding, I thought about it, and the only explanation I could come up with was that Hudson talked his way out of that house to keep me safe. I couldn't have been more than ten minutes behind him. If someone came for him, he'd have tried to get out of there as fast as possible to make sure I didn't get caught up in it."

Hudson may have talked them out of the house, but they'd come back, and they'd found what they were looking for.

Following the same thought, Christina said, "I came back. I was going to dig up the chest and go public with the records. Chuck had gotten there first, so I had to come up with a new plan."

"Diana," I said. The woman Christina had blackmailed to try

to get copies of everything related to the Diamond Pharmaceuticals case out of the law firm. The woman who was in critical condition after being bludgeoned by Chuck. The woman whose heroic efforts saved everyone.

Christina swallowed thickly. "I didn't go to her first. I tried to get into the Diamond Pharmaceuticals headquarters. I tried to get a janitorial job, but they're so secretive they do background checks on every single person who enters that building, no matter their role."

I tried to picture Christina in coveralls, sneaking around with a broom.

"I swear I didn't mean for anything bad to happen to her," Christina said, openly crying now. "I hated her for the affair I thought she was having with Hudson, but I wasn't trying to get her hurt."

She broke into sobs, her body trembling as she pulled in tiny sips of air. I held her until she could take a full breath, then whispered to her, "Christina, Diana isn't dead."

She blinked and slowly shook her head from side to side, like she couldn't let herself believe me.

"Detective Styles came to see me," I told her. "Diana's alive. Chuck hit her over the head with his gun. When I found her, I thought she was dead, and Chuck must have thought the same thing, but she was still hanging on."

"She's really not dead?" Christina breathed.

I shook my head.

"Oh, God!" She pulled me in tight, pressing my head to her chest and clinging to me with a startling strength. Her tears fell on my hair, and mine wet the hospital gown she wore.

My back seized up, pain traveling up my spine and out toward my shoulders. When I twitched within her grasp, Christina pushed me away and frowned.

"You're hurt," she accused.

I leaned back down to continue holding her. "I'm fine," I lied.

"I'm mad at you," she said, pushing me back up. "Or, I will be once I get over being so fucking relieved my stupidity didn't get you killed."

With a laugh, I assured her, "Don't worry. Once I process the fact that I'm alive and not in jail for aiding and abetting a murderer and you're alive and not in jail for a murder you didn't commit, I'll be plenty mad at you, too."

I'd spent a fair portion of the last weeks angry at Christina, and that anger would return, I knew. She'd lied and kept things from me, and her insistence on keeping me in the dark put me through absolute hell. But in that moment, all I could feel was a relief that cracked my chest wide open.

Dave stepped awkwardly into the doorway. "Um, the detective—"

Styles walked in before he could finish his introduction, breezing past him as if he weren't there. She gave Christina a curt nod, then turned to me.

"I thought I might find you here. Ready to show me that recording?"

64

Sunrise from the roof of Christina's pool house was something special. I sat with my knees tucked up against my chest, looking over the back wall of her property and past her neighbors' homes to where the mountains glowed golden, giant cacti dotting the land between here and there.

"Brought you coffee."

I turned to see the top of Francisco's head clear the roofline, his dark curls grown out and hanging in front of his eyes. A hand came into view, putting a mug of steaming dark liquid on the edge of the roof. I reached over and grabbed it while Francisco climbed the rest of the way up the ladder with his own cup.

We'd had one awkward conversation when I'd been released from the hospital. I'd apologized for the lies and deception, and he'd said he really liked me but wasn't sure he could trust me after everything we'd been through together. The next morning, I woke up tangled in his flannel sheets. We said we'd take things slow and then proceeded to spend almost every night together, pretending we weren't in over our heads and overdue for another conversation about what we were doing. I was content to delay that conversation as long as possible, happy just to enjoy watching the rise and fall of his chest while he slept and being wrapped in his arms while standing at the kitchen counter, even if it meant my heart may suffer for it later.

My phone alarm blared in my back pocket, and I silenced it, then kissed Francisco on the cheek before climbing down the ladder and returning to the pool house-turned-art studio-turned-apartment. He followed me down, pulling me into an embrace while I flipped through the closet of work clothes Christina had insisted on buying for me.

"Stop," I giggled. "I'm going to be late. I need to make a good impression on my first day back."

I'd been fired, of course, for not showing up to work, but then once Wendy had seen the news reports she'd called me and begged me to come back when I was able. My replacement was a disaster and she wanted me back.

I'd agreed, though I wasn't planning to stay indefinitely. The surfaces of the apartment were all covered in career quiz printouts and books on identifying your strengths. I was done staying in situations just because they were easy or comfortable. For the first time, I was trying to figure out what I actually wanted. But while I did that soul-searching, I was happy to have a paycheck and some structure to my weeks.

On my way out the door, I pulled a gift bag out from under the bed and thrust it at Francisco's chest.

"What is this?" he asked.

"Open it and find out!"

He pulled the tissue paper out, then lifted out a picture frame. His mouth fell open, and when he looked at me I could see his eyes were misty. He held it up so I could see the framed page, the first page of his article. He'd blown up headlines nationwide with his article exposing Diamond Pharmaceuticals for fraud and the Pima County Board of Supervisors for their kickback scheme with Warner's law firm. He'd had his pick of serious reporting jobs after its publication, and there was a new fire in his eyes.

"Thank you," he whispered, then pulled me in to kiss me deeply. I let his tongue brush my lips open and rub against mine, then pushed him away.

"Late!" I repeated, then kissed him again quickly before running out the door.

I ran around the side of the house, through the gate where Dominic and a partner had carried the chest after digging it up. With Dominic dead, his partner hadn't ever been identified. Chuck wasn't talking.

For his part, Warner was cooperating with the police, though he was mostly in the dark. He'd warned Chuck that a partner at his firm was digging into the Diamond Pharmaceuticals case, and after Hudson approached Chuck, Chuck had taken matters into his own hands. Warner seemed remorseful, but I had a hard time finding any sympathy for him even after he'd ensured Diana got her job back along with a significant pay raise.

Christina was paying for Diana's bar exam preparation course along with Ethan's college tuition. He was re-enrolled in a computer science program and would start classes in the fall. And she was teaching again, having transformed the formal living room into an art studio while I occupied the pool house.

"I've always hated that room," she'd insisted when I pushed back against taking up her studio space. "The entire house, really, but especially that room. We've already got a living room! Why do we need a second, less comfortable one?"

She'd sell the house eventually, she said, but even though she hated it, I knew it would take time before she would be ready to leave the last place she and Hudson were together.

When I arrived at the administration building, Wendy greeted me in the lobby and waved me past Benny, the security guard, who gave me a leery stare.

"I'm *so* happy to have you back. You truly couldn't overestimate how absolutely awful Leanne was. Poor girl was here two days and couldn't produce one decent memo, and she cried at the drop of a hat!"

The other admins raised their brows when I took a seat back

at my desk, but they didn't say anything, just buried their faces in their own work.

My to-do list was miles long, and before long I was in the flow, fingers flying over the keyboard. I skipped lunch, eating a granola bar at my desk instead, to finish one task, and then immediately dove into another. I'd have stayed late not to try to make a good impression but because I was genuinely invested, but my phone reminded me that I had plans tonight: Ariel's school choir had their end-of-year concert.

When I slid into the back, the lights were already dim in the auditorium. A teacher opened the door, and fifty middle schoolers in black pants and blue polos with the school logo filed in. The audience broke into applause, parents pulling out phones and tablets to record the performance, and I searched for Ariel in the group.

I found her in the back row, black choker around her neck and hair done in a pair of braids. She searched the crowd just as I had been looking for her. I saw the moment she found her family. She gave them a small smile, lips parting to reveal new braces. Then she resumed her search, and when her eyes lit on mine, that smile pulled back even further. I waved at her and she pulled her shoulders back, standing taller.

The choir director spoke a short welcome into a microphone, then turned her back to the crowd and raised her hands, and pride welled up in me as I watched Ariel open her mouth alongside her classmates and begin to sing.

Thank you for reading this book. I hope you enjoyed it. If you did, please consider leaving a review or sharing it with a friend.

ACKNOWLEDGMENTS

Writing a book, while done largely in a room alone, is a true example of "it takes a village." I want to acknowledge my village and the part they played in bringing this book to life.

Thank you to the kind souls who let me bounce ideas off of them for this book. Mom, Andrew, Carlee—you were the first ones I shared this idea with, and your enthusiasm encouraged me to make it happen.

Leselle, I know I already dedicated the book to you, but I need to acknowledge again the impact of your love and support of this idea. When I was deep in the messy middle and losing sight of what this book could be, your belief brought me back. Victoria and Shraddha, your encouragement buoyed me as well. Thank you.

I want to acknowledge the help of my early readers. Your feedback made this book better and I am deeply grateful for it.

To everyone else who listened to me talk about this story, asked questions or pointed out flaws and holes, encouraged me to write when I was procrastinating, and made me believe this book was worth writing, thank you. It would not exist without you.

ALSO BY KATE MACLEAN

The Breeze Village cozy mystery series:

Pension for Murder

Bingo, Bribes, and Alibis

Third Crime Lucky

Garroted in the Gallery

www.ingramcontent.com/pod-product-compliance
Ingram Content Group UK Ltd.
Pitfield, Milton Keynes, MK11 3LW, UK
UKHW042002230426
12048UKWH00009B/497